PRAISE FOR

THE
LIGHTHOUSE
LAND

"This exciting and beautifully crafted book will
have readers sitting on the edge of their seats
wondering what is going to happen next . . .
powerful and unforgettable." —*Through the
Looking Glass Book Review*

"[Readers] will enjoy this first book in a planned
trilogy, for its intriguing story, warmth of the
characters, and pop culture references." —*VOYA*

"While the action will keep the pages turning, it
is the dialogue between Jamie and Ramsay . . .
that makes this such an enjoyable trip."
—*Publishers Weekly*

THE LIGHTHOUSE LAND

THE LIGHTHOUSE TRILOGY
◆ BOOK I ◆

ADRIAN McKINTY

AMULET BOOKS

New York

The Library of Congress has cataloged
the hardcover edition as follows:
McKinty, Adrian.
The lighthouse land / by Adrian McKinty.
p. cm.
Summary: Thirteen-year-old Jamie is overjoyed when a bequest sends him and his mother to live on an Irish island, where he and his new-found friend Ramsay travel to another planet to help a young girl save her people from certain death.
ISBN-13: 978-0-8109-5480-9
ISBN-10: 0-8109-5480-X
[1. Time travel—Fiction. 2. Magic—Fiction. 3. Ireland—Fiction.]
I. Title.
PZ7.M47869l5Lig 2006
[Fic]—dc22
2006019783
Paperback ISBN 13: 978-0-8109-9361-7
Paperback ISBN 10: 0-8109-9361-9

Originally published in hardcover by Amulet Books in 2006

Text copyright © 2006 Adrian McKinty
Map illustration copyright © 2006 Bret Bertholf

Book design by Chad W. Beckerman

Printed and bound in U.S.A.
10 9 8 7 6 5 4 3 2 1

harry n. abrams, inc.
a subsidiary of La Martinière Groupe

115 West 18th Street
New York, NY 10011
www.hnabooks.com

For my nephews and nieces, Oliver, Patrick, Erin, Lara, Samuel, Molly, and Sam. And for my children, Arwynn and Sophie. *Go raibh maith agaibh.*

CONTENTS

THE OTHER WAS ALSO THE LIGHTHOUSE. FOR NOTHING WAS SIMPLY ONE THING. THE OTHER LIGHTHOUSE WAS TRUE TOO.

—VIRGINIA WOOLF, *To the Lighthouse* (1927)

IT'S SEVEN A.M. in Harlem and the letter is waiting near the bottom of the mailman's sack. You're in bed asleep and outside is the darkness, the cold, a shroud of ice covering the city from river to river. You don't know that this is the morning on which your life will change.

Through the window is the uncoiled arm of the Milky Way and the moon the color of narcissus. Duct tape has stopped the snow from falling on your head and the airline blankets form a barrier against the frozen air. The new day is coming, but it's not quite here yet; just a clear navigator's sky and a red tongue of light in the east, beyond the Triborough Bridge and Long Island and the Atlantic Ocean.

In Central Park the weather station reports a temperature of minus five and the news says the subways and the buses are running slow.

Because of the cold and the delays, the mail carrier arrives late at the Manhattanville post office in Harlem. He's called Freddy—a nice guy, but even on the best of days not the fastest person in the world. He was born in Jamaica and, though he's lived in New York since he was a child, he has never gotten used to the winter.

He has a coffee, toasts a bagel, wraps himself in four layers of clothing, and finally starts doing his rounds just before 7:30 a.m.

He appears outside your building at 8:15 and shakes his head.

Freddy always shakes his head when he comes to your address. It's the worst building on his route, near the corner of 125th Street and Broadway. Most of the apartments have been boarded up and there are holes in the roof. The fire escape is rusted and hangs on the front of the place like an iron skeleton.

The heating never works, and when Freddy goes inside, he keeps on his thick USPS coat and wool hat.

He unloads his bag, stamps the snow off his boots, and whistles a Britney Spears song while he opens the big mailbox frame with his master key. Freddy's late, but he's not worried; this building never takes him long. Since the pipes burst and flooded the fourth floor, most of the tenants moved out. A few did stay, because you couldn't get rent this cheap anywhere else in the whole of New York City.

Freddy throws in the mail and then pauses when he sees the letter with the English stamp that's addressed to Anna O'Neill. He's glad that he came back from vacation today because, slow as he is, at least he knows the route and the replacement mailman wouldn't have understood that this is your mother's maiden name. He might not have delivered the letter at all and instead returned it with a "Not at This Address" label.

But you and Freddy are pals, and occasionally the pair of you take turns losing chess games to Thaddeus at the library. In a homemade card, your mother gave Freddy a Christmas gift of ten dollars, which he knows was a lot of money to her.

Usually he only puts bills in your mail slot, but not today. Today it's definitely something different. He holds up this letter for Miss Anna O'Neill—a watermark says MCCREAGH AND WRIGHT SOLICITORS AT LAW. He reads a couple of lines through the envelope.

"Looks like it's good news for a change," Freddy mutters to himself.

He puts the letter in your box, locks the big metal mail frame, and waits there for a minute or two. Sometimes you come down early to check the mail. Apart from the landlord's bad seed, you're the only kid left in the building. Freddy looks at his watch. He can't wait anymore and so he walks back out onto 125th Street, where the sun is over the East River and the city is well on its way to work.

It's a good thing he didn't wait. You won't be down this morning to get the letters at all because last night you stayed up late trying to fix the hole in the ceiling of your bedroom. It was a new hole, and you didn't tell your mother about it because it would only have worried her. You noticed it when snowflakes started coming in. You repaired it easily with duct tape, but you know that won't last forever.

Anyway, you're still in bed when your mother goes down to the ground floor just before nine o'clock in her heels and black business suit. She opens the mailbox with her key and looks inside. She's expecting a check from your father. He promised last week he would send it the day after Christmas. But it still hasn't come. In her heart she knows it's never going to come. She looks at the rest of the post: bills, a late Christmas card, and then a letter—*the* letter.

"Huh," she says, the water vapor in her breath making a little puff in the frigid air.

Just as Freddy did, she lifts up the letter and examines it. The envelope is creamy white and made from light but expensive-looking paper. The stamp is British—a painting of Santa Claus standing on a rooftop with a pair of reindeer. The letter is addressed to Miss Anna O'Neill, Apt. 33, 555, 125th Street, Harlem, New York, USA 10027— which puzzles her. No one calls her *Miss* O'Neill anymore. Not for years and years. Even after the divorce she was still called Mrs. Smith (your father's name) at work and on the payment demands for the maxed-out credit cards.

"I wonder what on earth this is," she says aloud.

She throws all the bills unopened into the recycling bin, puts the letter in her jacket pocket, and carries it upstairs. By some instinct she knows she'll need to be sitting to read this one.

She walks back into the small apartment on the third floor, closes the door, pours a mug of coffee, and sits down at the kitchen table.

The light is flickering above her head, so she turns it off and opens the blinds. The view out the window is of the elevated 1 subway line on Broadway, and a little bit farther beyond she can make out the Hudson River and the snowy shore of New Jersey. Just then, a subway train comes past and rattles dishes in the apartment, but she hardly even notices.

Her heart beating fast, she tears open the letter.

She reads it.

She gasps and nearly spills her coffee.

She reads it again and carefully puts it back in the envelope.

She writes a note on a piece of paper: JAMIE, I'VE LEFT FOR WORK. THERE'S CEREAL IN THE CABINET. IF YOU GET BORED TODAY, GO SEE THADDEUS AT THE LIBRARY.

She grabs her thick winter coat, gloves, and a hat and heads to work. She takes the train to 59th Street. She walks quickly over the salt-encrusted sidewalks to the lawyers' office on Central Park West. She takes the elevator to the twentieth floor and finds one of the partners whom she likes—one of the younger ones.

At 10:15 a.m. she shows him the letter and he tells her exactly what it means.

That afternoon, when your mother finally comes home after making some phone calls, buying a bottle of champagne, and quitting her job, she'll hand the letter to you.

You'll read it. You'll have just talked to Thaddeus at the library and he'll have told you that there is no magic in the world. He's told you that before. Thaddeus doesn't realize that he repeats himself a lot, and of course you like Thaddeus and would never embarrass him by mentioning it. But also that's because you and Thaddeus don't have conversations. He talks and you listen. He likes to talk.

You'll read it and you'll give the letter back.

"Well, Jamie? What do you think?" your mother will ask after a long pause. She'll look tired but not as exhausted as she's looked in a long time. Pale cheeks, gray creeping between the long strands of red hair falling over her face but an excitement in her dark green eyes. Green eyes, although you heard a man once say that they were emerald. Blinking, hopeful, emerald eyes.

"Well, Jamie?" she'll ask again, her hands deep in the mended cardigan pockets. "Do we go to Ireland?"

And you won't speak.

You never speak.

Not since the surgery.

But you'll nod your head and your mother will smile. She faked one on Christmas Day, a little quiver around the edges of her mouth, but this one is real. And you can tell because it's followed by a big, throaty laugh. The first one of those you've heard in a long time. And you won't laugh, but you will reciprocate the smile, and by this time next week you'll be on a plane that's taking you to a new home, in a new country, three thousand miles away from here.

☉ ☉ ☉

But that was in the future. And this was the now. Jamie shivered in the bed and woke. Another long New York winter day lay ahead. He looked at his watch. Early. Only 9:30. The library wasn't even open yet.

He closed his eyes and tried to go back to sleep.

He'd been in the middle of a dream. Something that had really happened to him and he'd forgotten about. It was summer, years ago. He was with his mother and father at Coney Island. They had ridden on the bumper cars and were strolling on the boardwalk eating cotton candy. His mother was happy, his dad was happy. He was touching his mom's cool fingers with his left hand, his right holding that big stick full of pink spun sugar. A nail had been sticking out of the boardwalk and he hadn't seen it. He'd tripped, fallen, and the cotton candy had splatted on the sand-covered planks. He cried and his father picked him up and kissed him on the cheek and told him not to worry, they would buy him another one.

Unfortunately, Jamie had awoken before his father had had the chance to purchase the replacement cotton candy.

He groaned and pulled up the blankets and burrowed deep underneath them. He tried for another moment to finish the dream, to give it a happy ending, but he couldn't fall back asleep. From somewhere down the hall there was a loud, repetitive banging noise.

He opened his eyes.

It was a stupid dream anyway. None of that could ever happen again. His father was in Seattle, married to someone else. And the cancer had made the rest of it impossible too.

He sighed. The noise was someone thumping at the

front door. He'd have to get up. His mother had obviously left for work already. Probably on the train by now.

He raised the big down comforter and pushed away the half a dozen blankets his mother had piled on his bed when winter had really hit at the beginning of the month. She'd gotten them all from airplanes—technically it wasn't stealing, the airlines gave you the blankets and if you wanted to take them home with you that was OK with them. Still, it was embarrassing to have them on his bed and he carefully made sure they were out of sight when anyone came over. Not that many people ever did.

He rubbed his eyes and looked out of the window.

The sky was a light blue, and ice was hanging in great stalactites from the fire escape. The city of New York was quiet, or at least the part of it he could see as he looked north across 125th Street. The subway tracks, the M60 bus to the airport, yellow cabs, gypsy cabs, not too many people. It was the week after Christmas and before New Year's, so nothing much was going on.

He stared at the hole in the ceiling he'd covered with duct tape. He'd have to tell his mother about it, so she could get someone to fix it. But he could wait until after that check came from his father. No point in worrying her unnecessarily.

Wrapping himself in the comforter, he climbed out of bed.

The banging from the front door was getting louder.

He'd have to get the door since he was the only one

there. It sucked being an only child, no little brothers or sisters to force to do things for you. Still, at least it meant that he had his own room, which he had decorated in his own way. He'd painted his walls deep crimson and then put up his posters at carefully chosen spots.

He had disdain for the musical tastes of his contemporaries and he felt that one poster of Sigur Rós or Franz Ferdinand was worth ten of Britney or Christina or Avril.

And anyway, he'd be too embarrassed to have a woman on the wall. His father had teased him so much at their old apartment, he'd finally taken down the poster of Katee Sackhoff from the new *Battlestar Galactica*.

The room was small but packed. He had a bureau, a desk, a reading lamp, and a bookcase full of books. Good books too. Thaddeus always tipped him off when the library was having a sale, so that he could pick up a *Harry Potter* or a *Times Atlas of the World* for fifty cents.

He walked into the living room. The apartment had two bedrooms, a narrow living room, a kitchen, and a bathroom. His mother kept it clean, but since the flood, everything had a mildewy smell, and it was always either too hot or too cold, depending on whether the heating was working or not.

The banging continued.

He knew it was Eric. No one else would thump on the door like that.

He trailed the comforter across the living room and flipped on the TV to get the weather. They were probably the only family in North America who didn't have cable, but Jamie didn't like TV much anyway. It annoyed him. TV people didn't inhabit the real world. In TV land people lived in houses with yards and fences and they had siblings and stupid problems that always got solved in either half an hour or fifty-eight minutes. Apart from the wonderfully gloomy *Galactica*, the only TV program he watched was *The Twilight Zone*, where everything was totally screwed up and weird and in black and white. That show from the 1950s seemed a lot more realistic than all the stupid reality shows of today. Twenty-five degrees, channel 1 said. Not too bad.

He found a note from his mother on the TV table. He read it, turned off the set, and walked down to the bathroom.

Since his mom was gone he could safely do his ritual.

He dropped the comforter and looked at himself in the mirror.

He did this every day.

And the shock hit him every time.

His hair had grown back since the chemotherapy. It was long, curly, and reddish blond like his father's, not real red like his mother's. He had his mother's imperious nose, but none of her regal authority, because his face was thin and his blue eyes looked frail and sad.

"I can hear you in there, Jamie," Eric said from the hall.

Jamie continued his inspection.

Yeah, his hair was back to where it had been a year ago, longer even, and he was putting on weight again.

But one thing would never be the same.

Because of the cancer in his bones, the surgeons had sawed off his left arm at the elbow. It had been the only way to save his life. Surgery and radical chemotherapy. And they'd been right. It had saved his life. The cancer was not just in remission but, in fact, was completely gone.

Gone.

Along with his arm.

And something else: his voice. For Jamie hadn't spoken a word in the last year—not since he'd woken up and looked at himself that first time.

In the beginning, no one had thought his silence would last long. The surgeons said it was quite common for amputees to be in a state of shock for the first twenty-four or forty-eight hours. Sometimes for even as much as a week or two. But at the end of a month, when he had still not spoken a single syllable, his mother, Anna, began to get worried.

She took him back to the hospital and they examined him. They put him through a whole battery of tests, but everyone said that there was nothing physically wrong with him. He wasn't speaking because he didn't want to speak. He was choosing not to.

Anna's health plan did not cover psychiatric care, but she used her savings and borrowed money and sent him to psychologists and mental health professionals—kindly men and women who were gentle and patient with him, but after many sessions still could not get him to open up.

Months had gone by and the months turned into a year and Jamie stubbornly refused to say anything.

He would nod or shake his head in answer to a question, and he and his mom had invented a few hand signals that meant "I'm going out" (his fingers walking) or "Thank you" (a double nod of the head) or "I love you" (a touch of the heart). And if he really needed to tell Anna something, he would write it on a piece of paper in a little spiral-bound notebook he carried. Always in block capitals, always very deliberately and slowly.

Of course everyone had been sympathetic at first, but as they learned that there was nothing physically wrong with him and he wasn't speaking out of choice, the sympathy began to drain away. Kids began calling him names at school, trying to bait him into a response. Any response. The teachers too were irritated by Jamie's refusal to speak in class or answer questions. In the end they recommended that he be moved to the Harlem School for Children with Special Challenges. He had been there since September. It hadn't helped. There were deaf kids in his class, mentally impaired children, but none with his own brand of self-inflicted disability. Jamie made no friends.

And then his mother had gotten desperate. She had written to celebrities and the Make-A-Wish Foundation and she'd received kind replies from Bethany Hamilton, the little surfer girl who'd had her arm bitten off by a shark, and also from the climber Aron Ralston, who'd had to cut off his own arm to survive a fall in the canyons of Utah.

Both offered to meet Jamie and talk to him. But Jamie had refused. He didn't want to meet anyone. He didn't want to talk to anyone. He just wanted to be left alone.

Perhaps this was the final straw for the family, and it was about this time that his father had left. There were tears and fights and arguments and man-to-boy talks.

His father explained to him that none of this was Jamie's fault, that he had fallen in love with another woman and they were moving to Seattle.

Jamie knew, however, that he *was* to blame. His father had always been the one telling Jamie to get a grip on himself; his mother had always been his defender. It had caused big arguments. His father's move to Seattle made him more convinced. That city was pretty much as far away from New York as you could get in the contiguous forty-eight states.

His father left, his mother couldn't afford their old apartment, and they had moved to this building on 125th Street. For the last four months they had been living here, more or less hand to mouth. His mother worked as a secretary in a law firm and it was a good job, but what with the cancer treatment and everything else, she had acquired a lot of debts. Food stamps meant that they wouldn't starve, but the rest of their existence was precarious.

"Get the lock, Stumpy!" Eric screamed.

Jamie had delayed long enough. He opened the door.

Jamie was tall for his age, but Eric, a couple of months younger, was taller still. Easily six foot and just turned thirteen. Eric shaved his head for his school swim team and he had powerful swimmer's arms and shoulders. Tall, bald, muscular, with deep-set caveman eyes, he looked like an escapee from a clandestine government experiment. Not a nice kid either, he'd been on a secret baby-sitters' blacklist from the age of seven and although he didn't have a police record, the police had probably cleared space for him in the hard drive. For Jamie, all that mattered was that Eric was the landlord's son and he lived in the basement in the only decent apartment in the building.

"Why didn't you open the door, gimp boy?" he asked.

Eric knew Jamie wouldn't answer, but he didn't care.

"My dad sent me up to see you deadbeats. He wants to know why your mother's stealing from him," Eric snarled.

Jamie saw that he was being goaded. He looked at Eric and shook his head.

"Oh, she's a thief all right. Anyone who doesn't pay their rent when they're supposed to is a thief. Your mother is stealing from us and I'm not going to stand for it anymore."

Jamie stepped back into the apartment and tried to close the door, but Eric was too fast. His long, rangy arm shot out.

"Where's our money?" Eric demanded. "You owe us five hundred dollars. We want it. I want it."

There wasn't anywhere near that amount of money in the apartment. They lived on fifty dollars a week and there was never much more than that in the pink piggy bank his mother kept in the kitchen. Still, it might be enough to keep Eric happy for a while.

"You better let me in to look for our dough," Eric said, shoving the door fully open.

Jamie made a decision. He wasn't going to let him have the piggy bank. Whatever else happened, he wasn't going to let Eric have a single cent.

"Are you going to let me in?" Eric demanded.

Jamie shook his head.

Eric didn't wait to debate the point; he pushed Jamie backward and stomped inside. Jamie clattered into the wall and fell. When he got to his feet, Eric was in the kitchen. He knew what he was looking for. He made straight for the cabinet above the fridge and grabbed the piggy bank. Which meant he had obviously sneaked in here before with his father's key. Jamie jumped him from behind and tried to pull him down, but Eric reacted fast and elbowed him in the stomach.

Winded, Jamie collapsed to the floor.

Eric kneeled down, put his hand around Jamie's throat, and squeezed. Jamie tried to push him off with his right hand, but Eric was just too big and too strong. Eric's powerful fingers locked around Jamie's windpipe, cutting off the air to his lungs. Jamie began seeing stars; he couldn't breathe. He kicked at Eric, but it was no good, the big kid moved so that he was kneeling on Jamie's chest.

"If you ask me, I'll stop," Eric said.

He squeezed harder, his muscly face lighting up with glee.

Jamie coughed and struggled for air.

"Go on, ask me; all you have to do is ask me and I'll stop," Eric said again. Jamie shook his head.

"Go on. Speak," Eric demanded.

But Jamie could take obstinacy to Olympic levels.

He made up his mind that he would rather die than give in.

He started seeing white lights, blood rushed in his ears, his heart pounded, and then all went black.

He woke in the same position in the middle of the kitchen floor. He couldn't have blacked out for more than two minutes. Eric had fled, taking the piggy bank with him. Hopefully, Eric thought he'd killed him. Let him be terrified for a while.

Jamie sat up and rubbed his throat. But even if Eric was cowering in the basement right now, afraid the cops were going to call at any moment, it wasn't enough for Jamie. Eric had broken into their apartment, had attacked him, stolen their savings, and insulted his mother. Something needed to be done. Eric had to pay. This was true, obvious. Any normal kid would be up already and out there plotting revenge.

But Jamie wasn't any normal kid.

Jamie's existence was stalled. It was as frozen as the figures on a paused DVD.

He'd had a life before, and maybe he would again, but now he was on the darkened stage between acts.

He sighed. There were some things you had to do even if your heart wasn't in them. You had to breathe, you had to get out of bed, you had to be nice to Thaddeus because he was a lonely old man.

You had to follow the rituals and pretend that your life had a forward momentum even if it didn't.

And, yes, you had to make Eric pay the price.

Jamie sat there for a while weighing the competing forces in his head, groaned, and stood.

He shuffled back into his bedroom. He pulled on a pair of jeans, a black T-shirt, his coat, and a wool Yankees hat. Finally, he slipped on his army surplus boots and tied the laces using his right hand and his teeth. He opened up the first volume of the old 1910 *Encyclopaedia Britannica* that Thaddeus had given him and took out the emergency twenty-dollar bill he'd been saving for an occasion such as this.

He walked out of the apartment and locked the door.

He limped down the three flights of stairs and went out onto 125th Street. It was around eleven o'clock and busier now. A lot of people heading to the subway stop or the various lunch places and diners on Broadway.

Although it was barely above freezing, the sun was

shining brightly and casting big shadows on the sidewalk. Jamie had lost his sunglasses a week earlier, and he was sorry he wasn't going to be able to use the twenty-dollar bill for a new pair, but what he had in mind was more important.

He crossed under the elevated subway tracks and walked west, past the chop shops and tire stores, in the direction of the Hudson River. Once he was across Broadway, he turned right and headed for the Hispaniola Bakery, which made delicious cakes but eked out a precarious existence between two vacant lots under the girders of the West Side Highway. For Jamie this block was a special place, almost no one ever came here who wasn't homeless—and certainly no kids. It was here, though, that he could let the whole city wash over him, as he stood in the middle of the empty street, with the river on his left, Manhattan on his right, the cars and trucks thundering overhead. It was peaceful and almost quiet in a way, the massive iron I beams and struts that held up the road like the bones of some vast beast lying undisturbed and unnoticed by New York's populace.

Jamie stood and appreciated his special place for a while and then remembered why he'd really come.

Let's get on with it, he told himself, then crossed the road and went into the bakery.

It was a small, ill-lit shop, with Caribbean travel posters, a dozen cakes in a glass case, and a selection of tarts, doughnuts, and éclairs in a refrigerator.

Papa Sorrel was reading the sports section of the *Daily News*. On another morning Jamie would have written a note and asked Papa what his thoughts were about the Rangers and the Knicks, but he didn't have time for that today. Today, he meant business.

"*Bonjour, Jamie, ça va?*" Papa Sorrel asked.

Jamie made the "OK" sign.

"*Oui. Moi aussi. Il fait très bon aujourd'hui. Maintenant, Jamie, tu as faim?*"

Jamie shook his head and took out his pen. He put his notepad on the counter and wrote I'D LIKE TO BUY A DOMINICAN BIRTHDAY CAKE. CAN YOU ICE "HAPPY BIRTHDAY SAMMY" ON TOP? He gave Papa Sorrel the note and put a twenty-dollar bill on the counter.

Papa Sorrel selected one of the best-looking of the cakes, a huge pink affair with alternating layers of cream and chocolate filling. He gave it an extra dusting of powdered sugar and iced it as per Jamie's instructions while he talked to Jamie about his eldest son, who had just come back from serving with the First Infantry in Iraq.

Jamie's mother had given Papa Sorrel some catering business at her law firm, and at first he refused to take the twenty-dollar bill, but Jamie insisted with a rigid stare. The old man had no choice but to comply. Jamie picked out a simple white box that could not be traced and Papa Sorrel tied it with string. There was five dollars change. Good, he'd need that.

Jamie nodded and left the shop, carrying the cake. He

walked back to Broadway and entered the pharmacy on 125th Street.

He wrote a note for the pharmacist:

I AM A MUTE. MY MOTHER IS VERY SICK. SHE CAN'T GO TO THE BATHROOM AND SHE NEEDS THE STRONGEST LAXATIVE YOU'VE GOT.

The pharmacist looked at him, read the note, and nodded.

"I know you, you're Jamie aren't you? I was very sorry to hear about your arm," he said slowly and somberly.

YOU SAVE A FORTUNE ON GLOVES, Jamie scribbled in his notebook.

The color drained from the man's face.

NOW, PLEASE, MY MOM'S NOT WELL, Jamie wrote.

"Mom's stuffed up, huh? She should take the Extra Strong Lax Aid. It's only for emergencies, not too much, one tablespoonful at the most."

Jamie bought the laxative and a simple plastic syringe with a plunger. He carried the cake back to his apartment and, using the syringe, injected the cake with the entire bottle of laxative. He covered the syringe holes with icing and wrote SAMUEL MARTINEZ, 555 125TH STREET, #22, NY, NY 10027 on the plain white box.

He carried the cake box downstairs and left it in the lobby. He went outside, rang the bell for the basement, and ran across 125th and entered the George Bruce branch of the New York Public Library.

He allowed himself a smile as he climbed the library stairs.

The Martinez family had left over a month ago, but he knew what would happen.

Eric would hear the doorbell, come up from the basement, see the box, open it, find the cake, and devour the whole thing himself.

The laxative bottle had said on the side GUARANTEED RESULTS WITHIN THE HOUR.

Excellent. With some difficulty, Jamie set the alarm on his digital watch for one hour.

For the first time in the last eleven months, Jamie had made a plan of his own and actually done something, not just drifted. It could be that Jamie was gradually changing, gradually coming to terms with his disability, gradually snapping out of his stupor. Or it could simply be that Eric had pushed him over the edge and was finally about to get what was coming to him.

Or it could be something else entirely.

It could be—if you're a believer in things like tipping points, catastrophe theory, chaos theory—that the letter's mere presence had already changed Jamie's universe a little, had already altered the way events were supposed to be, had already worked a little of its influence.

Maybe.

Jamie opened the door onto the second floor of the library. Thaddeus was the old black guy at the window slowly making his way through today's copy of *The New York*

Times. Except for the gossip column, Thaddeus read every single story and practically every word. The news depressed him, but he said it was better to know than to live in ignorance. He did the crossword in pen but often got stuck over the *Times*'s references to sitcoms and makeover shows.

Thaddeus was an interesting guy. Originally from Georgia, he had come to New York City after the war with a letter of recommendation from General Patton, with whom he had served as a sergeant in the Third Army. He had gone to City College on the GI Bill and become a schoolteacher. He had never married and never had kids. He had retired from teaching in 1985 and had spent the last twenty years reading, traveling, and playing chess. He helped out in the library now and again, stacking shelves and berating people who wanted to check out *The Five People You Meet in Heaven* or *A Million Little Pieces.*

He was an old, thin man with white hair and dark eyes. Today, he was wearing a blue shirt, a blue bow tie, and a black suit that seemed slightly too big for him. But he always dressed well, and on Sundays he went to church in a silk jacket and carried a cane.

Jamie sat down opposite him. Thaddeus nodded, carefully folded the newspaper, and took out the chess set. Jamie helped him set up the pieces.

"You been up to no good, boy," Thaddeus said. "I can see it in your eyes. Don't bother to lie about it. I can see it."

Jamie looked flustered.

"What's the matter with you? The queen goes on her square, hurry up," Thaddeus said.

Jamie fixed the pieces and moved his knight forward as his opening. Thaddeus thought for a long time and moved a pawn.

Jamie liked Thaddeus. He had known him since they had moved to Harlem. Unlike almost everyone else, Thaddeus had never asked him why he didn't want to speak. Thaddeus was not interested in the answer to that question. His mind was on higher things. Philosophy, science, politics. A squirt kid who didn't want to blab his uneducated opinions to everyone was a good thing, as far as he was concerned. In his day, in rural Georgia, children were seen and not heard.

Jamie moved his other knight.

"You know what I read today?" Thaddeus asked, moving a second pawn.

Jamie looked into Thaddeus's dark, watery eyes, his own way of encouraging the old man to continue the conversation. Thaddeus, however, did not need prompting.

"I read today that the Mayans believe that the world is going to end on December twenty-first, 2012. That's when their 'Long Count' runs out. Do you believe that, boy?"

Jamie thought about it and then made a question mark in the air.

"Huh. I wonder about you sometimes. Well, I personally do not believe that myself. You think a people who didn't even invent the wheel can know when the world is going to end? It's hogwash. That's what it is," Thaddeus said angrily, and moved another pawn.

Thaddeus tut-tutted over Jamie's next move.

"You believe in UFOs, boy?" he said.

Jamie shook his head and examined the board. Sometimes Thaddeus tried to distract him so that he could do a sneak attack on his pieces. Jamie inspected his lines of defense, but they seemed OK.

"You don't believe in UFOs? No, I don't believe in them either. If aliens wanted to kidnap us, they'd fly right down Broadway scooping people up with a net. I don't believe in any of that stuff. I know real life, son. I was in the war with George Patton . . ."

Jamie rolled his eyes. This was one of Thaddeus's favorite topics.

"I was in the war with George Patton and let me tell you, if a shell was going hit your tank, it didn't matter if you had up your Saint Christopher, Saint Jude, Saint Catherine, made no difference. One of them little statues didn't do nothing against armor-piercing high explosives."

Jamie nodded and moved his knight up to take a pawn.

"Remember what the Bible says, Jamie: 'It's better to hear the rebuke of the wise than the song of fools.' Fools aplenty you will find, Jamie, whether you be staying here or going to somewhere else," Thaddeus said, a little more mysteriously than usual.

Again, Jamie checked his defense. He didn't really

care about the game, but it made life easier if he gave the appearance of trying. Even when your life was stalled, you had to do a lot of work to find the path of least resistance.

Thaddeus yawned and read his newspaper. He seemed confident of his position, but this was another tactic the old man pulled sometimes. He read an article, shook his head, and seemed to think for a moment. He stared at Jamie until Jamie could feel the gaze and looked back.

"Sure 'nough. There ain't no magic in the world. Everyone thinks there's magic, but there ain't. We mortals are a little superstitious; we can't help it. Everyone is afraid of death and hopes that somehow they can escape it when it's their turn. And that's why they all believe in hexes and stuff, even if they deny it. But they all wrong. There's no magic. None. We live, we die, that's it. Everything passes, including you and me."

Jamie nodded and waited for Thaddeus's usual explanation about the laws of physics and the laws of chemistry, but today it wasn't going to happen. Thaddeus was pondering something else now. Jamie saw that he'd been thinking about it the whole game and had come to it finally, in his own roundabout way.

"I talked to Freddy this morning," Thaddeus said after a long silence.

Jamie knitted his eyebrows and made another question mark.

 25

"The mailman," Thaddeus said. "I talked to him this morning."

Jamie nodded. Of course. Sometimes, when he wasn't too tired, Freddy the mailman came over to the library. Jamie waited for Thaddeus to continue and when he didn't he offered Thaddeus a pawn in the center of the board.

"I talked to Freddy," Thaddeus said again with more emphasis.

Jamie looked at him to see what he was driving at. Thaddeus absently moved his queen.

"I talked to him and I have a feeling that I ain't going to be seeing you no more, Jamie. It's a shame. I hate chewing it with the old-timers that come here, always moaning about something, always complaining. Hate that. At my age and with my background, I want to be around kids. You want to be around the future, not the past. That's what I think. And you're about the only kid who ever comes in here. Look around you. Median age is about sixty."

Jamie nodded and moved his rook so that he could check Thaddeus if he was tempted by the pawn.

"Yup, I see the way it's going. Well, son, I'll miss you. You come see me before you go. You hear me, boy?"

Jamie looked into the old black man's graying, wrinkled face. Thaddeus was being a little more confusing than usual today. Jamie wondered if he was getting senile. He hoped not.

Thaddeus moved his bishop.

"That's a check on your king, boy. You're going to have

to move that king, and when you do you're going to lose your queen," Thaddeus said.

Jamie studied the board. He was amazed and a little disbelieving, but, of course, Thaddeus was right. He'd been paying so much attention to his own attack that he had neglected his defense. With the queen gone, Thaddeus would have checkmate in two, no, three moves. Jamie had no other choice but to resign. The old geezer had outwitted him again. Jamie knocked his king over. He offered Thaddeus his hand. Thaddeus held on to it longer than was necessary.

"You heard what I said about coming to see me, right?"

Jamie nodded. He thought that had been just part of Thaddeus's tactics, but obviously the old man was serious.

"Yup, you better come see me before you go. I've been thinking about you and I got something I want to give you as a temporary solution to your problem. So you come over before you go anywheres, you hear?"

Jamie blinked, still very puzzled by what Thaddeus was talking about. What problem? Going where? The alarm on his watch beeped.

I HAVE TO HEAD, THADDEUS, Jamie wrote in his little blue spiral notebook, then tore off the page and put it on the chessboard.

Mrs. Moore, the librarian, stopped him at the desk and gave him a book for his mother. Mrs. Moore and his mom were both divorced and without partners. The book was called *Are Men Necessary?* and was by a woman who apparently dyed her hair the color of tomato soup. Jamie nodded a thank-you, grabbed the book, put on his coat and hat, and ran outside.

He could hear the howling even before he had made it across 125th Street. And when he got to his building, it sounded as if someone was being tortured down in the basement. Jamie almost felt bad for a moment but then he remembered what Eric had done to him today and on previous occasions. Yeah, let *him* suffer for a while. Jamie walked upstairs and opened the door. His mom was back early.

"Hello, Jamie," she said, and hugged him.

When he had taken off his coat and hat, she handed him the letter.

"I got this letter today. It's very important. I want you to look at it right now," she said. Jamie sat down, unfolded the letter, and read it:

> McCreagh and Wright Solicitors
> 27 High Street
> Belfast, N. Ireland
>
> Dear Miss O'Neill,
> The ruling of the Special Master being formally lodged with the High Court on December 20th of this year, 2005, and the Testament of Mr. Samuel O'Neill Esq. late of the County Donegal being uncontested by said Court, we,

the solicitors for the probate judgement do hereby inform you, Miss Anna O'Neill of New York County, that you are the sole beneficiary of the late Mr. Samuel O'Neill Esq.

The properties, monies and other items being severally divided thus:

Fees, taxes and other monies being deducted, we hold on Trust for you a sum not less than five thousand pounds sterling.

A house known as the Lighthouse House, to be held on entailment for direct descendants of the O'Neill family. Given to Miss O'Neill for the term of her life and conveyable by Miss O'Neill on her death only to her descendants, or if she has no issue, to her closest living relative provided that relative has the surname or maiden name of O'Neill, Ui Neill, or a variant thereof.

A stipend of ten thousand pounds per annum for upkeep of said house on condition that Miss O'Neill live in said house for at least 300 days in a calendar year.

The island on which said house stands, Muck

or Mugg Island, a ten-acre island off the coast of Ireland in the County of Antrim in the parish of Portmuck.

The causeway linking said island to the mainland. All fishing and gaming rights for Muck Island and the rights to minerals or precious metals found therein.

Yours Sincerely,
Arthur John McCreagh
Arthur McCreagh LLB, MA solicitor at law

Jamie hesitated for a moment and then handed the letter back to his mom. There were a lot of questions, but he was not the boy to ask questions.

Anna answered some of them.

"My grandfather came from Ireland, but he never told me that we had property or were related to people who did. Even so, I guess we were the closest living relatives."

Jamie nodded.

"Do you understand the letter? Do you understand what it means?"

Jamie nodded again. *It probably spells the end of my promising career as a teenage poisoner*, he thought with relief.

"Well, Jamie, what do you say?" Anna asked.

He closed his eyes to take it all in, and when he opened them his mother was crying.

"Well, Jamie?" Anna asked. "Do we go to Ireland and live in the Lighthouse House?"

He gave his mother the OK sign and the joy broke through on her face. She smiled happily through the tears.

"Good, because I quit my job this afternoon," she said.

He touched his heart, which meant "I love you, Mom" in their secret sign language, and then he took out his notepad and wrote AND NOT JUST BECAUSE YOU'RE AN HEIRESS, which made his mother laugh.

They stayed up late and ordered pizza, and in bed that night Jamie thought of what Thaddeus had said. Thaddeus was an intelligent man and more than that, he was a wise man. He had lived a long life. But he didn't know everything. And the proof was the letter. There *was* magic in the world. Even if it only existed because you believed in it. Even if magic was only a wish for things to be different and a chance for that wish to come true.

WIND SCREAMED through the rafters, spray from huge breakers thundered against the windows, and mountainous waves shook the building as if some terrible monster had been released from the ocean floor and was now angrily tearing the lighthouse to pieces.

The rain coming down the chimney had extinguished the fire, the candles had been blown out, and the lamp was impossible to relight with a sodden tinderbox. The girl could see nothing. Not the round walls. Not the bed. Not the white of her hand held a few inches from her eyes. And the storm clouds were so thick, they even smothered the lightning that crackled into the raging sea.

The darkness was like the stories she had read of the end of the world, when the stars were supposed to fall from the heavens and the sun would shine no more.

Maybe this *was* the end of the world.

Maybe she would never see her father or her home again.

She heard the boom of icebergs crashing into one another. Normally, they didn't come this far south, but the heavy weather had disrupted everything. The ships at sea would definitely be having trouble tonight.

This wasn't her first storm here, but this was the worst one yet. Water was pouring in through the smashed window, and the noise of the waves was terrifying—an endless stave of music on which the only note was the constant pounding of white water against the rocks.

She was sitting in the middle of her iron bed with the sheets wrapped around her like swaddling clothes.

The dark frightened her and the sound of the water sloshing against the furniture on the floor below made her more afraid. She knew the sea was unlikely to get this high, but she couldn't help but be anxious. She had never learned to swim; her father was a very busy man and hadn't had the time to teach her.

She thought about it for a moment or two and then she smiled ruefully to herself. She remembered what the sailors had told her. Even if she could swim, it wouldn't matter. The freezing-cold ocean would kill her long before she had a chance to drown.

If the lighthouse was ripped from the rock and the debris tossed into the waves, it would all be over in a few seconds.

She closed her eyes and opened them.

Open, closed—it made no difference; the pitch-blackness was the same.

She held the brooch against her chest and shook her head.

No, she would not be afraid.

This was not the end of the world.

This was an arctic gale, a low-pressure weather pattern, typical for the latitude and time of year. It was nothing more than that, and it too would pass. She knew all this because she was the daughter of a scientist and was beyond irrational fears.

"It is going to be fine," she whispered to herself.

A comforting thought as she heard tiles being ripped from the lighthouse roof and flung against the granite walls.

"It will be fine."

Just then a colossal wave smashed against the lighthouse, breaking another window and sending seawater cascading into the far side of the room. She held the brooch tighter and buried herself deeper under the blankets.

As she'd done before, she forced herself to think back to happier times with her father at the university. They'd gone hiking in the Basky Wood and once all the way to the summit of the Divide Mountain. From the mountaintop you could see thirty miles in all directions. To the west more mountains, some with snow; to the east a pleasant farming country and the river.

Yes, think about things like that.

She remembered a birthday. There had been a party and exotic food, and a conjurer.

She tried to recall her mother's face, and when she concentrated hard, it came back to her: blue-green eyes, yellow hair, and a smile that made everyone around her smile too.

If her mother were here right now she would be telling her, "Be brave, hold on, you can do it."

If her father were here he would be saying the same things, but he would also be talking about wind speed and how, if it was blowing this hard, it had to be a fast-moving storm and would therefore soon be done. Lorca (who had warned her not to come here in the first place) would be the most supportive of all. "Do not be afraid, little one," he would be saying in that honeyed accent of his.

"I will not be afraid," she said softly to herself, her tiny voice lost in the screeching gale. And she tried hard to be brave, but eventually she could contain the tears no more and began to sob.

She cried and cried and the sea roared and the thunder bellowed, and after a time her sobs were louder than the wind outside.

She wiped her face and listened.

The rain had stopped.

The central vortex of the depression had passed over the island and she knew the storm was ending.

She peeked her head out from under the covers and, a little later, got out of bed. She walked across the room and looked through the broken window. The sea was crashing on the rocks at the eastern shore of the island, but was no longer breaking on the lighthouse itself.

"It'll be over soon," she said to reassure herself.

She went back to the bed and lay down and waited for the morning.

Daylight came an hour later and by then the storm was gone.

But there was no time for celebration. She had a lot to do.

First of all, she checked the stores. The floor was drenched, but the cereals were in wax-sealed tubs and had not been damaged. The thick glass jars of flour were fine, and, in fact, her whole pantry was more or less intact except that the only bag of taka was ripped apart, soaked, and spoiled. Still, things could have been a lot worse.

Next, she would have to check the well.

She made her way down the spiral staircase and walked outside through the flotsam, jetsam, and the long lines of brown seaweed that had been cast up everywhere over the island. She threaded her way over the moss and the sharp, black volcanic rocks.

The spring was inland, about five hundred paces from the sea. The well cover was four-inch-thick cast iron and seemed OK, but she knew from previous experience that the water would taste brackish for a day or two.

She lowered the bucket, brought up some water, and took a drink.

She grimaced. It wasn't pleasant, but it wasn't too bad, and at least it wouldn't make her sick. She went back to the lighthouse and climbed to the top floor. She took the linen and her soaked bedding and carried them down-stairs. She stretched them out on the heather, hoping the sun and wind would dry them before nightfall.

She spent the whole of the morning and afternoon repairing the lighthouse and tidying the island as best she could. The only thing she couldn't fix was the roof. She'd need scaffolding or a ladder to get up there and she had neither. But a ground-level inspection showed that only a few tiles were missing and most of the roof was intact.

The sun was warm and it was so clear now that a hundred miles to the north she could make out the eerie glow of the sea ice reflecting the polar sun.

She worked hard and ate and drank, and in the evening when her chores were done, she opened one of the final jars of salt beef and cooked it slowly over the spirit stove. She boiled some well water and added a few *fala* leaves to take away the saline taste.

When night came, she went outside and walked around her little domain. A tiny island on which stood a solitary lighthouse in the middle of the frigid sea, hundreds of miles from land.

She sat on the rocky beach and watched the stars. The constellations comforted her. Perhaps her father was looking at the sky right now, at the Tree and the Ranta's Claw and the Serpent.

And then the moons rose: first Atmos, round and yellow, the older of the two, and then the smaller, potato-shaped Callis, which was white on one side and gray on the other.

She was tired. She took her dried sheets and walked to the top floor of the lighthouse to the great room where the fire and the lenses had been, years ago when the city had had the wealth to maintain this place and protect the shipping lanes.

Of course this also was where the Lords had come from, and, according to her father, would come again. She didn't know if she believed that or not. All she could do was wait and see. She yawned, and then in defiance of her father and in homage to her more superstitious mother, she prayed for deliverance from the invaders.

"Protect us from Alkhava and the iceships," she said, then blew out the tallow lamp, carefully remade her bed, lay down upon it, and slept.

❋ ❋ ❋

The sky was the color of a Giants hat, the kind of blue you only got in New York on a crisp winter day, very early, before the cars and the buses had pumped exhaust fumes and spent hydrocarbons into the air.

Jamie blinked. They weren't going to be seeing this particular patch of sky for a long time. His mother was standing beside him next to the suitcases while they waited for the airport taxi service to come. Two suitcases each. The rest of their meager possessions already sent on to Ireland.

Ireland—Jamie could still hardly believe it. They were going to Ireland. They were going to their own private island. "Muck," they'd called it, or "Mugg," Jamie thought, remembering the words in the lawyer's letter that he had read about twenty times by now.

On a map that he had downloaded from the Internet,

Muck Island appeared as a tiny speck of land off a place called Islandmagee. Islandmagee wasn't an island itself, but was really a peninsula, joined to the rest of Ireland through the town of Whitehead. But if you pretended it was a real island, then they were going to be living on an island called Muck, just off an island called Islandmagee, which was off an even bigger island called Ireland, off an even larger island called Great Britain. What was cooler than that? It was almost as if they were relocating to the edge of the world.

Except that it didn't have the inconveniences of the end of the world, because once on the mainland, they were only about an hour's drive from the big city of Belfast.

Muck looked very small, just a speck of green in the Irish Sea, but even if it was only half the size it wouldn't have mattered to Jamie or his mom. It was theirs. Their own personal kingdom to do with as they wanted.

For Anna it was a godsend. The check never came from Jamie's dad, but it didn't matter; they had a place to live for free, they would get money for upkeep and board, and if they were careful and didn't spend a lot, they could certainly save enough to send Jamie to college one day.

The lawyers sent a surveyor's chart showing the island, the Lighthouse House, a ruined tower next to the house, and a causeway linking the island to the mainland. Jamie had spent hours memorizing the layout of the island and although he was standing on a sidewalk on 125th Street in the heart of Manhattan, in his mind he was already there, walking along the windy shore, the rain beating on his back, with maybe a dog beside him carrying a stick in its mouth. The very first thing he would do on arrival would be to skim a stone on the sea. That would be something. A stone from his own beach on the Irish Sea.

His mother was looking at him.

"Did you hear what I said?" she asked.

He shook his head.

"I said, do you mind standing here for a sec while I leave the key? If the car service comes, tell them I'll only be a minute," Anna said.

Jamie gave her a thumbs-up, but he wasn't really paying attention. He was thinking about the other things he had learned. At first he'd been worried that the name "Muck" meant that the island was dirty or covered in bird droppings or something, but that wasn't it at all. "Muck" itself was a corruption of the Irish word *mugh,* which meant "pig" in some dictionaries and the more inexplicable "passage" in others.

So it wasn't some crappy mess. Quite the contrary. It was all good. And to add to their growing excitement, just yesterday the lawyers in Belfast had e-mailed Anna some recent pictures of the house and it looked windswept, wild, and wonderful. Two floors, like they'd said, white-painted walls, a tiled roof, and big windows facing out to sea. The lighthouse was a round stone tower about forty feet high that looked very, very old and in a bad state of disrepair; but that didn't bother Jamie. That only added to the romance of the whole thing.

Jamie blew hot air into his fist and stamped his feet on the New York sidewalk.

A bunch of kids walked past him in the direction of the subway stop.

He looked at them with disdain. No back to school and the depressing trudge through freezing January, February, and March for him.

Of course, he would have to go to school in Ireland. As his mom often reminded him, even in Ireland that was the law. But those would be different kids who didn't know him and with whom he could make a fresh start.

And he wouldn't go right away.

Anna said he could take a week off to adjust and then he was going to a school called Carrickfergus Grammar in the nearest big town. Anything was better than the Harlem School for Children with Special Challenges.

In a new country maybe things would be different.

His mom came back from the basement.

"Well, I've left the key with Eric, and we're done. The taxi should be here soon. I have to say, Eric looked terrible. He's been like that for an entire week. I'm glad we're leaving; there might be a flu bug going around."

Jamie smiled and sidled up next to his mother on the sidewalk.

"Are you going to miss anything?" Anna asked after a moment.

Jamie shook his head. Not much.

"I'm looking forward to some peace and quiet. The

New York noise—who needs it? Babies crying, sirens blaring, people yelling in English and Spanish, gunfire, smoke alarms, car alarms, air conditioners plummeting out of apartment windows, and, of course, the number 1 train rattling by at all hours of the day and night. Good to be going."

Jamie nodded.

Yes, things were good. It was New Year's Day, the sun was shining, the weather was mild, they were going on a trip and . . . suddenly a wave of panic went through him. He quickly pulled out his notebook, leaned on the suitcase, hurriedly wrote a note, and gave it to Anna: GOT TO GO TO THADDEUS, I COMPLETELY FORGOT, I PROMISED I'D SEE HIM BEFORE I LEFT.

"We don't have time, Jamie," Anna said, reading the note.

Jamie looked steadfast, his eyes fixed and determined.

"We don't have time," his mother insisted.

Jamie scrunched up his face to show that he was frustrated.

His mother looked at her watch and then relented.

"Well, only if you run. No chess games. And if he starts talking about World War Two, tell him you have to go. You have to be at JFK early to get through security. Go now. Hurry."

Jamie ran along 125th Street and, at a break in the traffic, crossed to the George Bruce Library. He sprinted up the stairs and looked for Thaddeus at his old window seat in the corner, but he wasn't there today. Breathing heavily, he jogged to the checkout desk, wrote a note in his book, and handed it to Mrs. Moore: DID THADDEUS COME IN TODAY?

Mrs. Moore shook her head. "No, Jamie, he hasn't been well, he—"

But before she could even finish, Jamie had turned and was sprinting out of the library. Fast down the stairs, between the taxis and cars, and up one block to Thaddeus's apartment on 126th Street.

When he reached the building, he was sweating and completely out of breath. He buzzed Thaddeus's number and waited. There was a cough over the intercom.

"Who is it?" Thaddeus asked.

Jamie didn't answer.

"Who is it?" Thaddeus asked a second time and Jamie again said nothing.

Thaddeus got angry now.

"You kids, you think it's funny to torment an old man with the . . . oh, wait a minute, is that you, Jamie? Buzz two times if it's you."

Jamie hit the buzzer twice. Thaddeus pressed the latch release button and let him into the building.

Thaddeus lived in a nice old place constructed in the 1930s mainly as a residence for professors and students attending City College. A gilded, spacious elevator took Jamie to the fifth floor.

He walked along the plushly carpeted corridor and knocked at 502.

"It's open," Thaddeus said.

Jamie went inside. He had been here on several occasions, but every time it looked worse. The large apartment was stuffed full of thousands of books, magazines, and newspapers. Even the leather chairs and the table were piled up with volumes—hardbacks, paperbacks, and hundreds of old *National Geographic*s and *Scientific Americans*. Thaddeus hated to throw anything away in case there was something he wanted to read again. The old man almost never opened the windows, and the place had a blended aroma of coffee, cat, old books, and tobacco smoke.

Thaddeus was still in his pajamas and bathrobe. He was sitting on the sofa by the window with a blanket over his legs and thick slippers on his feet. He was smoking a pipe and seemed pale and ancient.

"Come in, Jamie, sit down now," he said between coughs.

Jamie sat opposite him in a rocking chair. Concern flitted across Jamie's face as Thaddeus coughed again.

"Don't look at me like that, you don't have to worry about me; I've got a cold, that's all, I ain't going to die anytime soon. If the Nazis couldn't kill me, a cold ain't going to either. And I want to be around to prove those people wrong about the world ending in 2012."

Jamie wrote a note and handed it to him: I DON'T HAVE LONG, MY MOM IS WAITING OUTSIDE IN A TAXI.

Thaddeus nodded.

"Yeah, I know, you're leaving today, going to Ireland

and probably not coming back. I been to Ireland. North and South. Decent place. Wet. Can't get corn bread anywhere in the whole country."

Gus came over and jumped on Thaddeus's lap. Gus was the cat Thaddeus had adopted from the animal shelter. A nice, good-natured tabby cat that Jamie liked. Thaddeus liked him too, but he wasn't feeling up to having a cat on him today.

"Beat it, Gus, the kid's in a hurry and we ain't got much time," Thaddeus said.

Gus looked at Thaddeus philosophically for a moment, jumped off his lap, and found a cozy spot in a pile of newspapers.

"Well, Jamie, I ain't one for good-byes and I ain't one for giving out parting wisdom either, but I do want to give you something. I've been thinking about this for a while," Thaddeus said. He got slowly to his feet and went into a back room. He came out holding a box, which he opened and presented to Jamie. It was a shiny black tablet PC. Jamie had seen them before on TV. One of the kids in school had one; they were pretty cool.

Jamie shook his head. He wasn't sure if the old man could afford such an expensive thing.

"Take it," Thaddeus said.

Jamie shook his head again and this made Thaddeus really angry.

"Don't you shake your head at me, boy. This is a present for you and you are going to be gracious enough to

 45

accept it. In my day, we showed respect for our elders," he growled.

Jamie took the shiny black computer, which was about the size of a textbook. It had a flat screen with a stylus on one side and a keyboard at the bottom.

"Do you like it?" Thaddeus asked.

Jamie nodded.

"OK, good, now let me show you what it's for. Give it over. OK. Now, I know you've had a problem speaking to people, I know it's a problem upstairs with your mind, not with anything physiological to do with your body. And I know you and you're a good kid and you're going to grow out of it eventually. But this is until you do, in the meantime. This is what you'll do. It's just like your notebook. You take this stylus, the pen, you write on the screen whatever you want to say, and then you press this button and it speaks it for you."

Thaddeus wrote something on the computer screen.

"Hello, my name is Thaddeus," a slightly mechanical voice intoned from the tablet PC.

He handed the computer back to Jamie.

"Now, if you get faster at typing than writing, you can use the keyboard instead of the stylus. Otherwise, print in block capitals until the software recognizes your handwriting. The battery is good for eight hours, and you can recharge it every night. Eight hours. That should be a full day of conversations. You can even set the macro so that you can quickly play phrases you use all the time, like "hello" and "how ya doing?" There's a little handle at the top so you can carry it around, and you shouldn't have any trouble with it. I got the one that looked the most reliable. There's even a Velcro strap you can wrap tight around your left arm. Then you could even walk and have your right arm free for writing. What do you think? Is it a good idea?"

Jamie was stunned for a second, but then he nodded.

"Well, show me," Thaddeus said.

Jamie took the tablet PC and wrote a few words on the screen. He pushed the voice button and it said: "Thank you, Thaddeus."

A tear came into Thaddeus's eye and he turned his back so that Jamie wouldn't see. Jamie wrote something else on the screen.

"I have to go now, Thaddeus. My mom is waiting," the PC said.

"Good. You better run along now. Use that thing. And you can e-mail me on it too. I can check my e-mail every day in the library and I'll be waiting for a letter. Listening? OK. Thaddeus Harper at hotmail dot com. You got that, boy?"

"I got it," Jamie answered via the computer.

"Good. Now get out of here. And don't forget that you're a New Yorker and the Yankees are good for baseball no matter what anybody says. OK, now, git and give your mom a kiss from me. I wish you both the best of luck in Ireland. I was there in forty-three. I expect it's changed some, but I believe you'll like it."

Jamie nodded and, surprising himself, rushed forward and gave Thaddeus a hug. Thaddeus held him for a minute and let him go; he couldn't help himself anymore and was crying now. Jamie smiled at him, turned, waved, and ran out of the apartment.

❋ ❋ ❋

Jamie's first view of Ireland through the airplane window was of a green, misty country made up of tiny fields and small white houses. The sun was setting in the west, turning the sky a brilliant orange and the Irish Sea a deep pink tinged with gold.

The plane skirted over Belfast and flew over mountains and a forest and a huge lake that the pilot said was called Lough Neagh.

Despite his excitement, Jamie yawned.

It had been a long day.

They had flown from New York to London's Gatwick Airport, and then they'd taken a bus to London's Heathrow Airport, and there, eventually, they'd boarded a plane to Belfast. A lot of people were making the exact same trip, having been persuaded by Board Failte that the far north of Ireland (the wettest spot on the island) would be a great place for a vacation. Most of them were career New York firefighters and cops taking the holiday of a lifetime and bringing with them their wives and golf clubs: the wives destined to spend much of the trip sheltering from the perpetual downpour in overpriced wool shops and the golf clubs fated never to be used because of the very same rain.

Even though Jamie had only spent a couple of hours in England—and most of that in the airport—it was still very exciting to be in a new country. The first time Jamie had ever been anywhere outside America. People talked with a different accent, they didn't look like New Yorkers, and they certainly dressed differently too.

Jamie had explored the vast expanses of Terminal 3 and bought British candies, comic books, and even a Big Ben pencil case.

Anna had a so-called bagel, but it was really just a roll with a hole in the middle of it.

When they boarded a 777 plane for the final leg of their trip, Jamie took the window seat, so that he could see everything that the pilot talked about: Manchester, Liverpool, the Isle of Man, and now Ireland.

"Ladies and gentlemen, we will be touching down shortly. Please fasten your seat belts," the copilot intoned over the intercom.

There was a burst of applause from a few weepy sentimentalists.

Ireland, however, did appear lovely; although after eight hours in economy, perhaps any large land mass would have looked inviting.

"We're here," Anna said.

"I know," Jamie wrote and then replied via his computer.

Anna grinned at him. Here was real communication at last. Thaddeus's present was wonderful and, if it could bring Jamie out of his shell, she would accept it as a temporary solution.

And Jamie liked the tablet PC. It not only helped him talk, but there were games on it, maps, an encyclopedia, and an MP3 player for music. It was the best present he had ever received. Two great things had happened inside a week, and he hoped that a bad thing wasn't going to follow to balance them out.

The undercarriage extended and without any further announcements from the pilot, they touched down at Belfast International Airport, which was a good twenty miles from the city in the middle of the Irish countryside. There was no passport control, but an agriculture inspector asked if they were bringing in any animal products or had recently been in contact with any animals.

"We went to the Central Park Zoo, but contact was minimal. They frown on that sort of thing," Anna joked.

"Yeah, lions got my arm last time," Jamie said through the tablet PC.

The man was not amused, and confiscated Anna's bologna sandwich, which she'd packed in case the airline food was terrible.

They went past Agriculture and out into the busy and thronged Arrivals Lounge, with its strip lights, bad country Muzak, voices in barely comprehensible Irish accents, and dozens of people standing behind a rope waiting for loved ones and relatives.

They got their bags and found the stand for Ulsterbus. Unfortunately, there was some sort of problem with the bus to Islandmagee. This was not so unusual. As a transportation service Ulsterbus enjoyed a somewhat spotty track record. On occasion their timetables were fictitious, their vehicles dangerous, and their drivers oblivious to rules, regulations, speed limits, and scheduled stops. However, all of this was made up for by the quality of their excuses, which showed a great deal of creativity and imagination. "I'm sorry, but your bus has been hijacked," or "The driver has been abducted by unknown elements," were common refrains in the 1980s. The company's representatives were especially inventive when foreign tourists were present.

"Sorry, there won't be any service today, as the leprechauns are on strike," a complacent mustachioed man said deadpan to Anna.

"They are?" Anna asked, befuddled.

"I'm afraid so."

"And that means what, exactly?"

"No service. Earliest, tomorrow morning, if then," the man announced with grim certainty.

"How are we going to get to Islandmagee? All the taxis are gone and—" Anna began with indignation but was interrupted by Jamie tugging at her sleeve.

Jamie had noticed a tall, older man in a tweed suit

with gray unbrushed hair and round glasses who was walking around the airport holding up a sign that said ANNA O'NEILL.

"What, Jamie?" Anna asked.

Jamie nudged his mother in the ribs and pointed at the man.

Anna reholstered her indignation and went over to him immediately.

"Are you waiting for me?" she asked.

"Are you Anna? And is this Jamie?" the man asked.

"Yes," Anna replied.

"Oh, good. I'm so glad. I'm delighted to meet you. I'm Arthur McCreagh from the solicitors. I believe we have talked on the phone."

"Yes, we have, how kind of you to meet us. They didn't mention that anyone was coming to the airport," Anna said and offered him her hand. He shook it happily.

"Oh, I'm glad to do it. I'm the trustee of the settlement. I was going to send a taxi for you, but then I decided to come out myself. I wanted to meet you, see how you were doing, and, of course, I wanted to meet Jamie. The new Laird. Did you have a pleasant flight?"

"It was a long day, but everything was pretty straightforward," Anna said.

"Excellent. Come on now, I'll help you get your bags. I have my car parked outside."

When they'd gotten their suitcases from the luggage

carousel, they made their way out of the airport and walked to a large brown, mud-strewn Land Rover.

"This is the car, just pop everything in the back," McCreagh said.

The wet, dark sky was obscured by low clouds and the air was cold and damp. Jamie was only wearing his jeans and T-shirt and he shivered a little.

"Are you OK? Are you a wee bit cold? You get in the car, Jamie, and I'll load her up. Put the heat on if you want," McCreagh said. Jamie shook his head. He didn't want to look like a wimp; he nodded to show that he was fine and lifted in the heaviest of the suitcases with his right hand. McCreagh looked at him with admiration and loaded the other bags.

When they were all safely inside the vehicle, McCreagh turned the lights on and sped out of the airport, driving the car northeast toward Islandmagee.

Jamie sat in the back, the two adults in the front.

Jamie fiddled with the seat belt, but he couldn't get it to work. He took out his PC.

"Is it a long drive?" Jamie wrote and the computer asked in its metallic voice.

McCreagh stared at Jamie for a second in the mirror and blinked.

"It's about an hour," he said and, perplexed, he looked at Anna for an explanation.

"Oh, um, he has a speech problem," Anna said.

McCreagh looked puzzled for a moment and then

nodded, no doubt recalling what Anna had said about Jamie recovering from cancer.

"Aye, I see, sorry to hear that, Jamie. I heard about your arm of course. But not the voice. Very sorry," McCreagh said and turned to Anna. "Is it gone permanently? Be a shame if the Laird couldn't speak at all."

"We don't know, it might come back one day," Anna said, embarrassed.

McCreagh looked at her and shook his head.

"Excuse me, that was a very impertinent question. I apologize. Live in hope and all that," he said.

McCreagh turned around in his seat.

"You're bearing up very well, young man, under your—uh—illness. I'm sure you're a big help to your mother," he said.

"'Big help' might be overdoing it, but now and again he makes his bed," Anna said with a smile.

"You never make yours," Jamie said though the PC.

"What does 'Laird' mean?" Anna asked to change the subject.

McCreagh looked at her and cocked his head.

"You said that you wanted to come to the airport to meet Jamie, the Laird, and then you just used the word again. Is it just an Irish word? Does it mean 'lad'?"

"Oh, no, no, not at all. Didn't we tell you in the letter? Margaret was supposed to send you a copy of the coat of arms from the Order of Heralds in London. Did you not get it?"

Anna shook her head.

"Oh, dear. Well, it's very simple; Jamie is the sole male descendant of Topper O'Neill, Laird of Muck. So when he turns eighteen, he becomes Laird of Muck," McCreagh explained.

"What is that, exactly?" Anna asked. "Laird of Muck?"

"It's a hereditary order—a minor one, somewhere between a baronetcy and an ordinary peer. It's an old title in the gift of the Earl of Ulster; the English equivalent would be 'Lord'."

Jamie's eyes widened. His mother gasped.

"Jamie is a lord?"

McCreagh laughed.

"Not at the moment, but technically, yes, he'll become Laird of Muck on his majority. You and Jamie are both of the royal line of the O'Neills. O'Neill is the royal name in Ireland. O'Neills and Ui Neills were the last Irish kings before the English took over. Of course, most people have forgotten about that."

"Well, O'Neill isn't royalty in America, they're everywhere. Paul O'Neill, Eugene O'Neill, Ryan O'Neal, Tatum O'Neal. Pretty common name," Anna said.

"Shaquille O'Neal," Jamie wrote.

"It's the same here now of course, but regardless, Jamie is the closest relative of Topper O'Neill and Topper is a direct descendant of the Great O'Neill, Prince of Ulster."

All three of them sat quietly contemplating this for a moment.

"But like you said, it doesn't actually mean anything," Anna insisted, still unable to really take it in.

"Well, it does and it doesn't. The full title is, let me see if I can remember it—oh, yes, 'Laird of Muck, Captain of the Ui Neill, Guardian of the Passage.' Of course, in the old days he could have taken his seat in the House of Lords in London, but they scrapped all that a few years ago. Nowadays you can't do much with the title itself; you can't even sell it, although I daresay you'll get invited to dine with the queen when you turn eighteen, that's if there's still a monarchy by then. Now, hold on, I'll have to get some petrol at the filling station here and then we're really going to have to get cracking if we want to beat the tide."

He pulled the car into a gas station and ran inside to pay first. Anna turned to Jamie in the back, who was grinning in the darkness.

"I know what you're thinking. You're thinking the Laird of Muck won't have to do the dishes, the Laird of Muck definitely won't have to clean his room. Well, I'm the Laird-Queen-Mother-Lord, and what I say goes," Anna said with a laugh. Jamie had been thinking exactly that, and his mother's insight made him smile.

McCreagh filled the gas tank and got back in the car.

"What do you mean 'the tide'?" Anna asked as they drove out of the gas station and down a dark, one-lane country road.

"Well, Muck Island is an island, you know," McCreagh said.

"I know that, but isn't there a causeway or something out to it?" Anna asked.

"Yes, there is. And most of the time it's passable, but at the highest point of high tide it is completely underwater, and you are effectively cut off from the mainland. So it *is* a real island. But don't worry, that only happens twice a day for about an hour; the rest of the time you can walk across the causeway without any bother. And even at high tide, I suppose, you could wade across in an emergency. Old Topper O'Neill used to walk back from the pub in Wellington boots, time or tide regardless."

"You mentioned him a moment ago. He was the one we inherited from?" Anna asked.

"No, no. Topper died years ago. You inherited from his son who lived in Donegal. Samuel. He used the Lighthouse House only as a summer home, seldom came even then. Last month he died without issue at a hospital in London. He had some money which went to charity, but, of course, the house and the island are entailed upon direct descendants of the line. We had a job tracking you down . . . Anyway, what was I talking about? Oh, yes. The tide shouldn't really affect pedestrians, but driving over the causeway is a different proposition. It's not paved, and it's quite slippery. That you can only do at a reasonably low tide and I want to get you across with your belongings."

McCreagh looked at his watch.

"We've got about forty minutes."

Jamie had listened to the conversation intently and with growing excitement.

He was exhausted from all the traveling, but he knew that the words Laird of Muck, Captain of the Ui Neill, and Guardian of the Passage were going to keep him awake all night.

They arrived in the town of Whitehead half an hour later and drove north onto the peninsula of Islandmagee, reaching the hamlet of Portmuck about ten minutes after that. In the darkness, all they could make out were fields, a few sheep, a couple of cows.

Portmuck was tiny. A score of houses at the bottom of a steep hill right on the water. A pub, a grocery store, a bay with fishing boats pulled up on a stony beach.

McCreagh drove the car through the village and onto the causeway leading to Muck Island, which was the dark mass of land a hundred yards offshore. Before they reached the causeway, Jamie couldn't help but notice (and be slightly unnerved by) the DANGER—TIDES and MOTOR VEHICLES PROHIBITED signs.

McCreagh continued over the causeway, going slowly over the loose sand and gravel.

"Ooh, I see the house. Do you see it, Jamie?" cried Anna. "But I don't see a lighthouse at all. Where is it, Mr. McCreagh?"

"Well, the lighthouse is not a traditional example of

that form. It's an old round tower dating back at least to the Viking times, but in the nineteenth century, as this part of Ireland became a shipping lane, equipment was installed and it was used as a lighthouse for about sixty years. The round tower was far too small for a keeper to live there, so they had to build a house next to it."

"They don't use it as a lighthouse today?" Jamie asked via the PC.

"No, it's not necessary. They took out the bulbs and equipment at least half a century ago. The coast is well protected nowadays. There's a big light at Blackhead, one over on the Maidens, one on the Copelands. You'll count about seven or eight lighthouses when you look out to sea on a clear night. You'll soon learn to tell them apart; each light has a slightly different time signature between signals. Some have periods of four seconds, some of five and, well, they're all different—"

"Please tell me about the house, if you don't mind," Anna interrupted, not that excited about how to tell one lighthouse from another at night, although Jamie had been fascinated.

"Well, it's late Victorian," McCreagh said. "Built by the British government for a lighthouse keeper and his family. The government leased the whole island from the Lairds of Muck, converted the tower into a lighthouse, and built the Lighthouse House. But then when the more modern lighthouses were built, the government gave it back."

"So how old is the house itself?" Anna asked.

"The Lighthouse House dates back, I suppose, to the 1870s; but, like I say, the round tower probably goes back about a thousand years, perhaps more . . . OK then, folks, here we are. We're on the island. *Your* island."

"Our island," Anna whispered.

McCreagh drove across the tiny islet and stopped the car in front of the Lighthouse House.

"I hope you like the house. You'll have to do a bit of fixing up, but we got the fire going for you and did some repairs and I think it looks well. I had a cleaning service come in this morning and do a big tidy, and I took the liberty of throwing out and burning all the old bedding. Got in new sheets, new blankets. Paid for it from the trust, of course. Hope you don't mind. I've written down instructions on how to use the appliances. Oh, and I've stocked up your pantry with some basics."

"Thank you very much," Anna said.

"Nay problem," McCreagh said.

He turned off the ignition and immediately began unloading the suitcases.

"OK, folks, I'd love to show you around and I hate to leave you, but I really have to make this tide," he said when he was done.

"That's fine, thank you very much, Mr. McCreagh," Anna said.

"My pleasure. You'll be fine, but if you have any problems, give me a call. Just remember what I said. At high tide you'd be better not to use the causeway. The water only goes up to knee height, but the currents can be treacherous. I know that I said Topper used to wade across to the mainland in practically all conditions, but I wouldn't advise it."

"How high can the water get? It won't come in the house, will it?" Anna asked.

"On a spring tide—that's about twice a month—it can get up to eight or nine feet of water. The house is about thirty feet above sea level, so unless the polar ice caps melt, you'll be fine. I'll drop by tomorrow, but I have to go now."

McCreagh waved to Jamie and Anna, got in the car, and began driving to the causeway. He suddenly stopped, got out, and ran back to them. He reached into his pocket and gave Jamie an old and large iron key.

Jamie took it. It felt heavy and cold in his right hand.

"This is the key to the lighthouse, the old tower; its rightful owner is the Laird, and this key has been in the Laird's family for hundreds of years. It's yours now, Jamie, but you may not give it to anyone, and do not lose it. Keep it safe. Keep it very safe. Do you understand me?"

Jamie nodded.

"If you must go exploring, there's an entrance to the round tower at the back of the Lighthouse House. It's the big iron door. I have to warn you though, it's very danger-ous in there. No one's been in since they removed the bulbs and the machinery, and Topper had a very nasty fall in there which almost killed him. The spiral staircase is crumbling and the—"

"Thank you, Mr. McCreagh, I think I'll take that," Anna said and took the key from Jamie.

McCreagh nodded. "Maybe that's best until he's a wee bit older. Well, anyway, I have to go."

"Mr. McCreagh, you've been very helpful. Thank you," Anna said.

"Don't mention it. It was all my pleasure. Delighted to meet you both . . . Must fly," McCreagh said, then jumped in the car and drove back across the causeway. The water was already halfway up the tires and he was lucky he didn't stall, but in under a minute they saw him driving into Portmuck.

"Let's check out the house, Jamie," Anna said.

The front door was open, and inside the porch were the boxes they had sent from New York. There were surprisingly few of them. Books, dishes, clothes. Neither Jamie nor his mother cared much about possessions. Maybe because the things they owned were so crappy. Anna had few family heirlooms, and Jamie had grown out of his toys and games.

They walked inside the house itself.

At first it was a little disappointing. It seemed small downstairs. A living room, a dining room, a kitchen, a library, and a fireplace. Upstairs there were three small bedrooms, and a bathroom with a bath and no shower. The ceilings were low and although the place had been swept and a fire lit, there was still a musty smell.

But the advantages more than outweighed the problems. Each room in the house had huge windows that looked out to sea and the place was at least five times bigger than their old apartment in New York City.

Jamie helped his mother unpack their night things, then brushed his teeth and changed into his pajamas. There were three bedrooms to choose from, and he picked the one in the corner nearest the old lighthouse that Mr. McCreagh had called the round tower.

Within ten minutes, Jamie was snuggled up in bed in the empty room. He opened the windows and looked out to sea. There were lights in distant Scotland and as Mr. McCreagh had said, lighthouses all up and down the Irish and Scottish coasts. It looked amazing.

Jamie suddenly remembered his plan to throw a stone and got out of bed. His mother came in just as he was pulling on a pair of sneakers.

"Are you OK, Jamie? Do you think you'll be happy here?"

Jamie took out his tablet PC, leaned it on the bed and wrote: "Yes, I will. Mom, I want to go down to the beach just for a second, before I go to bed, is that OK?"

Anna was so happy to hear a question from him, even via a machine, she nodded.

He pulled on a robe and went outside to the rocky beach in front of the house.

A beautiful sight.

The sea was calm and quiet. Above, fistfuls of stars. Black water stretching out from the beach in front of Jamie's house all the way across to Scotland, where the twinkling lights of the town of Portpatrick seemed close enough to touch.

Jamie picked up a stone and skimmed it across the waves.

"Jamie, come on, it's time for bed," his mother yelled from the house.

Yes, I'm really here. This isn't a dream. This is our house now, and our lighthouse and our island, he thought and he felt almost as happy as he'd been before they had diagnosed him with cancer. With this big new house, maybe even Dad would visit now.

He turned and began walking back up the beach. And then an odd aspect of the ancient tower caught his eye. Although the moon was shining on both the house and the tower, the old lighthouse seemed to absorb the moonlight rather than reflect it, almost as if it had something to hide, as if it were lurking in the shadows of the night, waiting patiently for the right time to reveal itself.

Jamie stared at it a moment, smiled at his own silliness, shivered, and ran inside.

Chapter III
THE BOY

A CINDER SEA spooked and quiet under a pale sky. A nearly deserted Irish country road. A dungy smell from the damp fields.

Static was making the hairs spark on Jamie's wool blazer and the rising sun was scattering little white clouds and warming the cold air.

The morning was so clear that from the bus stop, Jamie could see Arran Island, Ayrshire, and the Mull of Kintyre on the other side of the North Channel.

Under the bus stop sign, a boy was looking at him with curiosity. Jamie didn't like it when people looked at him, but since his surgery nearly a year ago he was more than used to it.

The boy was different from most people who stared at him. They would generally do their gawking furtively, surreptitiously, no doubt whispering to their friends and wondering what had happened to this poor kid with one arm. But not this boy; this character was looking, unapologetically and boldly, right at him.

They were both waiting for the same bus to Carrickfergus Grammar and both were identically dressed in a uniform of black trousers, black blazer, white shirt, and a blue-white-

 65

and-red tie. Jamie felt a bit ridiculous, but as long as everyone had to wear these clothes, it would be OK.

The boy was about Jamie's own age, thirteen, very tall, with wild curly hair that was jet-black and seemingly unbrushable. He had a long aquiline nose, the palest skin Jamie had ever seen, intelligent hazel eyes, and a goofy smile plying about a friendly face. He was skinny but athletic, and if it had been America, Jamie would have pegged him as a basketball player, although Jamie didn't think they played basketball in Ireland. In general, the boy seemed as if he was a pleasant enough person, but even so, the stares were making Jamie very uncomfortable, and he was now doing his best to ignore them.

If the boy was trying to be rude, this would be the first negative experience Jamie had had since arriving in Ireland on that dark night a week ago. Everything else had been great. He had thoroughly explored his new house and the whole of the island that was to be his home. Apart from the ancient lighthouse tower and the Lighthouse House itself, the island was a treeless landscape of thick grass and moss-covered rocks. On the east side, facing the sea, there was one long stony beach and a small cliff. On the west shore, a few scrubby bushes and, of course, the causeway to the tiny village of Portmuck. There were bird's nests all over the island, and at the northern tip he saw seals playing in the water. It was always windy and cold, but that didn't matter. It was an incredible location, isolated and interesting with amazing views up and down the Irish Sea.

The one place he hadn't explored was the old light-house itself, the gray stone round tower. His mother had kept the key to the iron door and had refused to let him go up there because of Mr. McCreagh's warnings about the dangers of ascending the spiral staircase. He had wanted to investigate further, but his mother had been quite firm, and anyway the novelty of everything else had more than compensated for this one disappointment. Even Portmuck Village had been interesting. It had just one grocery store and one pub, but there were fishing boats in the tiny harbor, cows and horses in the nearby fields, and friendly people wherever they went.

Friendly, that is, until now.

The boy blew into his hands and continued gawking at him.

Jamie turned his back on the kid and stared into the fields. He looked at his watch for the tenth time in about two minutes.

"Don't worry, this bus is late on a regular basis," the boy said in a heavy Irish accent.

Jamie could feel the boy's gaze on his back, but he didn't turn around.

"The bus, it's always late," the boy said again.

Jamie decided he was going to pretend that the boy didn't exist. Sometimes that worked and the person bothering you would get bored and go away. And if you did that enough, you could build up a mental barrier against everyone.

It wasn't that Jamie disliked people, it was just that he

wanted to be left alone. He wanted to be left with his hurt and his anger at the world for what it had done to him. An anger that had admittedly lessened since he had left New York but which was still there in the background. A cold, simmering presence that he could never quite get rid of, not when he stared at himself in the mirror or nervously put on his new school clothes for the first time and had to tuck the left arm in his blazer pocket.

"I said, the bus is always late, wee lad," the boy repeated.

Jamie looked out to sea and watched a large sailing ship cutting against the wind and, farther north, a red-and-white ferry pulling into Larne Harbor.

And then he heard footsteps and he knew the boy was walking over. He tensed but still didn't turn, not even when the rude boy actually tapped him on the shoulder.

"Listen, mate, I have the advantage over you. I know who you are, but you don't know who I am. You're Jamie who moved into the Lighthouse House a week ago. My name is Ramsay. I'm telling you this because I know your name and a wee bit about you and it's not fair if you don't know anything about me."

He'd said this in such a reasonable way that Jamie reluctantly turned to look at him.

The boy was offering him a hand. A big, white, meaty, Irish paw sticking out of his blazer sleeve. After a moment's hesitation, Jamie shook it. Ramsay let go suddenly after just a second.

"Have you had the chicken pox?" he asked quickly.

Jamie nodded. He'd been vaccinated when he was little.

"Thank God for that, I'm just getting over it—see the little scratchy scars on my hand? Wouldn't like to contaminate you. Not a good way to begin a friendship."

Jamie shook his head.

"So you're Jamie from America," Ramsay said.

Jamie nodded.

"You don't speak?"

Jamie shook his head.

Ramsay nodded. His brown eyes blinked knowingly.

"You had cancer, didn't you?"

Jamie looked surprised.

"It's a small place, Portmuck. It didn't take long till we knew everything about you. Shall I tell you what we found out?"

Jamie shrugged his shoulders.

"OK, I will then, and if it's crap you can shoot me down. Well, first of all, you and your mum are from New York and you were related to old Topper O'Neill who owned the Lighthouse House. And his son died and since you're the closest cousins you get the house and you're going to be living there from now on. Second of all, you had cancer. Third of all, your name is Jamie. Fourth of all, you're going to be going to my school. Am I right about all of that?"

Jamie nodded again.

"What happened to your arm? Was that because of the cancer? You had cancer and they cut your arm off?" Ramsay asked.

Jamie normally didn't respond to that kind of question, but there was something about Ramsay's big open face that seemed to say that he had asked only in the spirit of inquiry and was not trying to be unpleasant, so Jamie nodded his head again.

"And what happened to your voice? Did the chemotherapy burn out your larynx?"

Jamie shook his head.

"Are you not capable of speaking?"

Jamie nodded.

"You are capable of speaking?" Ramsay asked.

Jamie affirmed this with a second nod of the head.

"I get it, you can speak but you choose not to speak, is that correct?" Ramsay asked.

Jamie nodded.

"Huh, well, that's pretty interesting," Ramsay said, squinting with concentration. "You are physically able to talk, but ya just don't want to. Is that with everybody or just with me? Oh, you can't answer. Still, I can tell. It's everybody, isn't it? Fascinating. Have you never spoken? Like when you were a wean?"

Jamie didn't understand the term "wean," but he got the question and again gently nodded.

"You used to speak and now you don't because you don't want to. In the Xbox of life you've deliberately selected *Degree of Difficulty: Hard*. Hmmm, you're a bit mental aren't you?" Ramsay said.

Jamie frowned.

"Oh, don't worry about it though. I'm a bit mental too. All the greats were a bit mental. It's a fine line between genius and madness. You know what someone said about Victor Hugo? 'Victor Hugo is a madman who thinks he's Victor Hugo.' See what I mean? And in his high school they thought Einstein was a special needs case as well."

Ramsay could see that one of the references had eluded Jamie. He looked puzzled. Ramsay couldn't imagine anyone who hadn't heard of Albert Einstein, so he assumed it was the former.

"You haven't heard of Victor Hugo? He's a French writer. *Hunchback of Notre Dame*? Does that ring a bell? Ho, ho, ring a bell . . .'"

Ramsay began to laugh. Jamie didn't get the joke. Ramsay wiped the smirk off his face.

"Well, that's not important. Like I say, I'm Ramsay, I'm practically your next-door neighbor. I live in that big blue cottage as you drive into Portmuck. You must have seen it."

Jamie nodded. Ramsay rocked back on his heels and smiled at him. They stood quietly for a minute or two.

"They say that silence also is a type of conversation. Do you think?" Ramsay asked.

Jamie nodded. Ramsay scratched his nose and agreed with himself.

"I don't like many people, Jamie. Most of them annoy me, but you know what, I like you," he declared.

Jamie raised an eyebrow.

"Aye, I like ya. You follow your own code. You can talk, but you don't want to and that's your prerogative, mate. It's fine by me. Too much useless talk in the world anyway? I mean, what's the point of saying anything to anybody? When my words enter your brain what happens to them? Most of the time you'll never remember them, and if by some miracle you do remember them and they get encoded into little chemical or electrical ones and zeros in your brain, so what? We're all going to be dead in a hundred years or so and then they'll be lost forever, so what does it matter what any of us say? My half-brother, Brian, says that in the great scheme of things our lives are just a tiny blip in the vast eons of time. It's all pretty meaningless, really."

Jamie looked at Ramsay with a growing sense that the amicable feelings were mutual, that he liked this tall, strange Irish boy.

"Let me tell you something about the meaninglessness of words. You want to hear? I mean, if I'm blathering on, just tell me and I'll shut up. Oh, wait, you can't tell me; well, just spit if you want me to shut up."

Jamie reached into his backpack and pulled out his tablet PC.

"Nice computer," Ramsay said with admiration.

Jamie sat on the ground and wrote, "I'd really like to hear, Ramsay," and the computer played it back.

"Huh? So you'll write notes to people and let the computer talk, but you won't speak yourself. Isn't that a bit of a contradiction? I mean, if you're trying to isolate yourself from the whole world, you should be consistent, wee lad. Still, it's your life and your set of rules. And we all got our own wee things. Anyway, it's none of my business, and I was going to tell you something about words. This is it. It's going to blow your mind. Are you ready?"

Jamie nodded his head.

"There are more stars in the sky than all the words spoken by all the humans in all of time," Ramsay said and let this sink in for a moment.

"Is that true?" Jamie wrote.

"Yeah, it's true. And every day astronomers are finding planets around the stars. Almost every star seems to have a planetary system. So that means there are billions and billions of worlds out there. I don't know about you, but it sort of puts things in perspective for me. You know, everything on this screwed-up planet is pretty darn insignificant in galactic terms. So if one little kid on one wee corner of one stupid little planet doesn't want to speak, who cares? It doesn't mean a thing."

Jamie realized that he liked Ramsay because even though they were completely different, Ramsay reminded him a little of Thaddeus.

Ramsay laughed and rubbed his hands through his thick curly hair.

"So, you're Jamie O'Neill. Jamie O'Neill. You know that's a royal name don't you?"

Jamie nodded his head. Mr. McCreagh had mentioned it last week.

"Oh, yeah, the O'Neills were the Princes of Ulster for a thousand years or more. My name's McDonald. Ramsay McDonald. You probably don't know, being an American, but I share my name with a lame British Prime Minister from the 1930s. He didn't do much and what he did, he did badly. My parents had never heard of him and no one remembers him, but even so it sucks having the same name as some wick politician from yesteryear. And even if he was some cool guy, if you were a parent, you'd try and think of a different name, wouldn't ya? I mean, if my surname was Heisenberg, I'd never call my kid Werner, would you?"

Jamie shook his head, although he wasn't quite following what Ramsay was suggesting.

"My only consolation is that they didn't call me Ronald. Ronald McDonald? Can you imagine it? I'd have to move to Botswana or somewhere. Did they tell you that you're the Laird of Muck? I mean you're not just descended from royalty, in a way you are like a kind of Lord."

"They did tell me that," Jamie wrote on the computer.

"Yeah, I'd keep that quiet though. The kids at school would probably take the piss out of you and call you Lord Muck or something. It's going to be hard enough for you as it is, being a new boy, American, having one arm, and not speaking, you don't need to add to your troubles. Did you ever read *Little Lord Fauntleroy*?"

Jamie shook his head.

"Me neither, but I'll bet you it's a similar situation and it probably didn't work too well for the poor wee lad, probably took lots of crap until the very last chapter, so I'd avoid the whole trauma if I were you and keep the Lord thing under your hat."

Jamie nodded.

"Of course, if I was royalty, it would give me more of a chance with Grace Park from *Battlestar Galactica*," Ramsay mused.

Jamie couldn't write fast enough. "Grace Park? You gotta be kidding. Katee Sackhoff," the computer said.

Ramsay smiled and nodded wisely.

"The kid knows his *Galactica* babes. Well, well, well. You are a rare find out here in the back of beyond, Seamus, old son . . . oh, hang about, think I see something."

Ramsay looked down the road.

"Aye, the bus should be here in a minute. We'll be the first kids to get picked up. Sit with me at the back and none of the wee skitters will bother you. OK, mate? We Portmuck kids have to stick together. They call us 'cultchies' in Carrickfergus because we're out here on Islandmagee—it means yokel or redneck. They think of themselves as sophisticated townies because Carrickfergus is a suburb of Belfast. It's really, really stupid because they're just as big hicks as the rest of us. But don't worry,

I won't let them pick on ya. Nobody messes with me, not even the upper school, not since I knocked that lower-sixth kid's tooth out in a fight."

"I can look after myself," Jamie wrote.

"I'll bet you can too, having to get by in the rough and tumble of New York," Ramsay said with a grin.

They were silent for another moment and Ramsay looked at him reflectively.

"Chopped off the old leftie. You're in distinguished company," he said.

"I know, the shark girl and the climber guy," Jamie said through his PC, wishing the machine could convey his bored feelings at this kind of attempt to cheer him up.

"The shark girl and the climber guy? I don't know who you're talking about. I mean Nelson and Cervantes. They both didn't have the old southpaw and they did OK."

Jamie was about to type a response, but the big blue school bus appeared in the distance, so he put his PC away.

The bus slowed, stopped.

"Two today?" the driver asked Ramsay.

"That's right," Ramsay said.

Jamie got on board and sat at the back with Ramsay.

They headed off, shunting through the countryside of Islandmagee, picking up kids at junctions, at farmhouses, and in front of little shops. When the bus was full of children, they headed southwest along the seafront.

As they drove into the town of Carrickfergus, Jamie

immediately noticed a large gray castle jutting into the waters of Belfast Lough. He discreetly took out his PC.

"What's that?" Jamie wrote, and showed Ramsay the question rather than playing it.

"Carrickfergus Castle. It's not as interesting as it looks and after a couple of million school trips there, you'll have had your fill. It was built to keep your ancestors out. The Ui Neill attacked the English garrison at Carrickfergus pretty much on a regular basis from the twelfth century up through the Flight of the Earls in the seventeenth."

"Flight of the what?"

"Flight of the Earls. When Ireland was reconquered by King James, your distant ancestors were the last hold-outs against the king. Finally they had to give up and they escaped in 1607. Most of them fled from Lough Swilly and went to France and then to Rome never to return. A few disappeared off the face of the earth completely. It's actually a bit mysterious."

Jamie nodded, feeling strangely proud of those defiant Irish men in his past.

"They were cool guys, huh?" Jamie wrote.

"They resisted a bit, sure, but then they fled. Left Ireland in the lurch. Saved their own skins at the price of their people. At least Sitting Bull and Crazy Horse made a last stand, you know?"

Jamie nodded soberly.

They turned right up North Road and eventually came to Carrickfergus Grammar. A large series of buildings overlooking a couple of rugby pitches and a running track. There were hundreds of kids milling about the entrances, all of them similarly dressed in black blazers and trousers for boys, skirts for girls.

"Well, Jamie, we're here. I'll ask Mrs. McCallister if I can be your orientation guide today. She'll probably say yes, unless they have someone else in mind," Ramsay said.

"What does that mean?" Jamie wrote.

"It means, wee lad, instead of me going to my classes, I'll take you to all of yours and show you the ropes of the school. It's a day off for me and it should make your day easier. You want to do that?"

Jamie nodded.

"Good. Well, OK, Jamie, take a deep breath, follow me, and don't get all eggy if anyone says anything to ya. I'll deal with any wee skitters you might come across, and I promise you, you'll be fine."

Jamie gave him the OK sign and followed Ramsay out of the bus into what was bound to be a very interesting day indeed.

⬧ ⬧ ⬧

Obviously, the teachers had been briefed about Jamie's problems, and, with an air of embarrassment, he had been introduced to each of his classes and then pretty much left alone. No one had asked him any questions or made any comments on his missing limb or the fact that he did not speak. In all of the rooms, Jamie had sat next to Ramsay in a window seat, Ramsay reading comic books and Jamie trying his best to catch up with whatever his classmates were doing. They had gone to history first and then geography and then English and it all had gone smoothly.

In the mathematics class, Mr. Bennett, a gruff-bearded man from Scotland, had ignored Jamie but had practically beamed with delight when he'd seen Ramsay.

"We have a new boy with us, Jamie O'Neill. And, of course, most of you know Ramsay McDonald, who won the Interschool Maths Cup last year and was even interviewed on the radio," Mr. Bennett said proudly. "Weren't you, Ramsay?"

"Yes, sir," Ramsay said in a monotone as he sat with Jamie near the steaming radiators in the far corner.

"Impressive," Jamie stealthily typed on his PC.

"It was nothing," Ramsay whispered.

"OK, everyone, take out your textbooks and turn to page 345," Mr. Bennett said, then walked to the back of the class to give Jamie a book.

"Page 345," Mr. Bennett said very loudly, as if deafness might also be one of Jamie's problems.

Jamie opened the book. Mr. Bennett began speaking, but the math class was impossible to follow.

They were doing calculus, a subject Jamie hadn't even remotely covered in New York. And even for the Irish kids who had studied this all term, it was obviously difficult. Within just five minutes, Jamie's attention began to wander. For Ramsay it was too easy, and so neither

Jamie nor Ramsay noticed when Mr. Bennett stopped writing on the board and began giving them the evil eye.

Both were staring out the window at the verdant, sodden rugby pitches, the smoky town of Carrickfergus, and the blue waters of Belfast Lough. The school was on a hill and Jamie was transfixed by the pumping chimneys of Kilroot Power Station and the hazy outline of Belfast in the distance.

"Our two guests know it all, apparently," Mr. Bennett said quietly, and both Ramsay and Jamie could feel the attention of the class suddenly turned on them. They snapped their heads to face the front of the room.

"Jamie, you're new so I'll let this slide. Just give me a five-hundred-word essay on the history of calculus for next Monday. But Ramsay, you should know better than to look out the window in my class. Perhaps you would like to come up to the front and talk to us about the importance of mathematics and the significance of paying attention during your lesson," Mr. Bennett said with heavy sarcasm.

Jamie looked at Ramsay in horror. It was an evil punishment. He would have been terrified to appear before anyone, to be the focus of this much attention. Ramsay, however, immediately got to his feet, walked to the front of room, bowed politely to Mr. Bennett, cleared his throat, and began.

"In my opinion, mathematics is the most important thing you'll ever learn. C. P. Snow said that not knowing the second law of thermodynamics was like never having read Shakespeare. I agree. Maths is just as beautiful as poetry. And, of course, if it wasn't for maths, there would be no science, no medicine, no modern world," Ramsay said confidently.

Jamie, who had been cowering in his seat, sat up a little bit and noticed that the rest of the students were looking at this lanky, wiry-haired boy with interest. Ramsay winked at Jamie and continued.

"A hundred years ago in a very simple formula, $E = mc^2$, Einstein proved that all matter is energy. An elephant, your mum, everything can be described as pure energy. And if that doesn't blow your mind, you're not thinking about it enough. Without calculus, we wouldn't have cars or suspension bridges or telephones. Newton invented calculus along with his German rival, Leibniz. Another famous German mathematician was Euler. For me, the most beautiful mathematical formula of all has got to be Euler's famous equation: $e^{i\pi} + 1 = 0$ and if you look—"

"Thank you, Ramsay," Mr. Bennett interrupted, more than a little annoyed that his attempt to chastise and humiliate Ramsay had backfired so spectacularly. Fortunately the lunch bell rang, saving everyone from further recriminations.

❀ ❀ ❀

In the school library, Jamie found a quiet corner to write an e-mail.

To: thaddeusharper@hotmail.com
From: jamieoneill47@yahoo.com

Thaddeus, I know it's been a week since my last letter and I promised I would write every week but that is just me sometimes, sometimes you promise to do something and it's hard to do it. Anyway I haven't written because I've been very busy. I haven't been on the computer much and I haven't even watched TV once since we got here. But that's not surprising because we can't get TV on the island. Oh, wait, I saw a show at a pub/restaurant, Irish TV. It was about Bono, an Irish singer who wears elevated sneakers. He's cool. He's one of the richest people in Ireland and doesn't have to pay taxes because he's an artist. He's worth 300 million dollars. On the show he was talking about poverty in Africa.

Anyway I didn't want to write about Bono, I wanted to write about school. I started school today and it's ok so far, but pretty hard. I think I've made a friend but I don't want to say too much in case he turns out like the others.

The Lighthouse House is great and the lighthouse on the island is an old round tower that goes back hundreds of years. It's pretty amazing and a real mystery. I'm trying to find out more about it. I know you're a history expert so if you could tell me the books to read, that would be super cool. Anyway it's lunch now and Ramsay has just come to get me,

he's my shadow, showing me the ropes. Mom is well.
Take care. Jamie.

Ramsay and Jamie walked together to the dining hall.
Jamie hadn't had much Irish food since arriving a week
ago. His mother loved to cook and she made him chili and
pizza and they had been so busy tidying the Lighthouse
House that they hadn't had many chances to eat out.

A long line of kids stood in front of the lunch ladies,
choosing either Irish stew or Ulster fry. Jamie took an
Ulster fry from the lunch lady and an apple crumble covered with a thin yellow custard.

The two boys sat together near a window in the long
and bustling canteen. There were hundreds of kids in
there now, talking, chatting, playing jokes on each other.
A few were looking in Jamie's direction, but most were
taken up with their own concerns.

Jamie looked at the Ulster fry.

It was fried potato bread, soda bread, eggs, sausage,
bacon, and black pudding, which is another name for
blood sausage. It was swimming in lard and smelled like
old socks. He pushed the plate away. Ramsay could see
the look of his disgust in Jamie's eyes.

"You'll get used to it. It's like being in prison, you get
used to anything," he said.

"People eat this stuff?"

"Aye, most people have it for breakfast every morning.
There's an old joke: 'Why is Belfast like *Logan's Run*? . . .

Because nobody's alive over thirty.' They all die of heart disease. See?"

Once again the reference escaped Jamie, but he could always Google it later.

"Have your dessert though, that's what they do best here," Ramsay said.

Jamie ate a mouthful of the apple crumble with custard, and Ramsay was right. It was hot, sweet, crunchy, and delicious. He had finished the bowl and was about to have another attempt at the Ulster fry when someone tapped him on the shoulder. He turned around. There were three boys standing there. Two of them looked like mini Frankensteins, their broad shoulders barely fitting into their blazers, their ties not quite making it around their thick necks. The third was a weasely looking character with a snaggletooth, a beaky nose, and black hair gelled to a point in the front of his head.

"Are you the new boy?" the weasely lad said, except to Jamie it sounded like "Ann nuu, naa nuu baa?" so strong was his Belfast accent.

Before Jamie could understand the question or do anything, Ramsay had stood and interposed himself between them.

"Shove off, Tonto," Ramsay said.

"I will not shove off, Ramsay. You know the rules. All new boys have to get ducked in the toilets. We all had to go through it, he has to as well."

The two gorillas made a move toward Jamie. He could

see what was happening now and he stepped away from the table, ready for a rumble. He didn't like the sound of this "ducking" in the toilet, and there was no way it was going to happen without a fight. Ramsay put up his hands to calm everyone down.

"Steady on, lads. You got the wrong end of the stick here. He is a new boy, but he's not a first-year. That so-called rule only applies to first-years. He's a third-year, so it doesn't count," Ramsay said, but Tonto and the other two clearly didn't care.

"He's American as well, isn't he? And just because he's handicapped, doesn't make him special. He's not getting out of this. Come on, lads, get him," Tonto yelled to his two henchmen.

Ramsay looked at Jamie, pointing at the two larger boys, as if to say, I'll take care of them, if you can take Tonto. Jamie nodded, and before Tonto could react, Jamie had punched him twice in the face, staggering him backward into the dining table. Through overuse, Jamie's right arm had become strong and powerful, and one more punch knocked Tonto flat onto the table and into a bowl of stew. Ramsay, meanwhile, in a big whirling arm motion, had hit the two large boys on the top of the head with his clenched fists. Both had immediately fallen to the ground.

Before the two goons could get to their feet, Ramsay stood over them menacingly.

"Now, listen, you two—you better leave us alone you arse-wipingly wretched excuses for human beings. Go now, or I will personally beat the crap out of both of you," Ramsay said with cool disdain. Both boys looked once at Tonto, scrambled to their feet, and ran for the exit.

Ramsay pulled Tonto off the table as the bully wiped Irish stew from his face.

"Listen to me, Tonto. See that boy Jamie over there? He's my mate and if anybody messes with him, they're messing with me. Is that understood?"

Tonto nodded.

Everyone in the near vicinity had stopped eating to watch the action, but just then a shout broke out from the nearest group of tables: "Prefects coming, prefects coming."

The prefects, Jamie learned later, were upper-sixth-classmen selected to be a sort of student police force. The kids nearest the prefects blocked their way, dropping trays, bumping into them, and spilling water. Ramsay dragged Jamie out of the dining hall before he ended up getting detention or suspension or worse, which wouldn't be the best of starts at a new school.

The bus dropped them at the top of the steep hill that led down into Portmuck. Jamie was glad to get off. He knew that he had been the topic of most conversations. The new boy, the weird boy, the American, the trouble-maker. Ramsay had done his best to keep Jamie occupied with observations on the route, but he had still noticed the gossip.

Portmuck looked damp, huddled, and cold. The sky

was the color of a hearse, and fog was creeping in from the sea. Little curls of smoke were drifting from the houses, bringing the smell of peat and lignite coal.

Jamie's teeth chattered involuntarily.

"Aye, you should always bring a coat. The weather can change pretty quickly 'round here," Ramsay said. "We're nearly at my house. You can get warm there."

Jamie had a thought and took out his PC. He strapped it to his left arm so that, with some difficulty, he could walk and talk.

"Do you think we hurt that Tonto guy?"

Ramsay snorted.

"Not feeling guilty, are you? Forget him, he's just another red-shirted extra making a cameo appearance in our lives."

Jamie cocked his head and wondered if Ramsay knew that there was a difference between *Star Trek* and real life.

"Instead of your house, you want to come to my house and maybe see the island?" he asked via the computer.

Ramsay grinned at him.

"Well, well, well. I'll admit I had a wee bit of an ulterior motive in befriending you, Jamie."

"What was that?" Jamie typed, unconcerned.

"Ever since I was a wee boy growing up here, I've looked across to Muck Island and I've seen your house and the lighthouse and I'll tell you the truth—it's always struck me as a toty bit strange."

"The house is strange?" Jamie wrote.

"No, no, the house is fine, a wee bit of a Victorian

architectural oddity, but fine. Nah, it's the lighthouse that makes me wonder."

"Why is that?" Jamie typed, remembering his first glimpse of the lighthouse and the peculiar feeling he'd had looking at it.

"No one knows when it was built, no one knows who built it. And remember, it was only a lighthouse for a brief period. Less than a hundred years, I think. Before that some people say it was a granary. Some say it was a watch-tower for looking out to sea to warn people about the Vikings. But it seems older than that to me. If you examine it, it doesn't look like a typical Irish round tower at all."

"No?"

"The mathematical proportions are all wrong. Too narrow, a flat roof. It almost seems Roman or Greek or more likely Phoenician. But like I say, nobody knows. Topper wouldn't allow any archaeologists to check it out, and his son wasn't interested. He was hardly ever here."

"So you've never been to the island?" Jamie asked through the computer.

"Oh, no. I've been over to the island dozens of times. Topper hated people, he was a real grumpy boots, but for some reason he didn't mind kids wandering around. We used to go over to play on the beaches. But we never got to go inside the lighthouse, no one I know has ever been inside it. It's always locked."

"It's still locked, my mom has the key. It's supposed to be very dangerous in there," Jamie typed.

"Probably one day it will fall into the sea, but if it's lasted for over a thousand years the chances of that happening when we go up there are about, let me think . . . say we go up for one hour, there are twenty-four hours in a day, three hundred sixty-five days in a year, multiply that by a thousand . . . that's about a seven-million-to-one chance that we'd be killed."

"Will you tell my mom that?" Jamie asked through the computer.

"Absolutely."

The boys walked through Portmuck and onto the damp stony causeway leading to Muck Island. They followed the path to the Lighthouse House. The lights were on and through the window Jamie could see his mother reading a book. They didn't have television out here, but they did have radio, and Topper had left a fine old library of several thousand volumes, even some children's books. Since they'd arrived, his mother had been working her way through the classics—books that she had always wanted to read but never quite had the time.

"Is that your ma?" Ramsay asked.

Jamie nodded.

"Where's your father? Is he dead?" Ramsay asked.

Jamie shook his head and, still walking, used the stylus on the PC to write a response. It was an awkward pose but one he was getting accustomed to, the Velcro strap of the tablet PC wrapped around the stump of his left arm, leaving him free to work the stylus with his right hand.

"No. He lives in Seattle with his new wife," the machine finally said.

"When did your parents get divorced?"

"Last year," Jamie wrote.

"Last year? While you were having your arm cut off and all that chemotherapy? That's when he left?" Ramsay asked, surprised.

Jamie nodded.

"Bit of a bastard then, is he?"

Jamie thought about his answer. His father had taken him to Yankee Stadium, he had taken him to Coney Island. He had bought him Rollerblades for Christmas. He'd been there for almost every birthday. But then again, he had run out on him just when he had needed him the most.

He typed a one word response. "Yes."

Ramsay nodded. "Aye, well, that can happen. My dad's OK, except that he's never really around. Any grandparents?"

"My mom's parents are dead, but my dad's mom lives in Kansas. She's in a home out there," Jamie said through the PC.

"So apart from your mother, you're practically alone in the whole world."

"Except for the voices in my head," Jamie said via the PC.

"You're kidding, right?" Ramsay asked.

Jamie grinned at him.

They walked through the front door. Ramsay was impressed by the interior décor. He had been inside the Lighthouse House once before when Topper had let him in to use the bathroom. The place had been a real mess, stinking of old clothes and old dogs; but in the week Jamie and Anna had been living there, they had cleaned the house, painted it white, and removed one of the doors from the kitchen into the living room. The downstairs was now an expansive, open-plan design of living room, dining room, kitchen, library, and study all facing the sea and all blending into one another through a series of open doors.

They had put up a few Irish watercolors, a Buddha, a Ganesh, and a big but not too creepy-looking African mask.

Anna saw the boys from the library and got out of her easy chair.

"This is my friend Ramsay," Jamie said using the QuickPlay button on his PC.

Anna's heart skipped a beat. Jamie had found a friend on his first day of school? This was news.

"Nice to meet you, Ramsay. I'm Anna, Jamie's mom," she said.

"I like the name Anna—it's palindromic," Ramsay said.

"I don't like it. I had jaundice in school and they used to call me Anna Banana. For years I tried telling people my name was Anne, but it never really worked. I always slipped up. I'd be no good in the Witness Protection Program," Anna said with a grin.

"It had crossed my mind that you and Jamie might be in the Witness Protection Program," Ramsay said. "But you can't be now, not if you would mention it like that."

"It could be a clever double-bluff," Anna said, to

Jamie's delight. He was glad that his mom and his new bud were getting on so well.

"Could be," Ramsay agreed.

"So now that I've blown our secret identity, tell me about yourself," Anna said.

"I live in Portmuck, I met Jamie at the bus stop and we shadowed, and then we saw off a couple of chavs in the school canteen," Ramsay explained.

"What's a chav?" Anna asked.

"An even dumber version of a spide," Ramsay clarified.

"What's a spide?" Anna wondered.

"Sort of like a pikey without the ugly ethnic overtones," Ramsay said.

"What's a pikey?"

"A tinker."

"What's a—" Anna began but stopped herself. "You'll go on forever with this, won't you?" she said.

"Well, not forever. No regression can go much beyond the Planck length," Ramsay said with a grin.

"What do your parents do?" Anna asked, something Jamie realized, embarrassingly, that he had forgotten to inquire.

"My dad is a rep for Hasbro, the toy company. It sounds cool but it's not really, he's gone a lot. I don't get all eggy though, it's just one of those things. But I do get a lot of free toys," Ramsay said quickly.

When he spoke fast he was a little hard to follow. Anna looked at Jamie, who shrugged his shoulders.

"OK, um, what does your mother do?"

"She works in Magheramourne. She's an environmental protection officer for Larne Council. They're clearing out Larne Lough. It's a long-term project, it's a real pochle. Ma's always late nowadays, knee deep in the sheugh."

Anna again looked at Jamie to see if he had understood any of that, but he shook his head.

"If your mother, er, isn't coming home till late would you consider joining us for dinner?" she asked.

"I don't know. Whatcha having?"

"Meatloaf," Anna said.

"Meatloaf," Ramsay said with wonder. "I've heard of meatloaf before and I've seen it on American TV programs, but I've no idea what it is. It sounds great."

"Prepare to be underwhelmed," Anna said dryly.

An hour later they were eating it in the big kitchen overlooking the sea. It was getting dark and they could see the lighthouses on the Maiden Islands and Portpatrick light up in Scotland.

Anna was a good cook. Ramsay ate his meal and enjoyed it very much.

Pleased, Anna opened a bottle of red wine and since neither boy was old enough for even a diluted drop, she polished off most of it herself.

After dinner, Ramsay phoned his mother to tell her that he was over on Muck Island. She said that that was fine but that he had to come home before the water began to rise on the causeway.

He went outside to check on the water level and saw that he had about two hours. When he came back into the house, Jamie had gone upstairs to change out of his school uniform. Ramsay helped Anna clear the table. She was in the mood to talk.

"I'm so glad Jamie's found a friend," Anna said.

"Aye. We 'bonded,' as they say on *Friends*, over an evil maths teacher and that wee jam in the canteen, but I liked him from the get-go. We both share the same world-weary attitude towards society," Ramsay said.

Anna raised an eyebrow. "We've had so much bad news in the last year. After we inherited the house and came to Ireland, I was hoping that Jamie would move on and stop this, this . . . you know," she said and paused, embarrassed.

"The not-talking thing," Ramsay said casually.

"Yes. The not-talking thing. And then I thought the computer would help too—gradually wean him back into it—but he seems just as determined as ever not to speak."

"And there's nothing physically wrong with him?"

"No. It's all in his head. He just doesn't want to speak."

"I don't blame him at all, too much jabbering in the world already if you ask me," Ramsay said.

Anna nodded. It sounded like he was making excuses for Jamie, but that was OK, because it meant he cared enough to make excuses.

"He's a very bright boy, very sensitive too. Maybe too sensitive . . . although, like I say, he's gone through a lot," Anna said apologetically.

"I hear he's the new Laird of Muck," Ramsay said, somehow knowing that this would lift Anna's somber mood.

"Oh, you heard that? Yes, they told us that. It's silly, of course."

"It's not silly at all. It's an ancient title of the Princes of Ulster. I think you'll find you'll get a lot of respect in these parts."

"Will we?"

"Oh, aye. You probably won't ever have to pay in the pub."

"Let's go over there right now." Anna laughed.

"You think I could pass for eighteen?" Ramsay asked hopefully.

"I was kidding," Anna said. "So, um, do you have any brothers or sisters?"

"Nah, not really."

"That's an interesting answer."

"Well, my dad was married before and technically I have a half-brother from that marriage. Brian. But I've only ever met him once. He and his mother lived in Scotland. Dad says Brian's the brains of the family. He's in America at MIT. It's some fancy university in Boston or something. He e-mails very, very occasionally. But, anyway, he's dead old—like twenty-eight—and he's still not famous, so he can't be that smart."

"At least you have a brother," Anna said, not picking up on the fact that this was a sore topic.

Ramsay nodded and slipped into silence.

Upstairs, Jamie had gotten some e-mail.

To: jamieoneill47@yahoo.com
From: thaddeusharper@hotmail.com

Jamie, I am glad that you are settling in. Next week I'll be going down to the big library on 42nd Street because they are having a book sale. I will certainly try and find some history books for you there about your little corner of the world. I've been reading the weather reports for Belfast in the NYT. It seems warmer than New York. I hope the food is good. I will send a longer e-mail when I have anything to say. Thaddeus.

Jamie typed a quick response.

To: thaddeusharper@hotmail.com
From: jamieoneill47@yahoo.com

Thaddeus, the food is terrible. It smells like old socks. And not tasty socks either. Ramsay says there's a Mexican restaurant in Belfast and I want Mom to take me. It would be nice to eat some American food after all this time. Jamie. PS. Thanks for the help on the books.

Jamie came downstairs in jeans and a #2 Yankees sweatshirt.

"Derek Jeter's shirt. Christmas present," Anna said proudly to Ramsay. Ramsay nodded, although he had never heard of the Yankee shortstop.

"Would you boys like some hot chocolate?" Anna asked.

They both nodded. Anna went into the kitchen, boiled up some milk and cream, and then melted real chocolate over a steamer.

Twenty minutes later, Ramsay was sitting on the Lighthouse House veranda, looking out to the foggy sea and drinking the most delicious hot choc he'd ever tasted. Jamie winked at him and pointed at the old lighthouse. Ramsay nodded, catching his friend's drift.

"Mrs. O'Neill, ever since I was a wee boy I've wanted to look inside the old lighthouse here, and Jamie says you have the key. If we bring flashlights and are very careful, I wonder if you might let us go up inside," he said, blurting it out, all at once.

"Mr. McCreagh said it's dangerous," Anna protested.

"It's been standing there for more than a thousand year. The odds of it falling down the night we go inside are pretty slim," Ramsay said.

Anna was about to say no. Indeed the word "no" had formed on her lips, but then she shook her head. Jamie had made a new friend, and she liked Ramsay and she didn't want to come across as the killjoy mom. And perhaps the red wine played a little part too.

"I'll tell you what," she said after a long pause. "I've been pretty curious about the lighthouse as well. We'll get the flashlights and our coats and we'll go over to it. But this is the rule: I'll go inside first and you boys can wait outside. If I think it's safe then we can all go up to the top. OK?"

"OK," Ramsay said and looked at Jamie as if to say, "Did I do well?"

Jamie grinned.

It was a cool, misty night and, shivering, Anna led the little party out of the Lighthouse House by flashlight. Jamie was behind her with another flashlight and Ramsay brought up the rear, carrying the heavy iron key. The fog was so thick, Anna almost walked into the iron lighthouse door before abruptly stopping herself.

"OK, all. Here we are, on a suitably spectral and creepy evening. Key, please."

Ramsay handed her the key.

"Well, here I go. I hope there's no rats," Anna said and, without further ado, put the key in the lock, which appeared rusted but turned surprisingly easily.

She looked at the two boys.

"You two wait here until I come back," she said seriously.

"What if you don't come back?" Ramsay asked, doing a spooky voice.

"You two wait here," she said firmly, then opened the iron door and went inside.

Jamie watched the light from his mother's flashlight disappearing up the spiral staircase. He wasn't worried. Ramsay's statistics had convinced him. Still, he could admit to a slight nervous feeling in his gut until he saw the flashlight come down again about ten minutes later. His mother's face was flushed and red.

"OK, you boys can go up, it seems fine to me. It's steep. I'm going back to the house to get a drink of water. Don't stay more than fifteen minutes, and when you're done make sure you lock up," she said, handing the key back to Ramsay.

"I'll go first," Ramsay said.

Jamie shook his head. It was his island, it was his lighthouse; he was going to go first. He put his hand on Ramsay's shoulder.

"You wanna go up ahead of me?" Ramsay asked.

Jamie nodded.

"OK, but if this tower was built to keep out invading Vikings, there's probably a trip step or two built into the spiral staircase. They have them at Carrickfergus Castle. Just be aware of it, or you'll fall down," Ramsay said.

Jamie nodded, shined his flashlight ahead of him, and began to ascend the spiral stairs.

They were narrow, designed for only one person to climb at a time, and some of the steps were worn smooth. Lichen coated the walls and the smell was musty, pungent, and got a little worse as he got higher—the stink a cross between a pet shop and a garbage barge on the Hudson. There were probably all sorts of dead birds and rodents lurking between the cracks in the stone.

The stairs curved steeply in a full circle and after only thirty seconds, Jamie was starting to get out of breath; he was glad that he had the flashlight because it would have been pitch-black otherwise.

 99

He felt cold and a little weirded out. He stopped and waited for Ramsay to catch up, but after a full minute, there was still no sign of his friend. The big guy must have chickened out. Should he go on alone?

Of course. He wasn't going back now.

The flashlight flickered and as he continued, the steps got even steeper. He paused to catch his breath and then finally he heard Ramsay on the stairs far below him. His heart was beating fast, the blood pumping in his ears.

How many more of these old, granite-hewn steps?

He began counting them. One, two, three, four . . .

Suddenly something appeared in front of him.

A screeching white form that was coming straight at him.

"Huuhhhhh," he gasped, dropping the flashlight. He slipped on the staircase and fell down five or six steps, tumbling on the curve.

He might have plunged right to the bottom of the lighthouse had Ramsay not been there to catch him.

"Gotcha. I knew those trick steps would do you in. When they take you on the tour of the castle they always point them out. An invader running up the steps would miss his footing, trip, fall, and break his neck. You're lucky I was here. Come on, let me help you up," Ramsay said.

Ramsay steadied him and pushed him vertical. Jamie was unhurt.

"I'll go first, if you don't mind, and find your torch," Ramsay said.

Jamie wanted to warn him about the creature, but of course he couldn't speak, and by the time Jamie had tried to grab him Ramsay was three or four steps ahead. Jamie scrambled to catch up.

Then he heard a scream. *Ramsay—oh, no,* Jamie thought.

He ran up the steps. Ramsay was looking at him, more annoyed than afraid.

"Bloody hell, Jamie, you might have told me, there's a great big white seagull up here," Ramsay said. "Go on scoot, get out of it, go on, ya great big ganch."

The bird flapped and battered around, but eventually it found an opening back into the foggy night.

Ramsay grinned at Jamie in the glow of the flashlight.

"Oh, my goodness, I nearly keeked my whips. Come on, Seamus, this is the top," Ramsay said, and then pulled Jamie up.

Jamie wasn't sure what he had been expecting, but it certainly wasn't this. A round, empty, featureless room. A large open window facing the sea that had once contained glass and was now exposed to the elements. Bird droppings on the floor, a few leaves and plastic bags, a damp cobwebby ceiling, a smell of emptiness.

Nothing of any interest at all.

Ramsay leaned up against one of the round tower walls. "Well, I've got to tell ya, after all these years of waiting this is a bit of a letdown," he said. "I mean, I thought there would be some old lighthouse equipment, or maybe something from Viking times, or, well, anything really. But this, this is wick. This totally sucks."

And as he looked around the strangely barren, vacant room all Jamie could do was nod his head in disappointed agreement.

※ ※ ※

In a similar room, in a similar lighthouse, ninety-six light-years from Muck Island, a girl called Wishaway was also feeling frustrated.

Three weeks she had been in this place and of course the Ui Neills had not returned. Why would they? They hadn't appeared in almost four centuries.

She nibbled at a piece of *draya* cheese and continued looking at a small vellum book dictated by Morgan of the Red Hand. It was popularly called *The Book of Stories* and contained many tales from Earth. It was in English. Wishaway had read it through many times, but it always gave her comfort. She liked the narratives that told about the adventures of heroes, princes, and kings. She didn't like the ones that described the perplexing and interminable wars of the Earth folk.

She read for a while, finished her cheese, drank some well water, and walked outside.

The sea was a frigid blue and the air was crisp. The ice in the distant north groaned and creaked.

Three weeks.

What had her father been thinking to send her here?

She should have refused to go. She should have stayed with him, her friends, and Lorca. She was missing out on her studies. And who would clean the house or water the hoxney trees in her father's tiny garden?

This was a fool's errand.

And in any case, who knew what the future would bring? Perhaps the Alkhavans would not come this year. Perhaps the rumors of a great fleet of iceships were wrong.

Perhaps.

Wishaway wrapped the shawl around her shoulders.

She sat on a mossy bank and watched the stars appear one by one in the moonless sky. She was lonely.

There was nothing on this island. Not even a lost *ranta* or a *keppy* snail.

She shivered and stood.

"I am weary of waiting for thee, Ui Neill," she said aloud.

She walked back to the lighthouse, threw some dried kelp on the fire, and watched it burn and crackle with a dull, yellow flame.

Another week, she told herself. Another week and she would launch the boat and sail back to the city. Whatever was going to happen or not happen she would await it in the bosom of her family and friends.

And if her father complained, she would tell him that the Ui Neill no longer thought of them here on Altair. He could forget the possibility of aid from that quarter, for it was plain to even a base creature that the Ui Neill would never come.

Chapter IV
THE SECRET

To: thaddeusharper@hotmail.com

From: jamieoneill47@yahoo.com

Hi, Thaddeus, things are going well. School is fine. The kids are ok and the teachers are ok, but the subjects are pretty boring. I've met a friend who lives in the village of Portmuck. He's named Ramsay. He's tall and he plays rugby which is a game like football except no one wears helmets. He's also on the school basketball team (the Irish do play it I guess) but when I asked him what was his favorite NBA team he said the Harlem Globetrotters and unfortunately I don't think he was kidding. Ramsay is good at maths though. Over here they call it maths instead of math. I don't know why but they do. It's going to be easy next week because a lot of teachers and kids are going on a ski trip, but I don't want to learn to ski so I'm not going. Even though it's almost February there's no snow in Ireland. The food is still weird. We went to a Thai restaurant and they give us curry with french fries and a deep-fried Snickers bar for dessert. And for breakfast you still can't get bagels, but people eat porridge just like in the Goldilocks story.

The island is great, the house is nice, and Mom now has a part-time job helping out at the local elementary school. And as I told you there's an old lighthouse on the island that was built in the time of the Vikings or even earlier. Ramsay and me like to go up there, so Mom gives us the key and we go up and look out to sea. We brought chairs up and do our homework. Ramsay still thinks there's something odd about the lighthouse, something that isn't quite right. You would think it was pretty funny. He's one of those people that believes in aliens and stuff like that, people that you don't like except that you might like Ramsay because he's so good at math/maths. He's good at chess too, much better than me.

I sometimes think there's something funny about the lighthouse too. And I know you don't care for it when people talk about hunches and feelings and things without science to back them up, but Ramsay and I have been doing research to find out all we can about the lighthouse. Not much yet. I'm sending you a picture as an attachment. Like I said before if you could find out anything about Muck Island or the lighthouse or tell me about any books, I would love to hear about it if you have the time. There's so much history here. Ramsay says that's the Irish's main problem, they're drowning in history. You'd like it though. Anyway I'm doing well and hope you are well too I promise I will e-mail

more often. I hope this e-mail wasn't too disinteresting.
Take care, Jamie.

Jamie held the computer to the window and pressed Send.
"Did it go?" he asked Ramsay.

Ramsay walked across to look at the screen.

"Aye, it worked; wireless is pretty good out here," he
said, but Jamie noticed his friend's brow furrow ironically.

"What?" Jamie wrote with the stylus.

"You should have cleared the e-mail with me first.
'Disinterest' is a good thing, it means neutrality; 'uninter-
est' is the word you're looking for. You Yanks are killing
the language," Ramsay said with a smile, then sat down
next to his friend at the table near the lighthouse window.
When it was daylight and neither foggy nor windy, Anna
let them use the top of the lighthouse as their study.
Despite McCreagh's dire warnings, it had looked very
solid and safe enough. Anna had even helped the boys
drag up a folding table, two chairs, a couple of old rugs,
and some wire mesh to place over the window hole to
keep out the seagulls. But they were only allowed to be
there as long as they used it as a place to do homework.
It wasn't to become a place to experiment with drugs.

Ramsay never had much homework to do because he
was far ahead in all of his subjects, but he enjoyed helping Jamie, who was behind in everything.

He got Jamie quickly up to speed on English, history,
and the arts, but in PS 125 and in the Harlem School for

Children with Special Challenges, Jamie had done virtually no math or science and he was struggling to catch up. Not only could he not get calculus, but he was even having trouble understanding basic trigonometry.

Ramsay was a good teacher when he could focus on the topic at hand and not go off on one of his rants, which unfortunately he was doing right now:

"Trigonometry is about finding the height of a triangle if you know the other two sides. It's very simple. You use the angle of the triangle and the sine, cosine, or tangent. Simple stuff . . . 'Course it only works in two dimensions. They won't tell you that in school. No way. That's the problem with people not considering the alternatives. Don't think deep enough. For instance, some people think there has to be a pattern in the distribution of prime numbers, maybe some secret meaning, a message from God or aliens or something. But why should there be? I mean our prime numbers are in base ten because we have ten fingers, but maybe the aliens use base six or base five or whatever. It's just a bias, Jamie."

"There are no aliens. My friend Thaddeus says so," Jamie wrote on his PC.

"He says there's no aliens? Your mate Thaddeus says that?"

Jamie nodded.

"And do you think that?"

Jamie shrugged his shoulders.

"Well, have you heard of the Drake Equation?" Ramsay asked.

Jamie shook his head.

"Drake says that if you take the number of stars in the sky and guess the number of habitable planets around them and multiply that number by a very slim chance that those planets will have intelligent life, then you're left with at least a couple of hundred intelligent civilizations we don't know about in the galaxy."

"Well, where are they?" Jamie asked through the PC.

"The galaxy is very, very big. Maybe we just haven't spotted them yet. It's like looking for a needle in a haystack, using a plane flying over the haystack field at ten thousand feet," Ramsay said.

The quest for extraterrestrial life was another one of Ramsay's obsessions and Jamie knew it was best to let it go. His friend was always contradicting himself. Sometimes Ramsay thought there *were* aliens and sometimes he said that if aliens were out there they should be here by now teaching people the secrets of the universe in return for a box set of *The Simpsons*.

"Are you going to help me with math or not?" Jamie asked through the computer.

"Yes, I will. It's easy, wee buns. Trigonometry is all triangles and squares. Oh, and speaking of squares, my dad's finally coming home tomorrow tonight. He's been in Europe for a fortnight. Do you want to meet him? He always brings me free stuff to make up for his lousy parenting."

"Yeah, I'd like to meet him," Jamie said through the PC.

"I think you'll like him, he's an OK bloke, but he's not

going to be a substitute father figure for you, mainly cos he's a crap father. Away all the time. Out of it when he's here," Ramsay said.

"I don't need a substitute father," Jamie wrote.

"Good, because he can't be one," Ramsay said.

"Well, I don't need one."

"Well, he can't be one," Ramsay said, almost a bit sad now, for behind the joking, there was something that wasn't really a joke. Jamie's dad was on another continent, six thousand miles away. That was his excuse, but Ramsay's father was often right here and yet they never did dad-son things, never played football, never went fishing. His dad was so disengaged that it almost didn't matter when he was home. He drank a lot of beer, but even that wasn't anything important. He didn't even have the dedication to be an alcoholic. It was just another distraction, another method to stop him thinking about his life. Ramsay shook his head and let out a breath. Well, that wouldn't happen to him. To them.

Jamie sensed his friend's mood change.

"Let's get back to trigonometry. What exactly is a cosine?" Jamie wrote.

But Ramsay couldn't help but blurt it out. "No. Listen to me, Jamie, we can't go down his road. My dad's problem is one of a disappointed future. I'm sure he didn't want to be a rep, never at home, always on the road, drinking bad coffee and eating buffet food. Started as an actor you know, but it didn't work out. His

109

life is a valuable lesson. Look at us, we're young, we're happening. We've got to do something with all those paths of possibilities in front of us."

"What are you talking about? Like what?" Jamie asked via the PC.

Ramsay thought for a moment.

"Well, I want to be an inventor or a scientist," Ramsay said breezily, his somber mood lifting as easily as it had come. "Aye, a scientist, I want to win the Nobel Prize for something. That'd be cool."

Jamie nodded.

"What do you want to do with your life?" Ramsay asked.

Jamie shook his head. He didn't want to think about that. For although he'd had a run of good luck, getting out of America, to Ireland, finding a friend . . . he still felt like his life was on hold at the moment.

"Come on, what do you want to do?" Ramsay persisted.

But Jamie didn't answer. Ramsay couldn't know. No one could know.

Thaddeus had come closest to understanding him in one of his monologues about the War. "Jamie, once you feel the flutter of those wings of the Angel of Death, it changes you."

Yeah. That it did. It changed you. It changed everything. And not for the better. It didn't make you stronger, it made you—

Ramsay hit him on the back. "Why the long face, grumpy boots? Jeez, I set you off, didn't I? Well, don't worry about it. You're not going to be like your da and I'm not going to be like mine. We're cooler than that. I mean, look at us. For a start, we're really hip up here in our own little den away from the world. We are the cat's pajamas," Ramsay said.

Jamie shook his head. He wasn't convinced he was the cat's pajamas, Laird of Muck or no. He still only had one arm, he still was the stupidest kid in school, he still somehow couldn't bring himself to speak, even to his mother or his best friend.

"There's only one thing missing, Jamie. What we really need is girlfriends," Ramsay said with a smile.

Jamie sighed. That was another sore topic. Last year he'd been on the verge of asking Audrey Martinez to go see the *SpongeBob* movie. It was a brilliant plan because although *SpongeBob* was a kids' movie, he'd noticed that Audrey wore a *SpongeBob* backpack when she went to volleyball practice.

Of course then he had started feeling pains in his hand and arm, and then after the tests he was diagnosed with bone cancer. That killed that scheme.

"Have you ever had a girlfriend, Jamie?" Ramsay asked.

Jamie shook his head sullenly.

"Me neither. But I want one. Not one of these pale as puce local Irish girls. I want to go out with a musician. Not an actress, actresses are stupid. A proper musician. Gwen Stefani or Björk or Avril Lavigne, someone that writes their own material."

"Yeah, that's likely," Jamie said via the PC.

"You never know, if they come to Belfast for a concert.

Our eyes could meet, we could hook up after . . ."

"It's called statutory rape; you're only thirteen, Ramsay," Jamie pointed out.

"I wouldn't prosecute," Ramsay said.

"No, but your mother would," Jamie wrote.

"Speaking of mothers," Ramsay murmured, for just then they heard a voice at the bottom of the lighthouse.

"Jamie, Ramsay, come down now, it's supposed to rain and I don't want you two up there in the rain," Anna shouted from the Lighthouse House.

"Let's go, I'll teach you your trig tomorrow; it'll liven up another wet, cold, boring January Thursday," Ramsay said.

Jamie nodded, grabbed his flashlight, and went down the spiral stairs not suspecting in the slightest that the next time he would be in the lighthouse his entire life would change again, even more significantly than the change that had brought him to Ireland. Tomorrow was coming. Thursday it would be, wet it would be, boring it certainly would not.

Jamie and Ramsay spent an uneventful day at school. From his teachers, Jamie got nothing but make-up homework and a few weary stares. The sad cancerboy act had worn thin for a lot of them and now they had few qualms about asking Jamie questions he could not answer and giving him extra work.

Jamie, however, got a great deal of respect now from his fellow students. He had acquired the reputation as the silent one-armed kid from America who could do a Bruce Lee on you just like he did on Tonto and his goons, beating the crap out of them in under ten seconds with his one good arm.

Even so, he was glad when the bus pulled up at the hill outside Portmuck and let them off.

It had been mild and sunny for a few days. However, now, near the end of January, Jamie could feel the change in the weather. The air had more bite and the water was a little whiter on the black, angled lines of the rocks. Cows and sheep were huddling in the corner of the fields and the snow geese wintering here in temperate Ireland (rather than the ice-blasted wastes of Siberia) were quiet and subdued.

Jamie was wearing a duffel coat, and, because the tide was going to be high later, he had Wellington boots for the trip across the causeway to Muck Island. His mother was in Larne looking for a new car—something with a big wheel base like a Volvo or a Land Rover.

"I think it's going to storm. You wanna go to my house?" Ramsay asked as they walked back from the bus stop.

Jamie nodded.

"My dad should be back. He works for Hasbro, the toy people, did I tell you that?"

"You did," Jamie wrote.

"He's only home for a few days before he has to head out again to Boston, but he'll have brought a present."

Ramsay took them into a cottage that backed onto the hill which overlooked the sea. It was a tidy little house, with watercolor paints and family pictures and a well-swept look.

Ramsay's father was in the bathroom, so Ramsay

showed Jamie his room, which was filled with mechanical toys, a homemade radio, a miniature steam engine, and a bubbling chemistry set that smelled terrible. When Jamie asked Ramsay what he was making, he said he was trying to replicate Newton's alchemy experiments, which didn't explain much. There were a few big books: *The History of Science*, *The Illustrated History of Mathematics*, *The Decline and Fall of the Roman Empire*, a novel called *At Swim, Two Boys*, but nothing that interested Jamie. As Jamie scanned further, Ramsay quickly threw a towel over his stack of ABBA CDs and his *Hazel Weatherfield: Girl Detective* books.

"You want to hang out or are you one of those peculiar people that thinks it stinks in here?" Ramsay asked.

"It does stink in here," Jamie wrote.

"OK. We'll go to the living room. Meet Da," Ramsay said.

Ramsay's father was a tall man, heavily built and completely bald. He was only about fifty-five, but he looked considerably older. Probably, Jamie thought, because of all the traveling.

"Hi, Dad," Ramsay said.

Mr. McDonald smiled when he saw the two boys, but he didn't get up from his chair and he certainly didn't give Ramsay a hug or anything.

"Ah, Ramsay, nice to see you, son. Got to warn you, I only came back to get a change of clothes. Heading off soon. So is this your friend from America?" he asked in a booming voice.

"Jamie, this is my dad, Arthur. Dad, this is Jamie, he won't say hello. He doesn't talk. He had cancer," Ramsay said.

"Doesn't speak. Huh. Well, well . . . You boys like Shrek? These are from *Shrek 3*," he said, reaching into a bag and giving the boys plastic Shrek dolls that could say various phrases from the upcoming movie. If both boys had been about five years younger it would have been a fantastic gift.

"Thanks," Ramsay said diffidently.

A car honked outside.

Mr. McDonald stood up.

"Well, lads, that's my taxi. Jamie, I'll probably see you around. Ramsay, take care, I'm off to the airport."

Ramsay was stunned.

"But you only just got here," he protested.

"Yup. Time and tide, Ramsay. Time and tide. Change of plans. I might see your brother in Boston. Don't worry, I'll tell him you're nearly at his level. OK, must dash. Explain to your mother and tell her I should be back on Saturday," Mr. McDonald said. And then without any further ceremony, he got a suitcase from the dining room, waved, and went out to the taxi.

Ramsay watched the taxi drive out of the village, then slumped into an arm chair. But before he could begin a bitch fest, Jamie's computer started to beep.

"E-mail. Probably from Thaddeus. You go on and read it, Jamie. I don't mind," Ramsay said, sounding very depressed.

Jamie took it out of the backpack and punched the Inbox button.

To: jamieoneill47@yahoo.com
From: thaddeusharper@hotmail.com

Jamie, I am pleased that you are well. I am feeling much better. It has been cold here in New York
but it has not snowed. I was happy to get the picture of your home in Ireland. And of course I was
glad to look things up for you. It is nice to be asked
to help. When you are my age, young people
sometimes think that you are incapable of anything.
I actually did find out information about your island,
Muck Island, in a book I discovered at the 42nd
Street Library called 'Ancient Legends of Ireland'
written in 1930 by JJ Rooney. I have scanned in the
relevant page below and I hope it helps.

If your friend Ramsay wishes, I would enjoy playing him at chess sometime on Yahoo! games. On a
more serious topic, I have to go to Georgia next
week to visit my younger sister who is feeling poorly
but I will talk to you at more length when I return.
Look after your mother. Thaddeus

ANCIENT LEGENDS OF IRELAND
BY JJ ROONEY

. . . There are two legends about Muck, a
small islet off the County Antrim coast. The first,
contained in the long 'Chronicle of the Fintoola,'
by Bard NacCallum of the monastery in Bangor,

concerns Finn and the Fianna and their flight
from their enemies:

> When Finn fled from the invaders, he
> came to the Isle of Mugh and to the Place
> of Passage. Finn's men were sore afraid
> of this haunted place, but Finn chided
> them for their womanish superstition.
> "The Salmon of Knowledge is old. Here
> since the days of our fathers. It glistened
> when the world was new and if the
> Patrician speaks the truth it shone here
> before the Fall and the Angels. But I will
> take it and use it and give it to one of you
> as trust or if there is no one who has
> courage to be guardian cast it into the seas
> and unmake it. For it is a danger, a thing of
> power. Ireland was not where it was made.
> It was forged in the Sun. On the anvil of
> Lugh. Ireland is were it rests. Sleeps, is
> passed down, becomes a story and . . .

Here the manuscript is illegible, undoubtedly
damaged by fire during the first and most serious
of the sacks by the Norse on the Bangor
monastery. In the second legend, which takes
place during historical times, Lord Morgan of the
Red Hand, Clan Chief of the Tyrone Ui Neill, ran

from the English armies to Muck Island in the year 1607. The rest of his family having escaped Ireland during the notorious 'Flight of the Earls,' Morgan and his retainers were left alone and hunted. The account is taken up by the grandson of his steward, Dermot O'Neill, who published the unsuccessful 'True History of the Ui Neills' in Dublin in 1713.

You have spake of it. The Salmon of Knowledge. The Stone of Scone. Excalibur. Lord Morgan, who was entrusted with its secret, led his followers to Muck Island on the far edge of his domain. Taking only the smallest retinue, he escaped from the window in the upper chamber to the Tír na nÓg, a Land of Wonders in the far west, sending a servant back with the Salmon so that others may avail themselves in a time of similar need. Morgan, Lord O'Neill, was ne'er heard of again and the English dominion over Ireland was made complete when MacSorley Boy, Lord of Antrim, accepted the title Earl of Ulster from King James.

Interestingly, Jonathan Swift, who once was vicar of Kilroot, a parish that includes Muck

Island, may have used this legend in his *Gulliver's Travels* wherein a sailor travels west to many lands full of wonders . . .

It was a long and fascinating e-mail, and, of course, Jamie showed it to Ramsay.

"I told you there was something odd about that lighthouse," Ramsay said, brightening up.

They sat for a while and before the depression of Mr. McDonald's departure could envelop both of them, Jamie remembered his responsibilities.

"Ramsay, I still could do with a little help on this math. Mr. Bennett will kill me if I hand in another bad trigonometry assignment," Jamie said via the PC, except the computer couldn't say the word "trigonometry" and instead suggested "trigger ass."

"Trigger ass," Ramsay said laughing.

Then, suddenly, he stopped mid-guffaw and whispered the real word: "Trigonometry."

He slapped his forehead. "Trig-on-ometry," he said a second time, almost to himself, his big eyes wide with wonder. He ran his fidgety hands through his hair and sprang up like he'd seen a ghost. He was excited. He was on the verge of discovering something. Jamie had seen him like this once before, when he had solved Mr. Bennett's weekly "Impossible Homework Problem" by discovering a branch of mathematics that he hadn't even been taught yet.

"Angles, height . . ." Ramsay muttered and grabbed a pencil and piece of paper.

Ramsay stared at the old lighthouse through the window. He started drawing a diagram of it, making the lighthouse the side of a right-angled triangle.

"What is it? What are you doing?" Jamie asked via the computer.

But Ramsay couldn't speak. The e-mail from Thaddeus and the thought of trigonometry had given him the fuzzy edge of a solution.

He looked at the lighthouse and examined his drawing. "I think I have it," he said in a croak.

He sprang to his feet, grabbed Jamie by the shoulder of his school blazer, and led him outside. He gaped at the lighthouse over on Muck Island, nodded, and punched his fist in the air.

"What the hell is it?" Jamie asked via the PC.

Ramsay was grinning from big, misshapen, rugby-playing ear to big, misshapen, rugby-playing ear.

"What is it, Ramsay?" Jamie repeated.

"I think I know what's wrong with the lighthouse," Ramsay said.

Ramsay slapped Jamie on the back, and before Jamie could protest, he dragged him back inside the house.

"OK, OK, what now? Yes, ladder, must get ladder," Ramsay mumbled.

Jamie started to type a response, but Ramsay had

already left. He ran to the garden shed and came back into the living room a few minutes later with a rusty stepladder and a digging trowel.

"We're going to Muck Island," Ramsay said in a high-pitched, almost hysterical voice. He was practically freaking Jamie out with his red cheeks and wild, excited eyes. Jamie looked at him with surprise—Ramsay and his father were such a contrast, the son extroverted and over the top, the dad introverted and subdued, but maybe that's why Ramsay was the way he was.

"You carry this trowel, Jamie, and I'll carry the ladder," Ramsay said. "Are there still flashlights at the bottom of the lighthouse steps?"

Jamie nodded, puzzled and irritated by Ramsay's provokingly mysterious ways.

"Good, come on, let's go," Ramsay said. "Come on, OK, I'll carry the trowel if you don't want to."

Ramsay set off with the little spade and ladder. Jamie used the Velcro to tighten the PC to the stump of his left arm and tried to catch his friend.

"Stop. Wait a minute, what are we doing?" Jamie wrote with his stylus, but Ramsay was way ahead and Jamie had to hurry to get near him.

They walked fast across the causeway. Jamie had written "Tell me" on his tablet PC and he repeatedly pushed the Play button, to no avail.

Ramsay practically ran off the causeway onto Muck Island.

 121

Jamie finally had to ram him with his shoulder.

"You have to tell me. Now," he wrote on the PC.

Ramsay nodded, took a deep breath, and talked fast: "I'll tell you. I think I've got it, Jamie. I know what's wrong. The lighthouse. It's too small. It's not tall enough. Do you see it? I figured it out using the trig. And that e-mail totally confirms it. Look at the window on the lighthouse and look at the huge gap above it."

Jamie looked up at the lighthouse, but he still didn't understand.

"Explain it slowly, Ramsay," Jamie said through the computer.

"Your mate Thaddeus, we owe him. Both stories in that book were about your ancestors fleeing to Muck Island using some kind of secret thing. You heard what that ancient document said, one of the O'Neills escaped from a window of the upper chamber. Upper chamber. Upper chamber? If there's an upper chamber, there's a lower chamber. There's two chambers, but we've only seen one. So that can only mean one thing. There's a room missing. That's why the lighthouse is too small. Look at it Jamie, look at the window and look where the roof starts above the window. The roof in our home-work room is about seven feet above our heads, but look at the lighthouse. The gap is at least fifteen feet from the window to the roof of the tower. I worked it out on paper."

"What does that mean?" Jamie wrote.

"It means, eejit, that there's a secret room above our room."

The light dawned in Jamie's eyes.

Of course. It all made sense.

"I tell you, Jamie, easy-peasy. It was that combination of getting the e-mail from Thaddeus and you having to do your trig homework. Both of those things at the same time made something click in my brain. If the timing had been different we might never have learned the secret. Come on," Ramsay exclaimed, "we've got to get moving!"

They collected their flashlights, then carried the stepladder up the lighthouse steps and set it up in their homework room. Ramsay climbed to the top of the ladder and began scraping at the ceiling with the trowel. Stone started crumbling onto his head.

Jamie wrote something with his stylus. Ramsay wagged his finger at him.

"Don't press Play. I already know what you're going to say. You're going to tell me that this is an ancient monument and we could get in trouble for doing this," Ramsay groaned, mocking him.

"I wasn't going to say that, I was going to say be careful," Jamie wrote.

"Oh, sorry. Well, I will be," Ramsay replied and scraped at the crumbling brick in the ceiling.

"Oh, aye mate. This is definitely a false ceiling," Ramsay said, "It's only half bricks and stones. Oh, my goodness, I'm through already. Look at this. Look."

Ramsay tossed down bricks and debris from the ceiling. Dust was filling the room. Jamie coughed and put his hand over his mouth.

In just a matter of moments, Ramsay had made a hole in the ceiling big enough to get through. He climbed to the top limb of the ladder and shone his flashlight into what really was an upper chamber.

Jamie waited for what seemed like forever.

"Bloody hell, Jamie, you have to see this," Ramsay said, hoisting himself up and climbing completely into the upper room.

Jamie didn't need to be told twice. He took the tablet PC off his arm, grabbed his flashlight, jumped onto the ladder, and ran to the top step. Ramsay reached down with his big powerful arms and helped lug him into the upper room.

Jamie blinked in the darkness and then remembered to shine his powerful flashlight. The upper chamber was, of course, identical in diameter to the room below, but it was only about six feet high, and Ramsay had to crouch to avoid banging his head. There was no window, and it would have been bare but for a pillar in the dead center of the room, on which sat a gold object in the shape of a boomerang or a half-moon.

"Jeez, look at this. I got to get a gander at that," Ramsay said as he started moving forward.

Jamie blocked him with his arm and shook his head. It was his lighthouse. It was his island. He was going to go first.

Ramsay nodded, bashed his skull against the low ceiling, cursed, and then whispered: "Of course you have the priority, you should look at it before me."

Jamie walked over to the object and stared at it. It was a curved gold device about ten inches across with ridges in the middle and jewels or buttons on either side. It was not symmetrical and it looked heavy. It resembled a fish without a head and Jamie remembered that in Thaddeus's e-mail someone had said something about a salmon.

Ramsay came closer, gasping in amazement.

"That thing is bound to be worth an absolute fortune. It is definitely gold. We're gonna be rich," Ramsay said. "Don't pick it up yet though, it could be booby-trapped. Remember Indiana Jones and the big stone ball."

Ignoring him, Jamie put down his flashlight, lifted the object, and held it tight in his right hand. It was very light and extraordinarily beautiful.

"My turn," Ramsay said.

Jamie handed it to Ramsay.

"Wow, it's not as heavy as you would think, and there's something inside it. Yeah, I think it's electronic," Ramsay said. "Machinery or something inside."

Jamie tired to grab it back.

"Let me see it for a bit longer," Ramsay complained, but Jamie snatched it from his grasp. In the commotion he accidentally pushed what appeared to be a gold divot or button on the right side of the device, and then, much to Ramsay's amazement, Jamie completely disappeared.

Chapter V

THE PASSAGE

THE ROOM BLURRED, went pitch-black, and for a moment Jamie felt that he was falling. He put his hand out to protect himself. What had happened? Had Mr. McCreagh been right—had the lighthouse collapsed? The place *had* been dangerous. Maybe Ramsay's excavations had been the final straw for the old structure.

But after only half a second, Jamie knew that wasn't the answer.

If he was falling, it was a great and impossible distance yet without the slightest sensation of physical motion. Weird. And then, abruptly, he stopped, his body shook like he was being electrocuted, and he suddenly found himself where he had started, back in the lighthouse.

What on Earth? Jamie asked himself. *Could I have had some kind of seizure? A relapse of my cancer?*

No. That wasn't it either. His breathing was good and he felt fine.

He shook his head, opened his eyes.

He looked for Ramsay, but Ramsay was gone. And then he noticed that the curved room was larger than it should be and that it was illuminated by starlight. *I must have fallen through to the lower chamber and been knocked unconscious,* Jamie thought. Ramsay must have been terrified that he would get in trouble and run away. Or maybe he'd been knocked unconscious too.

But Jamie could only hold this impresion for another second before realizing that although this was a lighthouse, it was not *his* lighthouse.

It was *much*, much bigger than the round tower on Muck Island and the room was filled with odd-shaped boxes and furniture and it smelled completely different— a cold, frosty stink with a hint of sulfur. But if all that wasn't enough, at the far end of the room there was a bed, an iron four-poster bed, and in the middle of it, half under a heavy white sheet, a girl.

Jamie held the fish-shaped device in his trembling right hand and looked at her with astonishment. She was completely asleep, curled on her side, wearing a long white nightgown. And then Jamie *really* felt amazed because behind the girl's head there was a window, a porthole in the round wall of the lighthouse and there in the sky were two moons—one yellow, one white—and a wide expanse of stars completely different from the stars in his own world.

Jamie gasped in horror. Somehow he was no longer on planet Earth. His knees felt weak and almost buckled.

To prevent himself from falling, he found that he was walking over to the bed.

The sleeping girl was about his age with blond hair and

a pretty, delicate face. He didn't know how he knew, but he saw instantly that, although she looked human, she was definitely not human. She was a completely different species. An alien. Her eyes were narrow, her nose was tiny—almost nonexistent, and her cheekbones were thin and sharp.

If her yellow hair hadn't been covering her ears, he would have seen that they were pointed. What he did notice was her hands.

She had four fingers on each hand. Two central digits and two things that looked like thumbs.

And it was while he was looking at the girl's strange nonhuman hand that Jamie discovered something about himself, and this was the most incredible thing of all. More unbelievable than the alien girl, than the two moons, than the fact that he had teleported across the galaxy. Oh, yes, more stunning than all of that, was the fact that there, hanging next to his left hip, completely restored to life again, was his left forearm and his left hand.

He was woozy. Sick. He had to steady himself on the four-poster to stave off a fainting fit.

His left hand?

Could this whole thing actually be a dream after all? Some wish-fulfillment fantasy that he was experiencing after a terrible accident in the old lighthouse? Maybe he was in a Belfast hospital right now, stuffed with tubes, teetering between life and death?

He flexed his left fist. He pinched a finger. Hard. He banged his left fist into his leg and it hurt.

He gasped again and knew it was the truth. It was real.

The alien device that had sent his molecules spinning through space had restored his arm.

His exclamation had woken the girl. Her eyes opened. She looked startled for a moment and then she got out of the bed and kneeled before him.

"*Dusha, call, faara ee ee eaway, macha Ui Neill,*" she said in a trembling voice.

Jamie looked at her in puzzlement.

The girl blinked and then remembered he would not speak the tongue of Aldan.

"Prithee, my Lord Ui Neill. My father was right," she said, trying not to sound terrified. "Thou hast come then in our hour of need, as he said ye wouldst."

Jamie backed away from her and looked at his restored left hand. It was all suddenly too much. The new planet, the moons, the girl, the alien words. He felt unnerved, frightened, nauseated. The girl sensed that something was wrong.

"Thou hast journeyed long? Marry, thou art in need of sustenance?" she asked.

Jamie shook his head.

He opened his mouth.

He was going to reply to her.

He was going to speak.

His tongue was dry and his vocal cords were rusty. He hadn't so much as said one word in a year. Why had he not spoken since the operation? The answer was obvious.

He had nothing to say. What could he say? This broken, depressed little boy. He had been in a state of mild clinical shock for eleven months. The imposing horror of death. The shock of losing his arm, the shock of being changed utterly and forever.

But now the arm had been restored to him. The world had been set to rights.

And he knew that he was going to say something to the girl.

"Who are you?" he asked.

"I am Wishaway, daughter of Callaway, Councillor of the City, Principal of the University, and Chief Logician of Aldan," she replied.

"I'm Jamie," Jamie said.

"Thou art of the Ui Neill?" Wishaway asked.

"Yes," Jamie said in wonder, and the girl nodded as if this was the most natural thing in the world.

"My father said thou wouldst come. Prithee, we beg thy forgiveness. He would have been here himself, but he is needed to defend the city. He entrusted this responsibility to me in the hope, nay, in the belief that thou wouldst come."

"Well, I am here," Jamie said stupidly.

"Thou hast journeyed long?" Wishaway asked again.

"It only took a second."

"Thou didst not tarry then. Ye used the Salmon?" she asked, looking at the object in his right hand.

"Yes."

"Does my lord need sustenance or rest?" she asked.

Jamie shook his head. Wishaway waited for a respectful half minute before continuing.

"Come then, Lord Ui Neill, we must prepare the boat. The city is in great peril—it may already be under assault."

"What are you talking about?" Jamie asked.

"The iceships come. If they are there, we must lift the siege. Thou hast brought weapons?" Wishaway asked.

"What siege, what city? What are you talking about?"

"The iceships plan to besiege our city. The host of Alkhava comes to take our land. My father said that, just as in the past, so again would the Lords Ui Neill return to save us in this time of need," Wishaway said sadly.

"I don't know what you're talking about. I haven't come to save anybody, I don't know who you are, or what place this is," Jamie replied.

Wishaway looked at him strangely.

"Thou art ignorant of our situation, Lord Ui Neill?" she asked.

"That's right, I'm ignorant," he said.

"I am Wishaway, daughter of Callaway, Councillor of the City, Principal of the U—"

"Yeah, I got that part," Jamie interrupted. "What city? Where the hell are we?"

Wishaway's nose wrinkled in disapproval.

"We are not in hell, mighty Lord, we are alive on Altair. My city, Aldan, is threatened by Alkhava. Their arts are strong and they will unmake us. My father took me to this lighthouse on the Sacred Isle. Verily in the past when our city was threatened, men came from here, twice, to save us. My father held that we would be saved again, in our time of greatest peril."

Wishaway breathed heavily after her long speech. In the moonlight he could see that her eyes were a deep cobalt blue, unnervingly penetrating and clear.

"I don't know anything about war. If anything I'm a pacifist," Jamie said.

"Mayhap it is difficult for thee also, Lord Ui Neill. When my father sent me here, I did not believe him," Wishaway confessed. "The last time people came here was over three hundred years ago. I thought that he sought only to protect me so that when the city fell, I would not be sent into slavery with the rest of my kinfolk. But now I see that my father wert wise, for thou hast come."

"I have, but like I say, I'm not a warrior," Jamie protested.

"But thou art Lord of the Ui Neill?" Wishaway asked.

"Well, technically, I'm a kind of a Lord, it's kind of embarrassing and not really until I turn eighteen, but I suppose so, yes."

Wishaway nodded.

"Come, the tide is with us, Aldan awaits its savior. I will prepare the boat," Wishaway said.

"The boat?"

"Verily, it was not damaged in the storm save a spar on the main mast. But I will not be able to launch it alone," Wishaway said.

"Wait a minute, this is all happening pretty damn quick for me. Just let me get my bearings for a while," Jamie said.

"No, my Lord, the boat can only be launched at highest tide. If we wish to go tonight we must go now," Wishaway leaned forward and grabbed Jamie by the arm of his Carrickfergus Grammar blazer. His left arm, the arm that wasn't supposed to be there.

He felt a sudden panic writhe through him. His head was spinning. She pulled harder on the arm, she wanted him to get in the boat, she wanted him to leave tonight, to save her city, her country.

And then he had that feeling again. It was too much. It was all just too much.

"No, don't touch me," he said.

He backed off.

"Lord Ui Neill, ye must come, we need thy help," Wishaway said desperately.

"No, no," Jamie said, close to panic. He lifted the alien teleportation device, he pressed his thumb on the button on the right hand side, the room spun, the walls blurred, the ceiling dissolved. Everything went black and he felt as if he were falling into a dark tunnel. But only for a moment, and then he was in the lighthouse again, Ramsay was looking at him, daylight was creeping in through the hole in the floor, and his left arm was gone.

Ramsay patted Jamie on the back. He was ecstatic,

stunned, jumping with amazement, waving his big arms about excitedly. "You went invisible!" he yelled. "That thing makes you go invisible. We're going to be famous. We're going to be millionaires."

Jamie opened his mouth to speak, to explain what had happened to him, but no words came out. He couldn't do it, the joy of finding out that his arm had been restored had now turned to ashes in his throat.

The arm was gone and everything was as it was before.

"You went invisible," Ramsay repeated, his eyes wide with wonder and talking a mile a minute. "First we'll keep it a secret, so we can influence the outcome of football matches, sneak backstage at the Britney Spears concert, break into Mr. Bennett's house and convince him there's a poltergeist. That kind of thing. Then we'll have to tell people. It's an incredible discovery. We should go to the press, otherwise the government will use it as a secret weapon and kill us to keep the secret safe. After we have a press conference, we'll sell it to the highest bidder. The Americans will buy it for millions. Where do you think it came from? You don't believe in Atlantis, do you? I don't either. I say it's proof, finally, that there's aliens. That's another reason we'll have to go to the media. The government would only cover it up to prevent widespread panic and then they'll probably kill us again or jail us in some secret dungeon. My parents won't mind, but your mother will be devastated after all she's gone through. You know?"

Jamie wanted to tell him to shut up, he wanted to

scream at him. He wanted him to know the truth. But the renewed blow of losing his limb a second time had robbed him of a desire to communicate even this.

Ramsay was in his face, and nausea began making his head spin. He felt trapped and claustrophobic in the tiny, enclosed space of the lighthouse's upper chamber. He stumbled to the hole Ramsay had made in the floor and went down the stepladder. He needed light and air. He needed to get the facts straight in his head. He had either had a very convincing hallucination or he had somehow journeyed off the Earth.

He grabbed the flashlight and ran down the lighthouse steps and kept running until he reached the sea. The waves were crashing on the stony beach; he sat and sucked in the heavily oxygenated air in big throaty breaths.

A minute later, Ramsay came outside and sat beside him on the stones. He looked concerned. From Jamie's reaction he had an inkling that something even bigger than invisibility had just happened. He would take it easy with him.

"Are you OK, Jamie?" Ramsay asked.

Jamie nodded. Ramsay's mouth opened and closed.

They sat in silence for a moment, watching the wind whip over the gray Irish Sea and in the distance a big tanker making for the docks in Belfast.

Jamie was still holding the artifact in his hand.

Ramsay looked at it closely.

"I'm telling you, wee lad. That thing. It's not human.

It wasn't made on Earth, or at least, not by human beings," Ramsay said gently.

Jamie nodded. That was for sure.

"Something's up. You didn't go invisible, did you?" Ramsay asked after a while.

Jamie shook his head.

"What did happen?"

Jamie looked for his tablet PC, but it was back at the top of the tower. He put the Salmon device on the ground and made a walking man with two fingers.

Ramsay cocked his head and stared at him for a moment, but then suddenly, he understood.

"You went somewhere?" he asked in wonder.

Jamie nodded.

"Where?" Ramsay asked.

Jamie pointed up into the sky.

"You flew?"

Jamie shook his head, waved his hand dismissively and pointed way in the distance above their heads.

Ramsay's eyes widened with astonishment. He was too stupefied to speak.

"Space?" he said finally.

Jamie nodded and made his finger man walk on the stony beach.

"Another planet?" Ramsay asked, after a long pause.

Jamie nodded.

Ramsay stood up, walked around in a little circle, sat down again.

"Can I look at it?" Ramsay asked.

Jamie gave him the thing that Wishaway had called the Salmon.

"If that's true, it's the single greatest event in the history of mankind," Ramsay said in a whisper. There was a hint of skepticism in his voice and Jamie knew there was no other way; he was going to have to show him.

He stood, took back the Salmon, and beckoned Ramsay to follow him.

He walked to the lighthouse, Ramsay close on his heels. They climbed to the secret room and Jamie stood where he had stood before, next to the pillar, where the Salmon had been resting. He took Ramsay's left hand and placed it in the middle of the device.

"What are you doing?" Ramsay asked, fear creeping into his voice.

Jamie pressed the same jeweled button on the side.

It took longer this time.

They fell together, the walls blurring, the room exploding briefly in a black light and then, after only a moment, they were both standing in Wishaway's lighthouse on the planet Altair, light-years from Earth.

Jamie saw that the bed was empty and that Wishaway had gone somewhere. He put his finger over his lips to tell Ramsay to be quiet. Ramsay looked horrified, confused and a little afraid. Jamie showed Ramsay his restored left arm and Ramsay had to put his hand over his mouth to stop himself from crying out.

"Ssssh," Jamie whispered. "I want to show you something."

"You're talking?" Ramsay said, stunned.

"Shut up, Ramsay, I want you to look out the window and tell me what you see, quietly now, I don't know where she went," Jamie said.

He led Ramsay to the lighthouse window and showed him the two moons and the completely different star formations. Ramsay nodded and looked at Jamie with wonder.

Through the window, Jamie saw Wishaway taking a walk, presumably to clear her head. The meeting must have been just as traumatic for her as it was for him. Eventually, though, she'd have to come back to bed. They couldn't stay here.

"Who's that?" Ramsay asked.

"Let's go somewhere she won't see us. There's a set of stairs over there, we can go down to the floor below," Jamie whispered.

Ramsay nodded and Jamie led him down a wide set of spiral stairs to a storage room filled with wooden cartons and barrels. There were strange foodstuffs in glass jars, a flint tinder box, a grinding wheel for sharpening knives, a mill stone for crushing grain, a heavy ax. All of it damp, decaying, rusting. Whatever this place was, it wasn't a hive of activity, Ramsay thought to himself.

"We're on another planet, aren't we?" Jamie said, sitting down on a barrel.

Ramsay looked at the Salmon and the strange stars through another porthole window. He nodded.

"How come my arm came back?" Jamie asked. "And yet when I went back to Earth it was gone again."

"And your voice. Why are you speaking?" Ramsay asked.

"I don't know, I suppose because on this planet I'm whole again. I want to speak. It just seems that it's the right thing to do," Jamie said.

Ramsay walked to the window and looked out at the stars.

"We're on another planet, in a completely different part of the galaxy. I don't recognize a single star. Bloody hell, we might not even be in the Milky Way anymore."

Ramsay picked up some of the tattered equipment lying around the storage room. He started fiddling with what looked like an old oil lamp.

"Don't touch anything," Jamie ordered.

Ramsay put it down and sat next to Jamie.

"What do you think happened, Ramsay?" Jamie asked.

Ramsay shrugged.

"You can't move instantly across eons of space. It's impossible. Nothing can travel faster than light. Nothing. Even if you were moving at light speed it would take four years to get to the nearest star, Alpha Centauri," he said.

"So if it's impossible, how did we get here?" Jamie asked.

Ramsay scratched his forehead.

"That device we found must have created a wormhole,

a tunnel, a passage between two regions in space. It's the only way to go such a vast distance instantaneously," Ramsay said.

Jamie held the Salmon up to the light of the two moons.

"The O'Neills, my ancestors, did they make this?" Jamie asked.

Ramsay shook his head. "I doubt it. If I had to guess, I'd say this is an alien artifact, from a very, very advanced civilization," Ramsay said confidently. "The aliens may have left it behind in the tower as a method of jumping between worlds. It could be that it's site-specific. It only works from that one location. From there to here. The Princes of Ulster must have found it and kept it secret in the old tower. Remember Thaddeus's e-mail? It said that the O'Neills had twice used the tower as a place of escape. It didn't make any sense. If you were being pursued by enemies how could you escape from the round tower on Muck Island?"

"I guess now we know," Jamie said.

"Yeah," Ramsay agreed.

"But I still don't understand how it works. Why did my arm come back? And when she spoke to me, at first she spoke in alien, but then in a kind of old English."

Ramsay punched Jamie on the shoulder.

"Wait a minute. You spoke to her? Are you kidding me?"

"Yes, I spoke to her," Jamie said casually.

"What did she say?" Ramsay asked, close to bursting.

"She said that her father had sent her here to this

island to wait for me, to wait for an O'Neill to come and save her city from attack just like they'd done in the past. She was really intense and I panicked a bit and pressed the button again and came back to you."

"Wow."

"But she was speaking English, old English."

Ramsay nodded. "Obviously, humans have been to their world before. Maybe twice before, if we can believe Thaddeus's e-mail. Even though it's a secret, people must have known about this device, this world, its existence must have leaked out. In Ireland there's a legend about a hidden world in the sea called Tír na nÓg. And there's all those magical things they talked about in the e-mail: Excalibur, the Stone of Scone, the Salmon of Knowledge. They could all be names for the same thing. Maybe the O'Neills taught the people English when they came. It might have caught on. When Columbus went to America with a couple of hundred Spanish soldiers, everyone spoke Native American languages, but within a generation everyone spoke Spanish."

This was too much information for Jamie. "Slow down. What did you say about the thing?"

"When Columbus went—"

"No, the Salmon of what?"

"The Salmon of Knowledge. That's another Irish legend," Ramsay said.

"She called the device the Salmon," Jamie said.

"Yes," Ramsay replied, waving his arms excitedly.

Jamie put his finger to his lips. They heard footsteps on the stairs. Wishaway was returning to bed. They waited until she had settled down before continuing their conversation in whispers.

"But, but who made it, how does it work, what's happening?" Jamie asked, running together some of the million questions going through his head.

Ramsay thought about it for a moment. "Our sun has three worlds capable of supporting a form of life: Earth, Mars, and an icy moon of Jupiter called Europa. On one of these worlds at least, we know, life has developed and become sentient. Some people say this was a unique event in the galaxy, but we know now that's not true. An alien civilization must have arisen and discovered wormholes throughout the universe. They made these devices to allow them to travel through the wormholes and explore the universe," Ramsay suggested.

"Wishaway's people," Jamie said.

"She's called Wishaway?" Ramsay asked.

Jamie nodded. "Yeah, did she make this?"

Ramsay thought about it and looked skeptical. "I suppose it could be these people, but if so, they've forgotten how to do high technology. Look around you; oil lamps, a wood-burning stove—there isn't a single electrical device in the whole place. If her people made the Salmon, they must have fallen spectacularly from grace."

"OK, maybe, I'll buy that . . . But what's it doing here? Who made it?"

"I don't know. Maybe the wormholes and this machine were the way aliens used to travel throughout the galaxy. Maybe they were alien geographers charting the universe or something.

"So it creates a wormhole between Wishaway's planet and ours. And we step through it. It still doesn't explain my arm," Jamie said.

"I think it does. You'd need an incredible amount of energy to create and sustain a wormhole that a humanoid can fit through, but if you break that humanoid into his constituent molecules and reassemble him on the other side of the fold in space, it would take much less energy. The Salmon device must have a highly advanced computer inside. The Salmon scans your DNA, stores your pattern, and uses that to reassemble you on the other side of the wormhole. Your DNA only contains a pattern for a two-armed Jamie, not a one-armed one."

Jamie shook his head. "I'm still not getting it, Ramsay. When I returned to Earth my arm was gone again."

"Of course. The computer in the device didn't need to guess what you should look like on our world. No DNA scan necessary, because it already has your pattern for Earth. When you got reassembled on the other side of the wormhole on Earth, you returned to the original, could-not-be-improved-on formula for Jamie O'Neill."

Jamie nodded. "So as long as I'm on this planet— Altair, the girl called it—I'll have two arms and as long as I'm on Earth I'll only have one," Jamie said sadly.

143

"It's wick. But that's about the size of it, I think, mate," Ramsay agreed.

"Well then, I'm going to stay here," Jamie said.

Ramsay scoffed. "You don't know anything about this place. You don't know if you can eat the food. Drink the water. You don't know if the people are friendly."

"There's one good way to find out," Jamie said and pointed upstairs.

The color drained from Ramsay's face, but then he nodded. "Let's go talk to her. I've always wanted to meet an alien," he said nervously.

❁ ❁ ❁

When they went upstairs, they discovered that the girl had gone back to sleep. Jamie and Ramsay crept quietly into the room. They stared at her for a while, building up the nerve to wake her up.

"Look at her fingers," Jamie whispered.

Ramsay nodded. Four fingers on each hand. Here they would use base eight for their mathematics. This knowledge pleased him enormously.

"And her nose is different too. But it's amazing that she looks humanoid at all, really, when you consider all the evolutionary pathways her species could have taken. To have a face, limbs, and so on—it's remarkable. They call it convergent evolution on Earth when two different species end up looking the same."

She rolled over on her side.

"Do you see her ears?" Ramsay asked.

144

Jamie nodded.

"She looks like one of the faerie people from Irish folklore. Man, that's weird, it's more than a coincidence if you ask me. Maybe the traffic between worlds hasn't all been one way."

Jamie had been whispering, but as Ramsay spoke he got louder and more excited. It was enough to wake her up.

Wishaway looked frightened for a moment but then got out of bed and bowed to them.

"Thou hast brought assistance, Lord Ui Neill," she said to Jamie.

"This is my friend, Ramsay. Ramsay, this is Wishaway," Jamie said.

"Lord Ramsay, welcome to Altair," Wishaway said.

"It's not Lord Ramsay, and I'm not Lord O'Neill. Call me Jamie, call him Ramsay," Jamie insisted.

Wishaway bowed.

"So you're Wishaway. Jamie tells me your city is under attack," Ramsay said happily.

"Yes. The Alkhavans are coming in their iceships to lay siege to Aldan. They are many, we are few. My father hast been organizing the defense. He hast sent me here in the hope that ye would come," Wishaway said.

"In the past, hundreds of years ago, people came, didn't they? They brought muskets, and swords, isn't that right?" Ramsay asked.

Wishaway nodded. The Lords knew this already and they must be testing her, she thought.

"Forsooth thou knowest. A dozen men of the Ui Neill came here to the Sacred Isle. They brought the tubes of fire and they aided us in our fight against the Perovan attack. Now the enemy comes from the north in an even more fearsome form. Prithee, my Lord, we must make the tide and hasten for the city."

"What weapons do the Alkhavans have?" Jamie asked.

"They come in huge iceships, they have spears, bows . . . they have great machines that throw rocks. They are many in number. Thousands," Wishaway said softly and gazed outside to see if there was still something left of the high tide. The reefs around the island went on for miles; you would need at least a half-full tide to get the boat away from here.

"Why do they attack you?" Jamie asked.

"We are traders, my Lord. We are wealthy, we have traded with the Alkhavans in the past. They are curs. We have given them metals and wood to aid them in their struggle against the ice, but they always want more."

"Tribute never works," Ramsay muttered and looked at his friend for a contribution.

Jamie had run out of questions.

Both boys were still struggling with the situation.

"This is unbelievable," Ramsay said under his breath.

Jamie nodded. Wishaway drummed her fingers on the side of her leg in what was obviously a sign of impatience.

"How far is the city, Wishaway?" Jamie asked.

"Less than two days' sail, perhaps one if the winds are

with us, more if we must detour around the ice," Wishaway said.

"Sailing boats? You don't have engines?" Ramsay asked.

Wishaway looked puzzled.

"She doesn't understand, Ramsay," Jamie whispered.

"Mighty Lords, will you help us?" Wishaway asked, her hands clasping in front of her in a desperate, pleading gesture.

Both boys were taken aback.

"We, um, we'll have to think about it," Jamie said, looking at Ramsay.

"Aye, Wishaway, we'll need to talk about this *in private*," Ramsay said.

Jamie nodded. "Yes, excuse us, um, Wishaway, we need to have a chat over here," Jamie said. Wishaway looked disappointed and frustrated, but she said nothing.

Jamie led Ramsay to the far side of the lighthouse.

"My head's spinning. This is all a bit much to take in," Ramsay said.

"You're telling me. I've done it twice now."

"OK, we'll just relax and take it easy. Let's get our facts sorted out first."

"Shoot," Jamie said.

"First, we have discovered an alien teleportation device. An alien artifact. We've actually met and talked to an alien. Which is definitely the greatest discovery in the history of mankind."

"It is," Jamie agreed.

"If we were being responsible, we'd turn this discovery over to the government. I mean, we have to let scientists examine the Salmon and the wormhole, they'll need to send through teams of anthropologists, geologists, biologists to check out Altair. It'll cause revolutions in the history of science, in theology, in astronomy, in physics. If we were responsible adults we'd let the authorities know," Ramsay said.

"But we're not responsible adults," Jamie protested.

"No, we're not," Ramsay agreed.

"So we keep it a secret," Jamie said.

"Secret," Ramsay said, and offered Jamie his hand.

They shook on it.

"So, first thing solved. Now what do we do about Wishaway? About helping her?" Jamie asked.

"What do *you* think?" Ramsay asked, dodging the question.

Jamie thought for a moment and looked at the beautiful, strange little girl sitting on the edge of the bed, impatiently waiting for them.

"I think we can trust her, don't you?" Jamie said.

"Well, to use Dungeons and Dragons parlance, faeries are mostly Lawful Good. You know, they like law and order, and basically they do good. Unlike goblins, who are Chaotic Evil," Ramsay said.

Jamie shook his head with mild despair. "Seriously, Ramsay, talk like that is why you'll never get a girlfriend," Jamie said.

Ramsay shrugged. Would a girl be worth having if she wasn't into D and D?

"Anyway, back to the point," Jamie said, seeing his friend's eyes begin to glaze over. "This could be dangerous. This is a war. It isn't like Dungeons and Dragons, buddy. If we die here, we're dead."

"I know," Ramsay snorted. "When my thirteenth-level cleric died, I knew there was no bringing him back, even with a resurrection spell, which I didn't even have, but ironically I would have got if I'd made it to fourteenth level."

Jamie groaned, for unlike Ramsay, Jamie actually knew what death meant. He'd had had to confront death at the age of twelve when they had diagnosed his bone cancer. He had thought about his own mortality, what he would lose, what it would mean to him, how the world would continue on as before, with not even a ripple after he was gone. Ramsay needed to take it seriously too.

"I'm not kidding, Ramsay. It's not an adventure; we could die here," Jamie insisted.

"That's what an adventure means. Something out of the ordinary, something dangerous. I know we could die, but I also know that you're just talking for the sake of talking. You've already made your mind up about what we're going to do."

Jamie smiled at Ramsay's perception. He *had* already made up his mind. His forebears had somehow helped Wishaway and her people, and he felt that obligation. He wasn't going to let her down.

"We have to help her," Jamie said quietly.

Ramsay slapped him on the back. "That's what I was thinking, mate," he yelled with delight.

"But you don't have to come. It's my responsibility," Jamie said.

"I'm coming," Ramsay said with enough insistence to terminate that part of the conversation.

"What do we need to do?" Jamie asked.

"We've got to go back to Earth and get supplies and make a plan. These people seem pretty backward. Catapults and spears? With our knowledge of modern technology we could really do her people a solid. We could bring back books with schematics for cannons, that kind of thing."

"Excellent idea," Jamie said with a grin.

Ramsay suddenly looked troubled. "Wait a minute, though. I just thought of a problem," he muttered.

"What?"

"When you came here the first time, how long were you here, approximately?"

"I don't know, five to ten minutes."

Ramsay nodded. "That's how long I reckoned you were invisible. That means as real time passes here on Altair it passes exactly the same on Earth."

"So what?"

"Well, if we're going to go to Wishaway's city, we're going to be away for a few days, maybe a week or more. Back on Earth our parents are going to go crazy," Ramsay said with a cheeky smile on his face.

Jamie could read his friend's expressions by now. Just as Ramsay had thought of the problem, he'd already come up with the solution.

"So what's the answer?" Jamie asked, his voice bordering on annoyance.

Ramsay grinned.

"Just tell me," Jamie snapped.

"The ski trip."

"The ski trip?"

"On Monday the school's leaving on its annual two-week ski trip to Austria. We'll tell our parents and the bus driver that that's where we're going."

"It's too late to sign up for the ski trip," Jamie said. Ramsay's grin widened.

"Oh, I see, we don't sign up, do we? We tell our parents we're going on the ski trip. But we don't actually go," Jamie said.

"I'll set something up on the computer so we can e-mail them every day and they'll think we're away, but we'll have written all the e-mails in advance."

Jamie shook his head.

"Won't work. Our parents might be fooled, but the school will know we're not on the ski trip. And they'll see that we're not coming in every day and sooner or later they'll call our homes."

Ramsay was not perturbed in the least.

"No problem. We'll tell two different lies. We'll tell our parents we're going on the ski trip, we'll tell the school we're going to . . . oh, I don't know—we're visiting your family in America."

In the far corner Wishaway sighed.

Jamie could think of a dozen flaws in the plan, but he didn't bother to mention them. They were details obscuring the big picture. Here they were on an alien planet with an alien girl who wanted them to help her defend her city against invaders. Every other concern seemed suddenly irrelevant.

"Let's do it," Jamie said.

He and Ramsay shook hands again.

They walked over to Wishaway.

Behind her, and through the window, the dim red sun was rising from the icy waters of what looked to Ramsay like the western sea. He checked his pocket compass.

"Incredible, this planet spins counterclockwise as it goes 'round their sun," Ramsay began, but Jamie shushed him and stopped in front of Wishaway. Her piercing gray-blue eyes were looking at him with hope. Her nose twitched.

"We're going to have to go back to our world for a couple of days to get organized and bring supplies. But we'll be back. I promise. We're going to come, we're going to help you," Jamie said, and she nodded as if there had never been any doubt at all about their decision.

Chapter VI
THE GIRL

JAMIE HAD BEEN WRACKED with doubt and guilt all morning. His backpack was stuffed with sweaters, a new ski jacket, new sunglasses, and a thick wool hat. His mother had spent about two hundred pounds on clothes, and of course she'd had to write another check to the school for the ski trip. Fortunately that check would never get cashed; unfortunately that would take some explaining when he got back.

Anna drove him to the school bus stop.

Ramsay was already there. Also with a backpack, filled with winter clothes, waterproof clothes, a Swiss Army knife, a compass, and photocopied schematics for cannons, tanks, machine guns, and, on the verge of extreme impracticability, a B-52 bomber and the basic principles behind an atomic bomb. To impress the Altairians he was also bringing a small box of fireworks, his dad's pocket soldering iron, a harmonica, and a kaleidoscope.

On a more practical level, both boys had packed seasickness tablets, flashlights, and a first-aid kit.

Jamie got out of his mom's new car, a used Land Rover she'd bought at an auction in Larne.

"Are you going to be OK, Jamie?" Anna asked.

Jamie nodded and touched his heart, which meant "I love you."

"Well, take care, and make sure you keep your promise. E-mail every day, or get Ramsay to call so I know it's going well. Even if it's not going well and you're miserable I want to hear from you. OK?"

Jamie nodded.

"OK, darling, have fun," Anna said, then kissed him on the cheek.

Anna put the Land Rover in first gear, stalled it, and switched it back on again.

"Good-bye, Mrs. O'Neill. I'll look after him," Ramsay said.

"Good-bye, Ramsay, have a blast," Anna said with a wave as she drove off to her part-time job teaching kindergarten in the village of Ballycarry.

"You don't look so good," Ramsay said when Anna was gone.

Jamie took out his tablet PC.

"I'm not sure lying was the right thing to do," he wrote.

"It wasn't pleasant, but we were backed into a corner. We had no choice," Ramsay said weakly, and before he could think of any more mealymouthed excuses, the bus came.

The driver looked at the pair of them in mild astonishment.

"Not wearing your uniform, boys?" he asked, for both

of them were in jeans and sneakers, with Ramsay wearing a brown fleece over a T-shirt and Jamie in his black Yankees hooded fleece.

"Nah, we're going on the ski trip," Ramsay said.

The bus driver nodded.

"The ski trip, how long's that for?" he asked.

"Two weeks, so you don't have to come down to Portmuck for the next fortnight, unless we break our legs and they fly us out earlier," Ramsay explained.

"I don't hold with skiing," the bus driver said grumpily. Ramsay knew his theories. He didn't hold with skiing, abroad, foreigners, air travel, strange food, or cold. Ramsay and Jamie listened to a little speech about the perils of snow and how both boys should feel blessed that Ireland got the moderating currents of the Gulf Stream, keeping away hot summers and frigid winters. When the speech was done, they sat at the back of the bus, satisfied that he, at least, would not give the game away.

The driver picked up kids on the Islandmagee peninsula, in Whitehead, and other villages along the way.

The boys got off at the traffic circle for Carrickfergus Grammar, but they didn't go in. Instead, they avoided the prefects, snuck back out the school's front gate, and walked down the North Road.

They found a coffeeshop near the railway station. Ramsay had insisted that they carry PowerBars and a five-pound bag of rice in their backpacks just in case the food on Altair was completely inedible; and now he ordered them a huge breakfast in case it was going to be their last square meal for a while.

"There you go, love," the waitress said, plonking down two plates of porridge, toast, and fried liver and onions.

"What the hell is this?" Jamie wrote, looking with horror at the concoction in front of him.

"Protein and carbs," Ramsay said gleefully; he covered the whole thing in brown sauce and began to dig in.

"I can't eat this," Jamie wrote.

"You better. We don't know what we're going to find on Wishaway's world. Of course water exists there. H_2O is the same throughout the galaxy, but everything else might be poisonous for our immune systems. Eat your liver at least, might be the last bit of protein you'll get in a while."

Reluctantly, Jamie ate the porridge and took a few bites of liver. When they were finished the boys retired to a quiet corner to write their e-mails home.

To: annaoneill47@yahoo.com
From: jamieoneill47@yahoo.com
Dear mom, we got in safely. The resort is nice, full of kids, looking forward to skiing. It's very cold, everyone speaks English as well as German, will e-mail tomorrow. Jamie.

To: annaoneill47@yahoo.com

From: jamieoneill47@yahoo.com

Dear Mom, had my first full day of ski lessons today. I had a Disability Instructor so I could learn to ski with only one pole. The guy teaching me was American. He said that in Colorado he'd helped Bethany Hamilton learn to snowboard, which was very cool. It was hard in the morning because I kept falling over, but in the afternoon, it went really well. Ramsay took me on one of the blue runs and showed me the ropes. He is very good. I hope you don't mind but I'm going to have to e-mail you rather than get Ramsay to call. There are only a couple of public phones and there are big lines to use them (most people have cell phones (next year we'll bring one)). The food is very good, it . . .

Jamie and Ramsay continued writing until they had about a dozen e-mails full of incident and fairly convincing detail. Ramsay's parents had a computer at home and Jamie's mother could read e-mail at her school or at the Portmuck Arms, which had a pay-for-use Internet station.

"What do we do now?" Jamie wrote and played on the PC.

Ramsay looked at his watch.

"It's nine thirty. Your mother has left for work and by now my mom has gone too. We'll get the train from

Carrickfergus to Whitehead. Get off in Whitehead and then we'll keep off the roads and walk over the fields to Portmuck."

"What if someone sees us in the village?" Jamie typed.

"We'll stay in the fields, keep a lookout, and when the coast is clear we'll go straight to the causeway and up to the lighthouse."

"And how do we send these e-mails?" Jamie asked via the PC.

"That's easy, we'll take your computer to the lighthouse, make sure your battery is fully charged, and then I'll program a macro on your e-mail server to send the e-mail through the wireless hookup at the same time every day. That's the good thing about e-mail. You could think it's coming from Austria, but really it might be coming from just down the road."

"What if the battery runs out?" Jamie wrote.

"I'll make the computer go to sleep as soon as the e-mail is sent each day, and I'll make it wake five minutes before we're due to send another one. The battery could last six months that way."

Jamie nodded with grim satisfaction. Grim, because none of this was helping him shake the guilt and the feeling that he was a liar. A proficient, accomplished, thorough liar, but a liar nonetheless.

They took the train from Carrickfergus to Whitehead and walked along country lanes and over the damp fields to Portmuck.

There was no need to be worried about eyewitnesses. There was a typical Irish drizzle that kept gawkers to a minimum. And, besides, with their hoods up and their brand-new backpacks, they looked like a couple of Scandinavian hikers rather than two local schoolboys.

They cased the village for half an hour and, when the seafront looked deserted, they ran across the causeway to Muck Island.

They dried off in the Lighthouse House, had a final quick cup of tea, ascended the spiral staircase, set up the computer, and crawled into the upper chamber of the lighthouse. The Salmon was waiting on the pillar. Gold, gleaming, untouched by centuries of erosion or wet Irish air.

Jamie walked over and picked it up. Both boys were wearing their backpacks, had their hats on, were ready to go.

"Are we set?" Ramsay asked.

Jamie nodded.

Ramsay grabbed on to the Salmon too.

"I've just had a thought," Ramsay said. "What if we're carrying too much stuff and the Salmon can't handle it and it scrambles up our molecules with the clothes or the rice and we come out the other side of the wormhole half rucksack, half human?"

With that pleasant thought ringing through his ears, Jamie pressed the button on the side of the alien device and they fell through the vortex of compressed space-time from one part of the galaxy to another. The journey took a second or two longer than the previous times they'd jumped, and for a moment Jamie worried that Ramsay had been right about them carrying too much.

But even so, in only a few breaths they were back in the lighthouse on Wishaway's island, the icy sulphur smell in the air letting them know that they were no longer on Earth.

They were each in one piece, and a quick check showed that all their equipment had made it too. Wishaway wasn't there. Probably downstairs, Jamie thought.

"I guess we survived and, as patented, you got your arm back, good as new," Ramsay said. He looked at Jamie for a reply.

Jamie examined his restored left arm. It was as if the arm and his voice were somehow intrinsically linked. And now that the former had returned, Jamie knew he was going to respond verbally.

"Yeah," Jamie agreed.

It was early morning and the sun had only just risen in the western sky. A cool, red sun that seemed smaller than the Earth's home star.

"Do you think all planets have a distinctive smell?" Ramsay asked, sniffing the air and looking at the curious sun.

"I don't know," Jamie said, his own voice still sounding weird to him.

"Wishaway, we're here," Ramsay said loudly. "Where are you? Where do you think she is, Jamie?"

Jamie didn't answer. He was staring at the Salmon. There was something he hadn't noticed before. On the smooth surface near the gold button, there was a small, almost invisible red light, like a very tiny ruby.

"What do you make of that?" he asked Ramsay, showing him the Salmon.

Ramsay examined it.

"I don't know. It wasn't there before, was it?"

Jamie shook his head.

"Huh. Keep an eye on it. It might mean something," Ramsay said.

"It definitely means something, the question is whether it's something serious," Jamie said with a bit of exasperation at his friend's casualness.

"Where's Wishaway? Do you think she got fed up waiting for us and went back to her city?" Ramsay asked.

Jamie shrugged, still transfixed by the new thing on the wormhole device.

But then he shrugged his shoulders and flexed his left hand.

"Ten fingers," he whispered to himself.

It was good to be whole again.

Ramsay walked to the window.

"Wishaway, we're here, we made it. Wish you were here, Wish-a-way, ha, ha," Ramsay shouted before descending into giggles.

There was no answer but then they heard a breathless running on the stairs. Wishaway arrived, sweating, hyperventilating, and looking scared. She was wearing a heavy green dress, black boots, and carrying a long, brass telescope.

Jamie ran to her. "What is it? Are you OK?" he asked.

She was panting and although she was gasping for air, she was desperate to speak. "Iceship . . . coming from the north . . . Alkhavans," she managed. She grabbed Jamie's arm and dragged him to the window. Sure enough, there in the distance was a misshapen block of ice about a mile from the island.

"I think that's just an iceberg," Jamie said.

"No," Wishaway said, annoyed, then handed him the telescope. Jamie aimed it at the block of ice.

She was right.

Incredibly, what he thought was an iceberg was in fact a small sailing ship carved from a single block of glacial sea ice.

Jamie had never seen anything like it.

"That's amazing," he muttered, refocusing the telescope as it got closer.

Its hull was thick blue ice, thirty or forty feet long; the decks also were made of ice, as was the keel and even the small cabin at the stern. Everything in fact, save the wooden masts, cloth sails, and the ropes.

Jamie knew next to nothing about boats, but even he could see that the vessel was a warship rigged in the fashion of an old nineteenth-century clipper. A blood red pennant was flying from the main mast, and on the deck there were at least a dozen men dressed in furs, carrying spears, bows, and the occasional ax.

Jamie almost dropped the telescope.

"What is it?" Ramsay asked. "What do you see?"

"What are they going to do?" Jamie asked Wishaway.

"Prithee listen, Lord Ui Neill. They will strip the island of any wood or metal, take us prisoner, and then sell us in the slave markets of Afor," she said calmly.

"What do you see?" Ramsay yelled as he fumbled for the 10 x 50 binoculars in one of his backpack pockets.

"They are flying the flag of no quarter. If we resist, they will kill us," Wishaway said without letting her emotions take over.

Ramsay gave up looking for his binoculars and wrestled the telescope from Jamie.

"Is there anywhere we can hide in this lighthouse or on this island?" Jamie asked.

Wishaway shook her head.

"The boat is hidden in a cave on the far side of the island, but, forsooth, they will see us run to the boat. They are under full sail, the wind is behind them, and marry they will be here in a few minutes, not more," Wishaway said, this time her voice beginning to crack a little.

"Bloody hell. What on earth is that thing?" Ramsay said looking through the telescope for the first time.

"Haven't you been listening? It's an iceship. They're coming to get us," Jamie said.

Ramsay gasped, dropped the telescope, then picked it up again.

"Let me see, I'll count. There's about twelve, no, make that thirteen of them," Ramsay said. "All of them armed."

"What are we going to do? We can't hide in here, this place is too small. Can we fight them, Wishaway?" Jamie asked, trying to keep the fear out of his own voice.

The color had drained from Wishaway's face and she looked paler than ever. As white as a skeleton in the biology lab, Jamie thought. Obviously she was very frightened.

Jamie put his arm around her shoulders.

"Don't worry, we'll think of something," he said.

"Well, they're landing," Ramsay said.

Jamie snatched the telescope from Ramsay's hand.

"What are we going to do, Ramsay?" Jamie asked frantically.

There was a loud rumbling noise and through the window they could see the iceship skip onto the stony beach on the far side of the island, its frictionless hull allowing it to slide easily up onto the shore. Ropes were lowered over the side, then ten large men began climbing down onto the island.

"Under the bed," Ramsay said, finally coming to his senses.

"First place they'd look," Jamie snapped.

"Downstairs in all those boxes," Ramsay suggested.

"They're coming to take the metal and wood, they'll grab all of that," Jamie said.

"On the roof, can we get onto the roof?" Ramsay asked.

"They will see us, Lord Ramsay," Wishaway replied.

"Our only option is that boat of yours, Wishaway. If we can outrun them, could we get to the cave and launch the boat?" Jamie asked.

Wishaway shook her head. "It is low tide, Lord Ui Neill, we cannot launch the boat for another two or three hours," she said quietly.

The men had dropped to the beach and were making their way, without hurry, directly to the lighthouse. They were tall and light-skinned, bearded, most with ragged blond or red hair dangling down into their faces.

"OK, we'll have to fight them. Ramsay, what weapons do we have?" Jamie asked.

"I didn't bring weapons, I brought plans for weapons. Oh, wait, I've got my Swiss Army knife," Ramsay said.

"Lord Ui Neill," Wishaway said, but Jamie didn't hear. He was thinking. They were going to have move fast. It wasn't going to be much of a contest, but he'd never backed down from a fight in his life.

"Get out your knife, Ramsay, I'll break a chair leg and use it as a club. Wishaway, you better arm yourself, it's not going to be pretty," Jamie said, his eyes narrowing with determination.

The men were now at the bottom of the lighthouse, looking for the way in.

"We've no chance, mate, three kids against a dozen pirate berserker types. We're history," Ramsay said.

"They may be pirate berserkers, but I'm from New York City, and we don't give up that easily," Jamie said grittily. "Except against the Red Sox," he added in an undertone.

"If you're fighting, I'm fighting," Ramsay said.

"Lord Ui Neill," Wishaway said again, trying to get Jamie's attention. But Jamie was busy breaking off a chair leg and steeling himself. Ramsay unfolded the knife blade on his Swiss Army. Jamie took off his backpack. The Alkhavans were now at the bottom of the steps and making their way up the stairs.

"The slave market of Afor . . ." Ramsay muttered, "I don't like the sound of that one bit."

"Lord Ui Neill," Wishaway said loudly.

Jamie was balanced on both legs, and took a baseball stance with the chair leg.

"My Lord," Wishaway insisted.

Jamie looked at her. "What?"

"Lord Ui Neill, why do we not use the Salmon?" she asked.

Jamie turned to Ramsay.

"Brilliant!" both boys said simultaneously.

They scrambled to put their backpacks back on, then Jamie took Wishaway's hand and placed it in the center of the device.

"Grab hold, Ramsay," Jamie said.

The Alkhavans had reached the storage room below. A lone, tall, ax-wielding sailor appeared at the top of the stairs. For a moment all three of them stared into his black, terrifying eyes, then Ramsay grabbed the Salmon,

Jamie pressed the button, and they fell through the wormhole all the way to Ireland.

⬥ ⬥ ⬥

Both boys had gotten into the habit of closing their eyes when they jumped through the wormhole, and when they opened them they were back in the dimly lit upper chamber of the round tower on Muck Island. Jamie had lost his arm and Wishaway looked exactly the same.

"I was right," Ramsay said, staring at her. "Machine must have scanned her pattern, zoomed her through the wormhole and rebuilt her on the other side. Welcome to Earth, by the way. It's a bit squalid up here, come on downstairs. Have you ever seen TV? DVDs? We got incredible stuff on this planet. Make your iceships look like a big joke."

Wishaway said nothing. She was looking at Jamie with concern.

"Don't you get all Silent Bob on me as well. Tell me *you* can speak," Ramsay said to her.

"Prithee, Lord Ramsay, I can speak," she said.

"Thank God for that. One's enough, although wait till you see him chatting away through his computer. Hey, have you ever seen a computer? They're incredible. Wow, the Internet—you've never seen the Internet. You can play chess with kids in China, listen to music, and there's a webcam in this porn star's house in California that oh, uh . . ." Ramsay's voice trailed off, embarrassed.

Jamie wanted Wishaway out of this smelly, claustrophobic room, so he showed her how to get down to the lower level of the lighthouse.

Wishaway thanked him and stared about her in quiet wonder.

Jamie grabbed his PC, which he had left on a table near the window so they could send out wireless e-mails. He took his backpack off. "In this world, I can't speak," he wrote on the tablet PC and played the message for Wishaway.

The tablet PC was a little frightening, but she understood that it was Jamie trying to communicate with her.

"I see, Lord Ui Neill. Your voice comes from this box, as from a speaking trumpet," she said.

Jamie was pleased at how quickly she got it. "That's exactly right," he wrote.

"Jamie, we have to let her see everything. Planes and ships and TV . . . We got to—it'll blow her mind," Ramsay said.

Then Jamie noticed that the red light he had seen previously on the Salmon was dimmer now. He showed it to Ramsay.

"It's much less bright. Hmmm. That's pretty interesting, isn't it?" Ramsay said.

Then Jamie remembered how polite Wishaway had been to him when he had first gone through the wormhole.

"Would you like anything to eat or drink?" he asked through the computer.

Wishaway shook her head and kept near to Jamie. She

was still shocked. The Alkhavans' arrival had been an unexpected and terrible turn of events. They had come to the island. How had they known about it? Was it just a random attack, or had the city fallen and her father and the council told them where she would be? Either alternative was not good.

She was afraid and worried for her family.

And this world. The air was moister, heavier, and the planet smelled of burnt wood.

She leaned on the shoulder of Lord Ui Neill.

It was something she could never have done on Altair. When the great ones had come in the past, they had been described as being ten feet high with dark hair on their faces and booming voices. They had new ideas, spoke strangely, and had brought with them the thunder tubes—the weapons of death.

But this Lord Ui Neill was only a boy; he was her age. And on this planet he had an arm missing and he could not speak. She found him less intimidating. He was weak, vulnerable.

Jamie, the alert, young, thirteen-year-old boy that he was, could feel a girl's touch through any amount of clothing.

He turned to look at her.

He sensed that she was worried.

"How long will the Alkhavans stay on your island?" he asked via the tablet PC.

"They will not wish to spend the night, forsooth. The

Alkhavans are a superstitious people, given over to belief in spirits and ghosts. Our disappearance will have disturbed them greatly. They will water and take what they can and leave. Mayhap an hour, mayhap less."

Jamie nodded and saw the concern in her bluer-than-blue eyes.

"OK, then we'll wait an hour and we'll go back. I know you want to make the tide and get to your city," Jamie said through the PC. They couldn't stay much longer than an hour here anyway, in case his mother came back.

Ramsay looked up from the Salmon.

"I'm not sure that we will, Jamie. I think I know what the red light means," Ramsay said.

"What are you talking about?" Jamie typed.

"I think the Salmon is running out of power. It takes a tremendous amount of power to create or sustain a wormhole. We've made six journeys through the wormhole in a matter of days. The light is still on but for all we know, when we jump next time the red light might wink out and we'll be stuck there," Ramsay said.

Jamie understood. If they went back it might be a one-way trip.

"It doesn't have to be *we*, Ramsay," Jamie wrote.

"Don't insult me, mate. If you're going I'm going," he said with his trademark wide-faced grin.

They climbed down from the lighthouse and spent the next hour or so showing Wishaway the wonders of Earth. They walked to the Lighthouse House and, as Ramsay predicted, Wishaway was astonished by television, radio, and the other electrical appliances. She told them that nothing like these existed on her world, and this went some way to confirming Ramsay's belief that someone else—not humans, not Altairians—had made the Salmon.

It was the food, though, that really amazed Wishaway. She was not at all worried about being poisoned by alien food and tried everything. Some things like bread and cheese were similar to foods on her world. Other things she'd didn't recognize and found delicious, but it was when she took a bite of chocolate that she almost died from joy. They had nothing like that on Altair. Fortunately, Jamie's mother had a freezer full of chocolate chips and a bag of mini Snickers bars.

Wishaway gorged herself in a very undignified manner and finally ended up making a sandwich of bread, butter, jam, chocolate chips, and a sliced-up Snickers bar. Jamie thought it was disgusting but hilarious, whereas Ramsay just thought it was disgusting.

The greatest of Earth's delights, however, came when Wishaway learned that she could have hot water merely by turning on the faucet. On Altair a hot bath was a once-a-month luxury, even in a sophisticated city like Aldan.

She had to have one.

Jamie showed her upstairs to the bathroom, ran the bath, and discreetly left while she soaped herself and enjoyed the warm water.

He went back downstairs.

"How's she doing?" Ramsay asked.

"Good. Anxious to get back, though," Jamie wrote.

"It's a pity it's so cloudy today, I would've loved her to see an aeroplane," Ramsay said.

"Airplane," Jamie wrote with the stylus.

"Who invented the language?" Ramsay said sharply.

"Who invented the airplane?" Jamie replied through the tablet PC.

"I tell you what we should be doing," Ramsay said, ignoring this. "We should be playing her music. You know, like the greatest music ever, the Beatles or something. When she goes back to Aldan, she can play it for the locals on one of their instruments. She'll be famous."

Jamie thought this was a fantastic idea, but they spent so long arguing about what they should play her that Wishaway appeared at the bottom of the stairs, her hair dried, looking radiant in her green dress.

"You were only in for ten minutes; you can steep yourself for longer than that," Ramsay said.

Wishaway shook her head and looked at Jamie. He understood what the look meant.

"We better get back if we're going to make the tide," Jamie wrote.

They removed evidence of their visit and exited the Lighthouse House. They walked back to the lighthouse and climbed the steps to the lower chamber. Jamie had added chocolate and chocolate cookies to his backpack, so it was even heavier than before.

"Will they be gone by now?" Ramsay asked Wishaway.

"Prithee, Lord Ramsay. I knowest not. They will not stay long in what for them must be a haunted place. They are a primitive people," Wishaway said with disdain.

"You know, your English is fantastic, but you really have to cut out the forsooths, prithees, thees, and thous. No one uses them anymore. Copy the way I talk, not Jamie. I'm a real mick like the Ui Neills," Ramsay said.

Wishaway looked at Jamie for guidance.

"Your English is fine, Wishaway," Jamie typed, then set the PC back near the window. She nodded, but he could tell that she was going to be very careful about how she spoke from now on, and would attempt to exorcize the old words and redundancies from her speech.

They climbed to the upper room. Jamie lifted the Salmon off the pillar. Ramsay and Wishaway took hold.

"It really might not work this time," Ramsay said. One of his typical comforting thoughts, as they were about to jump. He pressed the button anyway, and they fell through the void.

This time as the wormhole appeared, they could see through it to the lighhouse on Altair and they could even hear the waves battering the rocky shore. For a moment Jamie wondered if they were going to make it at all, for it seemed as if the Salmon was really struggling to push them through the eons of space. The journey took almost fifteen seconds, perhaps even a little more. Both boys sighed with relief when they opened their eyes on the Sacred Isle. *Would the Salmon have the power left for more jumps?* Ramsay wondered but kept this further worry to himself.

On Altair it was almost evening.

They ran to the window to check on the iceship, but it was gone.

Wishaway's room had been destroyed. The bed had been torn to pieces, dismantled, and taken, along with all the fabric, food, paper, wood, and iron in the tower.

"They did their job fast and quick. Wow, they've left nothing," Jamie said. He was always the first to speak because he was always happy at getting his arm back.

"Aye, they did a number on this place," Ramsay said.

All they had missed was the glass in the windows and a few copper coins lying on the floor.

Jamie picked one up and was surprised to see an Elizabethan-dressed Irishman on one side and a city with towers and minarets on the other.

"Morgan of the Red Hand and the city of Aldan," Wishaway explained sadly.

"Look at the Salmon now, Jamie, see what I was saying?" Ramsay said breathlessly. When Jamie looked the red light was very dim indeed. "What do you think that means?" Jamie asked.

Ramsay shook his head. "I don't know. I'm starting to think it's a power gauge. A warning light like you have when your engine's overheating."

"What do you think it's telling us?"

"One more jump, if we're lucky," Ramsay said quietly. Jamie nodded with resignation.

"What do we do with it? Do we take it with us?" Jamie asked.

"We could hide it here. I'm pretty certain it's site-specific; the ends of the wormhole are in these towers. We'll need to come back here to go home, *if* we can go home. No point lugging it along, especially on a boat."

Jamie thought about it. There might be no point bringing it, but he'd feel better knowing it was nearby.

"We better take it just in case," Jamie said.

"Lord Ui Neill, I do not mean to be rude but—"

"'Course. Come on, Ramsay, we better get cracking." They walked outside.

It was cold, but not freezing—somewhere in the fifties, Jamie thought. "Next time we come we'll bring a thermometer and record things for science," Jamie said.

"If there is a next time," Ramsay muttered.

They walked across the small island to the eastern shore, Wishaway running ahead to check on the boat. She ducked down a trail that led to a small cliff.

"'Stairway to Heaven'—we should have played her 'Stairway to Heaven,'" Ramsay said ruefully.

"That's not even the best song on that album," Jamie replied. "'When the Levee Breaks' is much—"

"I should have played her my DVD of Zeppelin at Madison Square Garden—Jimmy Page's trousers would have totally impressed her."

"Not his guitar playing, his pants," Jamie said sarcastically.

Wishaway jogged back to them with a huge grin on her face.

"They did not find it. If they had, they would have taken it. Wood is rare where they live; a wooden boat would have been quite a prize."

"Wood is scarce and metal is scarce, is that right?" Ramsay asked as they walked down the little path. The tide was going out and the rocky beach was slick with water and long strands of purple kelp.

"Thou art, er . . . *you are* correct. Wood is not to be had in Alkhava, but in Aldan it is more common. Metal is scarce all over the world," Wishaway said.

"If only you could have stayed longer on Earth, I would have loved to have shown you an entire ship made of iron—put those iceships to shame," Ramsay said.

Wishaway said something in reply, but her response was lost in the surf booming against the shore.

They followed her around an abutment in the cliff and, sure enough, there was the cave, the black mouth almost invisible against the dark rocks. It was an exceptional hiding place. Wishaway walked over to the two boys and cleared her throat. She wanted to give them instructions, but she was still not sure of her position with them.

"Atmos will rise soon. We will have enough tide on the first moon for an hour or perhaps two. Thus if ye art rested, Lords, mayhap we should launch now."

"Now is fine," Jamie said, "but you've got to stop calling us Lords. Jamie and Ramsay, remember?"

Wishaway nodded.

Ramsay took the flashlight out of his jacket pocket and shined it into the cave. The boat was small. A single-masted vessel, not more than fifteen feet long. No cabin and very little shielding from the elements. He looked back at the gray-white sea behind him that was pounding roughly on the land.

"How far do we have to go in that thing?" Ramsay asked.

"A day or so, depending on how the wind and currents lie," Wishaway said, beginning to untie the boat from its moor anchors in the side of the cliff.

"You came all the way here in that?" Jamie asked, sharing some of Ramsay's skepticism.

Wishaway shook her head. "I have come hither in my father's boat; we towed this craft behind us," she said, as if it was a matter of small concern.

"You do know how to sail though, right?" Ramsay asked.

"Of course, I prithee, I have not sailed yon craft before, but I have crewed or captained ones that are similar," she said confidently.

"No more prithees or yons. Seriously, I'm pat with all the hep lingo. Copy me," Ramsay said.

Jamie's mind was on more important topics. "I don't know anything about boats. Does it look OK to you?" Jamie asked his friend.

"It looks fine, Jamie," Ramsay said, although he knew next to nothing about boats either.

"What's it called?" Jamie asked conversationally.

"What is what called?" Wishaway replied.

"The boat?"

"We do not give names to boats. That is an old superstition. We are not like the Alkhavans. We are a scientific people," Wishaway said a little snootily.

"We're much more scientific than you and we give names to everything," Ramsay said under his breath.

Wishaway told them to throw their backpacks into the boat and then she showed them how to undo the ropes and anchors that held the boat fast in the storms. When everything was untied, she climbed into the vessel and fitted a steering oar to the boat's stern.

"We are ready to launch," she said.

"How do we do that?" Jamie asked.

"We push the boat into the sea," Wishaway said, wondering if this was as stupid a question as it sounded or whether it was another test from the Lord Ui Neill.

Wishaway lowered two knotted ropes on each side of hull so they could climb aboard, and then Ramsay, Jamie, and Wishaway pushed the boat easily over the slippery rocks and into the retreating surf. When the boat was floating, Wishaway climbed nimbly up the side, followed much less nimbly by the two boys. Both of them were soaked from the knees down, and Ramsay grumbled something about his new shoes.

Wishaway, paying them no mind, attached a rope to a large blue sail made of a linenlike substance, and without further ado she hoisted it up the mast. She tightened the sail on the boom, dropped the steering oar in the water, and within a few seconds they had headway and were moving east.

Although Wishaway was an expert sailor, the seas were rough, the boat was small, and by dusk all three of them were drenched.

Wishaway's lighthouse supplies had been stolen, but the three of them ate PowerBars and sipped fresh water in jars stored on the boat. Ramsay warned Jamie about the possibility of diarrhea-causing microbes in the water, but both boys drank it without any ill effect.

The sea was cold and the wind from the north was freezing. It was hard to get warm, and the boys had the idea of spreading their sleeping bags over themselves as a kind of splash cover. It worked well, and they all sat together on the lee side of the craft, protected only a little from the waves, but much warmer than before.

The sun was sinking into the east, a redder sun than Earth's star, and because it was less massive, the sunsets were much less spectacular.

"Either their sun is smaller than ours, or it's much farther away," Ramsay said. "That's why it's so cold here, that's why everything's so marginal."

Wishaway looked at him with interest. Lord Ramsay was obviously versed in knowledge of the scientific arts.

"They say that in the past the sun was larger in the sky," she said softly.

"It's moving farther away?" Jamie asked her.

Wishaway nodded. She didn't understand the physics, but her father had told her something like that.

Ramsay shook his head.

"That can't be good. Maybe it's being pulled away by a binary star, or a gravity well, or even a black hole. Whatever it is, if it's moving away, it's just going to get colder here; things are going to get harder."

Wishaway looked distressed. Jamie gave Ramsay a dirty look. His friend took the hint.

"Oh, don't worry about it. That could take millions of years and I might be wrong. It might be in orbit about a binary star, it might move away for a while and then come back again. The important thing is to survive through the tough times. And we'll help you with that," Ramsay said cheerfully.

"Are there no birds here?" Jamie asked to change the subject. "I haven't seen a single bird since we got here."

Wishaway didn't really understand the concept of birds, although she had read a little about them in *The Book of Stories* written by Morgan of the Ui Neill. Jamie explained that they were feathered vertebrates that had colonized the air. Wishaway knew of no such creatures on her world, which saddened both boys immensely. She described a flying batlike creature called a *ranta* that could come in many sizes. However, they didn't see any of those. As some consolation, in the seas, they did spot what looked a lot like fish—which Ramsay explained was another example of convergent evolution. Fish and the occasional glimpse of much larger, hump-backed animals that Wishaway called *taaraas* and seemed to be either a type of whale or giant octopus.

"So your father sent you to the tower to wait for us?" Jamie asked after a while.

"Yes. It was his belief that the Ui Neills came from the tower on the Sacred Isle nearly four centuries ago," Wishaway said.

"Are there more towers like that on this planet?" Ramsay asked with interest wondering if the Salmon would work from other places on Altair.

"Yes, Lord Ramsay. One in the city itself, one in the domain of the Witch Queen in Balanmanik, but it was my father's belief that the Lords Ui Neill arrived here. Some of the records have been lost but—"

"Is that your father 'round your neck?" Ramsay asked, noticing the picture holder about her throat.

Wishaway blushed.

"This is my mother. She has died, since four years now," Wishaway said.

"Can I see?" Jamie asked.

Wishaway looked shocked.

"It is not considered decent to gaze at another's loved one, but if you insist, Lord Jamie, I will—"

"No, no, not at all," Jamie said, dreadfully embarrassed.

All three lapsed into silence.

Night fell and Wishaway steered them by the extraordinary collection of stars illuminating the heavens. The two moons gave off enough reflected light so that it was possible to read. Not that they had anything to read apart from Ramsay's photocopied weapons manuals. But certainly neither boy was tired. How could you be, sailing on a strange ocean, under a stranger sky, with an alien girl who was taking you into a war?

"Which star do you think is our sun?" Jamie asked, looking up into the heavens.

Ramsay shook his head in the darkness.

"It's impossible to say; none of the constellations look remotely like our own. They could be the stars in our neighborhood of the galaxy, but maybe we're seeing them from a different angle, so they make different patterns. I don't know if we're fifty light-years from Earth or five billion," Ramsay said.

Wishaway held on tight to the steering oar and said nothing. Her hands were cold and she would have liked to ask one of the boys to take the tiller for a while. They were heading, more or less, due east, which meant you kept the red star Firta behind the stern and the blue star Chichahora to the left of the prow. It should be easy for them to keep the boat on that course. But she decided that she would not ask either of them to relieve her. The boys troubled her. Ramsay seemed intelligent and Jamie was a natural leader, but neither of them looked like the great saviors of the country her father had promised. Their conversations were clouded by doubt and unknowing and it seemed (impossible as this was to take in) that they knew as little about the mighty Salmon as she did.

She decided that she would risk a question to assuage her mind. "Lords," she began uneasily, "you must know how far your world is from my mine. You made the Salmon, and it surely will have told you how far."

"We didn't make the Salmon," Jamie said. "At first we thought your people made it. Ramsay thinks there's a third party involved."

"Us? We did not make it. Such an engine is beyond our ken. You are jesting with me, Lord. Surely you constructed the great Salmon on your world of wonders?" Wishaway asked, deeply concerned.

"No, no, not at all. We didn't make it. We just found it when we were exploring. We're just a couple of kids, you know," Jamie said carelessly.

Wishaway was stunned into silence for a moment

"But you are the L-Lord Ui Neill," she stuttered after a while.

"We don't really have Lords anymore. They got rid of all that a long time ago," Jamie said.

Wishaway was struggling to process this information.

Her thoughts became articulated into words. "But if ye be youngsters, with no knowledge of the Salmon or of the higher arts, how will you save Aldan?" she asked, trying to eliminate the edge of panic in her voice.

"That's what I've been wondering," Ramsay admitted. "I mean, if metal is scarce, tanks are out, even guns probably, and there's nothing we could throw together quickly anyway. It's going to be difficult."

Wishaway pushed away the sleeping bag and slunk to the back of the boat. The full horror of what they had told her was beginning to sink in.

These were mere children. *Children.* Younger than her by the looks of it—youths who had simply stumbled upon the passage between worlds. They came from a busy planet, with many distractions and devices, but nothing of practical import.

And the threat to Aldan was a real threat. This was not a light matter. There were supposedly thousands of Alkhavans in dozens of iceships—bloodthirsty killers who would think nothing of slaying a pair of alien youths who stood in their way.

She had been pinning her hopes of deliverance on these two, but now the scales fell from her eyes. The last of her faith slipped away. She was seeing things as they really were.

The thought that these two *boys* could save her city, her country, suddenly seemed ridiculous.

It would be like asking Allaway, the miller's son, to become war master and raise the siege, or Arfair, of the fishing clan, to become President of the Council and negotiate a settlement.

It was absurd. She laughed bitterly, and after a minute she had to get a grip on herself to stop the laughter from becoming hysteria.

"Ramsay, you have knowledge of boats?" she asked.

"A little," he admitted warily.

"Then take the steering oar. I must rest. The red star always in the rear, the blue star always on the port side," she said then took one of the sleeping bags, wrapped herself in it, and lay down at the foot of the mast.

She spent the night curled in the bottom of the boat, rising only once to sheet the main when the wind picked up. She didn't sleep, not for a moment, kept awake by the sound of the boys chattering and the realization that Aldan and everyone in it could expect no help from her.

In the morning, she took the tiller again, and as they approached the coastal waters of the island of Aldan, the winds began to moderate and the chop left the sea. The water turned from an icy gray to a pleasant greeny blue. Sometime after noon Wishaway began to get restless.

"We are close now, we must look out for ships here," she told the boys.

"Where is here?" Ramsay asked.

Wishaway didn't answer but rummaged in the pile of her belongings she had kept stowed on the boat and finally picked up a tube of thick leather.

"This will help you understand," she said, and from the

tube she removed a map drawn on a weather-beaten parchment. It showed the known regions of Altair. Aldan was one of several island kingdoms in the broad circumference of the planet. It was the only temperate zone left in the world. Here they would not freeze if they fell into the water. To the north was the frozen country of Alkhava, almost completely covered by glaciers, and in the south was the ice desert continent of Perovan. Jamie looked at the map with fascination but shivered at its terrible consequences. Ice threatened the tenuous grip of civilization around the equator of this world, and whether the civilization could survive was an open question.

Wishaway carefully rolled up the map and put it away.

The sky was now overcast and it was difficult to take a bearing. It made her nervous, as she had no idea how far she was from land. She had sailed straight for her home city of Aldan because the intelligence agents in Afor and the north had told the Council that this was the ice fleet's first destination. And if the capital fell, the rest of the country would quickly follow. But now she began to regret her hasty course. Perhaps it would have been better and safer to land farther up the coast.

She had imagined that the mighty Lords would pull some trick, some magic like their "television," and destroy the enemy in a single blow.

She realized now that this was not going to happen.

They, like her, were vulnerable to an Alkhavan attack.

She had to protect them.

"Yes," she muttered under her breath, "farther up the coast." At the brine cove, or Black's Bay, or the old yellow harbor.

Land these boys somewhere quiet and then make their way into the city. Explain the situation to her father. He would be disappointed, but perhaps he could go back to Earth with the boys and plunder its secrets for something that might aid them in their struggle. Maybe she didn't even need the boys—obviously they had been ignorant of the Salmon until very recently. Perhaps she could even take it for herself.

Her dark thoughts were interrupted by a strangled yell: "Dead ahead, over there," Ramsay called, looking through his powerful binoculars.

"I do not see—" she said, and gasped.

She tied off the steering oar and brought the boat into the wind. The sail began to luff up. She found her brass telescope and stared through it.

They were ten miles west of Aldan, and the line of barges and cruisers guarding the city was gone. In the distance she could make out scores of gleaming white ice-ships near the walls of the inner harbor.

Jamie looked through Ramsay's binoculars. All he could see were a bunch of icy blobs on the horizon and what might be land beyond that.

"What is it?" he asked, noticing Wishaway's terror.

"The Alkhavans are through the outer defenses," she groaned.

"What does that mean?" Ramsay asked, excitedly.

Wishaway couldn't answer for a moment. There were tears in eyes. She was trying to stop herself from crying.

"What does that mean for us?" Jamie asked more gently.

"It means," Wishaway said, between sobs, "that we have arrived too late. The city is about to fall."

Chapter VII

THE SIEGE

A GREEN-TINTED SKY. The smell of smoke and ice. A cold, disturbing feeling under the shadowy penumbras of the two moons. The sailing boat moved closer to the port city of Aldan, gliding silently over the placid ocean in the last of the daylight. The sun was setting over the Aldanese countryside, giving Jamie and Ramsay at the prow an excellent view of what was happening in the city.

The iceships were attacking the port from three sides—huge, slablike mountains of ice that were being powered by sail into the portcullis across the harbor mouth.

The fortified harbor occupied a third of a large crescent-shaped bay, but the city was bigger still with the streets and houses extending well up into the hills behind.

Aldan was big and, doing a calculation in his head, Ramsay reckoned that it had to contain tens of thousands of people. Certainly they should be able to field thousands of defenders, and yet the momentum of the assault seemed to be with Alkhavans. Perhaps because of the ferocity of the attack from a people who were obviously battled-hardened, professional warriors.

Jamie wasn't thinking about strategy. He was watching the sky. On this planet there were no birds, but huge swarms of the *ranta* batlike creatures were flying west out of the capital, flapping great lizard wings three feet across and crying out in panic as their nests in the harbor walls were being overrun.

As the little boat nudged nearer, across the quicksilver sea came the sounds of war in the distance. The twangs of catapults, the crashing of masonry, drums, the battle cries of the Alkhavans and, on both sides, horns and trumpets. All of it combined to make a terrible music of destruction that frightened the boys and even Wishaway, who had heard it all before.

To get a better look, Ramsay raised his binoculars and Jamie grabbed Wishaway's brass telescope, extended it, and gazed through the eyepiece.

The city itself was a tapestry of glass buildings and domed structures made of red and white stone. It was an amalgam of cultures. Minarets and towers dominated the buildings near the port; an ancient, crumbling white tower lay in the center of town; and a large Irish-looking building on the hill (that was perhaps the university) certainly bore more than a passing resemblance to Trinity College in Dublin. There were few parks but many massive, weird-angled sculptures projected out from plazas and open spaces. Most of these were made from crystal or a kind of translucent stone. What they meant or signified was beyond Jamie.

He could have looked at the city for hours. But there were more pressing concerns.

Now they were close enough to see without aid. Dozens of iceships in close formation massing against the towers around the harbor walls. The little dots were defenders firing arrows, and hurling stones from sling-shots and catapults. But all these projectiles were bouncing harmlessly off the hulls of the great Alkhavan ships.

"Maybe we should lower that big blue sail," Jamie said. "We're still far out but we can't be too careful."

Wishaway nodded, slowed the boat, and turned it into the wind. They were in the west, in the gathering twilight, but even so it was possible they could be seen by a lookout on one of the iceships. She dropped the sail and with expert assurance disassembled and lowered the mast. She grabbed three stubby oars from the aft and offered them to the boys, but both ignored her, mesmerized as they were by the invasion.

She didn't feel, yet, that she could order these Lords from Earth to row, so she sat in the stern and paddled the small boat canoe-fashion, closer to the site of the attack.

"I don't understand why they don't go after the hulls of those big iceships. They're bound to do some damage. It's only ice for heaven's sake," Jamie muttered.

Ramsay shook his head. "Do you see the color of the hulls? They're a dense, transparent blue. That means it's very thick, supercooled ice. If water cools quickly without air bubbles, it can be as hard as iron, and of course lighter and more resilient. They must have carved these ships from right off one of the glaciers," Ramsay said with admiration.

"Won't the ships melt? It's warmer here than on Wishaway's island, and it has to be warmer than the north where these guys come from," Jamie said. He leaned over and dipped his hand into the ocean. The water wasn't exactly tropical, but it wasn't icy cold, either. "I'm sure it's above freezing."

Ramsay nodded, his eyes sparking with interest. "Yeah, you're probably right. It's definitely a bit warmer here and because of that they're bound to lose an inch or two a day from their hulls through evaporation and heat exchange," Ramsay explained.

Wishaway had been listening keenly to the boys' conversation.

"So if the ships are slowly melting, eventually they'll have to withdraw and go home?" she asked excitedly.

"Yes, but those hulls are twenty or thirty feet thick, so it won't be for a while," Ramsay said. "It would take a couple of months before they'd start to get seriously worried and have to head north again. And by the looks of it, this siege isn't going to last a couple of months."

Jamie grabbed Ramsay's arm and nodded at Wishaway, whose face had fallen into obvious despair. Ramsay got the message.

"Oh, yeah, though, I could be wrong. I mean, the

defenders are doing a great job. Look at those guys up there with the guns," Ramsay said, pointing to one of the topmost battlements.

Jamie trained the telescope and, sure enough, higher up on the city walls he could see little puffs of smoke from what appeared to be a squadron of men armed with rifles. Perhaps a dozen of them. They also seemed to have a small cannon and the balls from this, although few and badly aimed, were occasionally doing real damage to lines of invaders standing on the decks, waiting to disembark from their ships.

Jamie noticed that Wishaway was the only one rowing the boat.

"Come on Ramsay, we better row. Let Wishaway steer," Jamie said, grabbing an oar and fitting it into the oarlock.

Ramsay also picked up an oar and, still feeling guilty about his remark, passed Wishaway the binoculars. "Seriously, look at those guys with the guns. They're doing a great job," he said.

Wishaway took the field glasses and looked. "That must be my father's men," she said excitedly. "They have been working on making the powder for the fire sticks. Some of its components are very rare and very unstable."

"They obviously succeeded," Ramsay said.

"They're doing swell, Wishaway. Each volley seems to knock down half a dozen of the attackers," Jamie said.

Aye, half a dozen, out of thousands; it's too little too late, Ramsay thought, but he kept the observation to himself.

He was impressed by the Alkhavans' tactics. The city's weak point was the massive wooden portcullis across the harbor mouth, and this was where the Alkhavans were concentrating their attack.

This is no assault by marauding vandals. This is a well-thought-out and scouted invasion, Ramsay thought. They probably had spies living in Aldan for months, perhaps years, prior to this.

"There. Prince Lorca," Wishaway said with a gasp, focusing the binoculars on a desperate group of resisters on the battlements.

"Prince who?" Jamie asked, but before she could explain, suddenly an iceship under full sail smashed right into the portcullis. The big gate heaved backward, buckling under the impact.

"*Hurra tapra sas,*" Wishaway said to herself in horror.

"Here they come again," Ramsay muttered as a second iceship rammed the portcullis, which this time fell sickeningly off its hinges and crashed into the water at the harbor mouth.

The way to the harbor and the city was now open.

Some of the better-crewed iceships sailed immediately into the gap; others grappled onto the city walls. In five minutes, landing parties were being launched from the iceships and Alkhavan soldiers and marines were scrambling up onto the battlements.

The harbor was suddenly filled with hundreds of the invaders.

The Aldanese defenders on the piers were not so much overrun as engulfed in the Alkhavan throng.

"It's a bit like the invasion of Syracusa, don't you think?" Ramsay said.

Jamie scowled at him. He hadn't even heard of Syracusa, and he was in no mood for chat. This was serious. It was like watching a silent movie, a terrible, tragic classic of silent cinema. But worse, because these were people in a real war, doing real dying.

They rowed a little closer and the sound of the crashing portcullis reached them from Aldan.

Sound travels at the same speed as on Earth, Ramsay thought, his mind occupied by the invasion, but still able to think about the science of the new planet. And he'd already reached some tentative conclusions. He couldn't help but feel that gravity was a little bit less than on Earth, and that the oxygen content of the atmosphere was higher, which would be good for humans but bad for plants trying to grow and bad for anyone who wanted to stop the spread of the glaciers. It was global warming in reverse. As the planet got colder, glaciers increased, plants died, and the planet got colder still. Eventually it might balance as the carbon dioxide reached critical levels, but if it was true that the sun was moving away, no matter who won this invasion, the whole world was like a dead man walking. It was information he had to keep from Wishaway and probably even from Jamie.

"There," Wishaway said as another volley from the sharpshooters knocked down a dozen of the Alkhavans.

The boys rowed closer to shore, past several hulks of the Aldanese navy, which had obviously been overwhelmed and destroyed by the fleet of iceships. Small wooden vessels that had been plowed over, rammed, and then abandoned by the defenders. But the Alkhavans had chosen not to sink the boats because, of course, wood was too valuable.

What resistance was left was back in the heart of the city.

"We're getting too close," Wishaway said, her voice reduced to a hoarse whisper. Jamie turned to look at her. She'd been crying.

"Are you OK?" he asked.

She nodded, though her red eyes told a different story. "We should stop rowing now," she said again. "We do not want to get any nearer than this."

Jamie nodded and they pulled in the oars and let the boat drift while they watched the city's desperate attempts to beat back the invaders.

Wishaway wasn't really that worried about being spotted by someone on one of the iceships. Her little boat was much more maneuverable and much faster than the massive, lumbering Alkhavan vessels, and she could have the mast and sail up in less than a minute, but even so it was always better not to be seen at all.

And it wasn't until the sun had set completely behind

the eastern hills that Wishaway dared bring them nearer to the land.

By this stage, things did not look good at all for the Aldanese. They had given up the harbor to the invaders and retreated into the higher portions of the city, and now the fighting seemed sporadic and poorly organized. Some defenders had set up roadblocks and laid ambushes in the narrow streets running perpendicular to the port. But the most persistent threat to the Alkhavans was still coming from the small band of sharpshooters armed with muskets and a tiny artillery piece, who would launch a volley or a surprise attack from one rooftop or hilly promontory and then quickly move on to another destination before the Alkhavans had a chance to respond.

"That must be your father again," Jamie said in an unnecessary whisper.

Wishaway did not respond. She knew now the situation was hopeless. With the harbor and its battlements completely in their hands, the invaders could land their iceships at will, sending the entire army of ferocious fighters deeper and deeper into the city.

The Aldanese were traders, not warriors, and although they had begun raising a navy in recent months, it was obvious that they were no match for the Alkhavans.

It was fully dark now and Wishaway was cold. She wrapped herself in a sleeping bag, sat in the stern, and after a while she stopped looking at the city and began staring at the stars instead. The constellations were comforting, somehow, as always.

The boys watched the battle and continued to speak in whispers.

"Do you think Wishaway's father can pull it off?" Jamie asked in a hushed undertone.

Ramsay looked at the back of the boat to see if Wishaway was paying attention and in case she was he spoke very quietly. "They have the technology from 1607, which is muskets and cannons, and not too many of those because metal is so scarce on this planet, but that seems to be as far as they've got. A dozen men with muskets against an army? You do the maths. If it was a dozen blokes armed with machine guns, you might be on to something, but otherwise . . ." Ramsay's voice trailed off.

"Why do you think these people haven't progressed any further?" Jamie wondered.

Ramsay shook his head. "Well, let's say that when your forebears came here in 1607 they were up on the latest science and knowledge. That's pretty doubtful, but let's say they were. The Aldanese haven't really done anything with it. This planet still seems very backward. They've missed out on the Enlightenment, the progress of the eighteenth and nineteenth centuries. I'm sure they're just as smart as us; I think it's just a case of having very few natural resources. No metal, not much wood, no coal . . . so no steam engines, no trains, no industrial revolution."

Jamie nodded.

Perhaps if they had come here months ago, they might have been able to help the Aldanese prepare better defenses with their modern know-how, but it was much too late now to do anything.

Suddenly, from the city there was a massive cheer from the Alkhavans. A few minutes later, black flags were raised on the forts and turrets in the lower parts of the town.

"What's happening?" Jamie asked Wishaway.

She sat up and surveyed the scene. Jamie handed her the telescope.

She focused it and shook her head.

"The banners of Alkhava fly over the government buildings. It looks as if the Council has surrendered," she said, barely able to believe it.

"What will that mean for your people?" Jamie asked, reading her concern.

"If the Council has surrendered promptly, quarter will have been given and there will not be large-scale executions," Wishaway explained.

"What *will* happen?" Jamie asked.

"The people will be gathered together. The men will be separated from the women and children and transported to the holds of the iceships. When all are aboard they will be taken to Afor."

"What's Afor?"

"The slave market of Alkhava. The men will be sold as

slaves, for work in the Alkhavan mines or in the north where the Alkhavans are building dikes and walls as a defense against the glaciers. It is a death sentence. Conditions are known to be terrible in the northern outposts, and most will die within the year."

Jamie was aghast.

"The women and children?" Ramsay asked, horrified.

"They also will become slaves. Some will be given to the victorious ship captains and officers, the rest will be sold at Afor," Wishaway muttered courageously. It was such a simple thing to say, but what it meant was that her playmates at school would be crushed, beaten, and subjected to terrible degradation. It would be the end of their young lives.

What she hadn't told Ramsay and Jamie was what would happen if the Aldan Council had rejected Alkahavan offers to surrender promptly. If that had occurred and the offer of quarter had been withdrawn, then all the men in the city would be executed over the next few days. Her father, her uncle, all her friends and neighbors. It was a horrible prospect.

She turned her head away and pulled up the hood on her boat cloak so that the boys could not see her tears.

The full impact of what she had said was only beginning to settle on Jamie and now he began to be filled with guilt.

Why had they acted so selfishly when they had found the Salmon?

Perhaps if they had alerted the authorities—rather

than trying to do all this themselves, the U.S. government might have helped. They could have sent scientists, soldiers, marines. Flamethrowers would have done the trick against those iceships. A couple of torpedoes, even.

More black flags began appearing in different parts of the city. Wishaway knew it was hopeless, but she had to ask: "Mighty Lords, is there anything thou canst do to save the city. Some trick, some secret knowledge of the other world?" she asked formally.

Jamie hadn't heard the question, he was listening to the sea, when from somewhere there was a low rumbling noise.

Ramsay shook his head and said, "I'm sorry, Wishaway, there's nothing we can—"

"Lord Jamie, is there nothing you can do?" Wishaway asked desperately.

Before Jamie could reply, all three of them heard the noise. A huge rush of water behind them. The children turned.

It was the bow wave of an enormous iceship bearing down on them.

"They're ramming us!" Ramsay exclaimed in horror.

"No, they haven't seen us in the dark. Get the paddles, quickly," Wishaway whispered.

Desperately the two boys grabbed the oars and began rowing away from the prow of the oncoming ship. Ramsay and Jamie pulled hard and fast and completely without rhythm. They weren't moving nearly quickly enough and the iceship was almost on top of them. Its thick blue hull would certainly smash the little wooden boat in two, killing the three on board instantly, or sucking them down in its wake and drowning them.

"Hurry, please," Wishaway said.

Jamie knew they had to get their act together.

"On my stroke, Ramsay," Jamie said. "Pull with me, together, pull, pull, pull, pull, pull."

They began moving faster.

Wishaway steered them to the left of the huge oncoming bow wave.

"A few more hard pulls, my Lords," Wishaway begged.

They rowed together for ten brisk strokes and their momentum was just enough to take them to the port side of the iceship.

"Get down," Wishaway whispered. All three of them lay flat on the deck.

The iceship cruised past in the darkness, silent and terrifying. The hull was crystal clear, so they could see right through to the heart of the vessel. There was equipment, ropes, tubs of food, barrels of wine, and the Alkhavan sailors and marines, sleeping, eating, sharpening their weapons, carrying out repairs. All of them dressed in heavy furs to prevent burns on the ice that made up the decks, the bulkheads, and the hull. The masts were wooden and the sails were made of cloth, but the rest of the ship was carved from this lovely blue glacial ice.

One Alkhavan with a blond beard and shaggy hair woke momentarily from his fur bed and looked across at the three children staring at him through the thick hull. He rubbed his eyes, shook his head, and went back to sleep.

And then, just like that, the ship was past.

Without waiting to discuss it, Wishaway raised the mast of the little boat, hoisted a sail, and took them away from the iceships, the Alkhavans, the invasion, and the isolated sounds of battle still taking place in the besieged city.

Land was no longer in sight when Jamie woke the next morning. The sun was rising out of the haze in the western sea and it was cold.

Wishaway was sitting at the tiller.

"Where are we?" Jamie asked her.

Wishaway handed him a jar of fresh water; he drank and thanked her.

"We are north of the city. It is beyond the horizon, there," she said pointing to the southeast.

Jamie could see a faint outline of smoke in the distance. "They're burning the city?" he asked.

Wishaway shook her head. "They would not do such a thing. Plunder is too valuable. It must be an accident of some kind. They will quickly put it out. You will see," she said sadly. She looked exhausted. She hadn't slept all night.

"Maybe you should rest for an hour or two," Jamie said. "I'll take the tiller. I've been watching you, I know what to do."

Wishaway's blue eyes blinked drowsily. She shook her head.

"No, Lord Ui Neill, I am—"

"For the last time, my name is Jamie. And you are definitely going to rest," Jamie said. He ducked under the mast, took her by the hand, and led her to his sleeping bag.

"It's still warm inside. Get in," he said.

Wishaway was too tired to resist. Jamie helped her in and zipped her up.

"Sleep," Jamie ordered. "We're going to need your help."

Wishaway closed her eyes, her small nose wrinkled, and almost immediately she was out.

Jamie took the tiller and kept the sails filled with wind. Wishaway hadn't suggested any course, so he decided he would just go north for a while and then tack and head south again. He wouldn't take them any closer to or farther from the city until they had decided what they were going to do.

"What *are* we going to do, Ramsay?" Jamie asked when his friend woke with a grunt and a fart.

"I don't know," Ramsay said, for once completely bereft of ideas.

"We have to think. What are our options?" Jamie wondered.

Ramsay drank some water and took an energy bar. "We only have two choices. The first is to go back to Wishaway's island and use the Salmon and return to Earth. Maybe on Earth we can get guns or something and come back. The second option is to land the boat in Aldan, to make our way through the city and try to help."

"Help do what?" Jamie asked realistically.

"I don't know, lead a revolt, do sabotage, anything," Ramsay suggested. "I got tons of stuff in my backpack."

Jamie nodded gloomily. "This isn't Narnia. This is real life, Ramsay. We're just a couple of kids and there's every chance that if we go to that city we're going to die," he said.

"There are thousands of other people who are going to die if we do nothing," Ramsay said, and stole a look at Wishaway, who was sleeping fitfully in the middle of the boat.

Jamie nodded and a small, defiant smile began to creep from the edges of his mouth. If everyone who had the odds against them gave up at the first obstacle, there would have been no American Revolution, no landing on the Moon. What was it that Thaddeus had hinted? You have to make your own magic.

"As I see it, we're just a couple of punk kids, we have no knowledge of the city, no experience of war, no plan of any kind, no weapons, no tactics, no skills," Jamie said, and his smile became a broad grin.

"And?" Ramsay said.

"And, I say we bloody go for it," Jamie said.

"Absolutely," Ramsay agreed, and slapped his friend on the back not least because Jamie was beginning to sound like an Irishman.

When Wishaway woke around noon, they informed her of their decision. They had laid out the useful stuff from their backpacks. The knives, the plans, Ramsay's homemade fireworks. Some of it looked impressive.

Wishaway rubbed the sleep from her eyes.

"Wishaway, if your father is still holding out somewhere, we want to try to help. We've got schematics for weapons. We've also got fireworks, a pocket-sized soldering tool, flashlights, and, of course, twenty-first-century know-how. We really could help, you know," Jamie said.

"Do you know of a safe place to land the boat?" Ramsay asked before she had a chance to think of an objection.

Wishaway was confused and overwhelmed by their sudden enthusiasm.

"There is a cove and a small pier where my uncle lives, in the Pirra district. I doubt the Alkhavans will have got so far north. And there are many foreigners living there, perhaps they will not be harmed," she said.

"The Pirra district it is. Better to go there at night. We'll sit out the day here, eat, drink, build our strength until dusk, and then we'll sail in," Jamie said.

The others nodded, and Jamie noticed that if you sounded confident it was almost as good as actually being confident. And through this sense of conviction, unconsciously, he had become the person who made the decisions. It was an odd thing. He was frightened and he had reservations about sneaking into a city under attack, but he knew that from now on, as the leader, he would have to keep those reservations to himself. He would have to be a source of strength for Ramsay and Wishaway. He would have to hide the fear in himself so that they could be afraid and he could be a source of comfort.

They spent the day talking about anything but what was happening in Aldan. Wishaway's modern English improved, and she taught the boys a few words in Aldanese.

In the darkness after the sun had set and before the moons rose, Wishaway sailed the boat to the northernmost part of the city. Here the bay became shallow and there were many beaches and coves where a small craft could be landed. It looked like a prosperous part of town: big houses with balconies overlooking the sea, well-made terra-cotta roofs, neat little gardens. It seemed completely deserted, the residents probably having fled the oncoming Alkhavan onslaught.

They landed their boat against a small stone jetty. Ramsay used an oar to fend off the shore. They threw ropes onto a bollard and tied up. The boys shouldered their backpacks, and when the boat had come to a complete halt they stepped off the craft and into the city of Aldan.

Wishaway led them away from the water and up the hill. The street was cobblestoned, narrow, and, apart from a few small catlike animals with long furry bodies and disproportionately large heads, there was no sign of life at all.

"My father is most likely in the fort. I can take us a back way there, and we may be able to enter through one of the secret gates," Wishaway said.

Jamie nodded. "Though if we hear anyone coming, we've got to get off the road," he cautioned.

The streets were winding and complicated; within ten minutes of going up the steep inclines they had lost sight of the sea and their little boat.

For Wishaway it was home, but for the boys the new city was a source of amazement. The houses were packed closely together, almost on top of one another. Most had flat roofs on top of which gardens had been planted, bursting with many strange things. Spiny cactuslike plants with bright blue and red flowers; skinny, sunflowerish blossoms that were violet with three and sometimes four orange heads. Occasionally they would see a tree that was like no tree on Earth. They were all of the same type: narrow with yellow trunks and shrunken purple leaves. Though rare, they appeared to be much cherished. They were given water from little drip buckets and that had thick netting around them to keep off predators. None of the trees appeared to be very old or very tall and Jamie realized that after the Alkhavans were done with their work, all these trees would be gone.

Plant life was at a premium. Where the Aldanese had not planted trees or flowers, they had placed large glass and wooden sculptures that looked like falling stars or representations of the heavens. This was a people who looked up at the night and regarded the constellations with awe and trepidation.

Tiny towers and minarets were everywhere, perhaps serving some religious purpose.

There were a few Irish-looking buildings, but not

many. Churches or schools. All in the same translucent red stone, but with Irish arches and porticoes.

In the city it was warmer than down on the sea, and both boys stripped to their T-shirts as they walked and carried their overstuffed backpacks.

They came to a deserted market filled with broken pots and hastily discarded stalls and foodstuffs. The silence was eerie and was made more so by the knowledge that if there were any people around, they were hiding behind shuttered windows, watching them without making a sound.

"How old is the city?" Jamie asked.

"Forsooth, Lord Ui Neill, the White Tower stretches back into the dawn of history, like that on the Sacred Isle; but even before thy people, the Ui Neills, came, our ancestors had been here for hundreds of years."

"Old, then?"

"Yes."

"What are those little towers everywhere?"

"For saluting the moon gods. In the past, our people worshiped the moons. But when Morgan and the Ui Neills came bringing their religion, some were baptized into the new faith and some held fast to the old; but most saw that religion was a diverse thing and unbelief grew."

"So what are they used for now?"

"Now they are used to watch the stars and the moons."

"Observatories."

"Yes."

"Really kind of like the old use."

Wishaway shook her head fiercely. "No, this time we look up for science, not for fear of punishment by the moon or sun gods."

Jamie nodded skeptically. It sounded like they were embarrassed by their old beliefs, but they still couldn't quite let go.

They walked by a large dead animal strapped to a two-wheeled cart.

It looked like a cross between a buffalo and horse, with a huge, horned, black head and six squat, powerful legs.

"What is that?" Jamie asked.

"A *draya*," Wishaway said without further comment.

They saw more of the catlike creatures, which Wishaway said were feral *seechas* and which some considered pests but others encouraged as they kept away the rodents. These animals were dark-colored, lithe, and cautious, and the thought crossed Ramsay's mind that one specimen would assure his fame on Earth for generations to come.

There was no time to pursue these diversions, however, as they were obviously getting closer to the city center. From a street or two ahead of them they could hear the sound of shouting.

"You two must tarry here. I will see what is afoot," Wishaway said, and before Jamie could object she scampered off into the darkness.

The boys waited in the entryway to some kind of shop that sold pots and cooking utensils.

There was a small shuttered window covered with a strange Arabic or Hindi-like script that neither of them could make head or tail of.

"Weird, huh?" Ramsay said, pointing at the writing.

"There's many weirder things. What did you make of that dead horse thing back there. It had six legs," Jamie said.

"Aye, it's bound to all be bizarre at first. It's like when the Spanish conquistadors went to South America and everything was different. There were llamas instead of horses and they ate guinea pigs instead of sheep. It wasn't at all like Spain."

"Did they get freaked out?" Jamie asked.

"The Spanish? Not at all. They freaked the Indians out with their armor and horses and guns. Very interesting book I read about it. Lend it to ya sometime."

"At least a llama looks a bit like a horse. These things are totally different. It's more like when people saw the animals in Australia for the first time."

"Aye," Ramsay agreed.

Wishaway came back to them from across the street. "My Lords, the Alkhavans are up ahead, going house to house, rounding up people. They are taking them somewhere. There is no resistance. It seems that the city has indeed surrendered."

"Your father?" Jamie asked.

"It is likely that he will have surrendered too," Wishaway said sadly. "Come, we must hide or they will surely see us."

211

Wishaway and the boys climbed onto the flat roof of the pottery shop. They had only just laid down in the darkness when a roving band of Alkhavan troops burst into the street—yellow-haired men, dressed in furs, some now in looted leather or fabric clothes.

Systematically they kicked in the doors of houses and dragged out what Aldanese citizens they could find. Most of the people in this part of the city had fled but there were a few—older people and those too sick to run.

An Alkhavan officer wearing better boots than his companions and a red headband ordered the civilians searched and tied together.

"Aaach takala aarrnam!" he yelled, and a party of soldiers marched the prisoners down the street. The officer meanwhile searched the shops and houses for any valuables. He briefly scanned the pottery shop underneath the children's hiding place. For a moment he even examined the roof where they were crouched in terror. He sniffed the air, spat, and then shook his head before moving to a more promising locale.

The Alkhavans were disciplined and serious, which surprised the two boys, who'd been thinking of them as pirates and marauders.

"I thought it would be a scene of chaos and murder," Jamie said under his breath when the soldiers had moved to the next street.

Ramsay shook his head. "Nah, if they're going to sell

people as slaves, they don't want to damage the merchandise," Ramsay muttered.

When the torchlit band of soldiers was gone, Wishaway sat up. "He ordered the soldiers to take the prisoners to the arena. If my father is alive, he will be there," she said.

"How come he didn't speak English like you?" Ramsay asked.

Wishaway blushed. "English is only spoken by a very few, those who have been to the one of the universities founded by the Ui Neills," she said.

"How many languages are there on Altair?" Ramsay asked.

"I speak seven of them, but there are very many," Wishaway said.

"Only seven, huh?" Ramsay said with admiration.

"And you were criticizing her English," Jamie muttered to his friend.

Wishaway had no time for further banter. She climbed off the roof with the boys close behind her.

"You think this is wise?" Ramsay whispered as they got closer and closer to the sounds of trouble.

But for Jamie it was simple. If Wishaway's father was being held in the arena and she wanted to go there, then that's where they were going to go.

They went single file with Wishaway leading and Ramsay in the rear, stealthily making their way deeper into the city.

Wishaway desperately wanted to find her father, but she wasn't foolhardy; she took them by a circuitous route, high into the hills almost to the eastern edge of the town, near the walls.

"From this spot we can get to the cliffs behind the arena. It should be safe, the Alkhavans may not have come here yet," Wishaway said.

It was a logical guess. If the city had surrendered, the Alkhavans would search the easier parts first, around the port and on the main thoroughfares, not up these very steep lanes.

It was logical but wrong, and throughout their journey they could hear bands of soldiers marching through the streets. They had to duck into entryways or behind walls or lay flat in the shadows to avoid Alkhavan patrols. And here, too, there were some scenes of devastation. Many houses had already been looted. Windows were broken, doors smashed, clothes and valuable wooden items thrown into the street to be picked up later.

Wishaway had not wanted the boys to see her city this way. Deserted, shambolic, ruined. This was a proud trading town with a university and a thriving port, and she had wanted to show it off. Now the shame of defeat made her cheeks burn. Aldan was the only city in the whole of Altair that had underground sewers, but with bodily waste and other filth running disgustingly down the streets you would hardly know it.

Jamie could sense her despair and humiliation. He put

his hand on her back. The touch was comforting for both of them.

After several hours of cautious traveling, they came at last to a small mesa that Wishaway said was their destination.

"This way," she whispered, leading them to a point where the mesa backed onto a cliff that was filled with black, thorny shrubs which smelled like rotting food. The stench was so bad that both boys had to hold their noses, yet Wishaway didn't seem to notice it.

"We used to come to this place to watch the races for free," Wishaway said. "You can slide into the upper seats of the arena from here."

"The races? They raced those *draya* animals?" Ramsay asked.

"Oh, no, only *kalahars*," Wishaway said.

Kalahars, whatever they were.

The arena was originally a natural amphitheater formed under the mesa. At a later date it had obviously been expanded into an oval with large marble-like stones forming seats and stairs.

"It's like a Greek amphitheater," Ramsay whispered.

Wishaway led them through the shrubs until they approached a small drop-down onto the upper deck of the arena.

The three of them scrambled from the thorny cliff into the stadium itself and skulked immediately into the shadows.

 215

Lit by hundreds of torches, the amphitheater beneath them was as clear as day.

Alkhavan soldiers ringed the perimeter, while thousands of Aldanese civilians stood in a frightened huddle in the center of the massive oval itself. Women, children, men, all awaiting the next step on their grim journey from freedom into bondage.

For a while there was a general hum of excitement, and then from the north gate a parade of black-clad Alkhavan marines marched into the arena, followed by an Alkhavan soldier mounted on an animal that resembled a rhinoceros, if rhinoceroses could be green and six-legged.

"Is that a *kalahar*?" Ramsay asked.

"No, that's a *yasi*," Wishaway said.

The soldier dismounted and walked proudly to a reviewing stand. The Alkhavan troopers hissed and whipped the frightened Aldanese into silence.

"He must be some sort of general," Jamie said, and took out his binoculars. He focused them on the Alkhavan laboriously climbing the final steps to the podium.

He was a tall man, with a purple cloak over his furs. Unlike most of the rest of the Alkhavans, he had black hair that was elaborately clubbed and tied behind his back. He had a pinched, narrow face and a dangerous sneer to his attractive mouth.

There was something about the man that chilled Jamie to the bone. Jamie didn't have time to think more about it, because the general immediately began to speak.

"Shabba Alkhava, nixi tara shabba Alkhava, treekka, Aldan ukor!" the man yelled, and drew a huge cheer from his troops. The arena was well designed acoustically, and although they were high on the upper deck, Jamie could easily hear the speech. And there was something about the man's voice, too, for although it was harsh and guttural, it had almost a refined tone about it.

"What did he say?" Jamie asked Wishaway.

"Soldiers of Alkhava, brave soldiers of Alkhava, this night you have conquered," Wishaway said.

After the cheering there was a drum beat for silence and then the general addressed the assembled mass. Wishaway whispered a simultaneous translation.

"'People of Aldan, my name is Protector Ksar. Your city is now under my complete control, and be assured that those of your fellows who have fled into the hills and mountains will be captured quickly. Already I have sent ships to the city of Krikor on the eastern side of your island. It, too, will soon fall. You can expect no help and no rescue. But because of the wisdom of your Council, you will not be killed. Your lives will be spared and you will be taken to Alkhava to be sold as slaves. You will be well treated, and if your capacities are of use to us, you will be allowed to continue in the profession to which you have been trained. If you resist the deportation order, or any order of my men, you will be executed. If you attack or harm any Alkhavan, you and your family will be executed. Any dissent, resistance, or revolt will be punished by death.'"

There was a loud groan from the assembled mass of Aldanese civilians. Some of the children began to cry, and it was only after the Alkhavan officers cracked their large leather whips into the crowd that Ksar had sufficient silence to speak again. He barked an order to one of his subordinates, and a group of chained prisoners were brought into the arena. There was about a dozen men and several women, most of them elegantly dressed in long robes.

"That's my father," Wishaway gasped, pointing to a gray-haired, bearded man in a white cloak. He was exhausted and he could only stand with the assistance of a woman next to him.

Ksar continued his oration and with a trembling voice Wishaway translated.

"'Foreigners from Oralands, Perovan, and Kafrikilla, we will respect your neutrality and you will be allowed to return to your own countries after a small donation to our coffers. Citizens of Aldan, you are another matter. Your Council was wise to give me your city while the generous offer of quarter was still in effect. However, these Council members who opposed the surrender and who resisted our best efforts of peace, these warmongers and traitors will be given to you as an example. When the sun rises over the first day of the new Alkhavan city of Aldan these enemies of peace will be— Oh, no . . ." Wishaway whispered and her lungs filled with air to scream.

Jamie put his hand over her mouth and pulled her down. Wishaway fought against him and bit his finger. Ramsay held down her arms, and then she broke into sobs.

"What did he say?" Jamie asked.

"They're going to be executed," Wishaway cried.

The boys looked at each other.

"There's nothing we can do at the moment," Ramsay said, trying to comfort her.

In the arena, the rebel Council members were led to a large ceremonial iron gate from which had been hung many trophies and symbols that the boys could not read. One by one, the councillors were chained to the gate to await the first rays of the new day coming from the west.

Wishaway fought violently against the two boys.

"There's nothing we can do," Ramsay said. Wishaway scrambled to break free. She kicked at the boys, but they were too strong for her.

"Not yet, anyway," Jamie said.

Wishaway stopped struggling.

Cautiously, Jamie took his hand from her mouth.

Wishaway sat up and brushed at the dust on her green dress.

"Not yet?" she asked, wiping the tears from her cheeks.

"We'll save your father. I promise you that. But we need a plan first," Jamie said.

Wishaway's face filled with hope. "Thou wilt save my father, Lord Ui Neill?" she asked very seriously.

Jamie nodded. "I will," he said simply.

"How?" Ramsay said, looking at the hundreds of soldiers guarding the people in the arena.

"We'll think of something, Ramsay. Won't we?" Jamie said.

"Oh, oh aye, 'course, yeah, we'll think of something," Ramsay replied.

"He's as good as free. I promise," Jamie said, wondering if Wishaway could tell that this was a lie, even bigger than the one he'd told his mother to get himself here in the first place.

"We can't fight them," he continued. "There's not enough of us. Maybe we create a diversion or spook them somehow. What do you think, Ramsay?"

Ramsay didn't reply, but then Jamie noticed that Ramsay had that grin on his face. That grin which Jamie knew well by now. That wide, crooked smile that meant something was cooking in that big Irish brain.

"What is it?" Jamie asked him.

Ramsay ignored the question and turned to Wishaway.

"Let me get this straight: The Alkhavans are very superstitious, right?"

Wishaway nodded. "The people are not schooled in the sciences. There is no university in their country. Every day they make useless sacrifices to the ice gods who threaten their homeland. My people no longer believe in spirits, witches, demons. Not so with the Alkhavans," Wishaway said angrily.

"What is it, Ramsay? What are you thinking?" Jamie asked again.

Ramsay took off his backpack. "OK. This is what we're going to do," he said, and began explaining the plan.

It was an hour before the dawn. Most of the captured population in the arena was sleeping or resting on the clay racing tracks. Some of the guards ringing the perimeter were sleeping, others were laughing and quietly passing bottles from one to another. The discipline of the Alkhavans under Protector Ksar was extraordinary, and Wishaway noted that the city on this night was quieter than it had been in decades—perhaps ever. Ksar himself had retreated to one of the captured houses.

The two boys looked at each other.

"Do you want to synchronize watches?" Ramsay asked nervously.

"What for?"

Ramsay shrugged. "I don't know, people always do in the movies," Ramsay said.

"Do you have anything sensible to say?" Jamie muttered.

"Sensible? No, not really," Ramsay admitted.

Jamie turned to Wishaway. "How many of your people do they have now?"

Wishaway looked at the desolate crowd of civilians. Trickles had been coming in all night. It was hard to estimate numbers. There were perhaps fifteen or twenty thousand people there.

"Half the population of the city," she whispered.

Jamie nodded.

"There's maybe a thousand guards. We should have enough to swamp them in a general panic."

"I'm ready," Ramsay said.

"Let's get started," Jamie said, anxious to end the waiting and begin the rescue attempt.

Light would be coming soon. There was no sense in delaying it anymore.

"OK, then, on my mark. One, two, three, go," Ramsay said.

Jamie ran along the line of fireworks they had laid down, lighting the slow and fast fuses. Ramsay had only brought one box of rockets and mortars, but it might be enough to scare the wits out of the superstitious Alkhavans.

"How long we got?" Jamie asked when he got back to Ramsay.

"A minute," Ramsay said.

The boys reshouldered their backpacks.

"We'll go straight for Wishaway's father," Jamie said.

Ramsay nodded, but before he could respond, the first rocket went off into the air with a huge bang and a flare of light.

Ramsay had gone to Sunday school until asked to leave when he mathematically disproved the existence of Noah's Ark. But the scene instantly reminded him of the story of when Elijah showed the prophets of Baal a thing or two about pyrotechnics.

Everyone in the arena immediately woke up.

Then a second rocket exploded with an even bigger bang and a brilliant shower of falling green streamers.

"That's got their attention," Jamie muttered.

"Yes," Wishaway said.

Some people began to cry out.

When the third and fourth rockets went off together and a homemade mortar exploded with an enormous crash, Jamie, Ramsay, and Wishaway seized their chance and ran down the stone seats of the amphitheater. People had begun screaming, and many of the guards had deserted their posts and were making for the overhang under the reviewing stand. A fifth rocket went off with a massive, thundering explosion, and that was the tipping point that started the stampede. Guards, civilians, Alkhavans, Aldanese, yelling, running in all directions.

For the Alkhavans, unaccustomed to gunpowder and such terrible noise and light, it was as if the heavens were enraged, perhaps angry at their attack on the Aldanese city. Putting their hands over their heads they tried to sprint for cover, but then the *yasi*, tied in a corner, broke free from its handler, gored several Alkhavan soldiers, and stomped toward the exit.

That only added to the confusion.

Soldiers scurryied this way and that, throwing down their weapons, cowering from the erupting sky. Some of the officers were trying to keep their men calm, but others were also bolting for the exits.

An eighth rocket exploded prematurely, low to the ground in a blue flame. There was a massive group yell, and now everyone was scrambling for the way out.

Jamie, Ramsay, and Wishaway battled through the throng and made for the iron ceremonial gate where Wishaway's father and the other rebel Council members were being held. Using his big rugby-playing body as a wedge, Ramsay pushed people out of their path. But in the melee, even the strong Irish boy found it hard to keep his balance, and he would have fallen to the ground had Jamie not been right behind him to steady him before he got trampled.

As the ninth and tenth and then the final rocket exploded in the air, the Alkhavan rout had become a full-scale general panic. A good number of soldiers were paralyzed by fear, others were begging the heavens for forgiveness, still more were attempting to dive under the stone seats, or running for nearby houses. Some were even sprinting all the way back to the safety of their ice-ships in the harbor.

Wishaway and the boys made it across the quickly emptying arena to where the councillors were still shackled to the ceremonial iron gate.

Wishaway reached her father and threw her arms around him.

"Oh, Father," she said happily in Aldanese.

Callaway was a thin man, with a wispy white beard and dark, intelligent eyes.

"Father, we have come to save you," Wishaway said.

"No, Wishaway, you must run while you have the chance," Callaway said in a frail, willowy voice.

"No, Father, my friends will save you," she insisted in English.

Ramsay and Jamie nodded.

"Who are these strange—" Callaway began, but his voice trailed off as recognition dawned. At first he was too stunned to react, but then, even chained as he was, he tried to bow.

"You were right, Father. The old lighthouse island is indeed the Sacred Isle. These are the Lords Ui Neill. They have come from Earth to save us," Wishaway explained.

Just then, a breathless, dazed, and half-naked Protector Ksar appeared at the top of the viewing platform.

"Arrrkkacak bulllow, shaddd, gury, akdrka ras!" Ksar bellowed in a commanding voice.

Wishaway translated, "He said, 'These are only tricks and shadows.'"

He was unheeded by the broad mass of the soldiers, but some of the Alkhavan officers stopped running immediately.

"Are there any more rockets to come, Ramsay?" Jamie asked.

"No, we're all done," Ramsay said.

"Well then, we better get cracking, we don't have much time," Jamie said.

Ramsay took out his pocket-sized soldering iron and

in ten seconds burned through the thin metal handcuffs chaining Callaway to the iron gate. Ramsay passed the tool to the next council member.

"Push this button and it will burn through the metal and free you, then pass it on," Ramsay said.

The Council member, an older woman, took it uncertainly.

"Mooga firaa, veela so masta Aldanekish car. Last tka kakk aa rill!" Ksar screamed at the top of his voice.

Wishaway did her United Nations bit again: "'The fires have now stopped. It is all an Aldanese trick. Stop the civilians from escaping.'"

The officers, noticing that the strange lights and fires had indeed ceased, began grabbing their men and organizing them into squads.

"Take this and push the red button," Jamie yelled, showing the councilwoman how the soldering iron worked. She still didn't seem to understand, but there was no more time now. Jamie turned to Callaway. "We have to go, sir," he said.

"I must stay and assist my fellows," Callaway protested.

"Now," Jamie yelled, grabbed Callaway, and pulled him through the crowd of fleeing Aldanese and panicking soldiers. They ran up the steps of the arena with Wishaway and Ramsay just behind. They only just made it, for by the time they got to Wishaway's secret entrance, Ksar had managed to take control of the situation. Alkhavan soldiers using sticks and powerful iron axes had corralled those civilians who had not escaped and were herding them back into the center of the arena.

Ksar was furious at the stupidity of his men. He pounded his fist on the wooden dias. "Find the escapees and hunt them down like vermin," he yelled in Alkhavan, and began ordering individual officers to send out teams of search parties.

But Wishaway and her father and the boys were out of the arena and on the mesa and were soon making their way through the upper town.

In ten minutes they were at one of the many gates through the city walls.

"What now?" Ramsay asked.

"We go through," Jamie said. Wishaway nodded.

Supported by the two boys, Callaway ran through the broken gate, and all four of them kept running until the city was five miles behind them.

They rested by a stream and drank and got up and ran again.

By noon they were safe, and the sound of the screeching *rantas*, and the yelling soldiers, and the whole terrible war was far behind.

Chapter VIII
THE VILLAGE

BASKY VILLAGE WAS DEEP in a hoxney wood about twenty miles inland from the city of Aldan. It contained barely six or seven houses, but since these were woodcutters' cottages and woodcutters owned the right to fell the precious timber, they were large, expansive dwellings, filled with all the modern conveniences: spinning wheels, a hand loom, toys from faraway Oralands and Kafrikilla.

Callaway knew they would be safe here for a while, but that safety wouldn't last forever. Sooner or later a patrol of soldiers would notice the forest. It was only a matter of time. It was like taking refuge in a gold mine. Eventually someone would come to get you. This could only be a temporary destination, a place to rest and think while he figured out what his next move was.

Callaway was not a superstitious or a religious man. His belief that the Ui Neills might come to save Aldan was based not on a prayer to a totem or faith in a divine power, but on the application of history. In the past when the country had been imperiled, the Lords from Earth had come. And now they had come again. It had been a slender hope and he tried to keep his surprise from

Wishaway. But what he couldn't conceal was his astonishment that the Lords Ui Neill were children. Bright, resourceful children certainly, but children nonetheless.

They had brought with them no weapons but many plans.

He had spent a day examining Ramsay's schemes for steam engines, balloons, flying machines, and repeating rifles and in theory they were ingenious, but in real terms they were utterly useless. If Callaway was back in the city with the full resources of the university behind him, perhaps he could have made one or even several of Ramsay's devices, but out here in the countryside, he could do nothing. At the coming of the Great Ui Neill, he and his followers had brought knowledge of the Earth poets Homer, Chaucer, and a contemporary called Shakespeare, but they had also brought practical ideas and many weapons. He owed the boys his life, but after spending two days with them it was obvious that they could do little to help liberate the city.

They were clever, but they certainly weren't soilders.

Rumors were confirmed that another fleet of iceships had landed at Aldan's second city, Krikor. The whole country would soon be under occupation.

Callaway and a score of other refugees talked tactics in the largest of the woodsmen's cottages, but as time went on, their conversations were more about evacuation than resistance.

Some felt that Perovan offered the best chance of

refuge, even though Perovan had attacked them in the past. It was a big country and many miles from Alkhava. Others preferred a voyage to one of the commonwealth of island nations which might welcome refugees with knowledge of the invaders' tactics. The booty and slaves from Aldan would keep the Alkhavans happy for a while, but not forever, and perhaps the other islands in the Middle Sea could be warned and a better defense prepared.

Callaway hadn't quite given up hope of somehow retaking the city, but he knew he had to accept the will of the majority, since his authority was somewhat diminished—if not gone altogether. The other councillors were either dead or on the run and the entire system of government had completely broken down. Now it was every citizen for him- or herself.

By their second day in Basky, as reports came in of brutal Alkhavan raids on outlying villages, no one spoke any longer of how to win the war, but rather how to save their lives.

A man called Arakar of the fishing guild knew where they could retrieve several trawlers that were in winter storage on an isolated beach thirty miles east of the city. The Alkhavans were unlikely to find them, and the vessels could easily carry the score of survivors here in the woods either to Perovan or wherever else they wanted to go.

Callaway knew they would have to make a decision soon, but the thought of abandoning the country to Alkhavans paralyzed him. The city of the White Tower of Aldan, the city saved by the Ui Neills, the city where they had spread English and the scientific arts to the rest of the world.

And yet, what else could they do?

As a sign that he hadn't given up all hope, he sent scouts to check on the situation in Aldan City, but he also sent Arakar to see if his boats were still there.

The teenagers couldn't help but be infected by the moroseness of their fellows. After the initial euphoria following the escape from Aldan, the harsh realities were beginning to set in.

They, too, heard the talk of evacuation, and that depressed them more.

If Wishaway and her father went to another island, where did that leave Jamie and Ramsay? Did they go with them, or did they get one of the boats to return them to the lighthouse island? They only had about another ten days before people would begin to miss them on Earth.

It was a hard decision not only because Jamie would lose his arm if he went home, but he would also lose her.

Her.

He didn't even want to think her name.

It was silly, but he couldn't help but feel that there was something between them.

The excitement and the stress of the last few days had brought them together. And now there was a little spark that was more than friendship. Neither of them spoke about it, but both knew it was there, lurking in the background, like a beautiful, dangerous tiger in the shadows of a tree.

And whether it would stay in the jungle or come out into the sunlight, only time would tell.

❋ ❋ ❋

Ramsay had lain the blueprints of the B-52 bomber on a large table inside of one of the smaller huts. He was staring at it intently when Jamie came inside.

"I've been looking for you, Ramsay," Jamie said cautiously.

"Oh, I've been up and about. There's a couple of new refugees, I've been talking to one of them. Big kid from one of the other islands. He's called Lorca. Did you meet him?"

Jamie shook his head.

"They say he's a prince; he's an old friend of Wishaway's."

"Yeah, I think I heard her mention the name before," Jamie said.

"Oh, he's a big goof, you'll like him," Ramsay said with a grin. "You know what he says to me when he hears I'm from Earth?"

"I can't imagine."

"'Out, out, brief candle.' Can you believe it? He knew a line from *Macbeth*. Incredible, eh?"

Jamie did not reply.

He'd been thinking things over.

Ramsay was his friend, and he was very intelligent, but there were some things that Ramsay couldn't yet grasp.

The boys were both roughly the same age, but Jamie felt older and Jamie knew that Ramsay still didn't see the seriousness of the situation. For Ramsay it was an adventure, a game, whereas Jamie knew lives were at stake, a country was at stake, an entire civilization. Cancer had given him a dark education into the ways of the world. They were both children, but if ever there was a time for them to grow up, it was now.

"Yeah, he's a big lad, too. He was at the university, so he even speaks English, old-style like, you know. But don't worry, I'm teaching him the new stuff. Anyway, the *Macbeth* thing blew my mind. One of the O'Neills must have been in London in 1606, seen the play or bought one of the cheap prints, taken it with him during the Flight of the Earls," Ramsay continued cheerfully.

Jamie again said nothing.

He was preparing himself. He had to communicate his sense of urgency.

He could feel it and he could sense it, but as yet he was not able to express it.

Actions would speak louder than words.

He walked over to the table, took the blueprint of the B-52 bomber, and ripped it in half.

"What the hell do you think you're doing?" Ramsay said, horrified.

"What do you think *you're* doing?" Jamie replied.

"What? Have you lost your tiny mind? Gimme that back you eejit," Ramsay muttered, grabbing the pieces of the blueprint out of Jamie's hands. "Jeez. You've totally wrecked this. What were you thinking?" Ramsay said furiously.

Jamie stepped back and looked at the Irish boy. "No, Ramsay," he began quietly. "You're the one who hasn't been thinking. You have to get your head screwed on straight. I'm sorry I had to be so dramatic, but you have to forget the B-52 bombers, forget the rocket launchers, forget that stuff. It's useless, do you see that? It's not going to help anyone. It's all too late. Callaway is talking about evacuating us from here. The Aldanese are beaten. The Alkhavans have won."

"We gave them a lesson the other night," Ramsay protested.

"No, we didn't. We didn't do anything to stop their advance. We were lucky to get out of there in one piece. What do you think's going to happen now while you pore over the plans of some completely impractical scheme? The Alkhavans are going to come here next. You see that, don't you? We're all going to have to leave here. Evacuate. Flee. And what will *we* do? We'll have to go home with our tails between our legs."

Ramsay crossed his arms defensively. "So what's your big idea, genius?" he said angrily.

Jamie shook his head. "I don't have any big ideas. I don't know what we're going to do, but I do know that we're going to have to do something. We're going to have to do it fast and it has to be something practical, something that will really help."

"By 'we' you mean 'me,' right?" Ramsay said, still with more than a hint of aggression in his voice.

Jamie smiled. "You're very clever, Ramsay. You're cleverer than me. I'll admit it. And I need that gray matter of yours, buddy. We need you. We all need you, Ramsay. You have to stop having pipe dreams of rockets and planes. You have to appreciate the seriousness of the situation we're in. You have to focus, dude, you have to focus," Jamie said as gently as he could.

"So first you rip up my blueprints and now you're giving me lectures. Who do you think you are? You're not my dad, you're not my brother. You can't tell me what to do. You're younger than me, for heaven's sake. Has all that Lord Muck stuff gone to your stupid head? Has it? Huh? Huh?" Ramsay said angrily.

Ramsay's eyes were watering and his cheeks were red. He seemed to be on the verge of crying or blowing his top. Jamie backed farther away and gave him more space.

"Are you trying to tell me what to do? Are you?" Ramsay demanded.

Jamie said nothing, but this only infuriated his friend all the more.

Ramsay smashed his fist down on the table, picked up the blueprints and ripped them into a dozen pieces.

"There, happy now? Happy now, Lord O'Neill?" Ramsay, said, throwing the pieces at Jamie.

"Ramsay, calm down, I was only trying to—"

"You were only what? You think I don't know we're

screwed? You think I don't know that? I know it. I'm doing my best. I'm doing my bloody best!" Ramsay yelled, and shoved Jamie to one side.

Instinctively Jamie clenched his fists and the two boys squared off against each other for a long moment before Ramsay stormed past his friend and out of the hut.

Jamie stared after him for a beat or two, but he didn't follow.

That would be only compounding the mistake.

⊛   ⊛   ⊛

Early morning. Cold, heavy shadow in the spaces between the revered trees. Dew-covered, glassy trunks glittering like looking glasses in the gentle, rising sunlight. Silvered mirrors that reflected the two young, excited faces as they slipped away from the settlement and walked into the quiet wood.

The strange stars were all but gone, and the stranger nighttime noises had ceased.

They walked together in the forest, talking of their childhoods, their favorite foods, music, and books— and most of all about the differences between their worlds.

Wishaway pointed out woodland creatures, things that looked like squirrels, colonies of flying reptiles, and animals that had no correspondence at all to creatures on Jamie's world. Jamie told Wishaway stories about New York, about movies he had seen, about the terrible morning in September when the city had been attacked, about how the doctors had given him a death sentence and then saved his life.

Then there was a time when they didn't talk at all, and perhaps that was when they said the most.

They arrived at a favorite spot, a waterfall, where legend had it that one of the Lords Ui Neill, Morgan of the Red Hand, had proposed to the Princess Royal of Aldan.

It was peaceful there. Blue blossoms fell from the overhanging trees, and the smell was like that of rosemary. Magenta fish flitted in the shallows, and the water over the falls sang a melody, beautiful and sad.

Wishaway sat on the springy turf and shivered.

Jamie put his arm around her.

"Tell me the story," Jamie said.

"I have told you," Wishaway protested.

"Tell it again," Jamie insisted.

Wishaway pretended to be bored, but she began the tale with undisguisable enthusiasm.

After the battle of Aldan Heights, the great Lord Ui Neill, Morgan Red Hand, had taken the Princess here to Basky Wood and this waterfall, and he had proposed and she had accepted him. They had ridden back to Aldan, as happy as any could be. But her family, the royal house, had been opposed (even though the Ui Neills had saved the city from attack), for he was a stranger, a foreigner, and although he said that he was a Lord, he did not claim to be of royal blood.

The alliance was impossible.

The Princess rejected suitors from Kafrikilla and also a Protector of Alkhava.

And it was even said that an Aldanese rival for the Princess's love visited the witches of Balanmanik to import a curse on Lord Morgan.

But nothing could prevent the strong-willed Princess from marrying her chosen one, and finally the family had to let her wed this stranger.

The couple was happy in all things except that they had no children.

They tried everything to conceive and after many years, on the verge of desperation, they themselves visited and brought gifts to the Queen of Balanmanik.

But none of this worked, and in the end they were not capable of bringing forth issue.

After their adopted daughter died in battle, the royal line of Aldan died out.

And now the city was governed by a Council. Or, at least it had been until two days ago, when after all these centuries of independence it had fallen to barbarians.

"That's a gloomy story," Jamie said with a thin smile. "You don't believe it, do you?"

"Of course," Wishaway said, shocked.

"Even in secular Aldan, where people don't buy into the gods or witchcraft, you're still falling for some crap about a curse?"

Wishaway did not reply. Whether there was a curse or not, it was a fact that of all the Lords Ui Neill who had come here four hundred years ago, none had managed to have any children and conceive an heir.

And although Wishaway claimed to be, like her father, a hard-nosed scientist, still, at this place, she couldn't help but wonder if the terrible witches of Balanmanik had really played a part in the darkness that had befallen the royal house of Aldan, the Ui Neills, and now the whole world.

Jamie would be part of the curse, too. Poor, innocent, lovely Jamie, the Lord Ui Neill, Heir of Morgan.

She examined his face, his long eyelashes, his tired but happy eyes. He caught her looking and she turned away.

"I know what you're thinking," Jamie said. "And there's a good reason I got you to tell me that yarn again. Yesterday I ran it by Ramsay, and he has a better explanation."

"Yes?" Wishaway said skeptically.

"When Ramsay heard that story, he scoffed at the notion of a curse, saying that because humans and Altairians are completely different species, it isn't surprising they can't make babies. It would have been far more amazing if they had. Ramsay says our DNA is bound to be completely different, if indeed you Altairians even possess DNA, or some other complex molecule that carries your genetic makeup. You see? So there's nothing magical about it. It's just biology."

Wishaway looked at him with interest.

Why was he telling her this?

Was he trying to reassure her? Was he trying to remove barriers between them? Or was he just talking, trying to show her his knowledge, showing off, as all boys do, especially young boys?

They lapsed into silence and they sat together looking at the growing sunlight bending over the waterfall.

They didn't speak and the unspoken thing between them was the future.

Neither would think about it.

Neither could contemplate it.

So they didn't.

They lay there on the mossy yellow grass, and when the silence became uncomfortable Wishaway cleared her throat and talked again about her childhood and how, after her mother had died, she and her father had taken a sea voyage to all the islands of the Middle Sea. Her voice a mixture of sadness, blended with the odd happy remembrance of an incident or a place.

She was beautiful in a way no human being could be beautiful. Her deep blue-gray eyes and pale skin. Her small nose so filled with expression when she talked. Her cheeks rosy with excitement as she spoke of a new city or some great beast she had seen in the ice deserts of Perovan.

She finished her story and Jamie leaned forward and kissed her.

Wishaway looked at him, amazed.

"Lord Ui Neill," she said, blinking rapidly. He couldn't tell if her tone was angry or pleased.

"Do you kiss on this planet?" he asked, trying not to sound like Captain Kirk.

Wishaway bit her lip and nodded. "Of course, but only those who are married, or betrothed," she said sternly.

"We're neither," Jamie said, and reached down to the grass and held her hand—her cool, odd, lovely four-fingered hand.

Wishaway nodded again. "We're neither," she agreed in a voice that was barely a whisper.

"If you don't want me to do it again, tell me to stop," Jamie said. He leaned forward and they kissed without breathing for a full minute.

And they might have kept on kissing till one of them passed out had they not heard talk and footsteps coming through the woods.

Wishaway rapidly pushed Jamie away.

Ramsay bounded up behind them. He was with Lorca, one of the survivors from the city who'd ended up with them in Basky. Lorca was a scholar from the island nation of Oralands. He had originally come to Aldan to study at the university. There were half a dozen universities on the planet Altair, but Aldan's was the oldest, the most prestigious, and the largest, with an enrollment of nearly five hundred students. Like many things in Aldan, it had been founded by one of the Ui Neills, who had gone to a place called Trinity College in a kingdom on Earth.

Ramsay liked Lorca, who was tall like him and black-haired, though with darker skin and deep green eyes bursting with life. He was almost sixteen years old, but since a year on Altair was four hundred days long, he was really over seventeen.

He had only been at the university for two terms when the invasion had come. This was not actually his fight. Because he was a foreigner and Oralands was neutral in the struggle between Aldan and Alkhava, he could have presented himself to the nearest Alkhavan patrol, and they would have had to offer him safe passage. Either that or risk a war with another island nation.

But even so, Lorca had sought out the rebels and was surprised and delighted to meet up with Callaway, who had been one of his teachers at the university.

Both boys stood looking at Wishaway and Jamie lying on the grass, cheeks fiery red.

"What were you doing? Were you running?" Ramsay asked innocently.

Jamie and Ramsay had long since made up from their fight, but even so, his friend's clumsy interruption was inopportune and pretty annoying.

"No," Jamie said, ticked off.

"Did we interrupt something?" Ramsay asked. "Were you wrestling?"

Wishaway blushed deeper. Jamie shook his head.

"Of course not. We weren't doing anything," Jamie said.

"Are you sure? Have you got a cold?" Ramsay persisted naïvely.

"Absolutely sure," Jamie said, trying to eradicate the irritation from his voice.

"OK, then. Well, I want to tell you something," Ramsay said, dismissing the weird thought that had just come into his head.

"Hello, Wishaway," Lorca said in English, the lingua franca of the elite.

"Good day, Lorca," Wishaway said formally.

"*Fura typalass, smaria, tal,* Wishaway," Lorca added in the honey-sounding tongue of his own country.

It was obviously a compliment, for Wishaway blushed deeper still and laughed a little. Wishaway liked Lorca, too. In fact, everyone liked him, except for Jamie, who found him irritating and pretentious. It wasn't as if he was handsome. He was very tall, but otherwise normal-looking. As normal as six-foot-six, pointy-eared, eight-fingered aliens got.

"Why don't we keep to the English language," Jamie said, annoyed.

"Certainly, Jamie," Lorca replied cheerfully. "Until you are able to speak the languages of our world."

"Listen, have I got news for you. Good news," Ramsay said excitedly. "We got to tell your father, Wishaway, I think I've found something that might help us."

Wishaway started to get up. Lorca reached down and offered her his hand.

"She can get up by herself," Jamie said. "She's not an invalid."

243

Wishaway took the hand and Lorca pulled her to her feet.

"Thank you," Wishaway said.

"It was my pleasure," Lorca said, beaming. Lorca had known Wishaway at the university. She had sat in on her father's lectures, and although she was much younger than him, he considered her most charming.

"What were you sayin', Ramsay?" Jamie asked his friend.

"Come on, I'll show you, it'll blow you away. Lorca found it, but I know what to do with it. I suppose you were right when you got all shirty with me about the B-52. I've been trying to come up with something a wee bit more practical, and I think we might have a way of defeating the Alkhavans," Ramsay said quickly.

"What is it?" Jamie said.

"A surprise," Lorca said a little smugly.

"A surprise? Surprises, secrets, sneaking up on people. You're quite the little complicated character, aren't you?" Jamie said.

"It's a tautology to say that someone is complex. That's a given—all people are complex," Ramsay said.

"Yes, that's what makes them people," Lorca added haughtily.

"These two are really starting to get to me," Jamie said to Wishaway.

Ramsay ignored him.

"Come on, follow us," Ramsay said, and he and Lorca jogged back into the woods.

Wishaway set off in pursuit, her long legs running in the thick blue-and-gold corduroy dress she had gotten from one of the village girls.

"There's no point following; I know it's going to be a bunch of crap, whatever those two have found," Jamie muttered to himself.

He watched Wishaway run deeper into the woods, sighed, and then reluctantly set off in pursuit.

Ten minutes later, Jamie's doubts were confirmed. When he caught up to them, Wishaway, Lorca, and Ramsay were staring at a vast pool of thick black liquid bubbling out of the ground.

Ramsay was excited. "Well, Jamie, what do you think?"

"You found a tar pit?" Jamie asked skeptically.

Ramsay nodded. "Petroleum, actually. Naphtha or heavy crude by the looks of it."

"Uh-huh, and your plan is what, exactly? Cover the pit with leaves, lure the entire Alkhavan army to this forest, and hope they fall into the pit and drown? Is that it?" Jamie asked sarcastically.

"Don't be ridiculous, that would never work," Ramsay said, failing to pick up on the sarcasm. Lorca scooped some of the black liquid into an earthenware pot.

"Are we all set?" Ramsay asked.

Lorca nodded and turned to Jamie. "If Ramsay's plan works, we might be able to defeat the invaders. Our scouts tell us that because of the fireworks incident, most of the Alkhavans are afraid and sleep on their iceships at night. We might be able to destroy their army in a single blow," Lorca said with a huge laugh.

Wishaway nodded. "We must tell Father," she said seriously.

"Come on," Ramsay said, and they set off running back to the village.

"Wait a minute. What plan? What are you talking about? Am I the only sane one left on this planet?" Jamie said, but the others were way ahead of him.

"All this running can't be good for you," Jamie muttered, and jogged after them. Much to his satisfaction, Jamie managed to catch and pass Lorca before they reached the village. When he entered the hamlet, it was obvious that Ramsay had started his pitch without him. Jamie saw that thirty or so refugees were crammed into the headman's hut for a council of war. With some difficulty, he squeezed into the back.

Ramsay was speaking to a skeptical audience. "Callaway, I know a lot of you want to flee in the fishing boats, but I think we might have a better use for them," Ramsay said and looked for Lorca.

"We found a huge pool of this substance in the woods," Lorca said breathlessly, pushing his way to the front of the room and handing the jar of petroleum to Callaway.

Callaway opened the lid, looked at it. "Yes, it is called *noori*, some use it as a lubricant, although it is not as effective as lard. I believe it is common in this part of the country," Callaway said dismissively.

Ramsay grabbed the jar and poured a little of it onto the hut floor. He took out his lighter, added some straw, and lit it. In the highly oxygenated atmosphere of Altair, the petroleum had a low flashpoint and burned easily.

Some in the hut gasped, but Callaway was unimpressed.

"Yes, I have heard that it burns," he said. "Of what use is that to us?"

"The iceships," Ramsay said.

Callaway smiled benignly. "Lord Ramsay, I appreciate thy idea, but allow me to demonstrate why this is not practical," Callaway said.

He took a gourd of water and poured it on the burning petroleum. It fizzled for a moment and then went out. There was a groan from the people in the hut who'd had their hopes briefly piqued. Jamie noticed, however, that Ramsay's smile had not abated. Indeed his grin had only gotten bigger.

"Let me tell you a story. In my world, a thousand years ago there were two peoples, the Greeks and the Turks, and they were fighting each other for the great Greek city of Constantinople. Like Aldan, it was on the sea and that was its strength and its weakness. The Turkish navy attacked it again and again, but the Greeks, although few in number, had a secret weapon that allowed them to beat back the Turkish attack."

"Yes?" Callaway asked, starting to get interested.

Ramsay continued excitedly: "What we need is something that can burn in water, or on ice, something that can burn right through the hull of an iceship and sink it. What we need is something that on my planet we call Greek Fire. This substance *will* burn on water, it will burn on ice. There are three components to Greek Fire. First is sulfur, second is quicklime, third is petroleum. Now, I know you have quicklime; it's that stuff all over the walls of your houses in Aldan. And I know you've got petroleum—that's what this stuff is—so the last component, the missing component, is sulfur. And I know for a fact that you have sulfur, too."

"How do ye know this?" Callaway asked.

"When the O'Neills came here four hundred years ago, they brought what you called fire sticks. Guns, we call them. Now, those muskets ran out of ammo pretty quickly and since then you and your predecessors have been working on gunpowder to make them work again. When the Alkhavans attacked, Jamie and I saw that you had some of the guns up and running. You must have made gunpowder."

"Sulfur is what we call coral flame, Master Callaway," Lorca added respectfully.

Callaway was looking at Ramsay with growing interest. "It burns on water and on ice?" he asked.

"It'll burn right through the hulls of those ships. On our planet the Greeks used it for seven hundred years to keep the Turks out of Constantinople," Ramsay said.

Callaway nodded and stroked his white beard.

"And these Turks were unable to take the city?" he asked.

Ramsay looked uncomfortable.

"Well, no, they did end up taking the city, but Greek Fire helped delay it," Ramsay said, a bit embarrassed.

"Father, we must seize the chance. We know that their foolish, superstitious army sleeps on board the iceships. We could use Alakar's fishing boats to sail amongst the fleet at night, and using Ramsay's fire we will sink their ships and drown their army," Wishaway said.

Callaway shook his head. "Quicklime can be had easily in the hills, and thy *noori* we also can find, but there is no coral flame in these parts. At the university we had to buy most of our supply from Frantan."

"Exactly. Lorca says you have buckets of the stuff," Ramsay said enthusiastically.

Callaway nodded. "What of it?"

"Well then. We've got to do a raid. Sneak into the city, get at least a backpack full of sulfur, come back here, and make the Greek Fire. Twenty-five of us here. We'll have a team making the quicklime, another getting pots of the petroleum. I'll mix it and we'll bring it to the fishing boats," Ramsay said.

"And then what?" Callaway asked, still not convinced.

"We sail among the iceships throwing pots of Greek Fire onto the decks; the pots break; the Greek Fire ignites on contact and burns all the way through the iceships, sinking them. There's about twenty iceships, but I reckon we could easily make a hundred pots of Greek Fire."

Callaway sat down on his chair. It was a lot of information to take in. Although he had been one of the champions of the resistance, he had been about to recommend that the refugees take the hidden trawlers and flee to Kafrikilla.

"I must think more about this," he said, then got up and walked out of the cabin and deep into the woods.

After a time, he came to Lorca's petroleum pool.

He sat beside it and looked at the thick, viscous liquid.

It would be a gamble. Apart from Wishaway, the other survivors did not look healthy. They were tired and depressed and a lot of them felt weak. Even Prince Lorca, who had boundless enthusiasm, was looking unwell. And going back to the city? Attempting to get into the university, getting past patrols and guards and then attacking the enemy fleet at night? A bunch of civilians against war-hardened warriors?

Very risky.

But as Great Ui Neill once said, centuries ago, when he led the attack on the Perovan harbor, the biggest risk is to take no risks at all.

Callaway smiled to himself.

He knew what he had to do.

Chapter IX
THE PROTECTOR

THE CITY GLITTERED under the light of the two moons. Protector Ksar sat in a comfortable wooden chair in the president of the Council's house, a spacious home overlooking a sandy bay and the blackness of the Middle Sea.

It was two days since Aldan had fallen and his men had relaxed their patrols. Already one iceship full of plunder had been sent back to the Alkhavan port of Afor. In the coming days more goods and eventually all the slaves would be sent to the ice kingdom in the north.

For Protector Ksar, things couldn't have gone much better.

It was true that he was beginning to feel unwell, that some of his officers and men were also feeling under the weather, but that could be explained by fatigue. Although it had been a short campaign, the planning had taken months, and the combat hadn't been without its difficulties.

There was also the humiliating escape of the prisoners after the city had fallen, but he had already made sure that no report of that would ever make it back to the Lord Protector. Deputy Sara had been the only one of his lieutenants who had felt the Lord Protector should know of such things, and Deputy Sara had met with an unfortunate accident while inspecting one of the higher portions of the battlements.

Yes, the rebels were being rounded up, the patrols were winding down, the other fleet had met no resistance at Krikor, and most of Ksar's men were already ensconced in their ships, anxious to weigh anchor and return home with their newfound wealth and glory. And also, he thought ruefully, because they were still fearful of sleeping in the strange city. Ksar shared none of their fears. Why sleep in a freezing hulk of ice when you could relax in luxury such as this? His men were fools. Ignorant, shortsighted fools.

All of them would acquire a small fortune from the sale of the slaves, wood, and precious metals that they had found in Aldan. Enough to set them up for life. And of course it would all be gone within a year. Wasted on women, drink, banquets. And where would they be then? Broke, penniless, anxious for more plunder.

The cycle would begin again.

Protector Ksar smoked a small pipe of *akla* weed and drank some of the excellent Aldanese wine.

"No," he said to himself and blew a smoke ring out the window.

Why should they go back to the frozen country of Alkhava—where every year the glaciers advanced, the cold got more severe, and life became more precarious?

Why should they return at all?

He'd had this very conversation with the Lord

Protector before the invasion fleet had left. Instead of a pillaging mission, why could this not be a colonizing mission? Instead of the Alkhavans stripping Aldan of its resources, would it not be better to leave those resources intact and establish Alkhavan control over the whole island?

"We could migrate from the frozen wastes and live on this temperate island as lords and masters. Live and prosper and multiply," he said aloud to the empty room, repeating the argument he had lost to the Lord Protector a month ago.

But the Lord Protector would have none of it.

He was as superstitious as the basest of the soldiers.

He feared Aldan.

The great band of chiefs, the Ui Neills, had come there from who knows where. And Aldan was the site of one of the three ancient towers. The White Tower of Aldan, the tower on the so-called Sacred Isle, and the tower that the witches guarded in Balanmanik.

The Lord Protector was afraid.

But then the Lord Protector was . . . Dare he say it? Dare he think it? Yes. The Lord Protector was also a fool.

And perhaps he would have a fool's end.

Perhaps after Ksar and the fleet returned to Alkhava, the Lord Protector would meet with an accident just as Deputy Sara had done.

There was a knock at the door.

Protector Ksar was startled from his murderous and

treasonous thoughts. He choked on his pipe and had to take a sip of wine before he could answer.

"Yes?"

Deputy Krama entered. An ungainly fellow but a good, competent officer despite his young age.

"Sir, we have reports that persons unknown, possibly Aldanese, broke into the university. I have sent out patrols," Krama said in Alkhavan.

Protector Ksar bolted to his feet. "The university? Not the granary? Not the armory? But the university? Hmm. That's extremely interesting, don't you think, Krama?" Ksar replied in the language of the far north.

"Um . . . Yes, sir."

"It's not any of our men. Even the worst of our thieving soldiers would not think of going to the university. Books are not what interest our troops, eh?" Ksar said with a bitter laugh.

"No, sir."

"No, Krama, it's the Aldanese. They're up to something. They're plotting something. Possibly a repeat of that stunt that freed the prisoners," Ksar said.

"Do you want me to double the patrols, sir?" Krama asked uncertainly.

Ksar smiled in that way that made Krama think he was in trouble. "No, I do not want you to double the patrols, Krama. I want you to call out the entire garrison. Cordon off the university, seal the entrances to the city, rouse every man from the ships. All officers, all sergeants, I

254

want everyone up and searching for these rebels. Triple the guard around the slaves in the arena and make sure the port is secure. And I want updates from you every ten minutes. Is that clear?"

"Yes, sir."

"And send out my personal guard, too," Ksar said.

"Yes, sir," Krama said, shivering at the thought of the infamous black-clad veterans.

"Then why are you still standing here? Go!" Ksar bellowed. Krama scurried out and within a minute Ksar could hear trumpets blaring. The trumpets were followed by drums and the cries of troops as sergeants whipped them to their posts.

"You are clever, Master Callaway, but you won't escape this time," Ksar said in what was a surprisingly accurate guess as to who might be responsible for the night's disruption.

At that moment, a mile and a half from Ksar's balcony, Callaway was not feeling particularly clever.

Obviously something had gone wrong, because trumpets were being sounded everywhere in the city. Torches were being lit, and it looked as if the entire Alkhavan army was being mobilized.

It was the culmination of an unlucky series of events.

The night had not gone according to plan.

Callaway's original scheme had called for Lorca and

Ramsay to help him raid the chemical room of the university. Lorca and Callaway needed to be there to find the place, and Ramsay had to be there to see if the coral flame was really "sulfur."

They would go in, get the stuff, get out again quickly.

But the first complication was Jamie, who wasn't really needed but who had insisted on coming with his Irish friend. The second complication was the presence of Wishaway, who didn't want to remain behind if everyone else was going. Callaway had absolutely refused, but she'd always been a headstrong girl. A troublemaker. She repeatedly did the unexpected. Bringing the Earth boys was a good example. If he was being honest with himself, he'd have to admit that he had really only sent her to the Sacred Isle to get her out of the way, to save her from being killed or enslaved by the Alkhavans. For her to actually show up bringing two of the Ui Neill to save the country was incredible but somehow typical.

She had taken after her mother, who was from the mountains. She'd been independent and headstrong, too.

So instead of a party of three, now it was a party of five.

And perhaps it was the size of the group that gave them away when they were crossing the echoey inner courtyard of the natural philosophy building.

A guard had seen them and called a warning.

And now, ten minutes later, trumpets, drums, bells, shouting . . .

They ran across the small university campus and down toward the seafront.

They did have some advantages: it was dark, they knew the city (whereas the Alkhavans did not), and they were not filled with fear like the superstitious Alkhavan guards.

But Callaway knew that they had some serious disadvantages, too. There were hundreds of Alkhavans looking for them, and soon the thousands sleeping on the iceships would be on their way, too.

And there was one more thing. He wasn't feeling well. Perhaps it was age catching up with him, or exhaustion following the invasion, but whatever it was, he felt that he had aged ten years in the last few days.

Jamie and Ramsay were in the lead as they ran down a pitch-black alleyway. Wishaway was not far behind them and though Callaway was behind her as expected, what was surprising was Lorca lagging well back in last place.

"Tell your buddy to get a move on, he's slowing us all down," Jamie said to Ramsay.

"He's the one carrying the backpack," Ramsay hissed.

"It's got about three pounds of sulfur in it. I could carry ten times that and be faster," Jamie whispered back.

"We'll wait for him. I don't think he's feeling too good," Ramsay said.

Jamie shook his head, but they waited until Callaway and Lorca caught up.

"Thanks for the effort, but I think I'll take the back-pack, Lorca," Jamie said, rolling his eyes at Ramsay.

"I am sorry. I am unmade, *machat la mana*," Lorca said, panting, sweat pouring down his face.

Wishaway looked concerned. She touched his fore-head. "He is hot," she said.

"Yeah, we're all hot, we're running for our lives here," Jamie said, still finding it hard to be sympathetic. "Now, come on, no more wasting time. Where does this alley go?"

"It runs parallel to the harbor," Wishaway said. "And eventually to one of the north gates."

"Then we better get moving," Jamie said. "We're lucky not to have been spotted again, but that luck won't last forever."

"I'm not too happy about any of this," Ramsay mut-tered. "I'm just glad we left our stuff behind in Basky."

Jamie nodded. He knew what Ramsay meant, even though Ramsay was too spooked to say it.

He was glad that they had left the *Salmon* behind in Basky.

If they fell into enemy hands, they'd be in trouble. If the Salmon fell into enemy hands, they'd be lost for-ever—slaves in an ice land to the north, without hope of ever getting back to their homes on distant Earth.

"I've got a bad feeling, too," was all Jamie replied. He gave Lorca and Callaway one more moment to catch their breath and then all five set off running again.

One man's luck is another man's misfortune. And vice versa. And this night, Protector Ksar knew that luck was on his side.

For although the guards had lost the intruders at the university, and although the city was filled with a thousand roads and a hundred exits, for some reason the rebels were leaving a trail of yellow powder behind them. A trail of yellow powder that a child could follow.

It would only be a matter of time.

With some complacency, he sat at his desk, took up his pen, and continued his correspondence in the functional, squat Alkhavan script that was perhaps the ugliest of all the languages on Altair.

The first letter was another brief dispatch to the Lord Protector. Here he would be careful to write much but say precisely nothing.

Mighty Conqueror of the Seas, Great Lord of the North, Beloved One of the Ice Gods, Commander of the Alkhavan Armies, Lord Protector of us Thy Children, I, your humble servant, salute you.

We have made progress against your enemies and will be returning with great joy to your embrace. Your glory proceeds before us and your humbled enemies bow down in your powerful light.

We lack your physical guidance, mighty Lord, but your mere presence in our thoughts instills in us the courage and fortitude to win our task.

My men and I honor and salute you.

Hail.

PROTECTOR KSAR

The second epistle was to his sister, the Witch Queen of Balanmanik.

Sister. Despite your dire predictions, we have made much progress. The Aldanese resistance is crumbling quickly and I hope to have them rounded up very soon. The White Tower is in our hands and as per your instructions, I will have it searched in the coming days. Perhaps if you would deign to instruct me as to what I am seeking, it would help me in my task. But no matter. You may play your games as you will. This city and all of its contents will be stripped to the bare bones.

But now I must bring your attention to the most important of my finds.

This is a matter of the utmost secrecy. It is my belief that the Ui Neills, or an emissary of that clan, may, somehow, have returned.

Ksar paused over the dispatch to his sister and yelled for Deputy Krama.

Krama entered warily. "Yes, sir?"

"Krama, when the captives are caught. I want you to examine them personally. If any of them do not look quite right, have them brought here," Ksar said.

"What do you mean, sir?"

"I mean, you dolt, if any of them appear strange or in any way deformed, have them brought to me. Do you understand?"

"To your quarters, Protector Ksar?"

"Yes, have them searched and bound and brought here. I wish to interrogate them personally."

"They are to be brought in alive?"

"Yes, alive," Ksar said impatiently.

Krama raised an eyebrow, but he knew better than to further question the order. He went outside, leaving the Protector alone again.

Ksar picked up the reed pen.

Yes, my dear sister, perhaps a prize awaits bigger even than the capture of the city itself. We shall see. Tell this to none of your order and let not the Lord Protector's spies come to hear of these developments. I will keep you informed and I will trust your discretion.

Your brother,

Ksar, of the Ninth House of Alkhav, Protector and General of the Alkhavan People

He grinned and blotted the ink.

He sipped some wine and then walked to the ornate wooden cupboard by the window. He removed the pocket-sized soldering iron they had found at the arena. He turned it on and examined the blue flame for a moment.

"Yes, I wish to meet you, mysterious ones, for even your toys are most interesting," Ksar muttered to himself.

Jamie, Ramsay, and Wishaway were almost at one of the narrow pedestrian gates that led out of the city when they heard a yell behind them. They turned and to their horror they saw that Callaway was being wrestled to the ground by several black-clad Alkhavan soldiers.

"Caught," Jamie gasped.

"Can we fight 'em?" Ramsay asked.

Jamie peered into the gloom; it was difficult to tell, but there appeared to be at least a dozen soldiers shoving Callaway down and attempting to push past him in pursuit of them.

Two more caught Lorca, tackled him, and pulled him down too.

"*Jarma, triga* Oralands," Lorca shouted, trying to throw the soldiers off his back. But when a third guard clubbed him in the legs with a huge stick, they saw that Lorca would have no chance. He was going to be taken, too.

"*Vara tak, sna,*" another soldier screamed in Alkhavan at the three children.

"We've got to save them," Ramsay said.

Jamie shook his head. "It's too late," he replied and, gearing up for a sprint, tightened the backpack on his shoulders.

It was then that Jamie noticed the trail of sulfur that was flowing out of a hole in his backpack.

A trail that had led the soldiers right to them, a trail that meant they'd never had a chance to get away.

"I knew it. Look at this. Lorca set us up," Jamie said in horror. "Look."

He showed Ramsay the backpack.

"It's just an accident, Lorca's no traitor," Ramsay said.

"I knew there was something about him," Jamie said in disgust.

Behind them somehow Lorca had gotten to his feet, but he was quickly overwhelmed by the soldiers and they easily beat him and threw him down again onto the cobblestone street.

"We must help!" Wishaway cried and tried to run back, but Jamie held tightly onto her arm.

"Let me alone!" Wishaway screamed.

"What do we do, Jamie?" Ramsay asked.

Jamie looked at the squad of soldiers, who had now completely subdued Lorca and Callaway and were coming for them.

"We have to go," Jamie said. And, dragging Wishaway between them, the two boys ran for the north gate.

She struggled for a hundred yards, where they stopped in an alcove to catch their breath.

"Please stop fighting us, Wishaway. They've got your

dad and Lorca already. We've got to go and save ourselves," Jamie said.

Ramsay nodded. "He's right,"

Wishaway took a deep breath and nodded. "Yes," she said, and they started running again.

But the net was closing about them and, all around, horns were blaring and guttural orders being shouted out to the bands of soldiers and marines in pursuit.

Jamie knew there was only a small probability that they could escape now, perhaps getting through an unguarded gate and losing the search parties in the countryside. But even that small probability quickly evaporated when a squadron of soldiers appeared in front of them, blocking the narrow street.

"This way!" Jamie yelled, and he and Ramsay dragged Wishaway down a side alley. They only got about fifty feet before a blunt crossbow bolt hit Ramsay in the back. It knocked him flat.

"Ramsay!" Jamie yelled.

"I'm hit," Ramsay groaned.

Another crossbow bolt smacked into Wishaway, knocking her down, too.

"Wishaway, oh, no!" Jamie shouted.

"Uhh," Wishaway said, dazed but not seriously hurt.

"Go, go, Jamie," Ramsay said, struggling to get to his feet.

Jamie hesitated. He knew that *he* still had a chance to make his escape into the darkness of the alley—perhaps circle around the pursuers and then get over the city walls.

On his own he really could do it.

"Go," Ramsay said.

Jamie smiled. "I never told you, Ramsay. My great grandfather was on Iwo Jima with the Marines."

"What's that to do with anything? Run, you bloody eejit," Ramsay said, his Irish brogue coming on full force.

Jamie shook his head. "When I was really young, he told me the Marine code. You know what it is?"

"I don't care what it is. Run, you fool," Ramsay said, still trying to get up.

"The Marines say 'you never leave a man behind.'"

Jamie took the backpack off and let it drop to the cobblestones. He raised his fists. The soldiers came pounding up the street in their black boots, leather armor, and furs. They were yelling and carrying sticks and clubs.

It would be an unfair fight. But not that unfair. At least he would have two arms.

"Come on, then!" Jamie screamed then hit the first of the Alkhavan troops with a right hook so hard it put the man on his back.

Yeah, Jamie said to himself. *You bad.*

A plump Alkhavan took a swipe at his head with a heavy stick.

Jamie stepped to one side.

"That's the best you can do? Man, you so fat, your

butt should have its own zip code," Jamie said, laughing maniacally.

He managed to punch the plump soldier with another right and then he jabbed a third with his left. They swarmed around him.

"Come on then!" Jamie yelled again. "Come get a Harlem-style ass whupping."

He got in a kick on a fourth Alkhavan and a final left hook connected with a fifth, but the sixth and seventh dragged him down to the street and a half dozen more jumped on his back.

Within what seemed like seconds, his hands had been tied painfully behind his back, men were yelling at him in a foreign language, and he was being blindfolded, kicked, and hauled off to what could only be a choice between grim alternatives.

❋　❋　❋

Ksar looked at them with satisfaction. Yes indeed, he thought, this was quite a prize. He nodded to one of his troops to remove the blindfolds.

When the blindfold was ripped off, Jamie saw that he was in a large, well-furnished, and luxurious room. He saw wood furniture, expensive-looking carpet, a metal sculpture of a ship.

Ramsay was standing beside him. Both of them had their arms tied behind their backs.

Sitting in front of them were four guards and the Alkhavan general who called himself Protector Ksar.

Close up, he didn't look like a monster. He had a large lips, a generous mouth, high cheekbones under very pale skin and dark eyes that were both suspicious and intelligent. His black hair was severely braided behind his back, and he was dressed not in furs, but in a light cotton garment, like an Egyptian *galabia*—plain blue, with no decoration.

Protector Ksar examined Jamie and Ramsay with interest. "What are these?" he asked in Alkhavan, which to the boys sounded like: *"Arggcast taaraka."*

"Sir, they were with Callaway and the others," one of the soldiers replied. A squat man with a long scar on his forehead and deep-set eyes.

"Were they indeed, Krama? What do you suppose they are?" Ksar asked.

"You want my opinion, sir?" Krama replied.

"Yes."

"Freaks of nature. Or, um, maybe demons," Krama said.

"Demons, yes, perhaps," Protector Ksar muttered.

"Demons?" Ksar said in English to the two boys.

Jamie looked at Ramsay. *It's probably best not to speak,* Jamie thought, and Ramsay was obviously thinking the same thing. Both said nothing.

"They are talking with their eyes. Kill the demons, sir, lest they cast some spell on you," Krama said nervously.

"Lest they cast some spell on me?" Ksar said with a laugh. "You may go, Krama, and take the soldiers with you. I will question these two alone."

"But, sir . . ."

"You may go, Krama," the Protector said firmly.

Krama and the other soldiers filed meekly out of the room.

When they had gone, Ksar walked over to the window and stared out at the glittering, moonlit sea.

The iceships were bobbing in the harbor, and after all the noise of trumpets and running soldiers had ceased, the city had become deathly quiet again. Silent, save for the leather-winged *rantas* flying over the rooftops and a *seecha* crying in the street below.

Protector Ksar went to the cupboard and removed Ramsay's pocket soldering iron. He held it in front of Ramsay's nose.

"This is thine, I believe," Ksar said in English.

Ramsay did not reply. Ksar sat down on the edge of the large polished wooden table. He took a sip of red wine.

"Before I killed Councillor Trokar, she bespake an interesting story. She was chained to Councillor Callaway in the arena, awaiting her execution, when out of the chaos of that night, two youths approached Callaway and burned away his bonds with this machine," Ksar said, looking at the solder.

He tapped the device against Ramsay's face and continued: "As perhaps thou knowest, people say many things under torture. It taketh a stern hand to sort truth from gibberish. But I am well versed. She did say other things. Before she died, she swore that Callaway's daughter did speak something odd to her father. Thou wert there. Dost thou remember what she said?"

Ramsay remained expressionless under Ksar's gaze.

Ksar lit the solder and brought the blue flame close to Ramsay's cheek. The brightness of it alone sent terror through both boys. "She said, 'Father, Father, these are the Lords Ui Neill, come from Earth to save us.'"

Neither boy spoke.

Ksar smiled and watched Ramsay's skin blister a little under the powerful flame, though it wasn't even touching him yet. Ramsay gasped in pain.

Ksar stepped back. "Perhaps thy friend knows more."

Ksar put his hand around Jamie's throat. His four-fingered grip was slippery and powerful. He ignited the iron and brought the blue flame close to Jamie's right eye. Was he going to blind him? Jamie flinched and tried to back away, but Ksar was holding him tight.

"Do not resist. If I wished to kill thee, ye would be dead," Ksar said.

He watched with amusement as the solder singed some of Jamie's eyebrow hairs. He laughed.

"A wonderful toy, I shall put it to great use," Ksar said and switched the solder off.

He began probing Jamie's face roughly with his powerful fingers.

"Hmmm. The Lords Ui Neill? The legendary Lords Ui Neill come again, with misshapen ears and five fingers and gigantic noses and hair that burns like our hair? The Lords Ui Neill come again? And come from where, exactly?"

Jamie said nothing.

"Thou will not speak? Thou cannot speak? It is of no consequence. I am a patient man. Soldiers learn patience. Soldiers learn patience by following orders, no matter how foolish those orders may appear. My orders from the Lord Protector are that we must leave this city and return to Afor within three days," Ksar said, and shook his head with disgust.

"Three days is not enough time to get to the root of thy story. And in three days ye shall become the property of the Lord Protector. Is that what ye seek?"

Ksar leaned back and smiled.

"Thou art perhaps wise to remain mute," he said to himself.

He looked into Jamie's eyes.

"Kava lak tarmak," he muttered.

Ksar stared at Jamie's left arm for a moment. Something about it didn't seem quite right. He let go of Jamie's throat, stepped to the side, and regarded both of them.

"Shall I send thee to my master, or shall I—"

Just then, Ksar had a fit of coughing. He stumbled to his chair to sit down. He drank the rest of the wine to steady himself.

He was breathing hard when there was a knock at the door.

"Come," Ksar said weakly in Alkhavan.

Deputy Krama entered. "Sir, you were right, the— Are you well, sir?" Krama asked in Alkhavan.

"I am fine," Ksar replied. "Continue."

"Sir, you were right. The father talked when we threatened to behead the girl. The rest of the rebels are in a village called Basky, seven leagues from here. I have sent out a team of fast pickets to seize the others. We should have them all by morning."

Protector Ksar dismissed Krama with a wave of his hand.

He drank another glass of wine, stood, then slowly approached Jamie, apparently recovered now from his coughing fit.

Ksar's black eyes bored into him. "All of thy accomplices will soon be taken. We have found thy hiding place. A village called Basky," he said in English.

Jamie groaned.

Ksar laughed at him. "Thou art a knave. It would be easy to break you. Thy groan reveals thy understanding. Is that not so, mighty Ui Neill?"

Jamie bit his lip and Protector Ksar seized him by the throat again and squeezed hard, trying to force the boy to his knees. But Jamie was not so easily intimidated. He had stood up to Eric in Harlem and he would stand up to this creepy Alkhavan general. He refused to buckle, he would bend his knee to no man. Ksar would have to kill him first.

Ksar squeezed on Jamie's throat for another moment

and then abruptly let go. Jamie sucked in air and coughed.

"I like that," Ksar said. "Thou hast spirit, Ui Neill. Spirit and knowledge. Thou may be of use to us. Both of thee. It was thee, not Callaway, that made this trinket, this fire stick, and it was ye who wert responsible for the witchcraft in the arena. Is that not so?"

Jamie, who was well practiced in the art, again remained silent. Ramsay, who was new at the game but in the presence of the master of nonresponse, wisely followed Jamie's example.

It saved their lives.

If they had begun to talk, Ksar would have spent the night torturing them, extracting everything they knew. He would have learned about the Salmon. He would have taken it for himself, and to protect his secret he would have killed them.

Ksar shrugged. "If I had a week, I would know everything. But I do not have a week. Verily, though, of all the wonders we have taken in this city, it is my feeling that ye art the biggest prize of all . . . Nay, ye must not go to Afor. Thine existence must not become common knowledge. So what to do with thee? What to do?"

Jamie knew that Ksar had already decided exactly what he was going to do with them. He was merely toying with them now.

Jamie smiled to show that he was not afraid.

Ksar grinned and licked his lips.

"No, thou wilt not become chattels of the Lord Protector. He will never learn of thy appearance here. I will send thee to my sister, the Witch Queen in Balanmanik. She will know where thou art from. Whether thou art demon, or devil, or something else entire."

He smiled. It would also prove to her that he had indeed succeeded. True, she had been elected the Witch Queen, but he had taken Aldan in a single day and now had conquered the legendary Ui Neill. He had surpassed even the deeds of his father, a mere raider, a pirate, a man who blustered and bragged but seldom thought.

"Krama!" Ksar yelled at the closed door.

The deputy came in quickly.

"Sir?"

"Krama, send for Admiral Harn. Bring him here immediately," Ksar said in Alkhavan.

Yes, he thought, *it won't matter.* His sister would know what to do with them. She would know how best to use the alien witchcraft for their own purposes. If they were going to seize power from their doltish Lord Protector, anything that might give them an edge would help.

A few minutes later, the admiral entered. He was a short red-bearded man who had obviously just been woken up, for he had hastily draped a fur coat around his shoulders.

"Protector Ksar, I am at your service," he said in a guttural rumble.

"Admiral, look at these two—um—creatures," Ksar said in Alkhavan.

The Admiral turned and stared at the prisoners.

"What are they, sir?" he asked without emotion.

"We think they are demons, Admiral. Very dangerous. They are to be taken to Balanmanik to be presented before the Witch Queen. Perhaps she will sacrifice them to the ice gods."

"Yes, sir."

"Admiral, I wish you to leave with the first tide in your fastest ship," Ksar said.

"Yes, sir. We can be ready to weigh before noon."

"Excellent. Prepare your vessel, but be advised that this assignment is to remain most secret. You are to speak to no one."

"No, sir."

"Deputy Krama will meet you at your ship in the morning. There may be more of these creatures in a village called Basky. There may also be artifacts similar to this," Ksar said, giving the admiral the soldering iron.

The admiral turned it over in his hand and gave it back quickly.

"If indeed there are additional artifacts, they also are to be taken to my sister. They are to be sealed in a cabin. No one is to touch them. They are bewitched, and it will take all of my sister's power to safely handle them. Is that clear, Admiral?"

"Yes, sir, very clear."

"I will also send with you the demons' confederates that we seized at the city wall. Perhaps my sister can torture them in order to get the demons to speak."

"A brilliant idea, sir," the admiral said.

"However, these creatures are to be kept separate from Callaway, his daughter, and the prince of Oralands. They are cunning, Admiral, and may know the ways of the spirit world. Keep them separate and closely guarded."

"Yes, sir . . . But the demons are to be kept alive, sir?"

"Oh, yes, Admiral, alive, but secure."

"I'll have them watched 'round the clock, sir," Harn said.

"You have your orders, then," Ksar said dismissively.

"If they are demons, they will make noble sacrifices for the ice gods," Admiral Harn added.

"They will indeed, Admiral, they will indeed," Protector Ksar said with a wide, satisfied, and utterly terrifying smile.

AZURE ICE. Ship noise. The open sea. Moons pulling at the waters. The departing sun. Men lying down on furs. Silence. Night. Ghosts of constellations. Black water. Terrible cold. And then, finally, a cheerless dawn.

Their second day in the deepest hold of the iceship. The room was a seven-by-seven-foot cube, with air holes in the roof. There were old furs on the floor and they had a blanket each, but both Jamie and Ramsay were freezing and Ramsay was close to frostbite in his toes. The Alkhavan sailors, of course, had taken their fleeces and thick coats, leaving them only their sweaters and T-shirts.

They didn't know how long the trip to Afor was supposed to take, but Ramsay reckoned that if the journey was going to be more than a week, then it was likely that one or both of them would get hypothermia. He kept this information to himself.

They had been let out once to eat some dried meat and use the head—the ship's toilet was basically just a hole in the stern that they had to pee through. With sign language, an Alkhavan sailor explained that they had to be careful to get the pee down the hole and not to let the urine stream touch the ice deck, in case it flash froze. A disgusting prospect to the boys and the Alkhavans.

Fortunately, neither of the boys had needed to go.

It was weird, but if they hadn't been prisoners, journeying toward a terrible future and if they'd been much warmer, the iceship could have been an amazing place to spend some time.

It was entirely transparent, and from their cell, the boys could look into the many levels above them and down through the thick keel to the seas beneath. On the upper deck the crew went about their tasks with a grim proficiency. Trimming the sails, cleaning the ice, shaving rough portions off the deck, repairing holes and gashes in the hull.

Below them the scene was entirely different—a silent world of strange ocean creatures. Things like squid and octopuses and huge warm-blooded lizards and black-mouthed fish that had no eyes and kept in schools of a hundred or more.

The Middle Sea of Altair, however, did not have the variety of life that Earth's oceans possessed. Perhaps it was too cold, or the biology of this planet worked in narrower niches. There were no friendly dolphins or multicolored tropical fish to keep them company. Still, the journey on the transparent iceship would have been a dream vacation for an Earth oceanographer.

Another thing the boys did was examine the workings of the amazing vessel. How the sailors used furs to protect themselves from iceburns, how they prepared little spirit stoves to melt food and water, how the big wooden masts were freeze-welded into the rest of the ship, and how the big organic ship seemed to breathe and move with the sea rather than bob on top of it like an Earth boat.

As time went on they noticed that the Alkhavans grew increasingly ill-disciplined. There was a lot of grumbling, but the boys couldn't tell if this was special grumbling or normal sailor complaining. Once they heard the words "Ui Neill" mentioned in the harsh, guttural language of the north but then nothing more.

Ramsay would have loved to discuss it all, but most of the time, it was too cold to speak, and on top of everything else they began to succumb to an ever-increasing dread.

Wishaway, Lorca, and Callaway were in the hold next to their own. They could make out their faces, but the ice between the rooms was so thick that they couldn't converse.

You could tap the wall, but after several attempts to make a code they gave up in frustration.

One thing was certain, though. If Lorca was in the cell with the other two, he couldn't possibly be the traitor that Jamie had thought he was. Once Lorca yelled so loud about something the guards came and beat him with sticks.

Jamie had to admit shamefacedly that the hole in the backpack was probably an accident, not some deliberate ploy to get them captured.

Even so, he still didn't like Lorca very much, and he hated the fact that Wishaway was sharing her cell with him. Jamie wasn't much of one for examining his feelings and even if he had been, it was unlikely that he would have recognized jealousy among them. He was only thirteen and puberty had hit the same time as cancer, amputation, and silence. Jealousy was something Laurence Fishburne did as Othello at Shakespeare in the Park, not something Jamie was intimately familiar with. His feelings toward Lorca were just a confused mélange of irritation and resentment.

Jamie huddled next to his friend Ramsay, a fur beneath them, an old blanket on top. The sun was out now, and a little heat penetrated through the thick hull and the decks above.

"Sun's nice," Jamie said between chattering teeth.

"Yeah, I've been paying it close attention. We're heading northeast," Ramsay whispered confidently.

"Northeast," Jamie repeated. "Alkhava."

Ramsay thought for a moment.

"Only be the third country I've ever visited," he said after a while.

"Prisoners of war don't 'visit' countries."

"Good point."

"Well, I don't blame you anyway," Jamie said.

"Blame me for what?"

"For bringing Lorca. Traitor or not, he screwed us up."

"Let's not go back there, mate. He's no traitor. Do you see him through the ice? He's not well. Sick and in jail. That's no way to treat an ally. And secondly, when you had the backpack you left just as big a trail."

"Maybe I'm the traitor. Wait a minute—the raid on the city was your idea, maybe you're the traitor," Jamie said and laughed a little.

Ramsay laughed too, and for a long time both boys giggled for no reason at all except the misery of their circumstances.

"You know, if we're all going to our deaths, we *should* have played Wishaway Led Zeppelin," Ramsay said cheerfully. "Everybody should hear Led Zeppelin before they die. If not 'Stairway' definitely 'Kashmir.'"

"Nah, we should have played her Mozart. Not my cup of tea, but, you know, important," Jamie replied.

"No, better, the Beatles or the Rolling Stones," Ramsay muttered.

"Man, you're, like, trapped in the sixties. You should set fire to your draft card and burn us out of this ice cell. Or would that not be groovy?" Jamie said.

"Oh, you're funny."

"I am funny, and anyway, every Stones album since about 1974 has been a big, fat turkey . . . Hey, that reminds me of a joke. You want to hear it? It's sort of relevant to my situation."

"It's a joke about an American who smells and has no musical taste and is imprisoned on an iceship on an alien planet?"

"Easy on the smell comment, stinky. You ain't so tasty yourself. You wanna hear the joke or not?" Jamie asked.

"Tell it."

"OK, it's about a boy who doesn't speak. Like me. Sure you want to hear it?"

"Just tell it," Ramsay said.

"OK, so there's this kid and he doesn't speak. Not from birth, not ever. His parents are wealthy and they send him to specialists and the top doctors and no one can find anything wrong with him. Years go by and his parents love him and buy him presents and he does very well at school and he goes to college, and after his first time away ever he comes home for Thanksgiving. And his mom is so excited, she burns the turkey. Anyway, the boy is sitting down to dinner and he takes a bite of the turkey and he puts down his fork and he says: 'Oh, my God, this turkey is horrible.' And everyone looks at him in amazement, and his mom says: 'You can speak? How come you never spoke before?' and the boy says: 'Well, everything's been fine until now.' "

Ramsay laughed at the joke and Jamie laughed, and both boys made so much noise that Wishaway pressed her face against the five-foot-thick ice wall to see what was happening. As he sometimes did, Jamie put his hand flat on his side of the wall and Wishaway put hers on the other side, as if they were touching.

"I miss you," Jamie said, although he knew she couldn't hear him.

"Get out the violins," Ramsay said, and Jamie had to hit him to stop him from laughing again.

When night came, the temperature in the cell dipped even further and both boys found it impossible to sleep. There were few lights on the ship, and through the furs laid down by sleeping crewmen they watched the stars and tried to figure out if any of them were ones they could see on Earth.

"Here we are in another star system. Really, if it all does go horribly wrong we've had a pretty incredible ride," Ramsay said cheerfully.

Jamie shivered a nod of the head. "You know, I've had this thought before. You're going to think this is nuts, but this is all so incredible, sometimes I think it's all some sort of hallucination, you know, because of the chemotherapy and everything. Some sort of wish-fulfillment fantasy," Jamie muttered.

Ramsay shook his head. "You wouldn't wish to be here. You could never have thought of something like this. You ever see that episode of *Buffy* like that, or *St. Elsewhere*? You'd wish for comforting things. Not stuck on a frozen iceship. You'd wish for your dad and mum to be together or to be playing baseball for the Yellow Sox or whoever."

"The White Sox or the Red Sox, you mean. Yellow Sox—sheesh. And anyway, it would be the Yankees, and I wouldn't want my dad back now. We're better off without him."

"But in your fantasy he wouldn't be such an eejit," Ramsay replied after a long pause.

Jamie did not reply. Huddled against Ramsay for

warmth, he had fallen into a fitful sleep. Ramsay grinned, and after a time he let sleep take him too.

From a deep, dreamless place Jamie awoke suddenly with a start.

His heart was pounding.

His hands were soaked with sweat.

He sat up straight.

Something was wrong. He listened. There was no sound. He looked about him. The ship seemed the same.

And yet.

And yet, it didn't feel right.

He prodded Ramsay in the ribs. "Wake up," he said, the air so cold the water vapor in his breath almost froze to his chin.

"Is that you, Jamie?"

"No, your conscience. 'Course it's me, wake up."

"What? I'd just fallen asleep."

"Something's up," Jamie said.

"Unless it's the temperature, I don't want to know," Ramsay muttered.

Jamie listened to the ship. What was it exactly that was troubl—

He stood excitedly.

"I've got it," Jamie whispered.

"What?"

"We're not moving."

Ramsay opened his eyes.

"What do you mean?" he asked groggily.

"The ship isn't moving."

Ramsay sat up, rubbed the frost off his eyelashes. "You're right. We've stopped. Do you think we've arrived at Alkhava?"

Jamie shook his head.

"Look outside. We're in the middle of the ocean. Something's happened to the boat."

Ramsay saw that they indeed were surrounded by the great void of blackness that was the sea at night. He tried to peer into the upper decks, but it was too dark.

"If we've struck a reef or something and we're sinking, the crew will just abandon us and escape in that little wooden lifeboat they have," Ramsay said.

"Do you think we're sinking?" Jamie asked.

"I don't know. I don't think so. But you're right, something's up. Get on my shoulders and see if you can push open the hatchway."

"It could be just a trick, and they're waiting for us to make a move. They'll kill us for trying to escape," Jamie said.

"What do you think we should do?" Ramsay asked.

"Your plan, I guess. These people don't seem like the trick type," Jamie said, clambering onto Ramsay's back. The hold was only seven feet high, and the hatchway above their heads was a three-foot-thick slab of ice, punctured through with air holes. Jamie wrapped his hands in the sleeve of his sweater and pushed. He shoved hard, but the hatch was impossible to move. He got off Ramsay's back and sat down to take a breath.

"It's no good, it's too heavy," Jamie said.

Ramsay thought for a moment.

"Aye, you're right, it'll be too heavy. You could never push that slab away with your arms. It has to be legs. Legs are twice as powerful as arms."

"How am I going to get my legs up there?"

"Not your legs, *my* legs. Get on my back again. Put your hands over your head. We're going to use you as a battering ram."

"Like a blocker in football?" Jamie asked.

"Like a prop in rugby is what you mean," Ramsay said.

"Forget rugby. Do me a favor, just say it's like a blocker in football."

"Don't get me started. American football is a stupid game for big weans in motorcycle helmets."

"You wouldn't say that to any member of the New York Giants."

"Any member of the Irish rugby team could kick their butts," Ramsay insisted.

"Oh, I don't think so, I've seen your Irish rugby players and they're always too drunk to kick anything."

"Just get up there," Ramsay said, grinning in the dark.

Jamie got on Ramsay's back and put his hands over his head. Ramsay crouched low and jumped up. Jamie's fists and forearms went flying into the block of ice and the hatch lifted a couple of inches.

"Ow," Jamie groaned, trying to keep his voice down.

"Did it move?" Ramsay asked.

"A little bit. Try again," Jamie said.

On the next jump the block lifted five inches. On the third crash they pushed it out completely.

Jamie climbed through to the deck above. He waited for a moment to be beaten by one of the big Alkhavan sailors and then, when no attack came, he reached down and pulled up Ramsay.

"What do you think is going on?" Jamie whispered.

Ramsay shrugged his shoulders, which he realized was a pretty pointless gesture in the darkness.

They walked gingerly through what was a storage deck on the iceship, then ducked through a hatchway into the next deck up, which was sleeping quarters for the crew. A small oil lamp was burning with a meager flame. But it was enough to illuminate what had happened.

All of the crew were lying on their backs or sides, horribly ill, conscious but having trouble breathing. Some were groaning, but most no longer had the strength to make any sound.

The sickness, or whatever it was, had clearly moved fast because only this morning most of the men had seemed in good health, although a few seemed to be complaining about something.

The boys grabbed the lantern and, on a close examination, they saw that all the Alkhavans were covered with a red rash and raised bumps that looked a lot like chicken pox. Except this was a terrible version of it that was constricting their breathing and overloading their immune systems.

Ramsay knew instantly what had happened. "I've given them all the chicken pox," he said, aghast. "I was just getting over the chicken pox when I came here."

Jamie nodded. "It looks like it."

"Harmless on our planet, but deadly here. It's like Cortéz and the Spanish," Ramsay said.

"You totally *War of the Worlds*'d them," Jamie gasped. "Or that film where they kill the aliens with ordinary water, you know."

Ramsay nodded, horrified that apparently he had indeed done this.

"Wishaway!" Jamie suddenly exclaimed.

They ran to the deck below, found Wishaway's cell, pulled up the iceblock hatch, and lowered the lantern.

"Wishaway, are you OK?" Jamie asked.

Wishaway stood and looked at them, surprised for a moment before recovering her wits.

"I am well, Lord Ui Neill, but my father and Lorca are very ill," she said anxiously.

With some difficulty they pulled Wishaway and her two cellmates out of the hold and wrapped Lorca and Callaway in thick furs. They were both weak, unable to speak, and covered in the red rash. Wishaway and the boys dabbed water on their lips and tried to make them as comfortable as possible, but both Callaway and Lorca were completely unresponsive.

"If we don't get them help, they're going to die. We've got to do something," Ramsay said.

"Maybe there's a doctor on board," Jamie said.

They scouted the small iceship, but if there *was* a doctor he, too, was incapacitated. There were about thirty crewman on the ship and every single one of them was either grievously ill and weak, or, worse, had fallen into a coma. The admiral, in a separate cabin on the highest deck, was the only one who even had the strength to speak.

"Arghal, dadaafaggass, nia kull," he managed to say before slipping into unconsciousness.

This Wishaway translated as: " 'You have bewitched us, demons, you have slain us all.' "

Jamie looked at Wishaway and then at Ramsay. Ramsay's eyes were lowered with sadness and guilt.

"I'm sorry, Wishaway. He's right," Jamie said to her.

"Why do you say this?" Wishaway asked.

"Ramsay had the chicken pox. A disease. On our world it's harmless, but here it's deadly. I think we've infected your whole planet."

"Prithee, Lord Ui Neill, surely thou canst do something for my father?" Wishaway said, slipping back into archaic English, her eyes wide with concern.

Jamie put his arm on Ramsay's shoulder, but the big Irishman shook his head mournfully. "I don't know, Jamie, I don't see what we can do."

"You'll think about it though, right?" Jamie said.

Ramsay nodded. "I'll think about it," he replied.

"He's the smartest guy I know, he'll come up with something," Jamie said to Wishaway, and tried to keep the doubt of out of his eyes.

When the morning came, none of the crew had actually died, but many seemed on the brink of death, breathing hard, wheezing. Some with blood in their spittle, others contorting their bodies, clearly in a great deal of pain.

They had moved Callaway and Lorca to the admiral's room and his big, comfortable wooden bed, but although they seemed to be doing better than the Alkhavans, things still looked grim.

The one piece of good news was the discovery of all their stuff in a locker in the admiral's cabin. As the Lord Protector had commanded, the Alkhavans had raided Basky Village and found the boys' backpacks. Everything they had brought from Earth was there, safely housed, marked with a tag, ready to be shown to the Witch Queen of Balanmanik. Their clothes, the soldering iron, their first-aid kit, the Swiss Army knife, the flashlights—everything, including the most important thing of all, the Salmon.

Ramsay picked up the Salmon and walked out of the cabin. He beckoned Jamie to follow him. They stood on the ice rail and looked at the sea as the becalmed boat twisted in the wind.

"At least there's one thing," Ramsay whispered so Wishaway wouldn't overhear.

"What?"

"We might wipe out the entire planet, but we'll be able to get home," Ramsay said, his eyes tired and gray.

Jamie looked at the alien device and didn't answer.

"We came here to help the people, not to kill them all," Jamie finally muttered, almost to himself.

Ramsay nodded and thumped his fist into his hand. "I'm sorry, Jamie, it's my fault. I should have thought about the protocols. You know, they even made the Apollo astronauts get decontaminated after the moon landing, and they visited a lifeless rock," Ramsay said, his voice breaking a little.

"It's not your fault, you know. It's nobody's fault."

"If Wishaway's father dies, it'll be like I murdered him," Ramsay said.

"No. It won't," Jamie said and tried to pat his friend on the back. But Ramsay was not in the mood for consolation. He stormed off to the front of the drifting, listless ship and stared out at the empty water.

Jamie went back into the cabin. "Any change?" he asked Wishaway, who was anxiously holding her father's hand.

"No change," she said.

"What will we do, my Lord?" Wishaway asked.

"You can always come back with us," Jamie said, in a whisper so quiet Wishaway couldn't understand him. He wanted her to come to Earth. He wanted her to be with him. But he was afraid to say it again. Instead he looked at her soft skin and her blue eyes and a thought occurred to him.

"How come you're not sick?" he asked.

"I do not know," she said.

"You've been in contact with Ramsay for the longest time; you should be the most sick of everyone. You should practically be dead."

Wishaway gave him a thin smile. "And yet, I am as you see me."

Jamie took her hand and examined it. "You're fine, there's not a thing wrong with you."

"No, Lord Ui Neill."

"Wait a minute. It must be something to do with the Salmon. Right? The Salmon. Where's Ramsay?"

Wishaway seized Jamie by the sleeve of his fleece. "What are you saying, my Lord?" she asked.

"I don't know. But the Salmon did something. Whoever used this thing in the past to jump between worlds must have known that each planet has its own pathogens and bacteria. If you're not sick, it means that the Salmon must have adjusted your body to deal with the viruses that might kill you on Earth. The same with us—we've been immunized for Altair and we didn't even know it. If you'd sneezed on us without it, we'd probably be as dead as a dodo,"

"Who is this 'dodo'?" Wishaway asked.

"Flightless bird, exterminated by sailors, but that's not important. What's important is you."

Jamie ran outside the cabin, skidded on the icy deck, caught himself, and called out: "Ramsay, get in here."

"I'm thinking," Ramsay shouted back.

"Think on this. Why isn't Wishaway sick? What did the Salmon do to protect her? And why aren't we sick? The Altairian viruses should have killed us."

Ramsay turned to look at him. "What did you say?"

"The Salmon. Think about it. You said it probably scans your DNA and rebuilds you, right? Well, what if it doesn't just rebuild you but tinkers with you a little so that you can survive on each of the worlds the Salmon lets you go to. Even the super aliens who built this thing could be killed by bacteria. Yeah?"

"I guess."

"When the Salmon rebuilds your body on each planet, it adjusts you slightly so you can cope on that world and aren't killed instantly by hostile germs. If they're advanced aliens they gotta know about germs."

"That was always the flaw of *War of the Worlds* for me," Ramsay said.

"So, what do you think?"

Ramsay's eyes were big and animated again.

"It's a nice idea. It means Wishaway will live, but I don't see how it helps us in this . . ." he began and then his voice trailed away as an idea flashed in his brain. He ran across the icy deck, fell down twice, and grabbed Jamie by the shoulders.

"I think I might have something . . . Let's hope they don't have different blood types on this planet," he said excitedly.

"What?" Jamie asked, but Ramsay pushed past him, dashed into the admiral's cabin, rummaged among their stuff, and found one of the two first-aid kits the boys had brought with them. He tore open the seal on a set of syringes and needles. He fitted the needle into the syringe and looked at Wishaway.

"I suppose you don't know if you have different blood types on this world?" he asked.

Wishaway looked puzzled.

"That's what I thought, we'll have to take the chance. At least your father should be OK. Could you prick your finger for me, please, with something hygienic if at all possible?"

Wishaway looked at Jamie. Jamie was as puzzled as her but he nodded. Wishaway grabbed Jamie's Swiss Army knife and pricked the tip of her finger. Ramsay took the finger and let a little plum-colored blood drip onto an ice table.

"You have purple blood," Jamie said, impressed.

"Be quiet," Ramsay snapped, "I'm concentrating here."

Pulling the plunger back, Ramsay vacuumed the blood into the syringe. When he was done he turned to Wishaway.

"Wishaway, I have an idea that might save your father. There's a woman from Earth history, she was the wife of the British ambassador in Turkey—Lady Montagu I think her name was. Anyway, her son had smallpox and a Turkish folk remedy was to use a needle full of a healthy person's blood on a sick person. She did it, and the kid got better and she took the idea back to England and eventually they came up with the cure for smallpox. See?"

"I do not really see, Lord Ramsay," Wishaway said unable to understand Ramsay because he was talking so fast.

"I think I agree with Jamie that the Salmon reconstituted your body for conditions on Earth. Maybe your lungs are bigger, you metabolize oxygen better, I don't know, but you are definitely immune to our viruses. You definitely have antibodies in your blood that are protecting you. What I want to do is inject those antibodies into your father and help him fight the infection."

Ramsay had been speaking quickly and although Wishaway understood English there were a lot of words she didn't get. But Jamie did. He put his arm round her shoulder and nodded.

"Try it," Jamie said.

Wishaway trusted him.

"If you think it will help, Lord Ramsay," Wishaway said doubtfully.

Ramsay lifted the furs and exposed Callaway's pale forearm.

"You ever injected anyone before?" Jamie asked.

"Nah, but I seen it done on *ER*," Ramsay said.

He pushed the needle into Callaway's arm, slowly injecting Wishaway's blood into her father. He took out the needle and put a piece of cloth over the puncture.

"What now?" Jamie asked.

"Now we wait," Ramsay said.

At first nothing happened, but then Callaway's eyebrows began to flutter, and in half an hour his pulse rate had shot way up. His cheeks reddened and his breathing became more labored.

"He's getting worse," Jamie whispered.

"No. He's fighting the infection," Ramsay said.

Within another hour the redness had gone and his pulse rate had returned to normal. The sweat was drying on his forehead and his cheeks had retaken some of their pallor.

"I think it's working," Ramsay said.

Jamie paced the cabin and said nothing, but, soon after that, Callaway looked as if he was in a deep sleep and then, suddenly, his eyes fluttered and he woke.

Two minutes later he was sitting up in bed, sipping water, and eating a very little bread and cheese.

"It's a miracle," Wishaway said to Ramsay.

"Not a miracle. Antibodies," Ramsay replied.

They injected Lorca and he recovered even quicker. An hour later, both of them were weak but in improving health.

"Well, that solves the blood-type question," Ramsay said, slapping Lorca on the back. "There was a fifty-fifty chance Wishaway would have the same blood type as her father. But you're bound to be completely different."

"Thank you, Ramsay," Lorca said, not understanding Ramsay's words at all.

"Aye, if we'd killed you, it might have made things more complicated. But since Altairians don't apparently have different purple blood types, it means we can save 'em all," Ramsay said with a gleeful laugh.

"You saved me, Lord Ramsay, and to thou—to you—I owe my life," Lorca said, a serious look on the big student's face.

"You don't owe me anything, I was the one that got you sick," Ramsay said.

"I will repay my debt, Lord Ramsay, this I swear," Lorca said.

One hour later, when Callaway had examined some of the ship and the ailing Alkhavan crew, he gingerly approached the two boys. "Lord Ramsay, will the people in Aldan be similarly affected?" he asked slowly.

"I would think so, maybe even worse, I bumped into a lot of people when I ran through the stadium on that first night. Protector Ksar even touched your neck. Remember, Jamie?"

"I remember," Jamie said, shivering at the thought. "But he seemed sick already."

"Then we must return to the city, to save our fellow Aldanese," Callaway said.

296

"Of course, we gotta go back, we gotta innoculate as many people as we can. We got a bunch of needles. We don't have to use Wishaway's blood every time. Each new patient will have the antibodies. We can save everyone," Ramsay said, excitedly, beginning to lose some of the guilt that was hanging over him.

"Everyone but the Alkhavans, Lord Ramsay," Callaway said, his eyes narrowing.

Ramsay looked at Jamie for guidance and support.

"Everyone," Jamie insisted.

"But they attacked us, they have enslaved and killed our people," Callaway said angrily.

"Listen," Ramsay began. "The Spanish conquistadors brought European diseases to the New World and the diseases practically wiped out the entire indigenous culture. Is that what you think we should do here? Wipe out the entire planet? That would a terrible crime. We can't do that."

"But they were trying to kill us, Ramsay," Wishaway replied.

Callaway and Lorca nodded with approval.

"It is true, Ramsay. They would not spare our lives if they had been given the power," Lorca said.

"You explain it to them, Jamie," Ramsay said, getting angry.

"We should not be arguing about such things, we are not near the city, we have not even turned the ship," Callaway said.

Jamie shook his head.

He knew this wasn't a theoretical question. It was something they had to decide now. This was a moral choice that had to be made. Even if morality was going to trump their own personal safety. Even if it meant that the Aldanese wouldn't be able to exterminate their enemies. The Alkhavans, for all their barbarity, were sentient creatures too. They also were intelligent, living beings with motivations, ideas, families, and a unique culture. Jamie and Ramsay weren't gods, it was not for them to decide the fate of an entire people.

But on the other hand, the reason they'd come to Altair in the first place was to help Wishaway save her city. If the Alkhavans were taken out of the equation, Aldan would be safe for decades.

The others were looking at him.

He thought about it for another minute and made a decision.

"This is what we'll do. If, when we get to the city, everyone really is sick, we'll innoculate the Aldanese first. But, and this is important, eventually we'll have to do the Alkhavans. First we'll put them on their iceships with a crew of Aldanese sailors. Then we'll set sail for Afor, and then, when they're within sight of Alkhavan territory, we'll start injecting them and we'll show them how to save themselves."

"Then what?" Callaway asked skeptically.

"Then the Aldanese sailors will get in a fast boat and sail for home."

"That will give us only a few weeks before they can remuster and attack us again," Lorca said with disgust.

"That's all the time you'll need to make the Greek Fire. When they come again, you'll be ready," Ramsay said.

"Even with the Greek Fire, we will still have to fight them. This is an opportunity to destroy them forever," Callaway barked with frustration.

"My father is right," Wishaway said coldly and stared at Jamie with all the passion of someone who had seen her home destroyed.

"Yes, we must use this gift to save Aldan. And remember there is a second, smaller fleet in Krikor. When they hear that Aldan City has been liberated, they would surely come, but if we infect them with your sickness first, then all our enemies will be thwarted. Aldan will be safe," Lorca said.

Callaway and his daughter nodded with approval.

"Maybe we could kill some of them," Ramsay muttered, beginning to waver under the moral pressure.

Jamie knew he had to be firm.

This wasn't a democracy. They wanted him to lead, well then, he would lead, this was his call. He shook his head.

"No. I've decided. That is what we are going to do. We came to this world to save your city, not to kill all of your enemies. We'll save your city, send the Alkhavans back whence they came, and we'll make the Greek Fire. If the fleet at Krikor shows up, we'll be ready for them. We'll give them a lesson they'll never forget and then we'll go home," Jamie said firmly.

Ramsay nodded, and then, reluctantly, Wishaway and Lorca nodded, too.

Callaway wanted to object, but he saw now that he could not. Jamie and Ramsay had saved his life. They had laid low his enemies. He saw that he had been mistaken about them. When they had first appeared he had lacked faith in their abilities. But now he realized that they were not mere children. They *were* the Lords Ui Neill, come from Earth again to rescue his land.

He bowed his head and looked at the two boys.

"My Lords, it will be as you wish," he said with deference.

Jamie turned to Wishaway. "We have to get back. Can you pilot this big boat with just the five of us?"

It was a much larger vessel than she had ever sailed. It was made of ice, it was square-rigged, but she immediately assented.

She could at least try.

No, she would do more than try.

She would do it.

"I will have us back in Aldan within two days," she said.

Wishaway stood by herself on the prow of the ship.

"You look like Kate Winslet in *Titanic*," Jamie said,

coming up next to her, but of course she had never heard of Kate Winslet or *Titanic*. She shrugged her shoulders.

Jamie looked at her, but it was too much to explain.

He stood next to her awkwardly for a while, then, sensing she wanted to be by herself, he went back to Ramsay and Lorca, who were arguing about something.

Wishaway watched him go.

Good. One of the reasons she'd come to the prow of the ship was to be alone. She had told them she had to check the trim, but really it was to be in a place to think away from the boys and the sick men.

They were going fast enough to generate a huge bow wave, and white spray was bouncing off the ice and partially freezing before plunging back into the sea.

The rigging was tight, the breeze steady, the sails taut. Behind her, Ramsay and Lorca were now looking at a chart, Jamie was at the wheel, her father was pulling on a rope and shaking a reef out of the main sail.

She stared at the horizon.

The sea had lost its iodine complexion and was now a blue-green color.

She recognized these waters.

They were getting closer to Aldan.

A *juula* was swimming beside the ship, its big snout out of the waves looking for scraps. On previous ocean voyages she would have run to her cabin and thrown it a piece of bread or meat, but this time she hardly even noticed the large reptile.

"*Huusha ca, Aldan,*" she whispered to herself. "Nearly home."

The boys started laughing. She turned to look at them. Jamie was sticking his tongue out. Ramsay was pointing at something through the decks beneath his feet. Lorca started sticking his tongue out too.

She gazed back at the sea. The sails were full and they were making good speed with the northerly gale.

Yes, nearly home.

Jamie's laughter drifted forward.

Jamie.

She was thinking about what he'd said in the cabin. What he was going to do when they got back to Aldan.

Once the city was secured, Jamie said that they were returning to their own world.

She had heard him quite clearly.

"*We'll give them a lesson they'll never forget and then we'll go home.*"

Yes, he had kissed her, and for a time she had thought that there was something between them, a growing flower of mutual feelings, but now she realized that she had been mistaken.

They were not like the Ui Neills who had come centuries ago and sent one of their own back with the Salmon. Those men had been hunted, on the run, they had nowhere else to go. But Jamie and Ramsay had lives and families on Earth. It was natural that they would wish to return. They would not be staying here to live their lives and lead the people. They would be here only for a short while.

When their task was done, Jamie and Ramsay would desert them.

And then the people would have to find leaders of their own.

And if not the Ui Neills, who?

Her father was an old man, still recovering from the plague. Lorca was a foreigner.

Who did that leave?

The *juula's* black eye stared at her.

"Nahsta hura juula," she said. No food today.

The *juula* waggled its lizard flippers in disgust, spat water from its blowhole, and swam away from the ship, hoping for more amenable sailors in a new vessel. She smiled. The first time she had seen one of those creatures was on her father's diplomatic mission to Perovan. Years ago. She'd been so excited. The world seemed so amazing, so full of possibilities. She had only been a little girl. She was still only a little girl.

Wasn't she?

Her thoughts began to coalesce.

Aldan had had female generals in the past.

Hurga of Krikor had defeated the Kafrikillans at the battle of the Far Deep. And once Morgana of the Red Hand, the adopted daughter of Lilya and Morgan Ui Neill, had led a raiding party all the way to the Cloister of the Warrior Monks in Balan. And, of course, her own mother had become a respected teacher—one of the few female professors at the university.

Why not a woman?

Why not her?

That would show him she was not someone to be trifled with. That would show him.

She frowned as Jamie laughed at another one of Ramsay's jokes. Jamie was guffawing so hard, drool was coming out of his mouth.

Wishaway wrinkled her nose in contempt. There was something very childish about both of them.

Lorca threw a bucket over the side and, a moment later, hauled it up from the ocean floor. Lorca—he was more of an adult than either of them.

"Black sand and white shells!" he yelled to Jamie.

Black sand and white shells, Wishaway thought. Those boys wouldn't know what that meant, but she did. It meant they were on the Rejjo Bank. They were closer than she thought. In two or three hours they would sight the coast. An hour or two after that they would be at the city.

Yes, indeed, the time for frivolity was drawing to an end.

They needed a plan of attack. They needed someone to step up and decide what they were going to do.

She clenched her fingers together.

It is my responsibility, she thought.

She turned and walked back along the sticky, freezing

deck of the iceship. Ramsay and Lorca were giggling because Jamie had stuck his tongue to the frozen steering wheel.

Wishaway brushed the hair from her face.

"Look at him, Wishaway. He's gone and stuck his tongue," Ramsay said.

Wishaway stared at Jamie. How could she have thought there could be an emotional attachment between the two of them? The idea was ludicrous. He was a mere boy. He was from another world, yes, a Lord, yes, but a boy nonetheless. And although she was only slightly older than him in chronological time, she was clearly well ahead of him in maturity.

Lorca patted Jamie on the back.

She looked at the prince of Oralands, and their eyes met. Lorca smiled at her for a moment. Wishaway cleared her throat.

"Enough of this foolishness," she said. "We will be at the city in a few hours; we must begin making preparations for the fight."

"Why now? Isn't it better to sneak in after dark?" Ramsay said.

"No. We cannot wait until nightfall. We must act quickly if we are to save the population. We will sail into the harbor and attack the weakened forces. When the Alkhavans are destroyed, you will begin the process of helping my people."

"I tat I wuttth in chaarge heuh," Jamie protested.

"This is not the time for levity, my Lord. We must prepare for battle," Wishaway said sternly.

"Chill out. It's hours away yet," Ramsay said.

"He ruughtt, taak uh eeeesssy," Jamie added.

"No. We must prepare for battle, now," Wishaway said in such a commanding way as to make Ramsay jump and to wipe the smiles off all their faces.

Chapter XI
THE ATTACK

I N ALDAN AN ATTACK was the last thing on the mind of Protector Ksar as he lay on the fur-lined wooden bed in the president of the Council's house.

Everything had gone wrong.

His entire army had fallen ill with the plague. Himself included. No one had actually died, but it would not be long. Initially it had seemed harmless, everyone had come out in a mysterious rash, but it had progressed quickly—burning, itching, paralyzing—and now few had even the strength to drink or eat.

Hashat tal, they called it. The red death.

If the plague did not kill them, eventually they would starve to death. Ironic, to starve in the midst of such bounty.

At first he had thought the illness of his troops was some sort of Aldanese secret weapon. But the locals had succumbed just as easily as his own men. If it was a weapon on their part, it was a suicide machine.

He writhed under the furs, struggled out of bed and peered at his body in the looking glass. It was covered with a crimson rash and raised bumps that tormented the skin.

He drank a little wine and winced as it burned on the passage down his throat.

"A disaster," he muttered to himself.

And as if the ill luck of his army and his own personal failure hadn't been enough, a message had arrived by *ranta* from his sister in Balanmanik.

The creature was looking at him from its perch in the corner. It had a mocking, arrogant air he did not like.

"Foul thing," he said, and weakly threw a piece of stale bread at it, but it didn't move. It licked its leathery wings with its long tongue and hissed at him.

He picked up the note and reexamined that spiteful, spidery handwriting. No one could write in as small a script as the Witch Queen.

Since his capture of the city, he had been sending two sets of correspondence. Official reports to the Lord Protector in Afor and unofficial dispatches by *ranta* to his sister.

In the depth of his sickness, her latest reply had been a crushing blow. It had taken all his strength just to unroll the scroll from its carrybox on the *ranta*'s thick leg. Her words, written in the black blood of a *scarri*, struck deep into his heart:

> My brother, I will give you no warrants of pity. You have undoubtedly been beaten by some subterfuge of the Ui Neills. The fact that you have failed in your mission to take Aldan, the fact that the Lord Protector's army will be lost,

the fact that your disgrace will be known in the basest tavern, the fact that you will soon die, all of this is meaningless. Your biggest mistake was your first. You should never have sent the Uí Neills and their "toys" (as you foolishly called them in your letter) on the same iceship. Do you not see, brother, that if your entire army has succumbed, so has your admiral and the sailors of the Uí Neills' ship? The Earth lords are undoubtedly free and what we sought from them is lost. Incompetent man. What we needed of the Uí Neills was the Salmon. The Salmon of Knowledge. The Salmon of Power. The device that enables its user to leap between worlds. We sisters have been seeking it for hundreds of years and you had it within your grasp and let it go. You die as you lived, brother—a knave and a fool.

He reread the end and laughed bitterly.

He crumpled the note and threw it at the creature. This time the *ranta* flapped to the window ledge, but did not fly away, trained as it was to wait for a reply.

"A reply, yes," he muttered.

Protector Ksar took up a piece of paper, ink, and a quill. He dipped the wooden quill and, in a shaky hand, began a response.

My dearest sister, the fact that I am not privy to the plans of your brood is the reason you do not now have this Salmon on its way to you by ranta wing. Secrecy is the disease of your order and this is your failure, not mine. You will be happy to know that I am not dead yet. Nor do I plan to die anytime soon. Indeed, dearest one, I vow here and now that I will live to see you abase yourself at my feet, to see you humbled, to see your entire order bow before me as their new Lord Protector. Perhaps when that day comes I will show you more mercy than you have afforded me. Until then, dear sister, I bid farewell.

He blotted the note, rolled it up, and put it in the container on the *ranta*'s foot.

"Go," he said to the big black creature.

It hopped to the window, stretched its leathery wings, and lifted off into the Aldanese dawn.

"Well, well, the sun is rising, I made it through another night," Ksar muttered to himself then and noticed something on the horizon that caught his eye. He stared at it for a moment and caught his breath.

"Krama!" he yelled.

After a long pause the haggard deputy appeared at the door.

"Sir?" he replied weakly.

"Do we have any men left who can stand?" Ksar asked.

"Some in your personal guard have not yet fully fallen," Krama croaked.

"How many?"

"A platoon, no more," Krama muttered.

"That may be enough," Ksar said to himself and smiled. The Lords Ui Neill, like his sister, had made the mistake of underestimating him.

"Ready the men," Ksar said.

The gaunt lieutenant shook his head wearily.

Ksar anticipated his deputy's question and led him to the window.

"Look," Ksar said.

And now they could both could see it clearly.

The iceship was coming back.

They sailed into the great bay of Aldan expecting the worst. Wishaway's seriousness had snapped Jamie from his levity and he knew they had better prepare themselves.

Wishaway was armed with twin steel knives with which she had been trained since her early childhood; Lorca had a pole with an evil-looking hook on the end of it. Wishaway gave the two inexperienced Earth boys stout wooden staves—weapons that would do some damage to a weakened attacker but also wouldn't hurt the user too badly if mishandled.

Before they had even docked, they knew something was wrong, because there was smoke in parts of the upper city. Smoke meant fire and fire meant that wood or some other valuable combustible commodity was being destroyed.

They went through the harbor mouth and stood behind the ice walls of the ship, ready to duck for cover in case of attack. But no one hailed them or rained arrows or launched catapults.

It was eerie.

Row upon row of Alkhavan iceships lay silent and lifeless.

Wishaway barked instructions as Lorca and Ramsay turned the big wheel and sailed for the quay nearest the shore.

She ordered the sails dropped and they drifted alongside the long stone east pier of the inner harbor, the stern touching first and then the rest of the ship slamming slowly sideways into the quay. Ice was shearing off and making a terrible groaning noise as friction slowed the boat to a shuddering halt.

They tensed and waited for an attack, but again no assault came.

Jamie knew that they wouldn't keep the element of surprise for long. He looked at Wishaway. "Well?" he said.

She nodded. "Let's go," he said, and leaped off the side of the ship. Wishaway immediately jumped after him, annoyed a little that she hadn't been the first back onto her home soil.

The others followed, drawing their weapons.

They jogged cautiously along the pier but didn't see a

single soul until they reached the harbormaster's house. Inside they heard groans. When they broke a window and looked through, they saw half a dozen Alkhavan warriors lying prostrate on the ground, covered with the marks of chicken pox and very ill.

"We have to help them," Ramsay said.

"No," Wishaway replied. "Our own people first. Only when the city is secured can we assist our enemies."

Ramsay turned to Jamie to back him up.

But Jamie understood the sense of Wishaway's order. Now was not the time to have a bunch of marauding Alkhavans running around.

"Later," he said.

They made their way up through the docks and into the lower city.

The scene was one of devastation. The streets were littered with rotting food, dead *drayas* and *kalahars*, sick Alkhavan soldiers, spilled wine, and looted goods. Clothes, furniture, jewelry, rugs, china, tapestries—all in the process of being transported to the ships but hastily abandoned as the plague took over. The well-loved trees had been cut down and almost all the beautiful glass and wood sculptures were gone. Not to harvest their materials—this was just sheer vandalism.

Wishaway's heart was breaking from the horror around her. She didn't want to let it show. But Jamie knew her only too well.

"Are you OK?" he asked.

"I—I am well, Lord Ui Neill," she managed.

They threaded through the cobbled streets into the higher portions of the town, the sinister quiet punctuated only by the wind, howling *seechas*, and the shrieking calls of the nests of wild *rantas* near the sea.

It reminded Jamie of one of those episodes of *The Twilight Zone* when somehow all the people of the Earth get spirited away, leaving only one lonely man. Those episodes never turned out well.

At one of the city reservoirs they found several soldiers who had drowned themselves, perhaps trying to ease the pain or maybe deliberately committing suicide to escape the terrible suffering of the pox.

"It's awful," Wishaway said.

Jamie nodded.

"Do you want to go on?" he asked.

"We must find Ksar," Wishaway said firmly.

"Where do you think he'll be?" Ramsay asked.

"The Council residences are in the upper city," Wishaway replied, her eyes cold and determined.

"Let's go check it out, then," Jamie said.

They left the drowned Alkhavans and headed up the steep cobblestone streets.

"It is a shame, my Lords, that you cannot see our city in better circumstances," Callaway said, holding his nose against the smell of destruction.

"In a week or two, everything will be back to normal," Jamie said reassuringly. "I'll see to that."

Wishaway looked at him strangely for a moment. *He will see to that?* she thought. Surely *he* was going back?

Jamie grinned at her. "Come on, we should keep moving," he said.

The upper city was where the university, the fort, the Council president's residence, and the Old White Tower of Aldan were located. It was the logical place to find Protector Ksar.

It had been the most heavily guarded section of the city, and as they got closer they found more Alkhavans.

At a gateway, a large Alkhavan officer was still manning his post. He was propped up in a chair, but he stood when he saw the intruders.

"Arrag, as amata," he demanded, and lifted a heavy-looking wooden spear with a bronze point tied to the end.

Without waiting for a reply, he summoned the last of his strength and hurled it at the approaching party.

The spear crossed the air between the Alkhavan and them faster than anyone was expecting. It swished toward Callaway's chest and would surely have killed him or given him a mortal wound, had Jamie not shoved him aside. The spear glided between the old Aldanese man and the Earth boy and clattered to the cobblestones.

Holding his staff in both hands, Jamie ran at the Alkhavan. The soldier pulled a knife from his belt and lunged clumsily at him, but Jamie dodged the thrust, stepped to one side, and in one swift movement brought the staff down on the Alkhavan's head, knocking him to the ground.

He gurgled for a moment and then lost consciousness.

"Nice moves," Ramsay said with admiration.

"Thou didst well, Lord Ui Neill," Wishaway added, surprised at Jamie's deftness. He may have never used the weapon before, but he was obviously a fast learner.

Through the gate, in the next courtyard, they saw four people lying on the ground. Three were Alkhavan soldiers and the fourth, an Aldanese soldier, who'd obviously been captured and was being led away for interrogation. The pox had infected them, overtaken them quickly, and they had fallen as they walked. The Alkhavans too weak to kill their prisoner, the Aldanese soldier too weak to escape.

"Let's try our technique on your soldier," Jamie said.

"I will attempt it," Callaway said.

He pricked his finger with a knife, drew a little blood, and sucked that blood into the syringe. He injected the antibody-rich blood into the Aldanese soldier. They didn't have to wait long. Within five minutes, his eyes began to flutter and within ten he was strong enough to speak.

"I'll say one thing about your people, they fall fast, but they heal fast too," Ramsay said to Callaway.

Callaway nodded and questioned the soldier, who told them in a whispering argot (that neither Jamie, Lorca, or Ramsay could understand) that the plague had hit almost immediately after they had left in the iceship and then moved with devastating thoroughness through the population. Most of the Alkhavans were in a barracks at the fort or on their ships, most of the Aldanese were still in the arena. The soldier paused for breath while Wishaway translated what he'd said.

"What now?" Callaway asked, looking around at the plague-ridden city, anxious to begin his work but still deferring to Jamie.

Jamie did not hesitate. "I think we've seen enough. There is not much opposition here and what there is we can handle. We have to save the people. That's got to be our number-one priority."

Callaway nodded. "What do you wish me to do, Lord Ui Neill?" he asked.

"You'll have to begin an immediate program of inoculation. You've got to do the whole of Aldan and you've got to do it fast. We have a replacement pack of needles and three spare syringes. Is there any way you can make about a dozen more syringes, maybe out of wood or glass or something?"

Callaway looked at the syringe. He nodded. "I have devices such as these that may do, at the university, in the natural sciences room."

"The *sacha* jars. I know where they are," Lorca said excitedly.

Jamie nodded. "Get going, Lorca. You'll have to get them. Be careful, take precautions, this city is still pretty dangerous. When you get 'em, meet Callaway at the arena."

"I will do as ye ask, Lord Ui Neill," Lorca said, then nodded to Ramsay and ran up the hill in the direction of the university.

"I will go to the arena and begin the process of inoculation. Will you come with me, Wishaway?" Callaway asked.

She shook her head. "No, Father, we must find and capture Protector Ksar," she said.

Callaway reluctantly bowed. She was almost completely beyond his control now.

"I will go, then," he said, and affected a limping gait that he hoped would draw sympathy but alas did not. When he saw that his daughter really was not coming he muttered a curse and hurried to the arena to begin the process of saving his people. Wishaway's boldness and disobedience could be dealt with when the immediate crisis was over.

"So the three of us are going after Ksar?" Jamie asked her.

"Yes," Wishaway asserted.

"Who made that call?" Jamie asked.

"I did," Wishaway said firmly.

"Really?" Jamie said with a hint of a smile on his face.

"Really," Wishaway said with no smile at all on hers.

They climbed the rest of the steep hill in silence.

In this part of the upper city there were no people in the streets at all. Looting, too, had been minimal and everything was weirdly orderly.

The unfortunate Alkhavans were dying in their ships, the unfortunate Aldanese dying together in the arena.

It was a ghost town. But not yet a literal one.

Apparently they had arrived in time to prevent the pandemic from killing everyone.

The children entered a huge courtyard that led to the large, stone fort next to the White Tower of Aldan.

"Look at the tower. It's practically identical to the one on Muck Island," Ramsay said.

"This one's much taller," Jamie disagreed.

"Architecturally, it's identical."

"I don't know about that."

Ramsay muttered something about an "uneducated Yank" and Jamie responded with a rumble about a "crazy Paddy."

"This is the oldest part of the city. Aldan grew up around the White Tower, which has existed here long before our country was born," Wishaway said to silence them.

"It's pretty tall, isn't it?" Jamie said.

"It is the tallest building in the Middle Isles," Wishaway added with satisfaction.

They were relaxed now. They had encountered only a few Alkhavans and those were hardly any threat, all having succumbed to the terrible plague.

Jamie had his staff on his shoulder, Ramsay was dragging his along the ground, Wishaway had put away her knives.

The sun was shining brightly, glinting off the marble-like stone and making their eyes hurt under its glare. The city had an air of deathly stillness.

"Is the White Tower where you think Ksar is?" Jamie asked.

"No, not the White Tower. It is a ruin. We no longer even use it as a lighthouse. Sometimes we keep undesirables there. No, he will be in the Council president's house or the fort, if he, too, has not retreated to his ship."

The courtyard was empty but for a few upturned carts, a dozen prostrate Alkhavan soldiers, and a scattering of looted clothes, wine jugs, and shopware.

"So where's the president's house?" Jamie asked.

"Through the gates and up the stone steps," Wishaway said. "My father used to take me there often."

"Well, it should be pretty straightforward. Ksar is bound to be as sick as the rest of them," Ramsay said.

"His sister is the Witch Queen of Balanmanik, and his master is the Lord Protector of Alkhava. I would not so easily count out Protector Ksar," Wishaway replied cautiously.

"Unless his sister and his boss are genetic scientists, they ain't gonna be able to help him," Ramsay said with a laugh.

"Yeah, but we should still be careful," Jamie said, spotting that the other two had relaxed their guard.

Just then, Wishaway noticed an odd thing out of the corner of her eye. She stopped, turned, and examined the tableau: soldiers, cart, courtyard, and looted equipment.

What was it?

Something about the soldiers. They were all dressed in black, which meant they were an elite unit. Some were masked, which meant the elite of the elite.

But that was not completely unusual.

What was strange was that all of the Alkhavans lying in the courtyard had long bows or crossbows. And not just crossbows, crossbows with bolts sprung and ready to be fired at a moment's notice. She didn't like the look of that at all.

"Lord Ui Neill," she whispered.

"Yes?"

"Marry, I prithee take yon notice of this," Wishaway whispered. Jamie noticed that she always slipped back into Shakespeare talk when she got nervous. And that made him nervous.

"Why are you whispering?" Jamie asked.

Wishaway unsheathed her daggers.

"What's wrong?" Jamie insisted.

"These men, look at them," Wishaway whispered.

"What?" Jamie asked.

"Their weapons are primed."

Jamie saw the situation immediately. The blood chilled in his veins.

"It's a trap," he whispered.

"Come on you two, hurry up," Ramsay shouted cheerfully.

 321

"Make for the gate slowly. We got to get out of here. Don't do anything hasty," Jamie whispered.

"What?"

Jamie stared at Ramsay and tried to communicate his fears with a look. The big Irishman saw that something was up.

"What is it? What's wrong?" he yelled, but before Jamie could reply there was a whooshing sound and a hail of arrows and crossbow bolts flew at them as the men in the courtyard suddenly stood and fired their weapons.

It was close to point-blank range, but luckily the arrows skittered harmlessly into the cobblestones in front of, behind, and beside them. The most dangerous bolt was one that embedded itself in Ramsay's backpack.

The Alkhavans were weakened by plague and unable to put much tension into their bowstrings or strength into their aim; however, there were at least a dozen of them and sooner or later they'd do some damage. It would only take a few fortunate shots to kill all of them.

"Over here!" Jamie yelled, grabbing Wishaway and running with her behind the overturned delivery cart.

The men began to weakly reload their bows.

Jamie and Wishaway dived behind the cart, followed a second later by Ramsay.

Thock, thock, thock, thock. The arrows flew into the thick wooden sides of the vehicle.

"They're coming," Ramsay said, and they could see through gaps in the wood that the men were moving in on them in a semicircular pattern. There was no way to escape. They were trapped between the cart and the city wall.

The men were close, fifty yards at the most, and Jamie knew that if they tried to run back to the lower city, they'd be shot for sure.

"How many?" Jamie breathlessly asked Ramsay.

"A lot," Ramsay replied.

"That's helpful," Jamie said.

"That's my forte, being helpful. The Boy Scouts gave me a badge for helpfulness."

"What do you think we should do, my Lords?" Wishaway asked.

"I don't know," Ramsay said desperately.

Jamie grimaced. He had to make a plan and make it right now. He remembered something Thaddeus told him about the army: A poor decision taken immediately was better than a good decision taken too late.

"We have to take the battle to the enemy," Jamie said. "If we stay here, they'll kill us for sure."

Wishaway noticed the determined expression in Jamie's blue-green eyes. He had never looked more adamant or more handsome. They were outnumbered four to one, but there was no fear in his face at all.

"Thou art correct, Lord Ui Neill. If we attempt to run back the way we came, they will pick us off," Wishaway said.

"Whereas if we rush them . . ." Ramsay said.

"Let's get these backpacks off, for starters," Jamie muttered.

The two Earth boys unhooked the heavy backpacks and let them fall to the ground.

Ramsay grabbed his staff in both hands, Wishaway held her daggers, Jamie got ready to swing his staff.

Through the cracks in the wood they saw the bowmen moving closer and closer. When they were about twenty feet away, Jamie whispered, "Now," and ran at them, his staff above his head. Wishaway was close behind, her knives glinting murderously in the sunlight; Ramsay, no less enthusiastic, swung his staff wildly in the rear.

For a few seconds, the Alkhavans were stunned by the suddenness of the attack. A few seconds was all the children needed.

Wishaway leaped at the nearest bowman, a large blond-haired man with a bushy beard and a rash of chicken pox over the left side of his face. Her knife struck him in the chest, and he fell backward into another archer, knocking him down. A third crossbow man in the midst of loading dropped his weapon and tried pulling out a small bronze sword, but Wishaway was faster and stronger than the plague-weakened Alkhavan, and her knife slashed at and cut his throat. Purple blood spilled from the wound, and the soldier gargled horribly for a moment and then slumped forward, dead.

The archer who'd fallen grabbed her leg and dragged her to the ground. But Wishaway was ready. She dropped on him, stabbing him in the stomach with her left-handed knife blade.

Ramsay meanwhile, swinging his big staff, smashed into three of the Alkhavans, knocking away their crossbows and thumping into their arms and chests.

"For Ulster and for Ireland!" Ramsay yelled, and drove the point of his staff into the face of a sandy-haired, black-eyed Alkhavan.

Seeing Wishaway fall sent Jamie into a rage. He swung the staff and nearly cut the nearest bowman in half, instead knocking him completely unconscious.

He smashed the face of a second, breaking his nose and knocking him onto his back.

"For Harlem and New York City!" he yelled at the top of his lungs in such a terrifying voice that two more Alkhavans dropped their weapons and hurriedly limped away to the lower city.

In less than thirty seconds, three of the Alkhavans were dead, five more were wounded on the ground, and two had run.

But by now the remaining three Alkhavans had had time to draw their side weapons—ugly bronze short swords with hooks on the hilts.

The nearest one lunged at Wishaway in a clumsy sweep that she easily dodged, and parried, bronze clanging off bronze in a clash of sparks. She brought both her knives together, slamming them into the pommel of the Alkhavan's sword and knocking it out of his hand. The weakened Alkhavan groaned, stumbled, and fell to his knees. He was so sick, Wishaway didn't even have to kill him but merely kicked him in the back, sending him clattering to the ground.

A big, red-haired Alkhavan tried to skewer Ramsay with a spear, but missed and drove the weapon fast into the ground. Ramsay kicked at the spear, broke it in two, and thrust his staff into the man's belly. The man spat frothing purple blood from his mouth and dropped to his knees.

Ramsay hit him on the head and knocked him onto his back.

Jamie swung his staff at the last Alkhavan standing, but the soldier blocked the blow with a large wooden two-handed ax.

Jamie dodged as the Alkhavan launched an attack of his own, the ax slashing awkwardly into Jamie's left arm. For one horrible moment he thought it had been amputated.

He staggered backward. "No, not again!" he cried.

"Look out!" Wishaway called as, with an almighty burst of strength, the Alkhavan soldier raised the ax above his head and began to swing it down in an attempt to crush Jamie's skull.

Jamie was dazed, still looking in wonder at his left arm. Thoughts racing through his brain: What did it mean to lose an arm? What did it mean to get it back again? What had it meant to him in New York, and why had he reacted the way he had? The surfer girl Bethany Hamilton had surfed again. The climber boy Aron Ralston had climbed again. What had prevented him from moving on? Jamie was paralyzed by thought.

His arm.

He looked at it and saw that it was only a glancing flesh wound. A flesh wound, but still he didn't move.

The ax was searing toward his head.

"Look out!" Wishaway screamed.

I'm not the surfer girl and I'm not the climber guy, Jamie thought. *I'm not anyone else. I'm me. Jamie. But more than that:* "I am the Lord Ui Neill!" he yelled, and brought his staff up just in time to parry the blow coming.

"Get back!" he shouted, and hurled the blunted point of his staff at the startled Alkhavan soldier. The soldier was an elite member of Protector Ksar's personal guard, and a day ago he could have easily beaten a thirteen-year-old boy. He had killed several children on raids to Kafrikilla and Frantan.

But with the plague destroying his central nervous system and weakening him, all he could do was raise the ax handle in a defensive posture in front of his face.

Jamie's blood was up.

His rage drove his staff head through the Alkhavan's bronze handle, and the heavy blunt end smacked into the man's temple.

327

The soldier dropped the ax and fell to his knees.

"Who?" the soldier asked as he wobbled there for a moment.

"I am the Lord Ui Neill, Laird of Muck, Inheritor of Morgan of the Red Hand," Jamie spoke into the man's ear.

The Alkhavan soldier looked at him for a second more.

His eyes blinked twice.

"Bluuuuhhhh," he said and fell over unconscious.

"That's them all," Ramsay said looking at the wounded to make sure they were all staying down.

"I think you are right, Lord R—" Wishaway began, but then screamed as the masked Alkhavan she had kicked to the ground suddenly leaped at her and pushed a knife against her throat.

"Let her go!" Jamie yelled.

The Alkhavan soldier took off his black mask to reveal a face covered in red splotches and an orange rash.

Disfigured as the man was, Jamie and Ramsay instantly recognized him.

"Protector Ksar," they said together.

Ksar nodded and gathered his strength. "The Lords Ui Neill," he muttered in a mocking voice, his eyes weak, narrow, squinting from the morning sun.

"Let her go," Jamie said again.

Ksar shook his head.

"These were the last of my warriors," Ksar said. "The

only ones well enough to fight. Ye have destroyed all of us with your devilry," Ksar said, and pushed the knife a little deeper against Wishaway's skin.

"Kill her and you die," Jamie said, lifting his staff and coming closer.

"One step further, Lord Ui Neill, and she will die," Ksar said, and coughed sickeningly.

Jamie froze.

"Get him, Jamie," Wishaway said.

Jamie moved forward, but Ksar stopped him. "I have nothing to lose, Lord Ui Neill. Do not tempt a dead man," Ksar said.

"What do you want?" Jamie asked.

"I have received a message from my sister on *ranta* wing," Ksar said weakly.

"How nice for you," Jamie replied, and looked at Ramsay, trying to signal him to start moving behind the Alkhavan general. Ramsay took the hint and slowly began circling toward the cart.

Ksar coughed again and went on. "I made one mistake. Only one in my capture of this city and thee."

"Yes?" Jamie asked to keep him talking.

Ksar pushed the point of the knife deeper into Wishaway's throat. "I should never have sent the magical objects with ye on the iceship. I should have kept them for myself. My sister informs me that one of those objects is what she and her kind have been seeking all these years, all these centuries," Ksar said.

Jamie shrugged. "I don't know what you're talking about," he said.

"I have made a mistake, but that mistake will be corrected. Give me the thing that ye call the Salmon. Give it to me, or the girl dies," Ksar said.

He was a very sick man, but both boys knew he still had the strength to stab Wishaway and kill her.

"The Salmon? What do you mean *the Salmon?*"

"Quickly, Lord Ui Neill, I have no time for games. My sister says that ye will have it. And *she* does not make mistakes."

Ksar pulled Wishaway's hair back and pressed the point of the dagger against the artery in her throat.

"Don't give it to him, Jamie," she said. "It will cure him of the plague."

And he'll be free to run amok on our planet, get guns, weapons, anything he wants, Jamie thought.

"I will kill her," Ksar said.

Jamie knew he had no choice.

He ran to the cart, opened his backpack, reached inside, and took out the Salmon.

"I'm sorry, Ramsay, I have to do it," he said.

Ramsay nodded grimly. "I understand," he said.

Jamie threw the Salmon to Protector Ksar. He let it drop at his feet and then, still keeping the knife at Wishaway's throat, he bent down slowly and picked it up.

"Now let her go," Jamie said.

Ksar examined the device and noticed the jewelled button on the side.

"Let her go. We gave you the Salmon, now let Wishaway go," Jamie said.

Ksar laughed. "*You* are the Lord Ui Neill? You are the savior of Aldan? You are the Inheritor of Morgan of the Red Hand? You are none of these things. You are a fool."

Wishaway screamed and tried to break free, but Ksar held her tight.

"Good-bye, mighty Lords," he snarled, grinning at the two boys.

He pressed the jeweled button on the Salmon, and the atmosphere around them began to vibrate. Jamie ran forward, dived at the distorting forms in the miraging air, crumpled through the vector where they had been, and hit his head hard on the ground, retaining consciousness just long enough to see Ksar and Wishaway completely disappear.

Chapter XII
THE RETURN

THE COLD PERFUME of absence. The blue salt wind. A phrase repeating itself like a melody. The cradle rocks over the abyss. The cradle rocks over the abyss.

The cradle rocks—

The cradle . . .

Eyelashes.

Light.

Machines.

And there's no one here.

No nurses.

No mom.

Because you've woken early. Earlier than they were expecting. A winking star guarding the windows. Eyelashes spun from the moonlight.

No dad, certainly. Closing a house right on Puget Sound, has to be there to sign the contract, smack on the water, once in a lifetime opportunity, don't worry, son, we'll have you out, when you're better . . .

"Life is precarious. The cradle rocks over the abyss," was what the priest said, "but in the sweet hereafter we will find our reward."

The eager young priest who must have gotten that line from a book, because it sounded like stolen knowledge rather than learned wisdom.

And it was fine except that you didn't really believe in the sweet hereafter anymore.

"But if death is annihilation?" you asked him, quoting from your own book. "If evolution's right?"

"Darwin believed in God," the priest said with a kindly smile, and held your hand and prayed with your mother while, in the room next door, the surgeons scrubbed up to their elbows.

And you were too weak to reply. But you knew. The logic was inescapable.

Once you believe in evolution, you're sunk.

Evolution tells us that we were descended from simpler forms, from lemur-like creatures who hid from the dinosaurs; and before that fish; and before that blobs of single-celled life forms in the primordial soup. Do fish go to heaven when they die? Do frogs? When you take the cold medicine, does the cold virus go to heaven when it dies?

We were that virus a billion years ago. How, then, did we evolve a heaven?

What did that thought leave you with?

Fear.

And then it came.

The blackness.

The abyss.

The priest's words.

Your mother's kiss.

The anaesthetist counting.

"Five, four, three . . ."

There was no flutter of wings, Thaddeus.

Death isn't an angel. Death is a bulldozer flattening a shantytown. Death is an eraser . . .

Then the moonlight.

Machines.

Noise.

"You're awake," a voice says.

You don't reply.

"You made it through. No, don't try to open your eyes."

You open your eyes and where your arm was is now a shroud of bandages.

Another absence. What do they do with it? Do they burn it? Preserve it?

"I'll get your mom, she's just outside."

"Jamie."

A voice . . .

"Jamie."

"My arm, gone."

"No, Jamie. It's only a flesh wound."

He blinked.

"Jamie. Get up."

A flesh wound.

And he wasn't in Columbia Presbyterian a year ago, waking after his life-saving, life-changing surgery.

He was on another world, light-years from Earth, with his arm back and alive to fight another day.

And that's all you could do.

Live and fight and live again.

"Jamie!" Ramsay yelled.

"I'm OK," Jamie said and struggled to his feet.

"Jeez, you had a nasty fall. I think you knocked yourself out, are you OK?" Ramsay asked.

"I'm OK," Jamie replied, shielding his eyes from the harsh sunlight.

"Sure?"

"Yes," he said, and this time he meant it. Arm or no arm, speaking or not speaking, he lived and someone cared for him and perhaps that was enough.

Someone cared for him.

"Wishaway!" Jamie yelled.

"We'll get her. Come on, let's get cracking," Ramsay said, and grabbed a crossbow from a fallen Alkhavan soldier. He leaned it against his shoulder and sighted it along his arm.

"What are you doing?" Jamie asked.

Ramsay loaded a bolt in the crossbow, cocked it, and aimed at the place Wishaway and Ksar had just been.

"If I'm right about the Salmon, it won't work from just anywhere. The towers were built for a reason. The one we know about on Earth, the three here on Altair."

"What three? What are you talking about?"

"Didn't you listen to Wishaway when she was telling us

about the planet? Probably too moon-eyed. There's three towers on Altair. This one here, the White Tower; the one on her island, where we landed; and she also said there's one in a place called Balanmanik."

"Yeah, but so what?"

"You can't just go around creating wormholes in space willy-nilly. They're site-specific."

"And?" Jamie asked.

"And that means the Salmon will try and warp them through a wormhole, but the wormhole won't be there. Ksar needs to be in one of the towers."

"And?"

"And, Seamus, old son, the Salmon won't work. It'll hunt desperately for a wormhole, and since they're not in one of the three towers, it won't be able to find one."

"But they've gone," Jamie said.

Ramsay did not appear perplexed. "Yeah, interesting that. I imagine that there's some kind of emergency feature where the Salmon will break you up into your constituent molecules and transmit you to your destination without a wormhole. Of course without a wormhole you'll be going at lightspeed and it'll take decades, maybe centuries, to get to Earth."

Jamie was aghast.

Ramsay grinned.

"But somehow I don't think that's going to happen. The Salmon is very weak and it doesn't have nearly the power to do something like that."

"So?"

"So, unable to find a wormhole, unable to transmit their patterns manually, it'll simply reconstitute them and they should be appearing back here, just about—"

The air began to vibrate in roughly the same spot in the courtyard.

"You ever fired one of those things before?" Jamie asked.

Ramsay shook his head.

"I'll take it," Jamie said, grabbing the crossbow.

"Have *you* ever fired a crossbow before?" Ramsay asked, surprised.

"Hundreds of times," Jamie said.

Ramsay raised an eyebrow.

"I have Medieval Conflict Three on my PC," Jamie explained.

"I meant in real life. Give it back," Ramsay said, but before he could grab the crossbow, the vibrating air became a heat haze which became Ksar and Wishaway. Ksar's look of jubilation transformed first into puzzlement and then into pain as a crossbow bolt hit him in the shoulder blade.

"You got him," Ramsay yelled.

Wishaway shoved Ksar, broke free from his grasp, and ran to Jamie. He hugged her and kissed her on the cheek. Ksar tried pushing the button on the Salmon again, but to no avail. The Salmon's computer knew there was no wormhole in this location.

"Come on," Ramsay said.

Jamie loaded another crossbow bolt.

"Drop the knife, or I'll kill you," Jamie said.

Ksar hesitated, but only for a moment. He let the knife go and it clattered to the cobblestones.

Ramsay and Jamie ran at and jumped the Protector, ripped the Salmon from his grip, kicked him violently until he fell to the ground, curled into a ball, and began to whimper.

Jamie walked back over to Wishaway.

"I thought I'd lost you," Jamie said.

There were tears in her eyes. "It matters not. I have already lost *you*, Jamie."

Jamie looked puzzled.

"Why do you say that?"

Wishaway wiped her face.

"I heard what you said on the iceship. After the city has been saved, you are returning to Earth," she said, biting her lip and looking at him with despair.

Jamie shook his head.

"No. I'm not going anywhere. I'm staying here with you," he whispered.

"But your home, your country?" Wishaway asked, looking stunned, disbelieving.

"My home is here, with you," Jamie said softly. "I see that now."

When Ramsay turned to see what they were talking about, Protector Ksar, in a last desperate gasp, scrambled to his feet and tried to run. Ramsay sprinted after him and tackled the weakened Alkhavan general, hurling him to the ground.

"That's how we do it in rugby, Jamie," Ramsay said, wrestling Ksar onto his face, grabbing the nearest cross-bow, loading a new bolt and pointing it at the Alkhavan general.

Ramsay stood and threw the Salmon to his friend.

"You better hang on to this."

Jamie caught it and threw it back. "You should take it," he said, staring at Wishaway.

The situation was well under control a few minutes later when Callaway arrived with Lorca and half a dozen recovering captives.

The last of Ksar's strength had gone.

Blood was in his mouth.

He seemed close to death.

"Mercy, my Lord," Ksar said, his voice barely above a croak. The chicken pox had covered his face and was causing his immune system to overload. His breathing was labored, his eyes weak.

"I suppose we have to save his miserable life," Ramsay said.

Jamie nodded and looked at Wishaway.

"You are right. We must," she said. "Please, Father."

Callaway took a syringe, pricked his finger, sucked up some of his own blood and then injected Ksar with the antibodies.

"You'll be on the mend in an hour or two," Jamie said.

Ksar grunted but showed no sign of gratitude.

"Tie him and guard him," Jamie ordered.

Lorca nodded and several recovered Aldanese soldiers took the humbled Protector Ksar away.

"Are we making progress, Callaway?" Jamie asked.

"My Lord, we have in–inoculated several hundred people and we are making great strides. We have used thy replacement packet of needles. The glass divining tubes from the university make excellent syringes. We now have twenty functioning devices."

Jamie nodded. "What'll that take us?" he asked Ramsay.

"Say one person a minute, sixty an hour, times twenty, you could be doing a thousand an hour," Ramsay calculated.

"We are fortunate that much of the Aldanese are gathered in one place at the arena. We could have most of the city inoculated by morning," Callaway said.

"And the Alkhavans?" Wishaway asked.

"When they're all safely aboard their iceships and as soon as we have enough prize crews we're going to sail them under escort to Afor. Once there, we'll free the captains of the ships, innoculate them, and explain how the injections work; then our men will set sail for home," Jamie said.

"We should make them promise not to attack us before we give them the serum," Wishaway said angrily.

"Their word is worth nothing. They'll break it as soon as they have the chance," Jamie said.

"Then why must we help our enemies to become strong?" Wishaway asked, her eyes narrowing furiously.

Jamie was not going to get into this discussion again. He had already made the decision and, apparently, he was still in charge.

"I'm not going to be responsible for wiping out an entire culture. We're going to give them the serum because it's the right thing to do," Jamie said in a voice that made it clear that the debate was over.

Wishaway nodded. Jamie put an arm around her to console her.

"It won't matter anyway," Jamie said. "By tomorrow we will have begun making Greek Fire as per Ramsay's instructions. We'll deport the Alkhavans, and if any of them have the stupidity to attack the city again anytime soon, they'll be in for a nasty surprise."

"Are you certain, Jamie?" Wishaway asked skeptically.

Ramsay answered, "Greek Fire will stick to and burn right through their hulls. If any of the Alkhavans attack you again, we'll sink their whole fleet before they get within a mile of here."

Wishaway looked at Jamie to confirm this.

"We'll get working on it right away," Jamie said.

And it was fortunate that they did, since the Alkhavans came sooner than anyone was expecting.

Quiet on the face of the waters. The sea so calm it effortlessly reflected the moons and the infinity of stars in the still, dead night.

Calm, but not for long, Protector Ksar thought.

Coming across the bay were ships, bringing with them either triumphant success or terrible disaster.

The Krikor fleet.

The Alkhavans' last chance.

There in the distance, four massive objects out beyond the purple water.

Protector Ksar looked through the bars of his cell in the highest room of the White Tower and almost howled in frustration.

The scouts had spotted them hours ago, had lit the beacons and even he, a prisoner, saw that the iceships were returning.

His master, Lord Protector, was famous for his impatience. It had let him down again. Ksar knew that he was no general, no tactician.

In his fury at the failure of the attack on Aldan, the Lord Protector had redirected the Krikor fleet, sending back four boats against a city that was obviously waiting for them, willing them on.

"Arkgas, can arkgas," Ksar muttered in the tongue of his country. Fools are always fools.

He felt for the small knife he had sewn into the sleeve of his black robe. The Aldanese guards had not found it. He touched the expensive, rare steel blade. It comforted him. His father would have been proud that he had smuggled it into this room, even after they had searched him twice.

But that alone brought comfort.

For two days he had seen the Aldanese militias practice hurling their pots of fire. They had gotten better and better, and Ksar well knew what was in the store for the Krikor fleet.

"Arkgas, can arkgas," he said again and moved away from the barred window.

He sat heavily on the floor and closed his eyes.

This was something he didn't want to see.

A mile from Ksar's prison in the White Tower, Jamie, Ramsay, Lorca, and Wishaway were lying flat on the deck of one of the dozens of galleys lurking in the Aldan harbor. The crew were sitting quietly at their oars, and in the glassy dark the only noise at all was the burning of a slow match, which the marines would use to ignite the rows of clay pots filled with Greek Fire.

Everyone was tense, but ready.

The four lumbering iceships had been expected for hours, and the preparations for the ambush had been well laid.

Still, it would be folly to underestimate the abilities of the Alkhavans, the most accomplished pirates and raiders on the whole of Altair.

A south wind rippled the ink-black sea.

The iceships loomed closer.

"I'll say this for the Alkhavans. They're persistent buggers," Ramsay whispered.

"We should have infected and killed them all when we had the chance," Lorca muttered furiously. "We could have sent a boatload of dying men into the Krikor ships. None of this would have been necessary."

Jamie was taken aback by his ruthlessness but did not reply.

Two days trying to explain his actions to the skeptical Aldanese had wearied him of the whole business.

Indeed, in the city of Aldan, Ramsay had been given much honor as the inventor of the Greek Fire, but the feelings about Jamie were mixed. Yes, he was the Inheritor of the Great Ui Neill, yes, he had thrown back the invaders, but he had shown weakness in sparing the lives of their enemies, weakness that might come back to haunt them.

Everything would depend on tonight.

Still, win or lose, live or die, it was sufficient for Jamie that *he* knew he had done the right thing, even if no one else agreed with the decision.

"If they beat us back on the water, they will take the city easily," Lorca said.

"Quiet," Wishaway scolded. And Lorca, chastened, kept his mouth shut.

Fluorescent octopus-like beings bobbed beneath them in the water. On the harbor wall the *rantas* croaked and screeched their nighttime chorus.

The iceships were gliding slowly under full sail, unaware of the flotilla of barges, galleys, and fishing skiffs awaiting them.

The plan was to draw them in. Callaway had given strict instructions that no one was to attack until the Alkhavans were right among the little fleet.

And coming they were. They could even smell them now. That heady musk of furs, sweat, ice, and blood. The transparent hulls betraying every preparation of the nocturnal phantasms arriving to avenge their first defeat in a hundred years.

Closer.

And closer still.

One of the Aldanese marines stood, and Callaway, in a loud stage whisper, yelled: *"Tikki Malat."* Not yet.

"Not yet," Ramsay echoed quietly. "Suck 'em in."

Even Ramsay knew they had to be patient. And Ramsay wanted speed more than any of them, since he had a secret which he would only tell Jamie when the battle was over. But a secret that required the battle to be quick.

The impatient marine lay down again.

The wind picked up. A pink cloud moved in front of the yellow moon.

Two hundred yards from the harbor, at a silent command, the iceships turned together, swinging into the wind, pulling ropes on the lee side, and tightening their sails into attack formation.

And, now on this new tack, one of the big ships was bearing right down on Jamie's boat, the V of the bow churning up the sea thirty feet directly in front of them.

"Bloody déjà vu. These things are going to get me yet," Ramsay said in a voice that was trying to conceal his fear.

Some of the galley men grabbed their oars and began back-churning the water.

Jamie knew that he had to take charge of the situation. Yes, Ramsay was right, the ship was close, but they couldn't afford to make a big noise while maneuvering out of the way.

Quickly he turned and addressed the crew: "Stop it. Leave those oars. If they do ram us, no one is to cry out. We all have to remain calm, it's better to lose one boat than the element of surprise," Jamie said, and Wishaway translated into Aldanese for those who hadn't had the benefit of a university education.

"We could be killed," Lorca complained.

"Then we'll be killed," Jamie replied with satisfaction.

There was a grunt from the oarsmen and they nodded to one another and put down their oars. Better to lose one boat than the whole battle.

The iceship swept closer and closer, eerie and lit up, like the ghostly *Flying Dutchman* Jamie had read about in books.

Closer.

But then the light breeze freshened and took the

massive vessel a little to starboard, inch by inch until, finally, it passed a few yards from Jamie's galley.

The oarsmen let out a very human sigh of relief, and through the hull they could see a rough crew of Alkhavans preparing for the final assault, running to the deck carrying axes and spears, completely oblivious of the fate awaiting in the waters around them.

All four iceships glided past, and when they were deep in the throng of the hidden fleet suddenly a horn blew, a mighty cheer erupted from the Aldanese sailors, and the clay pots filled with Greek Fire were ignited from the slow match.

Immediately the night became alive with fire, and from the lead boat Callaway yelled loudly across the silent water. *"Ara tak! Ara tak! Ara tak, ca Aldan!"*

In thirty boats, thirty men stood with clay pots filled with Greek Fire—that highly combustible substance made of sulfur, naphtha, and petroleum—a deadly medieval form of napalm.

Each pot had a rag wick protruding from the top and was made from thin clay for easy breaking.

"Light them up and fire at will!" Jamie yelled as he dipped his own wick in the slow match, watched it catch, and then with a mighty two-armed heave, hurled the pot onto the deck of the closest iceship.

The burning pot arced through the clear night like a firework or a meteor going the wrong way.

It curved in a long parabola and then landed clean on

the deck of the iceship, exploding in a whoosh of terrible yellow fire.

Delirium. Panic. The Alkhavan sailors yelled, and the yells became screams as the burning pitch sizzled and melted through the thick ice deck and then, miraculously, kept on burning, down through the lower deck and through that into the cargo hold and then right through to the hull itself, where it carved out a large hole before being finally extinguished in the oxygenless depths of the Aldan Sea.

But the damage was done.

Ocean poured through the gash in the iceship's hull—a frothy, angry sea that burst the bulkheads and soared up into the holds.

The iceship groaned in agony and immediately began to list.

A cheer went up from the Aldanese, and suddenly the sky was alive with dozens of clay pots sailing through the crystal night, crashing onto the iceships, and igniting in jets of brilliant flame.

It was a dream of violence.

A nightmare.

Jamie gasped in horror.

Men on fire. Ships on fire. Sails combusting. Masts crashing down. For the Alkhavans, terror knew no bounds. They had been attacked by sea dragons. Demons. Ghosts.

The officers tried to maintain discipline, but even

they were terrified as exploding bombs of Greek Fire seemed to burst everywhere with deadly precision and horrifying noise and awful effect.

The panicked sailors were jumping into the sea, rolling on the ice, or sitting, paralyzed by fear and unable to do anything but pray to the ice gods to save them.

The confusion gave the Aldanese a chance to ignite a second round of pots, and only a minute after the first wave a new hail of seething Greek Fire landed on the Alkhavans.

"Baga kaak, naaa!" an Alkhavan admiral yelled, and some of the sailors and marines gathered their wits and began firing arrows and spears at the throng of tiny boats.

"Get down!" Jamie yelled as a hail of missiles came at them.

After the first wave, they stood and returned fire.

And this was the pattern for the next few minutes.

Sling shot and arrows roaring down from the ships, arrows and clay pots coming back from the boats. Everywhere the night punctuated with orders, explosions, and the screams of burning men—most now leaping from the decks and plunging into the water in a vain attempt to save their lives.

"Baga kaak, naaa!" the Alkhavan admiral cried again before a pot of Greek Fire burst in the rigging above his head, sending scalding petroleum on top of him, mercifully killing him in seconds.

In the chaos, one iceship lost its helmsman, the wheel spun wildly, and it collided with another. The entire bow split from the rammed ship with a sickening crash, sending sails, weapons, and men into the burning waves.

"Converge on the ships, don't let them get away," Jamie ordered, and they didn't need a translator to get the message. The oarsmen rowed close to the big vessels, and the two remaining iceships came under a relentless wave of fire. By now, however, the Alkhavans realized that they were besieged by men not demons, and they attempted a desperate resistance.

Jamie's boat was targeted by a squad of bowmen, and a throng of arrows thumped into the deck in front the Aldanese.

Thock, thock, thock.

A man to Jamie's right was hit in the throat and killed instantly. An arrow narrowly missed Wishaway, but Lorca was struck in the thigh and tumbled to the deck.

"Lorca!" Wishaway cried.

"It is but my leg, keep up the fight," Lorca replied.

Jamie took aim at the iceship and fired his second pot filled with fire. This time he missed the deck and instead smacked it into the hull, where it burst in a crooked splat of flame that drove the bowmen back.

Three more pots hit the ice vessel, and one must have burned through to the bottom because in a half a minute there was an awesome, disjunctive roar of water, and the entire ship rolled over on its side like a dying whale.

"We have bested them," Wishaway said.

"It's not over yet," Jamie said, and lit another pot.

But the oarsmen and everyone else knew that it was as good as done, and a feeling of elation rippled through the crew. They had to struggle not to cheer.

Jamie lit his third pot of fire and threw it at the final, faraway iceship. It missed and fizzled harmlessly into the water. But it didn't matter. The last of the four iceships was surrounded by the little boats, like an elephant encircled by lionesses.

It too fought bravely, but soon it had been holed and also began to list; and within moments the sizzling, burning ship buckled, upended, and began sinking under the black waves. The masts and rigging collapsed, entangling the screaming Alkhavan sailors, dragging them down down into the burning sea. Drowning them, incinerating them. It was death by fire or death by water, but death certainly.

The scene was dreadful and raw, and at last a great shout went up among the Aldanese. A hearty, happy bellow that became a song of triumph. A terrible dirge that almost but not quite silenced the cries of the dying warriors.

"We did it, we did it," Lorca said.

"Yes," Ramsay replied excitedly.

Jamie sat down on the galley and a wave of disgust passed through him.

"We've done it. Belisarius himself would be impressed," Ramsay said in Jamie's ear.

Jamie didn't reply. He had never heard of Belisarius and in fact couldn't have cared less what anyone thought.

This was one battle too many for him.

Suddenly his head felt light and then he gagged, leaned forward, and would have fallen into the sea had Ramsay not grabbed him.

"Are you OK, mate?" Ramsay asked, putting his arm around his friend.

Jamie looked at the scene of devastation and weakly nodded. "I'm OK," he said.

"Good. Because we better get to shore. I noticed something yesterday. Didn't want to tell you about it until the Alkhavans were taken care of, but it's something you should know."

"What?"

In the light of the burning sea, Ramsay took the Salmon of Knowledge out of his zip pocket and gave it to Jamie. At first Jamie couldn't see anything wrong but then he noticed that the light on the side of the device was winking. The power light. Life was ebbing from the alien artifact.

Jamie looked at his friend. "Which means?" he asked.

Ramsay put the device safely back inside his pocket. "We better get to shore," he said. "We don't have much time if we're going to do a jump."

"And are we going to do a jump?"

"If we don't and this thing dies, we'll be stuck here."

Jamie nodded. "I'll tell them. We gotta get back," he said.

Jamie stood and looked about him. Celebrations were taking place throughout the fleet of small boats. Drinking, singing, a few men even dancing. But more sinisterly, some Aldanese boats were rowing among the Alkhavans and battering the survivors with their long oars.

And again, the savage and feral expressions on the Aldanese made Jamie sick to his stomach. He had come here to help the Aldanese people, not to supervise a massacre.

He strode to the prow of the galley, pushing the oarsmen out of his way. He stood next to Wishaway, who was bandaging Lorca's leg. She saw his look of fury and recoiled for a moment.

"Jamie, what—" she began, but he ignored her.

"Stop the attack on the survivors. Your orders are to pick them up. Save all that you can," Jamie yelled at the top of his voice.

Everyone froze, and there was a long pause before the distant voice of Callaway relayed the order in the common tongue: *"Tarra, pa, falla, hass, meaya, na Ui Neill."*

A groan of disapproval, but Wishaway stood and echoed the words of her father:

"Tarra, pa, falla, hass. Pick up the survivors. Now."

The celebrations were curtailed and the crews went to their oars and began looking for Alkhavans who could be rescued.

And then, exhausted, Jamie sat and, unable to look further at the scene, turned his gaze to Aldan, where the stars were lullabying themselves to sleep and the first light of dawn was appearing on the temples and minarets of a city that knew victory was theirs.

❀ ❀ ❀

Jamie and Wishaway stood together on the harbor wall as the morning sun illuminated the dreary scene. A battle won was only slightly less dispiriting than a battle lost.

"I hope the war is over," Wishaway muttered almost to herself.

She shivered.

Jamie put his arm around her.

"After a disaster like this, the Alkhavans won't dare come near you again," Jamie said.

Wishaway walked over to the harbor battlements and looked at her war-ravaged city. It made her sad. But this was the lowest ebb. The empty city was already beginning to fill up with healthy Aldanese citizens who had been inoculated and were recovering from the Earth virus. And soon there would be a victory parade, a celebration, and then a great rebuilding.

Jamie came over to her and took her hand. "Honestly, by this time next month, it will almost be as if this whole nightmare never happened," he said.

She did not reply, but he was probably right. She smiled. And they couldn't have done it alone. She knew who had made the victory possible. Just as they had done in the past. The people from Earth. The Lords Ui Neill.

And now she felt almost a little guilty. She'd been doubt-ful at first. How could children save them from the Alkhavan army? Well, they may not have been adults, but they had done the impossible task. They had defeated the enemy and more than that, at the end of it, they had shown mercy, which was more than her father or she might have been capable of.

It moved her as she looked at him. She held his hand tightly.

Ramsay bounded over and began to talk so fast she could barely understand.

"Jamie lad, Jamie, listen to me, we gotta talk, like right now," Ramsay exclaimed.

And yes, she owed both of them.

She walked over to Ramsay and kissed him on the cheek.

"Thank you, Lord Ramsay," she said.

"Thank you," he replied with a huge grin.

She bowed to Jamie and kissed him chastely too.

"Thank you," she began, but Jamie gave her a look before she said the word 'Lord.' She cleared her throat. "Thank you, Jamie," she said.

"Thank you, Wishaway, for everything," Jamie replied.

He wanted to say more; he wanted to tell her what he felt about her planet, her city, about how he felt about her, but Ramsay interrupted him.

"Jamie, listen to me," he said.

"What?" Jamie asked with a touch of irritation.

"I'm not kidding, Jamie, look at the Salmon now," Ramsay said.

Jamie lifted up the alien device. The red light on the side indeed was blinking. But now even faster, more urgently.

"What does that mean?" Jamie asked.

Ramsay looked exasperated. He wasn't in the mood for long explanations.

"You know exactly what it means, Jamie. We have to go back. It's running out of juice. That last jump that Ksar tried, it's drained it. It's been draining for the last few days. We got to get going as soon as possible. I'd say we have a couple of hours tops, certainly by nightfall."

"And then what?"

"Do you ever listen, mate? If the power system dies, we won't be able to jump. We'll be stuck here forever."

"How are we going to get back to the Sacred Isle in a couple of hours?" Jamie asked.

Ramsay shook his head. "We don't need to go back there."

He pointed at the ancient White Tower of Aldan. Jamie looked perplexed, but Wishaway frowned.

"In the sacred writings, the Lords Ui Neill said that the White Tower was a holy place," Wishaway said sadly, as if she was reluctant to give out the information.

Ramsay grinned.

"See? Three towers on this world. Three places you can jump from. Good job Ksar didn't figure it out."

"He'd be on Earth right now," Jamie said, shivering at the thought.

"Come on, Jamie, we'll have to go there, the sooner the better," Ramsay said. "I packed our backpacks last night. Come on."

But Jamie shook his head and smiled at his friend.

He had known this moment would come and it was going to be difficult to explain. But there was really no other choice.

On Earth, he was incomplete. He was a cripple. He was voiceless. He was a freak.

But not here. This was the place where he could blossom and grow and become a man. And even if somehow he could get his arm and speech back on Earth it wouldn't matter because he belonged here, with her—with Wishaway and all the wonders of a new world.

And he knew that he was going to have to tell his friend that he wasn't going to make that jump. Ramsay was going to have to return to Muck Island by himself.

Ramsay was getting annoyed. "Come on, Jamie, snap out of it. I'm not kidding about this, we really don't have much time," he exclaimed, holding up the Salmon.

Jamie shook his head a second time. He reached out and took Wishaway's hand.

"No, Ramsay. I'm sorry. I've been thinking a lot about all of this. I'm not going to come with you," Jamie said.

Ramsay looked horrified. "You're kidding, right?"

"No."

"What? Are you out of your mind? This is a one-way trip, mate. The Salmon is running out of energy. If I go home now, I won't be able to come back and get you. You'll be stuck here. Marooned."

Jamie nodded and looked into his friend's big, disbelieving eyes.

"I know that, Ramsay. I understand. But you see, the thing is, I don't want to go back to Earth. I want to stay here. On Earth I only have one arm, I don't speak, I don't have anything going for me. Whereas here I have everything," he said, looking significantly at Wishaway.

She smiled and he put his arm around her waist.

Wishaway's heart was pounding. She hadn't been sure, until this moment, that Jamie really was going to stay.

Ramsay shook his head in amazement.

"Look, Jamie, if this is about Wishaway, it's no problem. She can come to our world. Things are better on Earth, anyway," Ramsay said.

Wishaway shook her head. "I am needed here, Lord Ramsay. We must rebuild the defenses, we are still in grave peril," she said.

Jamie nodded in agreement. "I'm needed here too, Ramsay. I can do good work here. We can make things.

Hot-air balloons and steam engines. I can contribute. On Earth I'm nothing. Here I can be a big help."

Ramsay was speechless.

"You must be joking, pal. You don't know what you're saying. This won't be for a week or two. If you stay here, it's for the rest of your life."

"I know. I've thought about it. The only thing I'll miss is my mother. Nothing else. Will you explain it to her, Ramsay?"

Ramsay shook his head. "You can tell her yourself."

"I'm not going," Jamie said definitively.

His mind was made up. He didn't want to return to Earth, where he was a voiceless cripple with nothing to contribute to society. And how could he leave her? It was impossible.

Ramsay looked shocked as the truth of Jamie's words began to sink in.

"I'm sorry, Ramsay. But please, you'll tell Mom? You'll explain everything, right? Promise me," Jamie pleaded.

There was a long silence.

"And is that your final answer?" Ramsay asked with a half-smile.

"It is."

Ramsay turned away. He didn't want Jamie to see that he was tearing up. He gazed out at the strange azure sea and the wrecks of great hulking iceships floating in the harbor. He'd miss this world too, but he'd miss Earth far more.

He looked at the Salmon. The red light was blinking furiously. He knew he didn't have long.

"Well, I better go. Can you get someone to show me how to get to the old tower?" he asked Wishaway.

"I will get my father, Lord Ramsay. He will wish to bid you farewell in any case," Wishaway said, and ran to find Callaway, who was supervising the unloading of the attack boats.

When she was gone, Ramsay turned to his friend.

"Do you really know what you're doing? You're not just lovesick or something? This is the biggest decision of your life," Ramsay said.

Jamie's eyes were firm, certain. "I made up my mind on the iceship, and I've been thinking about this for days," Jamie said without hesitation.

Ramsay nodded. "OK then, mate. Well, listen to me and listen good. I didn't want to say this while she was around, but you can't stay here, you can't. I've been watching the skies. This planet is doomed. It's a binary system and the sun is moving farther away as it progresses in an elliptical orbit about its companion star. Here on Altair it's going to get colder and colder until this world becomes one big snowball."

Jamie took in the information. Ramsay was telling him the truth, or at least what he thought was the truth.

"You understand now why you have to go back?" Ramsay said.

Before Jamie could reply, Callaway came breathlessly onto the harbor wall led by a red-faced Wishaway.

He approached Jamie, bowed. "My daughter says you wish to go to the White Tower of Aldan in order to return to Earth?" he said.

"Not me. Ramsay. He has to leave," Jamie replied.

"The White Tower is a very old structure. It is not safe. We are using it as a jail. No, Lord Ui Neill, I forbid it. Of the three towers on Aldan only the one on the Sacred Isle is safe and in some condition to use for your purposes," Callaway said.

Ramsay didn't want to discuss it. "Yeah, look, Callaway, we don't have time to sail to the lighthouse on that island. The light is blinking, the power is draining from our machine," he said, holding up the Salmon. "I have to leave right now."

Jamie nodded to show that it was serious.

"But Lord Ramsay, we wished to have a ceremony, we wanted you to meet the survivors of the Council and the Elders of the city, we wanted—"

"Please, just take me to the tower," Ramsay said with annoyance.

"Father, he must go immediately," Wishaway said.

Callaway bowed. "I will take care of it. We have some prisoners interned there, but they will be removed," he said, and hurried to the tower to make preparations.

"Uh, I need to talk to young James for a wee mo, Wishaway," Ramsay said, and led his friend to one side.

"So you understand now? This victory is a temporary one. None of these people have a future. You won't have a future staying here."

"How long have they got?"

"Before the ice takes over? I don't know. A couple of hundred years? A thousand? Ten thousand, I don't know. But it will happen. It's inevitable."

Jamie nodded. "Long enough. We'll think of something. We'll survive," he said confidently.

"No you won't. You don't belong here, the Earth's your home, not here on this dying planet," Ramsay pleaded.

But Jamie was done talking.

He placed his arm on his friend's shoulder. He looked at him for a long time and then in a voice barely above a whisper he said: "You take care now, mate."

Finally, after another long silence, Ramsay nodded.

"Aye, you too," the big Irishman said, and they walked to the White Tower for the final parting of the ways.

Chapter XIII
THE WORDS

I N HARLEM IT WAS a typical early February day. Cold. Miserable. The piles of snow on the sidewalk had assumed the color of wet concrete and the consistency of week-old porridge.

Thaddeus had just gotten back to the city after a visit to Georgia, where his sister's illnesses had been much less imaginary than usual and hadn't been helped by her foul-smelling home remedies and concoctions. But a trip to the doctor, a dose of antibiotics, and she had been right as rain.

After making sure that his apartment had not been burgled and the kid down the hall had not starved his cat to death, Thaddeus walked to Fairway, got some supplies, and popped in to the library to log on and see what Jamie was up to. Mrs. Moore said hello and gave him a look of apology because a teenager was on the computer playing Yahoo! poker. Although Thaddeus was an old man he could be quite intimidating, and after a minute the kid could no longer take Thaddeus glaring at him.

He got off, and Thaddeus sat down on the warm seat and checked his e-mail. Nothing. He was surprised and then a little upset. Jamie hadn't written to him in almost two weeks. He owed Thaddeus several e-mails and he had not responded at all. You could say a lot of things about Jamie. He was sullen, difficult, moody—but you couldn't claim that he was rude. There had to be something wrong. Maybe he was sick, maybe all that Irish weather had given him a terrible cold. Or perhaps, even worse, he'd had a relapse of his cancer. Thaddeus was worried.

He immediately began to type:

> To: jamieoneill47@yahoo.com
> From: thaddeusharper@hotmail.com
> Jamie, I hope you are well. I'm concerned about you. Please drop me a line as soon as possible. Thank you. Your friend, Thaddeus.

Thaddeus sent the e-mail, had dinner at the Soul Food Kitchen on 125th Street, caught up on two weeks' worth of the *New York Times* crosswords, and went to bed.

He woke at nine after a difficult night's sleep, filled with bad dreams and anxiety. He walked to the library and waited outside for Mrs. Moore to arrive and open up.

He climbed the stairs with her, listened to her gab about the state of the world, and logged on to the computer. There was still no e-mail response from Jamie.

Now he was really worried.

If Jamie had had a relapse of his cancer, Thaddeus wanted to know about it. Maybe he could help somehow. After all, he had money saved in government bonds.

He knew what he was going to have to do.

He was going to have to go home, find that phone number Jamie had given him, call Ireland, and get some answers.

Anna had just sat down to drink some tea when the phone rang in the kitchen.

She'd had a long day, teaching in the morning and then shopping for carpets in Belfast. She considered ignoring it, but then she realized it might be a phone call from Austria. Jamie was supposed to be back the day after tomorrow, but maybe there had been a change in the arrangements.

She closed the kitchen window to block the sound of the wind and rain and picked up the handset. "Hello," she said.

Thaddeus said hello and got immediately to the point. "Is Jamie OK? I haven't heard from him at all in nearly two weeks," he said.

"Jamie? He's doing great, Thaddeus, he's on the school ski trip to Austria, if you can believe it," Anna said with a grin.

Thaddeus pushed the cat off his lap. Actually, he couldn't believe it. Jamie skiing? It didn't seem to fit with all he knew about the boy. Could he have changed that much in a few weeks?

"You've heard from him then? He's OK?" Thaddeus asked.

"Yes, he's great. He e-mails me every day. He and Ramsay are having a wild time," Anna replied.

"He e-mails every day," Thaddeus repeated suspiciously. "Has Ramsay called *his* parents?"

A cold feeling ran down Anna's spine. "I don't know," she said nervously. "Why?"

"It just seems odd to me, I haven't heard from him at all. He hasn't sent me a single e-mail. That's not like Jamie," Thaddeus said.

"That isn't like Jamie. Hmmm. Look, let me call the school and check that everything's all right and then I'll call you right back, Thaddeus. OK?" Anna said.

"OK. You have my number?"

"Of course, Thaddeus, and even if nothing's wrong, I'll still call you back. I've been meaning to catch up, but I've been so busy."

She hung up, dialed the school, and in two minutes her whole universe was turned upside down.

The school secretary informed her that neither Jamie nor Ramsay was on the ski trip.

Anna called Ramsay's mother.

In another minute everyone knew what had happened.

Jamie and Ramsay had run away from home. Where they'd gone was anyone's guess. Britain? Europe? They'd been missing thirteen days. In thirteen days they could be halfway around the world.

Anna called the nearest police station at Carrickfergus, and they told her they would alert Scotland Yard and Interpol. They would need a description, photographs, could she come to the barracks right away?

"Of course, I'll be right there," she said.

It was raining outside. A storm was throwing white

water over the rocks, and because it was close to high tide, the causeway was completely covered with water. It didn't look safe, but Jamie's life was at stake. What choice did she have? And she remembered something the lawyer, Mr. McCreagh, had said. Topper O'Neill had crossed the causeway high tide, low tide, regardless of the weather, wearing only a pair of Wellington boots. And he'd been fine every time, even when he'd come back drunk from the local pub.

She ran to the car, fumbled for the key, and opened the Land Rover door.

She got inside and turned on the lights.

It really didn't look terrific weather-wise. It was a very dirty night, but this was a good car and she was an excellent driver.

"Here goes," she muttered, and accelerated out of the driveway of the Lighthouse House. For some reason she almost stopped when she was driving past the lighthouse itself. There was something about that old tower, that room where Jamie and Ramsay played . . . she slowed the car and changed from third to second gear.

But she dismissed the thought from her mind.

She had to stay focused on what was really important here. Jamie had gone missing. He was in trouble. She had to get to the police station.

She dipped the clutch, slipped the car back into third, and drove fast off Muck Island onto the causeway linking it to the mainland.

The water was indeed high, higher than she'd ever known it to be. It was coming up over the tops of the tires, but still the car had good grip. It was a tough old vehicle, and she was pretty sure she'd seen footage of this type of Land Rover crossing flooded rivers in Africa.

She kept going, and still wasn't worried when water came pouring in through a hole in the passenger-side door. She was nearly halfway across. Not much farther to go now, and it was less slippery as you got closer to the mainland.

That Jamie, what was he thinking? Was it Ramsay's influence? He seemed like such a responsible boy. She hoped drugs weren't involved. She hoped, above all else, that Jamie was safe.

She sped up a little bit.

The speedometer hit thirty, then thirty-five, then forty.

She was almost off the causeway.

Then, almost imperceptibly, she could feel the back wheels sliding sideways. She grabbed at the steering wheel, tried to correct the skid, but now the front of the car was spinning too. The Land Rover had been jolted by a sudden rush of water flowing through the Muck Island channel.

The vehicle lost all traction and was now being carried by the sea. It floated for a second, then flipped, Anna's seat belt prevented her from crashing through the windshield and being killed instantly. It protected her still as

368

the Land Rover rolled twice more and came to a halt on its side, right on the causeway's edge, on the verge of the deep water.

She'd been lucky. Anna was dazed but conscious.

She did a quick triage.

The pain was overwhelming.

Both her arms appeared to be broken, her collarbone felt cracked, and there was blood in her throat from where she must have bitten her tongue.

Fighting the pain, she tried to pull at the toggle on her seat belt, but it would not release because the car door had buckled inward onto the seat belt clip.

In the pitch-blackness, she tried desperately to pull at the seat belt, but it had jammed fast, trapping her tight in her seat.

She frantically tugged at it and then stopped.

The Land Rover had started to slide.

"No, no, no," she begged, but the vehicle slipped off the causeway and into the deeper water of the Muck Island channel.

The vehicle came to a halt on the rocky bottom.

Immediately the car began filling with water.

Panic went through her like a hot blade through butter.

She knew the tides by now, she knew how high the sea got when you were off the causeway.

It might take an hour, perhaps two, but at the absolute peak of the high tide the Land Rover would be completely submerged.

If she couldn't get out, she was going to drown.

The freezing cold Atlantic touched her ankles.

She began screaming.

"Help me, someone help me, please, please help me!"

But the crash had killed the Land Rover's lights and her voice was lost in the wind and rain. She tried to reach the horn but couldn't. She realized that on a stormy night like this, no one would be out for a walk and it was unlikely that anyone in Portmuck would see the car at all, certainly not as the water got higher and higher and the green Land Rover disappeared from view.

She scrabbled frantically at the seat belt clasp, but it was caught up in a twisted mess of metal against the door, and the door itself was wedged hopelessly on the gravelly sea bottom.

The only way she was going to get free was if someone could open the passenger-side door from the outside.

She screamed and tried to bite through the thick seat belt material, but after several painful bites she gave it up as pointless.

She began to cry hysterically.

"No, no, no, not this way, not this way," she sobbed.

And then after a minute, as the frigid sea began to rise about her legs, she decided that she'd better use her breath more constructively.

"Help me!" she yelled at the top of her voice. "Help me! Please. Please help me. Please, someone, anyone. Please help me!" But in her heart she already knew that there was no help coming.

Two hours after the battle, Ramsay was standing in the upper room of the old White Tower of Aldan. Like the tower on the Sacred Isle, the White Tower had been used as a lighthouse at some time in the past, until it had gradually fallen into a state of disrepair. The room was littered with oil lamps, kindling, mirrors, and other equipment. It was very dirty, as it had recently become a nest for *rantas*—the huge batlike creatures that dominated the skies on this planet.

Despite Ramsay's objections, about twenty citizens had been brought there to honor him and wish him a pleasant journey back to the stars. The stars—it was quite a concept. But the Aldanese were not a superstitious people, and they understood that Ramsay had come here using technology, not magic. Of all the countries and lands on Altair perhaps only here in Aldan would anyone have been brave enough to show up to see a person disappear into thin air.

The crowd was breathing hard and looking pensive.

The hastily assembled Aldanese university members, councillors, and guild representatives were still recovering from the chicken pox, the battles, and the long walk to the top of the White Tower.

Ramsay realized that most of them expected him to make a speech, but there wasn't time. The light on the Salmon was flickering, and if he didn't make the jump soon, he would be stuck there with Jamie. And he, for one, didn't want to live on a world where they weren't going to get TV or planes or video games for at least a couple of hundred years.

No speech, he thought. Just a final look about him. This was a moment he'd remember for the rest of his life, and he wanted to take it all in. His three friends: Lorca, Wishaway, Jamie. The strange and beautiful city. The elite Aldanese citizens talking, waiting for Callaway to call some sort of order. Everywhere the disgusting smell of *ranta* poop.

If the Salmon still worked, at least the jump would be straightforward. In the corner of the room, inlaid on the floor, there was a gold circle, and within that circle a gold square, and within that square a triangle. Of course it could just be a fancy design, but it looked significant.

If this isn't the place to jump, I'm a monkey's uncle, Ramsay said to himself.

He stood for a moment and then took out the Salmon.

His friends came over. Jamie offered him a hand, but Ramsay hugged him instead.

"You'll tell my mom what happened, won't you?" Jamie said.

Ramsay nodded.

"I will miss you," Lorca said.

"I'll miss you too, buddy," Ramsay replied. "How's your leg?"

"It will be well anon," Lorca replied between gritted teeth.

"Oh, Ramsay, you will be careful?" Wishaway asked.

Ramsay nodded. Wishaway kissed him and stood back.

Ramsay held up the Salmon.

"Well listen, folks, I better—" he began.

"Just one moment, Lord Ramsay," Callaway interrupted.

The assembled guests had recovered their breath and were ready for a ceremony.

"We must begin the *faraka*. We will be brief, Lord Ramsay, as we know you must depart," Callaway said.

"Hurry," Jamie said.

"Ladies and gentlemen," Callaway began in a loud voice. "Citizens of Aldan, survivors of the great attack and the great plague, we are here today to honor and wish a good journey to the Lord Ramsay of the Ui Neill. And to welcome into our city the Lord Ui Neill, Seamus, known as James, Prince of Ulster, Laird of Muck, Heir of Morgan of the Red Hand, Defender of the Shore."

When Callaway finished there was a round of applause. Callaway approached the two boys and gave them each a bright blue flower, the Sea Rose, the Aldanese symbol of victory.

"Jeez, it's getting like that scene at the end of *Star Wars* where they all get the medals," Ramsay muttered impatiently to Jamie.

"May we ask you for a speech, Lord Ramsay?" Callaway asked. "Most of us are familiar with your tongue."

The light on the Salmon was pulsing like a defibrilator.

373

"I'm sorry, Callaway. I really have to go," Ramsay said. Callaway nodded.

Jamie shook his friend's hand, Wishaway ran forward and gave him yet another kiss on the cheek.

"I'm quite the kissable mick today—it's that heady aroma of blood, sweat, *ranta* poop, and Greek Fire, it drives women crazy," Ramsay said.

"Don't try it on Earth," Jamie laughed.

"Well I might just—" Ramsay began, but then he noticed something he didn't like.

At the back, standing between half a dozen burly guards, was their enemy Protector Ksar and several other high-ranking prisoners.

"What the hell is he doing here?" Ramsay asked.

"Protector Ksar and his generals were imprisoned here. We do not intend to return them until there is a lasting peace between our country and Alkhava," Callaway said with some complacency.

Jamie nodded. It was one thing to save the lives of the Alkhavans, but he had to agree that it would be foolish to let them have their best commander back without some sort of treaty or security guarantee.

"I'd trust that guy as far as I could throw him," Ramsay said.

"Don't worry, Ramsay, I'll be here. I'll make sure he and his soldiers get the message not to come near us again," Jamie said.

Ramsay looked at Ksar. Here was a man who had lost everything, who was capable of everything.

"Lorca, you keep an eye on that guy too. These two lovebirds aren't going to be paying attention to anything," Ramsay said to his tall friend.

"Fear not, Lord Ramsay, we will keep that villain here a thousand years if necessity demands it," Lorca said.

Jamie was holding Wishaway's hand and they looked very happy together, but Ramsay knew he had to ask.

"Jamie, are sure you won't come with me?"

"I want to stay here."

Ramsay nodded and walked into the gold triangle within the gold square within the gold circle.

He put the Sea Rose in his pocket. He held the Salmon up for everyone to see. They were going to like this. Probably tell their grandchildren about it one day. He hesitated, to give Jamie one last chance to change his mind.

But Jamie didn't move.

Ramsay's finger touched the button on the Salmon and the beginnings of the wormhole opened from the old White Tower, in the city of Aldan, on the planet Altair, in the constellation Pegasus, to the old lighthouse tower on Muck Island, County Antrim, Ireland, Earth.

The Salmon began to vibrate and make a whining noise. There wasn't much power left in it, and Ramsay could tell that it was operating under capacity.

"Come on," he muttered under his breath.

And then the wormhole slowly began to open wider— very slowly.

"Thank goodness," Ramsay said. "Bye, everyone."

"Good-bye," Jamie said.

Ramsay waved.

The gap narrowed between Earth and Altair and, as the two lands were connected through space and time, from lighthouse to lighthouse, Jamie could hear the sound of rain. It was raining on Earth.

He smiled. Definitely the sound of sea and rain.

But then there was something else.

Jamie was sure that he could hear a voice screaming from the other side of the void: "Help me! Please someone help me!"

A hoarse woman's voice. Desperate. Panicked.

There was no doubt about it.

It was his mother.

She was in trouble.

"Help me, please, Jamie. Anyone," she called again.

Jamie knew what he had to do. His father was in Seattle and Anna had no one else.

Jamie turned to Wishaway.

She had heard the voice too. Indeed the voice had caused a general commotion in the room. Enough of a commotion for Protector Ksar to remove a small knife from the sleeve of his long gown. Following the inoculation his strength had returned. It wasn't all the way back by any means, but he knew it was now or never. Was he doomed to spend his whole life on this condemned planet, or could he escape to another world? A world of heat and warmth, a world where he could use his power and his cunning without interference from his sister, the Lord Protector, or these petty Aldanese.

With one swift, unnoticed slice, he cut the bonds about his wrists.

Jamie kissed Wishaway and Ramsay eased his thumb off the red jewel on the Salmon. He knew what Jamie was going to do.

"My mother is in trouble, I have to go," Jamie said.

Wishaway sobbed. "You won't be able to come back," she said.

"If there's a way I'll find it," Jamie replied, and kissed her a final time. Her blue eyes were streaming with tears.

"But Jamie I—I . . ."

"Come with me, Wishaway," Jamie pleaded.

"I can't. I'm needed here. I need to be here to look after my father. To rebuild my city," Wishaway said.

"Is there anything I can say to make you change your mind?" Jamie said with tears in his own eyes too.

She was too emotional to speak, she was sobbing uncontrollably.

She kissed him on the lips and held him tight and then she took the brooch from around her neck and slipped it into his jeans pocket.

"Once we are safe here in Aldan, I, too, will look for a way," she whispered.

Ramsay could feel the wormhole becoming slightly stronger. But this time the Salmon was really struggling to keep the pathway open. Still the seconds were precious. As soon as it was sufficiently stable, the Salmon would break him up into his constituent molecules and send him through to Earth. Jamie had to come, now.

"Come on, Jamie," Ramsay said.

Jamie let go of Wishaway, ran over to Ramsay, and grabbed hold of the Salmon.

"Come on," Ramsay said again to the Salmon.

And then Protector Ksar made his move.

He broke free of the ropes around his wrists and ran for the golden triangle, where Jamie and Ramsay were beginning to disappear.

"Stop him!" Wishaway screamed.

Lorca leapt on the Alkhavan general and threw him to the ground, but even weakened as he was, Ksar was a trained soldier and knew how to use a knife. He stabbed Lorca in the stomach, causing the big student from Oralands to yell and fall backward to the marble floor.

"Lorca!" Wishaway yelled, and ran to help.

Ksar scrambled to his feet and jumped into the golden circle just as the boys were vanishing. Desperately he grabbed hold of the Salmon and tried to wrestle it from their grip.

The Salmon groaned sickeningly. It was struggling to form a wormhole big enough to transport the three of them across the universe. It had almost no power left and the process was taking much longer than any of the previous jumps. Maybe it wouldn't work at all. Ramsay tried to push Ksar off the device, but his vise-like hand was too strong.

Protector Ksar raised his knife and swung it at Jamie's throat.

"Jamie, look out," Ramsay called.

But Jamie had learned a lot in the past two weeks. He blocked the knife with his left arm.

"Hold me, Ramsay. Don't let me go," he said to his friend, and he released his grip on the Salmon. Ramsay held on to the device with one hand and grabbed Jamie's back with the other to prevent him from falling into the void.

With both hands free, Jamie was able to grapple with Ksar. He punched him, and the blow connected with Ksar's nose. Ksar swiped at Jamie's face, but Jamie ducked out of the way and grabbed Ksar's wrist in two hands.

Ksar was snarling with rage, his black eyes glaring at Jamie.

The wormhole buckled and the Salmon made a whining noise. Ramsay knew they were pushing their luck.

"I will destroy you, Ui Neill," Ksar muttered, breaking loose from Jamie's grip and lunging forward with the knife. "You are a mere child. I am a warrior of the Alkhavan army."

There's a time for talking and a time for action, Jamie thought, and he let the Protector lunge toward him, watching the knife, almost as if it were in slow motion, inching closer and closer to his heart. Before it could stab into him, Jamie made his move. He thumped down on

Protector Ksar's wrist, knocking the knife away, and then he grabbed the general by the arm and let the Alkhavan's own forward momentum pull him completely off the Salmon.

Protector Ksar's eyes widened in terror and he tried desperately to regain his grip on the device.

"Get rid of him, Jamie, or we won't make it," Ramsay said as the wormhole in space finally opened fully.

Only Jamie's hold on his forearm was preventing Ksar from falling into the blackness of the fold in space-time.

"Now, Jamie," Ramsay said.

"No!" Ksar screamed. "No wait, no, we can make a de—"

Jamie punched him with his left hand, and before that fist disappeared forever, it did one last good service, connecting with Ksar's nose and hurling him into the gray-black void.

Protector Ksar screamed, vanished from view, and Jamie grabbed the Salmon just in time, as his molecules broke up, were transported across dozens of light-years, and re-formed across the galaxy in the old lighthouse tower on Muck Island.

Jamie and Ramsay opened their eyes, expecting trouble, but Ksar was not there—lost and vaporized somewhere between the two worlds.

Jamie took a deep breath and stared at his missing arm. It always took him a minute or two to recover from the shock of losing it again.

Ramsay held the Salmon up to the moonlight. The little red light had stopped winking and had now turned dead and black.

"Well, that's it, the light's gone out forever. I'm afraid our journeys are done," Ramsay said.

Ramsay saw that Jamie was having trouble coping with the arm again. He helped steady him on his feet. "It's OK, mate," he said.

Just then they heard the voice crying from outside.

"Help me. Please help me!"

My mom, Jamie thought.

He climbed through the hole in the lighthouse's upper floor and sprinted down the spiral staircase, almost breaking his neck in the process.

With Ramsay behind him he hurtled out into the storm.

"Over there on the edge of the causeway, I think I see a car," Ramsay yelled.

Jamie looked to where his friend was pointing, and yes, it was a car—his mom's green Land Rover almost completely submerged by the incoming tide.

Jamie dashed out onto the land bridge. The water was high, above his knees, and it was moving fast. He almost fell. Ramsay appeared behind him. Ramsay was taller and he had two arms to balance himself. He helped Jamie and they waded as quickly as they could through the freezing seas to the old Land Rover.

When they got there, the car was off the causeway, almost completely on its side and filling rapidly with water. The front end was under the water, but there was still a small and diminishing pocket of air. Anna was breathing, but the cold and the blood loss had finally caused her to slip into a state of shock.

"Hepmepasse," she was muttering incoherently between chattering teeth, the water now at her throat.

Ramsay climbed on the passenger-side door and tugged as hard as he could, but it wouldn't budge. Ramsay thought for a moment and deduced the nature of the problem.

"Water pressure is stopping us from opening it. Have to break the window, let the car flood with water, equalize the pressure, open the door," Ramsay said.

Jamie hesitated but then nodded.

Ramsay smashed the side window with his elbow. The frigid Atlantic filled the car.

Anna began to scream and her voice was muffled by the suffocating sea.

For a horrifying second, Jamie watched his mother disappear beneath the water and begin to drown.

But Ramsay knew what he was doing.

With the water inside and outside the vehicle, there was no pressure on the door and it was easy to open. He pulled it ajar, and both boys swam to Anna.

Ramsay tried to click Anna out of her seat belt, but it was jammed tight.

He took out his penknife and gave it to Jamie, signaling that Jamie should cut the belt while he pulled.

Jamie cut the seat belt in one fast movement and he and Ramsay tugged Anna out of the car, dragged her to the causeway, and carried her between their shoulders all the way to Portmuck.

She didn't need artificial respiration, but she had lost some blood and Jamie knew that sometimes shock and hypothermia can kill you, so he laid his mother on the beach, wrapped her in his jacket, and rubbed her hands while Ramsay ran into the nearest house and called for an ambulance.

❈　❈　❈

The hills a quiet emerald, the lough a darkening blue. A red sky illuminated by diminishing increments of golden light.

The sun had set over the Glens of Antrim, and night was creeping into Belfast. There were ferries on the water, trains on the tracks, and on the street below the window, newsboys and honking cars were vying for supremacy in the song of the departing day.

The door opened and Ramsay looked in. "How's she doing? Is she OK?"

Jamie shrugged.

There was no change.

Ramsay nodded. "I'll get some coffee," he said.

Jamie nodded and under his shirt, something cool brushed against his throat. Wishaway's brooch with the small carved portrait of the beautiful lady who had been her mother.

He smiled.

Time passed.

The traffic became quieter. The newsboys sold their last copies and ceased their calls. Peat smoke began corkscrewing from thousands of chimney tops.

Jamie looked at the coming night and waited for the stars. The first point of light was Venus and then Sirius and then he noticed the large and only moon in the friendly and familiar sky.

The view was unobstructed because they were on the fifteenth floor of the Belfast City Hospital and it was one of the tallest buildings in the city.

He turned his gaze back inside.

His mom was connected to a saline drip and a heart monitor. She had lost consciousness for a while and things had been touch and go in the ambulance, but now she was on the road to what the doctors expected would be a full recovery . . .

More time passed.

It was pitch-black out and Jamie had been sitting next to the bed for ten solid hours when Anna finally groaned and opened her eyes.

She looked around the room, focused, and saw him.

"Jamie," she gasped.

He smiled at her.

"Oh, Jamie. I'm so glad to see you."

He held her hand and pressed it.

Anna squeezed back, her grip filled with strength.

She was a tough lady, and it would take more than a storm and the terrible Atlantic to kill her.

Anna licked her dry lips and tried to speak.

She coughed and tried again.

"I don't care where you went or what happened. I'm just glad you're back," she said, and took a breath to recover.

Jamie nodded.

"You were up to something. I know that. Someday you'll have to write it all down for me," she said with a minute grin. "And then after that, I'll ground you for the next five years."

Jamie grinned and shook his head.

He wasn't going to write it down.

He'd been thinking. He saw it clearly. He'd had adventures, he had seen wonders, he had done wonders. But none of that really mattered, because the real journey, the real adventure, had occurred in his head.

He had changed.

He understood now that sometimes things don't happen for a reason. Sometimes things just happen because they happen. But you could use reason to make these things have a purpose. He could take everything that had been done to him and use it to reinvent the person called Jamie O'Neill.

And right at this moment he saw that his needs were not as important as the person lying in the hospital bed in front of him. His mom, who had been patient with him and kind and told him that he didn't need to speak, that he could take his time, that the words didn't really matter if the thought behind the words was there.

And it was true, you didn't need the words.

But sometimes they bloody helped.

He took a breath, gazed around the room, looked into his mother's emerald eyes, and said: "Mom."

Anna sat up in the bed. The drip almost flew out of her arm. She looked flabbergasted. Stunned.

"Did you speak? Did you say something? What did you say?" she asked quickly, and then immediately regretted it. This was a moment to be carefully shepherded. Not forced. Not pushed.

He looked at her. What had they called him in the White Tower on Aldan?

Prince of the Ui Neill. Last of his race. Not Jamie, but the Irish version of his name: Seamus. I am Seamus, the Lord Ui Neill, Prince of Ulster, Heir of Morgan of the Red Hand, Defender of the Shore.

He shook his head.

No, I am Jamie, from New York.

I am the lost boy back again.

"I missed you, Mom," he said.

Anna's eyes opened wide. He could see what she was thinking. Was this a one-off thing? Was it a dream? What was happening? The pulse on her heart monitor began to beat faster.

"Relax, Mom. Everything's fine."

"What? How? What happened, Jamie?" Anna asked. Jamie smiled.

"I'm going to tell you, Mom. I'm not going to write it on the PC. I'm going to tell you, everything," Jamie said.

Anna began to cry. To hear Jamie's voice, to hear him speaking after all this time was better than Christmas and her birthday rolled into one.

Outside the lights were on all over Belfast and farther down the lough into the mouth of the Irish Sea Jamie could see lighthouses begin their nighttime watch over the rocks and dangerous reefs.

He thought of that lighthouse on another world and the girl and the people he had left behind.

"Go on," his mother prompted gently.

Jamie sat back in the chair and cleared his throat. "Well," he said, "it all began when I was having trouble with my trigonometry homework . . ."

And then he talked.

And talked.

And talked.

ABOUT THE AUTHOR

ADRIAN McKINTY has been called "one of his generation's leading talents" by *Publishers Weekly*, and his books have been described as "unputdownable" (*Washington Post*) and "exceptional" (*San Francisco Chronicle*). Adrian was born and grew up in Carrickfergus, Northern Ireland. Educated at Oxford University, he then emigrated to New York City, where he lived in Harlem for five years, working in bars and on construction crews and enjoying a stint as a bookseller. He currently lives with his wife and daughters in Denver, where he teaches high school. *The Lighthouse Land*, his first novel for young people, is the first book in *The Lighthouse Trilogy*.

This book was designed
and art directed by
Chad W. Beckerman.
The text is set in 11 1/2-point
Adobe Caslon, a font designed
by Carol Twombly and
based on William Caslon's
eighteenth-century typefaces.
The display type is set in Eremaeus.

Enjoy this sneak peek at

THE LIGHTHOUSE WAR

BOOK TWO OF
THE LIGHTHOUSE TRILOGY

Five o'clock in Carrickfergus. Noon in Washington, D.C. The hour sounded with a tiny beep. Samuel Hutchenson looked at his watch. He was running a little late.

He quickened his pace.

It wasn't every day that the head of NASA got invited to a meeting of the War Cabinet. He was nervous. He knew what the president was going to ask him and he didn't have an answer. He walked into the Oval Office sweating buckets.

The president of the United States did not look up at first. He was having trouble with his pens. Twice he had tried to sign the executive order, twice the pen had not worked.

"What's the matter with these things? Can't anyone get me a pen that works around here?" he asked.

"Mr. President, Director Hutchenson of NASA," a tall aide whispered.

The president stood and offered his hand.

"Good to see you, Sam," he said cheerfully, "sit down."

Sam Hutchenson sat in the only remaining chair. Arranged in a semicircle around him were the four most powerful people in the world. The president of the United States, the vice president, the secretary of state, and the secretary of defense.

The presidential aide and a photographer left the room.

"What's all this nonsense we're hearing about aliens?" the secretary of defense snapped before Hutchenson's pants had even touched the seat.

"It's a very complicated situation," Sam Hutchenson began uncertainly.

There was a long and awkward pause.

"Well, Sam, why don't you begin at the beginning?" the president said helpfully.

"The beginning. Um. Of course. Well, it turns out that JPL, that's the Jet Propulsion Laboratory, a private body, not part of our agency, has picked up what they think is a message from an, um, intelligence in space."

The president narrowed his eyes.

"A nonhuman intelligence?" he asked.

"Yes, so they say, sir," Hutchenson said warily.

"And what does this message say?" the vice president asked.

"It's a long string of ones and zeroes. Ninety-eight

digits long. Some of that is the message repeated. The broadcast, if that's what it is, may have been going for weeks, possibly longer, but JPL's probe only caught the last couple of hours before it stopped."

"Where was it coming from?" the president asked.

"The constellation Pegasus. We can't be sure where exactly, but that's the general vicinity. We're trying to track it down," the NASA director replied.

"Are we certain this is the work of an intelligence?" the secretary of state asked.

"No, ma'am, not by any means. It may be the radio waves from a dying pulsar, it may be associated with a gamma ray burst, it could be ejecta from a spinning black hole. The truth is, we don't know exactly what it is. It was picked up by the JPL's *Cassini* probe around Saturn. *Cassini* thought initially it was a message from Earth and when it realized it wasn't, it sent the message back to Pasadena for confirmation. JPL jumped the gun a little bit, but they followed the protocols. They called us and we called you. Everyone wants to get an OK from the White House before the information gets released to the media."

The president leaned back in his chair.

"Do you have a copy of this so-called message?" he asked.

"Yes, sir, of course," Director Hutchenson said, took an envelope from his inside jacket pocket, opened it, and handed a piece of paper to the president.

The president looked at it and passed it around the semicircle.

This was printed in the middle of the paper:

11111111 11 1111 1101 101 10101 1001 1110
101 1001 1100 1100 11111111 11 1111 1101
101 10101 1001 1110 101 1001 1100 1100

The president took the note again and handed it back to Sam Hutchenson.

"If it is aliens, what do you think they're trying to tell us?" he asked.

The NASA director sat forward in his chair. He was on safer ground here and he was beginning to relax a little. "It's in binary, sir, the simplest way of transmitting a message across space by radio telescope. If you convert it to base 10, we think it means this," he said, handing the president a second piece of paper on which the number 255315135219145912122553151 3521914591212 was written.

"And what does that mean?" the president asked.

The NASA director grinned awkwardly.

"Um, we don't know."

"Could it be an alphabet code?" the secretary of state, a former specialist in security matters, asked.

"Well, if the aliens—if they are aliens—somehow know Earth alphabets, which is unlikely, it still produces a meaningless series of letters. Uh, let me see, I have it here on another piece of . . . where is it, ah yes, let me read it to you. 'AUAPCMTOPKK' is one of the more comprehensive solutions. We've had the FBI's Cray parallel computers run it through every known language on Earth, but it's still complete nonsense," the NASA director said with growing confidence.

The president took the third piece of paper and examined the word: "AUAPCMTOPKK."

"The computers couldn't find any code or message at all?" the president asked.

"No, sir, nothing. If it is a message, we don't know what it means. It might be music, it might be poetry, it might, on the other hand, be a scientific phenomenon unconnected to an intelligence."

"Like what?"

"Like I say, sir, we don't know—two stars colliding, the dying radio burst of a pulsar, something like that."

There was another long pause.

The vice president took the three pieces of paper, examined them intently, and passed them around.

No one could make head nor tail of any of it.

"How far away are these aliens? Could they be coming here anytime soon?" the vice president asked.

Sam Hutchenson laughed nervously.

"Oh no, not by any means. The source of the message is about a hundred light years from Earth."

"And to a layman that means what?"

"Oh, well, we estimate that the fastest a ship could

ever travel and still remain within the boundaries of the laws of physics is about ten percent of light speed. So it would take them a thousand years to get here," Sam said.

The president stroked his chin and smiled.

At first he'd been concerned, but this was beginning to look like less and less of a problem. Certainly not in the same league as the North Korea business.

"What's your hunch, Sam? Is it something we should be worried about?"

"I'm skeptical, sir. In the 1970s SETI—that's the Search for Extra Terrestrial Intelligence—claimed to have had an alien contact—the so-called Wow signal. It turned out to be nothing. During the Clinton Administration, NASA got egg all over its face from that Mars rock they said contained life but turned out to probably not be life at all. I think we may be looking at a similar phenomenon," the NASA head said, now completely at ease.

"You don't think it is aliens?" the secretary of state asked with a curious smile.

Sam had really not come to any conclusion, but he could sense the mood in the room: They didn't want to believe it was aliens. He, however, was not going to be badgered.

He shook his head. "I don't know. I just don't think we have enough information to say definitively one way or the other."

The president nodded. "So what do we do?" he asked.

"The story's already leaking. JPL only showed it to us first as a courtesy. And your order will keep them quiet only for so long. They want to release the message to the world. They will release it sooner or later. They don't really run a tight ship over there. Bunch of hippies, actually, very smart, but you know . . ." His voice trailed off as the president stood and walked to the window.

He looked out at the brown grass and the scrubby rose bushes. Someone wasn't doing a very good job with the gardening.

Was this really the answer to the question of whether humanity was alone in the universe? It was certainly too big to keep a secret. The NASA director was right about that. Secrets didn't last very long in this country.

On his inauguration day, no one had come to brief him about the Bermuda Triangle or the Kennedy assassination or Area 51. He learned, with a little bit of disappointment, that there were no big secrets hidden away. Oswald shot Kennedy, Area 51 was an ordinary aircraft base. There were no secrets and no conspiracies because Americans didn't do a good job at keeping secrets. Once free of the Puritan restraint, Americans had become blabbermouths. Everything that could leak would leak.

"Mr. President?" the vice president asked at last.

He turned to face them. "OK, I've decided what we're going to do," the president said to the expectant quartet.

"What?" the vice president asked.

"We're going to have a press conference. Let's tell the world before the hippies do. Sam, you'll run it."

"Me, sir?"

"You. You'll tell them we're not sure what it is. It might be a message from an extraterrestrial intelligence, it might just be a freak of nature. But we'll put it out there. Every time we've tried to hush things up, it's bit us on the ass," the president said and gave the secretary of defense a pointed look.

"What if the Chinese break the message first?" the vice president objected.

"We let everyone know. We'll put it out there. So what? Maybe the Chinese will break the message, maybe the French, hell, maybe two boys in a basement in Milwaukee will figure it out."

❄ ❄ ❄

Milwaukee, Wisconsin. A lovely spring day. Birdsong. Apple blossom. Kids bicycling under the trees. Women pushing jogging strollers in Congress Park. Teenagers playing street hockey in cul de sacs. A breeze off the lake rattling the air conditioners on the rooftop of the Harley Davidson plant and wafting the smell of pies cooling on window ledges.

A beautiful and arresting scene.

Spielbergian. Happy Daysian.

Something is going to happen.

Definitely.

But not here . . .

✦ ✦ ✦

Muck Island, Northern Ireland.

The dark sea, storm clouds, smoke from Ballylumford power station blowing over the rainy islet nestled off the Islandmagee peninsula.

The phone ringing in the Lighthouse House.

"What the fuuu . . ."

Jamie looked at the clock.

It was three in the morning.

"Somebody better be dead, or giving birth," he said.

He let it ring, but his mom was fast asleep.

Groaning, Jamie got out of bed, put on his slippers, walked downstairs.

He grabbed the phone.

"What?" he said.

"It is aliens. Check out the Internet."

"Do you know what time it is?"

"You know me and the old insomnia. Anyway, NASA held a press conference. They released the message. They're saying it could be a natural phenomenon. It's not. I've read it. It's dynamite. I think I'm onto something. I'll talk to you tomorrow," Ramsay said hurriedly.

"Say all that again slowly."

"I gotta go," Ramsay said and hung up.

"Wait," Jamie said, but his friend was gone.

Groggily he set down the phone.

"Kid's totally crazy," Jamie muttered to himself.

He stood there for a moment and then walked to the living room window and looked out to sea. In the channel the lights were bobbing on the Pirate Radio 252 ship, which was broadcasting pop and rock from beyond the three-mile limit. They wouldn't care if there were aliens or not, just as long as it didn't interfere with Britney Spears's or Jessica Simpson's ability to pump out horrible music.

Jamie stared at the lighthouses across the lough in Scotland. He yawned and inwardly swore at Ramsay, for he knew that, tired as he was, there was no way he was ever going to get back to sleep this night.

Keep reading! If you liked this book, check out these other titles.

The Lighthouse War
By Adrian McKinty
978-0-8109-9354-9
$16.95 hardcover

The Last Universe
By William Sleator
978-0-8109-9213-9
$6.95 paperback

The Telling Pool
By David Clement-Davies
978-0-8109-9257-3
$7.95 paperback

Look for book 3 in *The Lighthouse Trilogy* soon!